GHOST WRITER

Publishing
was his life.
But it might all
unravel over
an anonymous
manuscript....

Rene Gutteridge

BETHANYHOUSE
MINNEAPOLIS, MINNESOTA

Published by Bethany House Publishers
A Ministry of Bethany Fellowship International
11400 Hampshire Avenue South
Bloomington, Minnesota 55438
www.bethanyhouse.com

Printed in the United States of America by
Bethany Press International, Bloomington, Minnesota 55438

Library of Congress Cataloging-in-Publication Data

Gutteridge, Rene.
    Ghost writer / by Rene Gutteridge.
        p.   cm.
    ISBN 0-7642-2343-7
    1. Publishers and publishing—Fiction. 2. Ghostwriters—Fiction.
3. Editors—fiction. I. Title.
PS3557.U887 G47   2000
813'.6—dc21

                                                00-010081

For Sean

RENE GUTTERIDGE majored in screenwriting at Oklahoma City University and has written and produced over three hundred dramas for church worship services. *Ghost Writer* is her first novel. Rene makes her home in Oklahoma, along with her husband and son.

The author who benefits you most is not the one who tells you something you did not know before, but the one who gives expression to the truth that has been dumbly struggling in you for utterance.

—OSWALD CHAMBERS,
My Utmost for His Highest

CHAPTER 1

Nellie Benson placed her hands on his desk, leaned forward, and said, "We're dead."

Jonathan Harper rubbed the back of his neck. "Nellie, please. Don't do this. Everything is under control."

"Under control? Clyde Baxter is never going to write another book for us again. I'd hardly call that 'under control.'" She stood and paced the length of his office, then stopped and turned toward him. "Talk to him. Will you at least talk to him?"

Jonathan tried to smile. "He sounded fairly sure of himself, Nellie. I mean, he's written over thirty books. Can't you understand that he might not have anything else to say?"

Nellie leaned against his door, her eyes raised to the ceiling. "We haven't had a bestseller in three years except his novels. What are we going to do? What am I supposed to tell Ezra?"

"It's not like his books will stop selling overnight. Maybe his retirement will boost sales even more."

She laughed pathetically. "You're not in my world. Be in my world. Long-range goals, Jonathan. Think five years from now. I have to think five years from now because we've already spent money that Clyde was going to make us by renewing his contract." She took a deep breath and looked at him. "And I hate to be the one to say it to my golden boy, but this isn't good for you, either."

Jonathan folded his arms against his chest. "I'm capable of finding new talent, Nellie."

Her eyebrows raised. "Really? Because if I'm not mistaken, the last five authors you signed with us lost us money."

Jonathan tried to keep a steady expression, reminding himself that Nellie had a habit of overreacting. "It happens."

"Not five times." She loosened up a bit. "I'm not trying to scare you. I'm really not, Jonathan. But the pressure's on. Do you know what I mean? More than ever. On you and on me."

Jonathan nodded and leaned back casually in his chair. "You don't call me your golden boy for nothing." He smiled and she smiled back.

"Good. Then you'll have a sure bet for the next editorial meeting?"

Jonathan winked and Nellie walked out, leaving the door open, allowing for a perfect opportunity to see Sydney Kasdan walk by, glance in, and smile.

The smiles and lingering looks hadn't always been this consistent. Five months ago, Jonathan didn't even know her name. And perhaps five months ago, he wouldn't have wanted to. But temptation has a way of presenting itself in the most beautiful form and at the most vulnerable of times.

Working as a low-ranking editor, Sydney Kasdan blended in with everyone else walking the halls. But that soon changed when, upon delivering a manuscript to his office, she accidentally knocked over the entire stack of unread manuscripts sitting next to his desk.

It took them an hour and a half to put it all back together, trying to match pages to manuscripts and then put them all in order. But an hour and a half later, he knew this girl's name, age, dreams, loves, passions, pastimes, and a host of other miscellaneous information that would seem completely irrelevant if they didn't belong to Sydney Kasdan.

On this morning she returned his smile, as always, keeping her eyes on his a moment longer than necessary, then continued walking down the hall and out of his sight. Jonathan shook his head, trembled a little inside at the thought of a twenty-eight-year-old flirting with him, trembled again at the thought that he trembled thinking about her, and then sipped his habitual nine A.M. cup of Earl Grey. Their interaction hadn't proceeded any further than the smile and occasional touch on the arm, but it moved him in a way he hadn't been moved in years. It put a spring in his step, made him feel young again. It also brought a heavy cloak of darkness around him that he chose to ignore more times than not.

To her credit, Sydney Kasdan was no ordinary twenty-eight-year-old. She had graduated summa cum laude from NYU and held two degrees: one in English and the other in journalism. Her short black hair, delicate white skin, and classic beauty had, sadly, probably launched her further than her two degrees and promising editorial skills.

As this new morning-ritual thrill came and went, Jonathan found himself reflecting on his own successes. As a senior fiction editor for Bromahn & Hutch, the fifth largest publisher on the East Coast, he was, at age forty-five, one of the youngest and most successful in the business. As a twenty-six-year-old, he'd discovered one of the world's most celebrated authors: Clyde Baxter.

And it didn't hurt that he appeared to have the perfect home-life. Married for twenty years with three beautiful daughters, Jonathan was envied by all who knew him. He lived in a large two-story, cottage-looking house with a lakeside view, drove a new sports utility vehicle—a must for any upper-middle-class soccer dad—and was becoming very well known in the business.

His thoughts were suddenly interrupted by his secretary's deep, scratchy, pack-a-day voice.

"Mr. Harper, Clyde called."

Edie Darkoy leaned against the side of the doorframe, her large hip protruded in the perfect manner to form a shelf for her hand. On this morning, she was wearing fuchsia. Fuchsia and aqua were her favorites. Somehow, Edie had never learned the fine art of moderation. If she wore fuchsia, she wore it head to toe. From the large bow that held back her long, wiry gray hair, to the three-inch heels that stuck to the bottom of her swollen feet, she was one giant neon sign. Her lipstick matched, too, even when it ended up on her chin or front teeth.

"What did he want, Edie?" Jonathan snapped impatiently. She

always loved to play this game . . . withhold information from him until he asked.

"He said it was important. Said he wanted to have dinner with you tonight."

"What about?"

"Didn't say. Just said it was important."

"That's odd."

"Five o'clock at the Sienna okay?"

Jonathan paused. This would be his fourth night away from home—not that it had become any big deal to him. He and Kathy had been gradually drifting apart. He couldn't put his finger on the exact moment his heart wasn't completely hers, but he did know that the woman he had shared no walls with years ago was now a woman he feared sharing the dinner table with.

"Yeah. Fine."

Edie nodded, spit her gum into the nearby wastebasket, and said, "Great. I'm going on a smoke break."

Jonathan sighed, then became angry that he was somehow going to have to justify this to Kathy. That woman wanted it all! A nice house, plenty of money, and a husband at her beck and call! Well, he didn't earn the title of senior fiction editor by putting in a mere forty hours a week.

He picked up the phone and as he hesitantly dialed his home number, his mind replayed the horrific fight they'd had the night before over this very subject. *"All you care about are those stupid manuscripts you bring home night after night!"* she had yelled as she stomped upstairs.

After five rings, to his relief, the machine picked up. He left a quick, rambling message, making it sound as if he were flying out of the office, didn't know when he would be home, said something about an important meeting, and ended with a quick apology and a halfway sincere "I love you." If he sounded hurried, panicked, and perhaps even agitated, maybe she would back off, accept that he wouldn't be home this evening for dinner, and not call back. He could only be so lucky.

And perhaps his luck was already changing. As soon as he hung up the phone, he glanced up to find Sydney Kasdan standing in the doorway.

"Hi, Mr. Harper. This came for you. . . ." She raised a package in her hand. "I thought it might be important."

Jonathan smiled. "Come in."

Sydney walked in, her shoulders back in modest confidence. She held out the thick manila envelope to him, and he dropped it to his desk without even so much as a glance.

"Thank you."

"You're welcome. Sorry to disturb you."

She began to leave, but Jonathan stopped her with an abrupt but courteous, "Sit down. Please."

She took a seat directly across from him and crossed her long legs at the ankles. Her sharp eyebrows rose with her posture, and she asked, "What can I do for you?"

Her bright brown eyes brought a breath of fresh air into his mundane life. The way she smiled, the way she loved life and never seemed to tire, her intelligence and wit . . . it all brought energy back to him. But with the energy came the guilt.

He had to think of something quick. He reached over and grabbed a manuscript off the top of his large stack. He glanced down at it . . . a proposal from Embeth Wilkes, a down-and-out romance novelist trying to make a comeback with political thrillers.

"Here. I'd like your thoughts on this," he lied, trying hard to believe that's why he didn't want her to leave.

She looked at it for a moment, then looked up at him. "Before or after I read it?"

Jonathan laughed. "You're familiar with Ms. Wilkes's work?"

"Of course. I'm familiar with all the authors we publish."

"We haven't published any of her work in eight years."

"I know," she said with a small, confident smile, "but I think you can tell where a publishing house is going by where they've been."

"I see." His heart was starting to pound in his chest. "So I'm assuming you don't think she can pull it off?"

She glanced down at it again. "I don't think so. She tends to need definite heroes and villains in her romances, and I'm not sure she can depart from that. I feel readers are beginning to love the more ambiguous characters, characters that are both evil and good, simple and complex, you know?"

Jonathan nodded, resting his hands gently in his lap as he rocked back and forth in his plush leather chair.

"But," she continued, "I believe she deserves a chance to be read. You do, too, I'm assuming, since she's on the top of that stack." Jonathan's eyes narrowed at her observancy. She smiled, acknowledging his expression. "I've heard all the stories, believe me."

"Stories?" he asked with a short laugh.

"My favorite is the one about Naomi Yates—how you believed in her work, but you always got shot down. You even took it to different publishers as a favor to her, and they turned it down, too. So finally you helped finance a self-publishing deal yourself." She paused dramatically. "And you were right. She's become one of the most famous novelists ever. Everyone I know loves her work."

Jonathan smiled. That was a long time ago. "She's very talented. You know she just turned ninety?"

"Yeah. I hope to meet her before she dies."

"I can probably arrange that for you."

Sydney nearly leaped out of her seat. "Are you kidding? Would you? I'm a huge fan!" She stopped herself in the middle of her girlish excitement and cleared her throat in slight embarrassment. "If it wouldn't be too much trouble."

"I'd be glad to, Sydney."

"Thank you," she said in a softer tone. "Um . . . you're busy, so I'll get out of your hair."

Jonathan's first impulse was to stop her, but he felt himself treading into dangerous territory. These feelings were becoming stronger, the eye contact longer. So he just nodded, and she stood to leave.

"Let me know what you think," he said, pointing to the manuscript in her hand.

"I will."

His heart stopped beating quite so fast as he took in a deep breath to calm himself, then pressed two fingers up against his tightened lips. It was good to know he still had some control. His next reaction, though, was rationalization. Somehow, if only for himself, he had to justify what had just happened.

Did anything happen? Nothing visible to any other human eye. But inside he knew. He knew that he was falling. . . .

He erased those thoughts from his mind quickly and picked up the manila envelope she had just brought in. On the outside, he immediately noticed something. Something that stopped his heart. In a large font, on a white label, in the middle of the page was

```
Jonathan Harper
354 Lyons Rd.
Baxter Springs, Kansas 66713
```

Stamped across it was *Addressee Not Known*. And to his further astonishment, the return address had his name at the top with the address of the publishing house. Was this some sort of weird joke? Or a strange mistake? He hadn't lived at that address since he was a young boy. And even stranger were the words *Requested Material* printed in the lower right-hand corner of the envelope.

One habit he had since the first day he became an editor was to always open any envelope marked *Requested Material* as soon as it arrived. He did this for several reasons. One, it helped him nab authors he wanted before anyone else did. While their manuscripts sat in a pile somewhere on another editor's desk, he was already on the phone with the author. Second, it kept projects fresh in his mind. He knew anything marked *Requested Material* was something he at least had interest in.

He set the manila envelope aside, pulled out the pages, and looked at the front page. In the very middle of the stark white paper was the title *The Story of My Life*. He couldn't recall anything relating to this title, but that didn't mean anything. He had a lot of projects going, and he felt sure this one would end up on the stack. He flipped to the next page, and at the very top, in the center, it said *Chapter One*. He flipped back a page, looked at the title, then thumbed through the next few pages quickly.

He laughed out loud and shook his head. What kind of idiot would send what looked like about three chapters to his *childhood home* without an author's name? He flipped to the page following the title page one more time to see if he'd missed it but didn't find anything other than the beginning of the story. He was just about to toss it into the trash can when something caught his eye . . . the very first sentence.

The plow blades caught the sleeve of his shirt, though their mother had warned them time and time again to stay away from them.

He felt his stomach tighten in pain and his throat swell in rare emotion. He hadn't thought about the . . . well, it just had been such a long time ago. He took a deep breath to calm himself, slightly amused at the way all those childhood emotions suddenly came back in such haunting force. The editor in him wanted to toss it in the wastebasket, but something intrigued him. He read on.

The two boys were defiant at six and seven, so one could only imagine how they might turn out together. And imagination would be the only option for the younger one.

Sweat popped onto his brow. He rubbed his forehead with his hands as he stared down at the paper. A strange coincidence . . .

At first, the youngest didn't know what had happened. He heard grinding and a scream, but screaming was oftentimes just a hyped-up version of laughing. Turning around, however, he immediately realized what had happened. His feet felt like lead; his fear paralyzed him. He could only watch helplessly as the huge plow blades cut into his brother's limp body. He opened his mouth to scream at his father to stop the tractor, but nothing came out. He could only cry and watch—

Jonathan slammed the page down and covered it up with the title page. He swallowed hard and concentrated on trying to breathe. This story was so remarkably similar to his own that he almost felt dizzy trying to comprehend it all. They were five and six, though, and it was his uncle who drove the tractor. His older brother, Jason, had dared him to jump from one side of the tractor, over the blades, to the other. They'd done it a hundred times—and been paddled several times for it—while the tractor was stationary. But now came the real challenge . . . could it be done while the tractor was moving?

Jonathan slowly moved the top page off the manuscript.

It had started with an innocent dare.

The view from the rear window of the tractor had been obscured by mud that had accumulated over the years, making it easy to climb aboard the plow with no one knowing. The two boys watched from the tree line, waiting for the tractor to make another round.

"You gonna do it, Jon?"

"No way!" Jon laughed, and they pushed each other as boys always do.

"Come on. You get to pick anything from my room you want if you do it."

"I ain't doin' it, Jason."

"Scaredy-cat."

"You do it, then."

Jason's eyes watched the tractor as it made its final turn in the field and began to head toward them. "A'right. I'll do it."

The two boys stood breathlessly as the roar of the tractor thundered toward them, blowing debris high into the air. Their hearts pounded with the rush of the excitement. The tractor was so close now they could feel the earth tremble under their small feet.

"Don't do it, Jas," the younger one pleaded.

But Jason's eyes were set forward like a soldier on a battlefield. The fear was gone, and if not gone, then hidden. . . .

Jonathan threw himself back into his chair, causing the chair and himself to roll backward into the wall behind him. His whole body trembled in astonishment. How could this be? This couldn't be a coincidence, could it? The boys' ages were wrong, but the names were right. His brother's name was Jason. The events didn't exactly unfold as told in this story, for they had hidden behind some hay bales, not trees, and whoever won the dare got to keep the pet turtle in his room, but still . . . this was so unbelievably close to what had happened.

He rolled forward a little to grab his tea and take a drink, holding the cup with two hands in order to steady it. What was going on? Was this some cruel joke? But how could it be a cruel joke? No one he knew now knew about this. He was only five when it happened. It was long ago and long forgotten . . . wasn't it?

"Mr. Harper . . . Mr. Harper . . . ?"

Jonathan jerked his eyes upward to find Edie standing in the doorway. "What?"

"You okay?" she asked, her beady eyes narrowing.

Jonathan straightened himself in his chair, flattening his tie against his chest. "What is it, Edie?"

"Your wife's on line three."

Jonathan could hardly think straight, but one thing he knew for certain was that he didn't want to talk to Kathy right now.

"I'll have to call her back."

"She sounded as if she really needed to talk to you."

Jonathan's face snapped into a harsh expression. "And what's your point?"

Edie swallowed uncomfortably, waited a second longer for him to change his mind, then quickly turned and left.

Jonathan looked down at the manuscript, angered at how he reacted, angered at the thought of this memory so unexpectedly coming back to violate him. He hadn't thought of Jason in years. Without pictures, it was hard for him to even remember what he looked like.

Who was this from? Jonathan grabbed the manila envelope it came in, but there was absolutely no indication of an address. He grabbed the corner of it, where the postage was, to see where it was sent from. New York? Why would someone in New York send a manuscript for him to Kansas?

He needed a strong drink. He looked at his watch. It was only 10:30 A.M. He'd have to kill thirty minutes before any of the sports bars opened and he could get at least a beer. He hesitated. Kathy hated it when he drank. And he hated it, too. But . . .

Grabbing his jacket, he quickly walked out of his office, passing by Edie's desk in a manner that would repel any questions of where he was going. He glanced down the hallway for Sydney as he headed for the elevator, but she wasn't there.

The elevator door opened with the green Down arrow dinging. The doors simply wouldn't shut fast enough for him.

C H A P T E R

2

The drink Jonathan downed near lunchtime calmed him enough to return to work for a few hours before his meeting with Clyde. Edie dutifully handed him his messages as he strolled past her desk without hesitation. Kathy had called twice since he was out. His jaw muscles tightened at the thought of having to talk with her about being gone again this night. A few more messages from authors and agents followed, and he thought it was awfully deliberate of Edie to put the two messages from Kathy on top. Edie had a bad habit of sticking her nose where it didn't belong, and he could sense she was just about to do it again.

"Call your—"

He slammed the door to his office but finished her command in his head. *Wife. Wife. Wife.* He flopped into his chair and stared at the phone. Not returning phone calls was a cardinal sin in their relationship. Once, about ten years ago, she had called him at the office in the morning. He'd had a busy day and forgotten to tell her about a meeting he had following work. When he came home, he never heard the end of it, especially since she'd been counting on him picking Meg up from the baby-sitter's. Ever since then, no matter what, he returned calls. If he didn't, she was to presume he was dead.

He slid his hand from the top of his forehead firmly down the front of his face until it dropped off at his chin. The phone seemed to scream his name, yet picking it up would be like picking up lead. Why were they like this now? Why couldn't he just call and take the heat? Why couldn't she understand a little more?

While Jonathan mulled over that thought, his eyes locked onto the strange manuscript in the middle of his desk. Even with the alcohol's related effect, the words on those pages still bothered him. He then decided the best way to rid himself of the worry from this was to call his wife and create whole new worries. He was just picking up the phone when his door opened and Zippy walked in.

Zippy was a private nickname, unbeknownst to the poor man, who bore the name of Francis Flowers. Francis was a short man with a narrow, pasty face, large eyes, and thinning red-blond hair. His lips always seemed too tight, his cheeks too saggy. He was only in his forties, but he looked more like sixty.

The nickname "Zippy" first came about when Francis had accidentally come to an important meeting with his zipper down. But it also was appropriate because Francis had bad allergies, which ignited when he got agitated or angry or had any other extreme emotion, which was about all the time. So he was known to carry Ziploc bags full of tissues in his dress shirt, just in case. And third, he talked fast. So he was known to all but him as Zippy, and as far as Jonathan knew, no one had slipped yet.

"The door is closed for a reason, Francis," Jonathan said hostilely. One was always on the defensive with Zippy because Zippy was always on the aggressive. And when he was in the office somewhere, the air always seemed to thicken and cloud up like a cheap air deodorizer.

"Jonathan, always such a delight," Zippy said dryly, adjusting his thick glasses and pulling at the long wisp of hair that hung down past his brow. On a good hair day, that piece of hair was supposed to cover the bald spot on the top of his head. But Jonathan could not recall Zippy ever having a good hair day. "It's important. We need to talk."

"Francis, I don't have the time today. Look at this stack," Jonathan said, pointing to the slush pile next to his desk.

"You don't fool me," Zippy said quickly, scanning the desk with a narrow eye. Jonathan thought Zippy might be the closest thing to a troll he'd ever seen. "You've been avoiding me, haven't you?" His eyes scrunched up and blinked rapidly.

Jonathan threw up his hands in innocence. "Avoiding you?"

Zippy pointed a short, thin finger at him. "Don't give me that. You know I'm around. I've been wanting to speak to you for several weeks about this."

"This?" Jonathan again tried to mirror perfect innocence. He had, however, been warned by Carl Osburg, a nonfiction editor with the house, that Zippy had been wanting to abandon post.

Zippy, by occupation, was what is known as a ghostwriter. Admittedly, Zippy was a brilliant writer. He had ghostwritten nearly forty nonfiction pieces in their house alone. He was in demand by many celebrities whose names would sell but whose writing wouldn't.

Ghostwriting had sparked quite a controversy a few years ago when *Newsweek* interviewed a famous psychologist, who had written nine books on parenting, and ended up misquoting his writing throughout the entire interview. *Newsweek*, of course, uncovered the fact that this psychologist hadn't written a single word of the books he was selling, and not only that, on five of them he had not even been involved in so much as an outline. *Dateline* hit every ethical angle of it for a week.

Ghostwriters can make an exceptional living, especially if they're content writing namelessly and never getting credit when the sales soar. A few have tried coming out of the closet, so to speak, but most are not successful, because even if they've written a hundred books, they have to start over as if they've never written a book before in their lives, at least in the eyes of the marketing department. No house is going to be stupid enough to spill the beans on one successful author in order to launch one that, though talented, is virtually unknown.

Zippy had worked diligently for the publishing house for over twelve years. He was not only known for his impeccable writing style, but also for his ability to crank out a book in about half the time it takes other writers. He was brilliant to a fault, which was one reason he made such a good ghostwriter. His social skills were nil, but he could write on any subject handed to him.

But because of Zippy's inability to coexist with the human race, just a simple office visit from him was dreaded by all. His qualities—abrasiveness, defensiveness, and bitterness—were sometimes overlooked by the fact that he just couldn't seem to understand the concept of "personal space." And because his breath was on the verge of toxic, most everyone had developed an amazing skill of disappearing into bathrooms and cleaning closets just in the nick of time.

Jonathan carefully guarded himself behind his desk as Zippy approached and swiped a chair from the middle of the office, bringing it as close to the front of the desk as possible.

Zippy looked down his thin nose at Jonathan. "I suppose you are going to tell me you have no idea why I'm here."

"Sorry, it's true," Jonathan lied. Carl had forewarned him that Zippy had mentioned to him last month that he felt it was time to abandon ghostwriting and pursue the great American novel.

Jonathan nervously stuck a finger into the deep pits of his left ear and rattled it around as if that were his primary concern for the moment. Zippy crossed his arms and twisted his little face into a messy scowl. "Jonathan, you are lying. But I will overlook that shortcoming of yours for now. We have big plans to discuss."

"Well, if you talk as fast as you type, we should be done in thirty seconds."

The problem with Zippy was that he rarely caught an insult. "I'm from Iowa, Jonathan. We talk fast. And I type one hundred and twenty words a minute. Now, about my novel—"

Jonathan held up his hands. "Not now, Francis. I've got things to do. We'll have to discuss this later."

"Now! Now!" Zippy squealed, almost Yoda-like. Jonathan winced at the man's complete social depravity. He could quote entire passages of literature but couldn't ever seem to carry on a normal conversation or find a comfortable pitch to his voice. Jonathan's head pounded with intolerance.

"No, Francis. Not now. I told you, you can't just come waltzing into my office and expect my time to be available to you."

Zippy bit off a fingernail and spit it out onto the carpet as an afterthought. His eyes never left Jonathan's. "I've got a novel."

Jonathan spread a sneering smile across his face. "And I've got a headache. See Edie outside and we'll schedule an appointment, all right?"

"You're putting me off again, aren't you?"

Jonathan gulped quietly. Maybe it was the tone and pitch of Zippy's voice, but all indications were that Zippy was getting agitated. The end of his nose was twitching and his eyes were starting to water. When Zippy had an allergy attack, you were the one that needed an inhaler.

"Francis," Jonathan said smoothly, rising from his chair and sliding to the side of his desk. "Look, you and I will talk about this. I'm not putting you off. I'm just having a remarkably bad day, and I want to give you my full attention."

Zippy cocked his head to the side, tightened the muscles around his eyes, and pulled at his hair again. "It's going to be brilliant."

"Of course it is," Jonathan said, gently guiding him out of his office by the shoulder. "We'll talk soon."

Zippy pulled a tissue out of his Ziploc bag, blew his nose with enormous force, and then offered a hand to Jonathan as he said, "Of course we will. I'll be back. Count on it."

Zippy set his dirty tissue on Edie's desk, pushed his glasses back up his nose, and abruptly turned to walk down the long hallway. Edie handed Jonathan antibacterial gel before he even had a chance to think about what germs were now crawling on his right hand.

"Thanks," Jonathan sighed, squirting a few drops out. He still had three hours before he had to meet Clyde. He felt dizzy, despondent, and emotionally drained. His chest tightened in reaction to Edie's watchful eyes. But now that Zippy was gone, all he could truly think about was his brother's death and the manuscript that seemed to bring the whole incident back to life.

"You okay?" she asked. "You look like you just quit smoking."

"I don't smoke, Edie."

"Maybe you should start."

Jonathan sighed, walked back into his office, and prayed the rest of the day would go by in a blur.

———

Jonathan conveniently arrived at the Sienna an hour early and was on his second rum and Coke. He'd spent the afternoon buried deep in his work. Several times he found himself wanting to read the mysterious manuscript that now sat on the edge of his desk, but he fought the temptation, at least for now. He wasn't sure he wanted to know what the next paragraph held.

The short passage he'd read wrecked him in such a way that all he could think about was Jason and that horrible Sunday afternoon. In fact, that memory was one of his earliest. Whatever had happened before in his life melted away at the tragedy he witnessed at the age of five.

But now, several drinks later, any memory that might have wanted to survive in his mind was swimming in a pleasurable pool of alcohol. In college he had been a big drinker, but when he met Kathy, suddenly his party days didn't seem that glamorous. She'd insisted he come to church with her when they were dating, and the stability of that, along with her family and even their first daughter, Meg, had kept him away from the bottle for twenty years. Nearly twenty years, anyway.

He was just about to entertain some thoughts about Sydney when a large hand grabbed his shoulder. He didn't even have to turn around. He knew it was Clyde.

"Hey there, Clyde," Jonathan said as Clyde pulled up a stool next to him.

Clyde Baxter topped six feet, with silver-gray hair, a nice, intellectual-looking face, piercing blue eyes, and a mannerism that reminded you of your favorite great uncle. His always crooked bolo tie never looked quite right on him, and his western shirts made a tight fit over his large belly.

Whenever he entered a room, he always tipped his large-rimmed cowboy hat at all the ladies and gave them a special wink, and though Jonathan always felt embarrassed by his lack of style, it somehow never seemed to bother anyone else. He wore old Wranglers that were always too tight and was never, ever seen without his snakeskin boots.

At sixty-seven he had written thirty-six western novels, a genre that had been less than popular in the past few years but had not limited him the least bit. Twelve of those novels landed on the *New York Times* Bestsellers List, and the other twenty-four had sold over one million copies. To say the least, he had been Bromahn & Hutch's most successful novelist, and not only had Jonathan been responsible for finding him, he'd also been responsible for keeping him loyal to the house.

Over the past fourteen years, he and Clyde had become good friends, and admittedly, Clyde had been much of a father figure for him. In fact, there was really no one Jonathan respected more, although he'd been careful to always maintain a little bit of authority in the relationship, which for some reason, Clyde had been happy to afford him.

And so, throughout the years, Clyde had become part of the family. He'd attended all three of his children's baptisms and was even present for his youngest daughter's birth. Kathy loved cooking for him, and Clyde always enjoyed being cooked for. His wife had died of breast cancer shortly before his first novel was published, which allowed a lot of time for Clyde to write. On his thirty-sixth novel, he'd decided to retire after writing one final story in the life of his hero, Bartholomew Callahan. That single book had sold three million copies thus far and was still at number three on the bestsellers list.

"How's retirement, Clyde?" Jonathan asked him, pushing the last of his rum and Coke aside, as if Clyde wouldn't notice.

Clyde smiled, made a deliberate glance at the drink, and then said in his typical midwestern drawl, "Well, I'm comin' out of it for a short while."

"What?" Jonathan asked, trying to focus on the conversation. It would take him a moment, but eventually he'd be able to shake the buzz. Food. He just needed food.

"Yesiree! That's why I wanted to see—"

"Let's grab a table, shall we?" Jonathan said as he slid off the barstool and wandered into another section of tables. He found an empty one and sat down without bothering to ask a waiter. Clyde quietly followed him and took a seat across the table. Jonathan unfolded a napkin so he wouldn't have to focus his eyes on something steady, like Clyde, the saint of all saints. He decided to keep it light.

"Clyde, you can't come out of retirement. You killed Bart Callahan in your last novel, remember? The only people that get away with resurrecting the dead are those daytime soaps. By the way, we're still getting letters about his death. You crushed the hearts of about a million ladies, you know."

Clyde smiled but was unable to respond before a waiter approached with menus. "Can I get you something to drink?"

"Eat," Jonathan blurted. "I need something to eat." He glanced up at Clyde, who just looked at him curiously. "I mean, yeah, a drink—water's fine. But bring us an appetizer, okay?"

"Uh, yes sir, which one—"

"Whatever. Doesn't matter. Just something."

The waiter looked at Clyde, who quietly ordered tea. When the waiter stepped away, Clyde leaned forward on the table. "Jonny, you've been drinkin'."

"I hate when you call me that," Jonathan said in a mild, unthreatening tone, the best he could come up with at the moment. "I am of age, you know."

Clyde laughed a little, but concern lingered in his eyes. "I feel bad for takin' you away from your family tonight."

"Don't."

"Give Kathy my apologies. I should've called her to meet us."

"Well, the kids, you know, Clyde. It's hard to find a baby-sitter. And Meg refuses to baby-sit more than two times a week."

"You've got three beautiful daughters. Hope you know that."

"Thank you, Clyde. You know they love you."

Clyde nodded, and he seemed to gush at that statement. Every time Clyde would come over, he'd always give them each a ten-dollar bill. Of course, Sophie was still too young to know the significance. But Meg, twelve, and Leesol, eight, would always jump up and down and scream with giddiness. The waiter returned with the drinks and an order of chicken wings, then said, "Mr. Baxter,

I'm a big fan. May I have an autograph?" The waiter held out a pen and a napkin.

Jonathan waved his hand. "Give the man his priv—"

"Sure, sure," Clyde chuckled and quickly signed the napkin.

The waiter gratefully thanked Clyde, took their orders, and left.

"Jonny, I don't wanna keep you long. I know you wanna get back to your family. But what I have to tell you is quite significant. To me, at any rate."

"You say you're coming out of retirement?" Jonathan said as he grabbed as many chicken wings as his hand could hold and proceeded to eat them as fast as he could. If they were going to talk business, he was going to have to be alert. It wasn't until after he'd downed three of them that he realized they were *spicy* chicken wings. He grabbed his water and poured it down his throat.

Clyde watched with amusement. "You okay, big guy?"

"I'm fine, I'm fine," he said as he tried to flag down the waiter for another glass. "Continue, please."

Clyde took a dramatic pause, either to punctuate the fact that Jonathan was not himself or to emphasize his next statement. "I'm writin' one final book."

Jonathan focused on Clyde and nodded his head for him to go on. In his normal quirkiness, Clyde grabbed a chicken wing, took a bite, and licked his fingers one by one as if he were alone in his house and no one was around to care. "I had to write this, Jonny. It's something I had to write before I die."

Jonathan smiled at his mixture of passion and boyish quirkiness. The passion was something that had kept Clyde's last novels as good as his first ones. The quirkiness had somehow made him an American icon. "You're not planning on leaving us soon, are you, Clyde?"

"'Course not!" he replied in that famously loud, boisterous voice. "If the good Lord's willin', I'd like to stay another twenty years."

"Well, you look great. I wouldn't doubt if you lived to be a hundred."

Clyde smiled, but Jonathan could tell he wanted to go on about the book. "So what's this novel you *have* to write? Bart Callahan's dead. Are you going to do one with Cassandra? Make her the hero? You know how all the female readers loved her."

Clyde shook his head. "This ain't a western."

Jonathan paused, mid-chew. "Clyde . . . um . . . you don't write anything but westerns."

"How do ya know?" he said with a tilt of his large head. He raised his bushy eyebrows. "Maybe I write romance novels under a pen name." He laughed. "Maybe I'm Danielle Steele!"

"Clyde, seriously," Jonathan said, quickly sobering up, "westerns are what made you famous. No offense, but I'd hate to see your very last novel bomb because you tried to get into a new genre. Ask Embeth Wilkes. She's trying for political thrillers and, well, quite frankly, I'm not sure it's going to work."

"I understand." Clyde smiled softly, but his eyes were focused and demanding. "Jonny, I ain't tryin' to get into a new genre here. Believe me. I love westerns. But this story—well, it was inside me and I had to get it out. It's a story that needs to be told."

Jonathan, not meaning to, laughed out loud at his sudden seriousness. "Clyde! You're reminding me of some of these young writers that come through the house. They've got these stories 'living inside them' and they're just going to die if they don't 'come out.' That's another thing I like about you. Your stories are just stories. You don't write to hide an agenda, know what I mean?"

Clyde acknowledged the statement by laughing along and shrugging his broad shoulders a bit. Still, he seemed so determined. "I know it perhaps sounds foolish. I ain't a spring chicken. I should put my pen away and leave the writing world forever."

"You should have put your pen away a long time ago and gotten a computer, but that's beside the point. I never said you should retire. That was your idea. I could've stood you making us a couple more million. Nellie's having a nervous breakdown, you know."

Clyde laughed. "Yeah, well, there comes a time when you know it's over. I knew that *Mahogany Hills* would be it for me. At least as far as Bart Callahan goes."

"So what's this story you have to write?"

Clyde took out a manuscript from his briefcase. "It's got no title. Not yet." Clyde stacked the papers neatly in front of him, staring at the first page like he was looking at a newborn baby.

"It's a . . . thriller, I guess you would call it. A mystery. But it's about relationships, as well. It's not complete, not nearly, but I thought I'd give you what I have so you could start readin'."

"Clyde, listen. I'm sure it's a good story and everything, but you've never written a thriller. Why would you want to write one now?"

"Jonny, you've known me for a long time. And I've always appreciated your professional advice. A writer could have never hoped for a better editor than you."

"Thank you."

"And I know this is gonna be a gigantic risk for you and the publishing house. But I gotta do this."

The solemnness of Clyde's tone finally made Jonathan realize he was serious. He rubbed his brow and took a deep breath.

"All right. Fine. What's it about?"

Clyde bowed his head, then finally looked up at him. "I just want you to read it. I don't want you to know what it's about before you start readin'. I just want you to read."

Jonathan shook his head. "Clyde, you're acting very mysterious here."

"It's not mysterious. It's just that I think this is the most pure story that I could ever tell. And the most important." Clyde handed the manuscript across the table. "Please read it."

Jonathan sighed as he placed it carefully in front of him. "I'll read it, Clyde, but I'm not promising publication. Embeth Wilkes's attempt at political thrillers has everyone real nervous on this crossover thing."

"I understand. Just read it. That's all I ask."

Jonathan smiled. "Of course I will."

The waiter arrived with their meals, but Clyde stopped him. "I'll need a to-go box."

"What? You're not staying to eat?"

Clyde smiled as the waiter quickly returned with the box. "It was wrong of me to take you away from your family tonight. I was just overly anxious about this novel. Go home. Be with them. I'll talk to you later about it. And stick to water. It suits you much better."

"But—"

Clyde waved his hand up, refusing to hear his complaint. He took his box, said a quick good-bye, and left Jonathan sitting at the table alone.

The waiter stood over Jonathan and finally asked, "Would you like yours to go, as well?" He smiled a little and added, "Or would you like your privacy?"

Jonathan paused, then said, "I'll eat here." He hadn't called Kathy back, so he might as well be dead on the side of the road somewhere.

The waiter left, and Jonathan looked down at the manuscript. He turned to the first page of the novel, eager to read the first sentence. Clyde Baxter was famous for his first sentences. A few years ago, Jonathan had learned that in his spare time Clyde would go to bookstores, open up books, and read the first sentence of as many as he had time for. Clyde had the ability to capture his readers with his very first sentence because, perhaps, he spent more time on that first sentence than he did the whole first chapter.

Jonathan took a bite of his sandwich and began to read.

Chapter One

I suppose more than anything I wish I had known that Dietrich Donomar had decided a long time ago, from the solitude of his prison cell, to kill the innocent; he was, after all, already condemned . . . and apparently bored.

Jonathan smiled. Clyde never ceased to amaze him.

C H A P T E R

3

Jonathan sat at the table and watched Kathy silently place the dirty dinner dishes into the dishwasher. He tired of this routine, but nevertheless he had accepted it. And perhaps it favored a shouting match.

It was always the same. A single cold plate would be left on the table for him when he arrived home. Kathy would always refuse to warm it up to make her point. And Jonathan always refused to eat it, to make his.

Tonight was no different, although Jonathan did feel different inside. The manuscript he had received in the morning still echoed powerfully and redundantly in his head. A part of him wanted to go back to the office and continue reading, but he wasn't about to make *that* mistake. Another part of him wanted to tell Kathy, but the timing was all wrong. Besides, not even Kathy knew about what had happened to Jason, and he wasn't sure he wanted to talk about it with her or anyone, for that matter. So he just sat there, trying to give the children the impression that everything was okay.

When they finally left, Meg to her room, Leesol to the living room TV, and Sophie to bed, Jonathan rose from the table and his untouched plate of food and entered the kitchen, where Kathy emphasized every move she made with an edge of harshness.

"Kathy, I—"

"I know, I know, Jonathan. You had to work late."

"It was Clyde. He said he *had* to meet with me. He told me to tell you he apologized for taking me away from my family."

Kathy softened a bit at that moment. She loved Clyde. But her body soon stiffened again, and she turned her back, deliberately avoiding eye contact, to put the leftovers in the fridge.

"Kathy, what do you want me to do? It was Clyde."

Kathy finally whirled around, her fists punched into her hips. "So? So what, Jonathan! So what!" She lowered her voice when Leesol's giddy laugh at some sitcom made them realize they were not alone. "This is the fourth night in a row! And to top that off, you don't call me back?!"

"I know." He was tired and weary and longed for the day when Kathy was "Katherine" and their marriage was a fairy tale. Even at a time like this, when she was cold, her eyes dark with fury, he would never forget how it used to be.

He sighed and leaned against the counter. Her once light brown, shiny hair was now darker, shorter, grayer, pulled back out of convenience, where it tended to stay most of the time. He watched her tug at her old ragged T-shirt, pulling it over what used to be model-thin hips. And as she wiped away the sweat from her face and turned the oven off, he wondered when was the last time he'd seen her in makeup.

They heard Leesol giggle again from the living room, and Jonathan couldn't help but smile. Leesol most reminded him of Kathy, back many years ago, that is. Kathy had been happy and vivacious, free-spirited and passionate. That was one of the things that attracted him. She laughed. All the time she laughed. He missed that.

He glanced over at the trash, overflowing, squeezed to the maximum. That was one of his jobs, but he rarely did it. Should he do it now? That might make her angrier. He knew taking out the trash wasn't going to reconcile anything anytime soon. And he figured if he tried to do it now, it would send some sort of mixed-up, coded message that he couldn't interpret. He seemed to send those awful messages more and more these days. So he decided to just leave it alone for now.

"Well, don't just stare at it, Jonathan. It's not going to get up and take itself out, you know."

Jonathan sighed heavily. Okay, bad call. He should've gone for it.

"Oh, thanks for the big sigh," Kathy growled, nearly pushing him out of the way. "I'll do it if it's that big of a burden for you."

That's not what he meant! He wasn't sighing because—

Kathy stormed past him with the full trash can, pieces of it dropping in a trail behind her. Forget it. There was nothing he could do. He heard the garage door slam and decided to go into the living room to see what Leesol was up to.

He sat down next to her on the couch, but she didn't budge. She was watching an episode of *I Love Lucy*. Jonathan watched it for a little bit, and when a commercial came up, he grabbed Leesol and threw her into his lap. She looked up at him with her large brown eyes and laughed, not resisting his insistence that she lay her head in his lap.

"How was your day?" she asked in her pretend mature voice. She had been doing that lately, trying to be a woman. In reality, it wasn't too far off. At eight, and being the middle child, Leesol had for some reason chosen to skip Barbies and tea parties. At four she announced she wanted to be an architect, and she had spent hours since then drawing houses of her dreams.

Jonathan smiled down at her and ran his fingers through her long, curly hair. "It was okay, honey."

"Anything exciting happen?" she asked with very real curiosity . . . the kind that only comes from the purity of an eight-year-old.

Jonathan paused. It sickened him to think that the only exciting thing that had happened to him was a twenty-eight-year-old named Sydney Kasdan walked into his office that morning. How could he explain that to a child? And the manuscript—well, he would hardly call that exciting. More like . . . disturbing.

"Just the same old stuff."

"Sounds boring."

"How was your day?" He noticed Leesol fiddling with something small in her hand. "What's that?"

"Uncle Earl sent it to me today." She opened up her hand. "It's a miniature voice-activated recorder. See? It's so small it can fit in a pocket! And it doesn't even have a tape. It records it *digitally*," she said proudly.

Jonathan smiled at her enthusiasm. Uncle Earl, the husband of his only living aunt, his mother's sister Eleanor, loved to spoil the girls. He was always sending them obscure gifts that Jonathan guessed he bought on the Home Shopping Network. Eleanor always complained he stayed up late, "watching that silly channel."

Leesol went on excitedly. "He bought Meg an alarm clock that tells the time in every country in the world and says it in the language spoken there! He got Sophie a microwave bacon cooker, but Mom says she's too little for it."

The commercial finished, and she rolled off his lap and propped herself up on her elbows to watch the rest of the show and play with her new toy. He kissed Leesol and went upstairs to see Meg.

On his way to her room, he peeked in on Sophie, who was finally in her "big girl" bed. She held on tight to her stuffed tiger and had two of her free fingers stuck in her mouth. He suddenly longed for the days when he could sleep without worry as she did.

A few steps down the hallway led him to Meg's room. He quietly knocked on the door before entering. Meg was on her bed, reading something. She looked up at him, then looked back down.

"Hi, Meg."

"Hi." She didn't bother looking up. Jonathan sat down next to her on the bed.

"What are you doing?"

"Studying."

"Already? You've only been back to school two days."

"I'm studying my Sunday school lesson, Dad."

"You have homework in Sunday school?"

Meg sighed and set down her pen. "You would know these things if you came to church with us."

Jonathan bit his lip and looked away. He hadn't been in a while. At first it started out a week here, a week there. Then a month at a time. Now, as he tallied it up in his head, he guessed it had been over a year.

Meg continued, leaning back against the soft pillows that lined her headboard. "Mother's mad at you."

Mother? Jonathan shifted uncomfortably. She was growing up too fast. A year ago she would've never picked up on this. "I know, baby. She should be."

"She says you're never home for dinner. Why not?" She crossed her arms emphatically.

"Meg, I'm busy. I'm a senior fiction editor now. I've got a lot more responsibility. I'm trying to get some more time at home, but it's hard right now."

"My friend Robyn said that her dad's married to his job. Is that what you are? Married to your job?"

Jonathan grabbed her hand. "Meg, no. I'm not. I'm just busy right now. That's all. Things will calm down. I promise."

"My friend Katie's dad divorced her mom because her mom had an affair with her boss. Are you and Mom getting a divorce?"

"Where do you get these friends?"

"Daddy, don't change the subject."

Jonathan sighed. It seemed she had grown up overnight. She was asking too many questions. Too many *right* questions. "We are not getting a divorce."

"Good." Meg finally released some of the tension and anger as she tilted her head to one side. "I think you and Mom should have another baby."

Jonathan laughed and choked all at once. "W-w-what?"

Meg smiled, obviously proud of the fact she had shaken up her father. "My friend Isabelle's parents just had a new baby. She said it's cool. They're, like, young again. And she likes having a baby around."

"Well, what about Sophie?"

"Dad, Sophie's three. I'm talking a newborn."

Jonathan pulled Meg to him, gave her a strong hug, and then stood. "Well, I don't think you're going to be able to convince your mother of that."

Meg laughed and said, "But I've got you convinced?"

Jonathan pointed his finger at her, winked, and said, "Meg, you know you've got me wrapped around your little finger." He stepped to the door and flipped out the overhead light, leaving her reading lamp as the only light. "Don't stay up too late."

"I know. You either."

Jonathan nodded and quietly shut the door. In the next room he could hear Kathy putting Leesol to bed. He quietly walked across the hall into their bedroom and quickly changed clothes. He hopped into bed and pulled out Clyde's manuscript from his brief-case. He was finding the place where he'd left off when Kathy came in. She glanced at him, the manuscript, and then went to the bathroom, shutting the door behind her. Although he felt guilty, Jonathan hoped she would stay in there awhile. At least maybe he could get some work done. He'd only been able to read bits and pieces of Clyde's novel, and wanted to read more in hopes of getting a better idea of what Clyde was doing with this story. He was hesitant about telling Nellie of it until he knew more. He shifted through the pages to find the place where he left off.

I walked down the long corridor as if it were my first time, though I'd probably walked it twenty times or more. The guard's keys clanged loudly against the steel door as he un-locked it, and another guard methodically flipped a switch. The heavy door moved slowly to the left, and I walked through it.

"Need me, Agent Spade?" Mitch Richards, the guard on duty, asked.

"No, thanks, Mitch. I'm okay. I could do this in my sleep," I lied.

Mitch smiled, but as he locked the door behind me, he said, "I know, Keaton, I know. Just remember to stay away from the glass, and don't give him *anything.*"

The first time I ever made this walk, ten years ago, my feet had felt like lead, and the only thing that had kept me walking was my dignity. I was just about to make special agent in my department at the FBI, and I wasn't about to let some quirky freak like Dietrich Donomar ruin it for me.

My heart had pounded so hard in my chest I thought surely everyone could hear it. It amazed me how hard it was still pounding.

A lot of people liked to compare Donomar to Charlie Man-son, but I always thought that was an understatement. On the street, one might mistake Donomar for some type of male model or maybe a business executive. He was tall and domineering, and he had chiseled features that seemed to me to be like what one of those mythical Greek gods might look like.

He was, oddly, clean-cut and well mannered, his hair cut above his ears and his body language gracious and smooth. Not only that, he was brilliant.

He could multiply six-digit numbers within seconds. His mathematical capacity was equivalent to that of a computer on board a NASA space shuttle, so a few people had said. He also had a remarkable appreciation for classic literature and oftentimes in the middle of the night could be heard reciting Shakespeare, and even playing the different character voices.

He'd captured the dark imagination of the world. Several movies and books had been written about him, and whenever he was featured on a news magazine, their ratings would soar. The vice president of the United States had been quoted as saying, "Not even Stephen King could have thought up something like Donomar."

He'd finally been captured ten years ago, and after more than forty hours of questioning, we had concluded that Dietrich Donomar was probably responsible for more than 150 murders inside the United States.

The strange thing about Donomar was that he didn't fit any particular serial-killer pattern. Most serial killers killed their victims in the same way or followed some other distinct pattern, like the look of their victims, or a location, or some other constant. But Donomar killed both male and female, young and old, every race, from poverty to the richest of the rich. And he never killed in the same manner, either. Sometimes it was horribly bloody, and other times it seemed to be peaceful and painless. Some women he raped. Others he didn't. One of his most notorious killings was that of an older woman in a nursing home who was dying of cancer. The papers had reported that she was suffering, but the family wouldn't allow euthanasia. Donomar walked into the nursing home late one night and killed her by suffocation. Yet another time he killed a vibrant, healthy young athlete who had a bright future in front of her. He only had one weakness. He had to brag. And so he kept something from each victim to remember them by. That was it.

I had worked closely on the case with Pierce Jenkins, an FBI profiler and a good friend. In Donomar's trial Jenkins had been the foremost advocate for keeping Donomar alive. He wanted to study him, try to find *something* that made him tick, some sort of pattern, some sort of childhood tragedy . . . *something* . . . that made Donomar who he was. But in the last few years, Jenkins was growing increasingly frustrated and had finally told the press, "I don't know. He's probably the closest thing to pure evil I've ever seen. I've been doing this a long time. I've seen a lot of horrible things. But Donomar scares me the most."

Later that evening, over drinks, I'd asked Jenkins why Donomar scared him so much.

"Because he doesn't fit into our box, our definition of evil. He breaks all my rules. And I suppose that's why it took us so long to find him."

Those words echoed in my mind as I continued down the corridor. I didn't know why my nerves always got to me like this, and I certainly wouldn't have admitted it to anyone, though I suspect most everyone felt the same way, especially judging from the almost absurd precautions the prison took to keep him secured.

Unlike the famous fictitious serial killer Hannibal Lecter of *The Silence of the Lambs*, Donomar was very conversational, and what made him even more eerie was that he wasn't eerie in the least bit. It wasn't out of the question that you might've had drinks with him at a bar. Maybe a few of his victims did.

I took in a deep breath and reminded myself to keep my guard up, however "friendly" Donomar might appear. Three years ago one of the guards had taken a liking to Donomar and had foolishly been reckless by not going through the entire handcuffing procedure used by the prison to move Donomar from his cell to his one-hour recreation time. The guard was found hung by his own uniform in the hallway leading to the rec area, Donomar simply standing there waiting for someone to come get him.

Curiosity kept nudging me closer. I hadn't visited Donomar in over a year, so I was pretty surprised when I got the letter from him asking me to come visit, that we needed to talk "urgent business."

As I approached his cell, I couldn't quite see him, but I

could hear him. Breathing. Probably reading. I clenched my fists together one final time before Donomar came into sight. I closed my eyes as the glass window came into view, and then, with one final step, I approached the front of the cell and saw—

"If you're going to read, go downstairs."

Jonathan about jumped out of his skin. "What?"

"I'm tired. I can't sleep with your light on. You know that," Kathy said as she climbed under the covers.

Jonathan laid the manuscript on his bedside table. "Kathy, I'm sorry. If it had been anyone other than Clyde, I would've insisted we reschedule."

"If it had been anyone other than Clyde, you'd be sleeping on the couch."

They looked at each other, then Kathy let a little smile slip. Jonathan grabbed the moment and started laughing. Kathy laughed, too, and they shared a light moment together. It was like old times, when fights were just fights and not permanent records etched into the stone of their hearts. The laughter died down, and then Kathy turned to him.

"You should've come home tonight, Jonathan."

Jonathan suddenly grew very anxious, tired of continually explaining, convincing, apologizing. "Kathy, what do you want me to do? We've got three children, and you insist they go to private schools. We've got bills to pay."

"I know that. But you're not paid by the hour, you know. You don't have to work eighty hours a week."

"I didn't get where I am by slacking. And besides, Nellie's pressuring me. My last five books have—"

"I'd hardly call forty or even fifty hours a week slacking!"

Jonathan felt it coming . . . that horrible, irritated feeling that usually accompanied some sort of striking verbal explosion. "Let's just drop it," he managed under clenched teeth.

"Yeah, fine, let's remain silent and dysfunctional, Jonathan. Let's just pretend we don't have any problems. I'll put a smile on my face and tell Pastor Gregory on Sunday that you're 'working again.'

And you can spend a couple of minutes a week with the children just to pacify them. And the whole time you're making your stupid publishing house a ton of money, your family is falling apart."

Jonathan silently begged himself to remain in control. For his own sake, he had to remain in control. "The family is not falling apart. You're overreacting."

Tears filled Kathy's eyes. "You and I are falling apart. Can't you see that? It's not the same. We're not the same."

Jonathan felt himself turn ice-cold. "Kathy, for crying out loud. We've been married twenty years. I'm not going to get goose bumps and giddy when you walk through the door."

Her tears started flowing, and Jonathan immediately regretted saying that. But she always pushed! She pushed and pushed and pushed until he finally broke in some way! Why did she always have to do that?

Predictably she threw the covers back and hurried off to the bathroom, slamming the door behind her. At least the tightness in his chest would subside now. It always did when this sort of situation finally met some sort of resolution—even if that resolution was his wife locked in the bathroom.

Eventually she'd have to come out. And until she did, he could rest. He leaned his head back against the headboard and at that exact moment came to a monumental conclusion in his life.

He was tired.

At forty-five, Jonathan Harper was worn out, exhausted, completely drained of life. He was tired of trying to love his wife. He was tired of trying to be the best editor in the industry. He was tired of trying to please everyone. He was tired of turning down the things that would make him happy. He was tired of all of it.

He rubbed his face in his hands and felt his throat swell with tightness. He tried to hold back the tears as long as he could, but they finally fell. He prayed Kathy wouldn't come out of the bathroom at this moment of pathetic weakness.

But if he didn't let this go now, he was afraid he might just have a heart attack or a stroke or some other stress-related illness. And besides, he was feeling for the first time in his life absolute hopelessness, most especially in his marriage. He couldn't feel anything for Kathy anymore . . . at least nothing close to what he'd felt for her when they were first married.

He'd never *once* considered divorce, and if he were honest, he was too much of a coward to consider it now. Nevertheless, for the first time in the twenty years they'd been married, he wasn't sure he could see another option. Kathy was miserable, and he obviously wasn't providing what she needed. He, in turn, was restless and suffocating.

He turned his head to the side and picked up a picture of his three girls. Meg was holding a five-month-old Sophie, and Leesol had her arms wrapped around Meg's waist. Just looking at them brought the purest joy imaginable, and it was because of them that he would not leave. Only because of them.

He sighed and suddenly realized he had to go to the bathroom. He flipped the covers back, stood, and made the long walk downstairs.

CHAPTER 4

Jonathan left the house early, before Kathy was up. He'd opted to go ahead and sleep on the couch, not as a sacrifice or even a peace offering, but simply to avoid any more conflict. Plus, it made it easier to leave in the morning.

The office was quiet, void of the hectic busyness that buzzed around him on a typical morning. He had opened the blinds to his large window, letting the soft, glowing rays of the early sunrise filter hazily into his roomy corner office. He relished the moment's serenity. Although he didn't have any peace on the inside, he was, at the moment, able to control his surroundings to some degree.

He had the choice not to pick up that ominous manuscript that sat on the edge of his desk, and for several moments he resisted the urge. But the more he looked at it and the more he remembered what he'd already read, the more his curiosity began to get the best of him. He slowly reached for it and noticed his hand trembling.

Why am I so scared? Jonathan thought. *What am I afraid of?*

He flipped a few pages to where he'd left off. He had almost convinced himself this manuscript was an entire coincidence when yet another sentence grabbed his attention.

Young Jonathan had found his solace by spending the

majority of his time in the barn. Nearly a year had passed since his brother's death. Jonathan had retreated inward, not able to handle his own grief, and certainly unable to handle his parents'.

On this particular night, the air was notably cold, and Jonathan had left the house in only a thin sweater and his pajama bottoms. He hardly noticed the crunching snow on his bare feet as he kept his hands warm by tucking them deep within his armpits. He wondered if anyone would even notice if he just kept walking and never came back.

He glanced back at the large old house he called home. Over a year ago it had always seemed welcoming and warm. The chipped exterior blue paint gave it character. The screen door hanging on one hinge simply showed the house was used to its maximum.

But now it was all different, and in the dark the house loomed over Jonathan like a nightmarish beast. He carefully walked in its shadow, hiding in the darkness so as to escape safely to his barn.

He opened the large barn door with a hefty pull, and it creaked in a way Jonathan had never noticed before. He closed it behind him and felt around for the lantern he'd left hanging on the wall by the door. He found it with ease and lit it quickly.

Over him he heard a faint rumble of thunder, a sound that had calmed and soothed him ever since he could remember. Most kids his age were terrified of storms, but Jonathan embraced them, and at the first sign of a threat, he would race to the window and watch the falling lightning. That's when he felt close to God, when God's voice rumbled overhead in the clouds.

The three horses in the barn acknowledged his presence by shaking their heads. He walked over to his favorite, Spice, and stroked her long nose.

Without warning he heard the barn door creak. Turning around, he held the light above his head. He hoped with the approaching storm it was just the wind, but soon enough he could see his father entering.

"Jonathan? What are you doing?"

Jonathan didn't budge, his back against one of the stable

doors. *His father moved forward, and Jonathan lowered the lantern down next to his knees, casting a strange mixture of light and shadow on his father's face.*

"Jonathan?" his father repeated, now only feet from him. Jonathan felt himself growing reticent, humiliated that he'd been caught. He wanted to turn and run, but there was nowhere to go.

His father's tall figure stood over him, and Jonathan could only peer up, speechless. But he knew he couldn't remain silent for long. His father would demand an explanation.

"Son, I'm talking to you. Answer me."

Jonathan's grip tightened around the lantern's handle. "I was checking on Spice."

His father walked around him and touched the horse, checking her quickly and authoritatively. He finally bent down to Jonathan's level.

"Jonathan, I know you miss your brother."

Jonathan swallowed hard. He felt the hardness in his heart lifting. His father had hardly talked about Jason's death, and because of that Jonathan had held everything inside. But now, as his father's eyes, bright with reflecting orange and yellow light, stared into his, all he wanted to do was cry and be held. He felt his father reach out and wrap his large hands around his own.

"Jonathan," he said softly, "I need to know something."

Jonathan nodded, tears rolling down his face faster than he could've wiped, if he'd wanted to. At last, his father seemed like his old self, and Jonathan felt like a normal kid again, vulnerable, fragile, and loved by his father.

His father took a deep breath, tilted his head to one side, and asked, "Jonathan, did you dare your brother to jump the blades?"

At first, floating in the preciousness of the moment, little Jonathan wasn't sure he heard the question right. "What, Daddy?"

His father's back straightened and he let go of Jonathan's hands. "Did you tell Jason to jump those blades?"

Jonathan panicked. Did his father . . . was his father actually saying . . . no! No!

Jonathan answered as his entire body shivered. "No."

But that didn't seem to satisfy his father, whose eyes turned icy even with the warm light deep inside each pupil. "You must tell me. Did you make your brother do that?"

"No! No!" Jonathan screamed, backing away slowly, shaking his head and crying harder.

"Jonathan! Answer me! Tell me the truth! Jason would have never done that! He was a good boy! He would have never disobeyed me!"

"I didn't, Daddy! I didn't!"

His father, now standing, marched closer to him, a long, single finger extended toward Jonathan. "Whose idea was it, Jonathan? Tell me!"

"No!!!!" Jonathan cried, trying to back up more quickly. As he did so, he suddenly stumbled a bit on a lone two-by-four hidden in the hay and immediately dropped the oil lantern.

It shattered instantly and the flames spread gracefully in two directions, trapping Jonathan against the stables. He could hear his father screaming on the other side, and all he could scream back was "No! No! I didn't, Daddy! I didn't!"

Spice whinnied, her hooves kicking the air, then crashing down onto the stable wall, cracking the wood. Jonathan ran to the other side of the barn, away from the horses, and now his father was only a shadow as the flames rose higher. Spice anxiously clawed at the door, and the other two horses seemed to instantaneously go insane.

The roar of the fire was so loud that Jonathan covered his ears and closed his eyes, barely aware that the smoke was making it hard for him to see and breathe. All the horses were bucking, and Spice finally kicked through one of the sides of her stable and ran toward him. He moved to the right. The other horses found their way out as well, and now all three of them ran in circles of complete terror.

Jonathan's small body was huddled in a corner, and with his ears covered, he watched the fire silently crawl above him, destroying the ceiling of the barn. Small pieces of fiery wood began to fall, and the horses started coming closer to him as they ran in what were now becoming smaller and smaller circles.

Jonathan's eyes rolled back in his head, and he suddenly realized he couldn't breathe. The fire, the horses, the barn . . .

they were all turning black. "No, Daddy ... I didn't ... it wasn't my fault...."

Jonathan was barely aware that two hands had grabbed him under his arms and were dragging him across the ground until he came to and saw the barn in the distance, completely engulfed in flames.

He looked up to find his father over him, saying something to his mother, who was crying. His chest was tight, but he could breathe. "I didn't..." he mouthed, but no one seemed to be paying attention to what he needed to say. His father placed his ear close to his mouth, all the while screaming, "Jonathan! Jon—"

"—athan? Um . . . Mr. Harper? Jonathan?"

Jonathan opened his eyes, and at the door stood Sydney Kasdan.

"Are you okay?"

Jonathan slapped the pages of the manuscript together and pulled in as much air as he could in one breath. "Of course. I'm sorry. I didn't see you there." He glanced at his clock. It was only 7:30 A.M. What was Sydney doing here?

"I was just going to get some coffee. Want some?"

Jonathan leaned back in his chair, trying to regain his composure. He wasn't sure what he looked like on the outside, but on the inside he felt himself crumbling. How could anyone have known about that conversation? It was only he and his father. No one else was there! And his father had passed away five years ago. How could anyone know about that?!

"Is that a 'yes'?"

Jonathan snapped back to reality and nodded at a question he didn't even hear.

"Black?"

"Yes," he said. Sydney left.

Jonathan rubbed his face in his hands and moaned. What was happening? Was this all a joke? But even if it were, no one could've known all of that. He barely remembered it himself. There were vivid images in his head, but no details. He remembered the barn engulfed in flames and that dreaded question his father had asked him—

"Here you go," Sydney said, handing him a small Styrofoam cup across his desk.

"Thank you, Sydney," Jonathan replied, noticing for the first time how the morning light made her skin and eyes glow. Her smile was drenched in sweetness.

"I've been looking over the Embeth Wilkes manuscript you gave me."

Jonathan's heart pounded, whether from Sydney or the manuscript he did not know. He did know his feelings were growing stronger for her, though, and there was nothing he could do to stop them. Nothing at all.

"Tell me." Jonathan rested comfortably in his chair and waved his hand for her to have a seat.

"You'll be shocked," she grinned as she sat, gracefully crossing her long legs. "But I'm impressed. So far this story looks promising."

"Really?" Jonathan asked, leaning forward.

"Yes. It's as if she's acquired an entirely new writing style. I wouldn't have known it was her writing if you hadn't told me."

As intrigued as he was with Ms. Wilkes's sudden transformation as a writer, Jonathan Harper wanted to know more about Sydney Kasdan. In fact, he wanted to know everything.

"Sydney, you seem very intelligent to me."

Sydney locked eyes with him but at the same time blushed, a very odd combination, Jonathan thought. How can one be bashful and still look you in the eye? Jonathan continued, saying, "I'm not wrong, am I?"

Sydney's smile became a little more confident. "Well, Jonathan, I suppose I do have some intelligence."

Jonathan nodded. She was so mature. And so beautiful. So very beautiful. "What do you like to do in your spare time?"

Sydney again locked eyes with him. "Why?"

He paused, his heart stinging with a sudden fear that perhaps the chemistry he thought they'd had was all in his head. Was she not pushing for this? Why, then, would she be in his office at seven-thirty in the morning getting him coffee? Had he gone too far? Was he getting personal when she'd wanted to talk business? He loosened his tie a bit.

"Just curious," he said with as much confidence as he could muster. "I mean, you seem to be an odd combination of intelligence, beauty, and personality. A rare find these days."

What? Was he crazy? Why would he say that? What in the world could've led him to do something like that? He watched, trembling, as Sydney tilted her head to one side and with a small smile replied, "I like sports."

Jonathan relaxed a bit. Maybe he wasn't as off as he thought he was. "Sports? You hardly seem like someone who'd be interested in sports."

"Why is that?"

Jonathan smiled at her, and she smiled back. They connected in an instant, and he knew beyond a shadow of a doubt that there was something there. He stood and walked around to the front of his desk and sat on the edge, near the corner. "I don't know. I suppose it's the way you carry yourself. Very feminine. A lot of girls . . . um, women . . . I know who are into sports are sort of, well, you know. . ." They laughed at his inability to find the choice words.

"Hard?" she asked.

"Yes." He rubbed his hands together like a nervous teenager at a prom. "Just looking at you, it's just hard to imagine, that's all."

"Well, I've never played a sport in my life. But I do enjoy watching them. How can I prove it to you?" She playfully twiddled her thumbs a bit and then said, "No National Football League team that plays its home games in a domed stadium has ever won the Super Bowl." She winked. "At least not yet. And the only two days there are no professional sports games—basketball, football, baseball, or hockey—are the day before and the day after the Major League All-Star games."

He laughed, genuinely impressed. "Wow. You sound like—no offense—one of the guys."

She shrugged. "On the weekends you can find me on my couch, in my sweat shirt, wrapped in a blanket, watching football.

49

But don't be too impressed. I have a talent for retaining facts that can make me look like an expert on just about anything."

"Really?"

"Yeah. Don't ever play me in trivia. I'll smear ya."

Jonathan laughed, completely amused, intrigued, and captivated by her. "Like what?"

"Like anything. I just have a head full of useless facts."

"Come on, spill some out."

She shrugged girlishly. "If you insist. I feel sort of silly."

"Really. I want to hear this."

"All right," she said with a hefty sigh, her eyes moving upward as if searching the vast amounts of information in her head. "Got one. The name 'Wendy' was made up for the book *Peter Pan*."

Jonathan folded his arms together. "Impressive. But you're going to have to do better than one."

She laughed. "You can lead a cow upstairs but not downstairs. The first TV couple ever to be shown in bed was Wilma and Fred Flintstone. Iceland consumes more Coca-Cola per capita than any other nation. And Coca-Cola was originally green." She raised her eyebrows. "Shall I continue?"

"Yes!" Jonathan said, laughing.

"In 1987 American Airlines saved forty thousand dollars by taking one olive off each salad they served. The San Francisco cable cars are the only mobile national monument. Each king in a deck of cards represents a great king in history: spades, King David; clubs, Alexander the Great; hearts, Charlemagne; diamonds, Julius Caesar. Please don't make me go on! I bore myself with these useless facts!"

Jonathan slid toward her on the desk. "Okay. Let's put these 'useless facts' to the test, then. I'll ask you a question and see if you can answer it."

Sydney smiled at him. "Ah. A true test of intelligence, eh?"

"Simply application, my dear," he joked.

"Fire away . . . by the way, the term 'get fired' is a term that actually refers to clans long ago, who would burn the houses of unwanted people to get rid of them. Hence the phrase 'to get fired.'"

"All right, Ms. Trivia, what was the first novel ever written on a typewriter?"

She pretended to yawn. "*Tom Sawyer.*"

"First president ever to win a Pulitzer Prize?"

"John F. Kennedy, *Profiles in Courage.*"

"Only two people signed the Declaration of Independence on July fourth—"

"John Hancock and Charles Thomsen. Come on, Jonathan," she said, resting her chin on her hand. "Challenge me, will you?"

Jonathan smiled and suddenly couldn't remember the last time he'd had this much fun. He threw his arms up in the air. "Smartest dog?"

"Scottish border collie."

Jonathan tilted his head, and this time he locked eyes with her. "I'll have to take your word for it. I have no idea."

Sydney suddenly seemed to become self-conscious at Jonathan's relentless stare and lightened the moment with a chuckle. "Well, as fun as this is, I'm sure you have better things to do with your time than listen to me ramble off facts."

"Not really," he said, although that wasn't true. Still, he could sit with her all day, and he longed to know more about this woman who seemed to be an endless inventory of facts. "But I suppose I do have a real job."

Sydney rose from her chair elegantly and grabbed her coffee cup off his desk, her arm brushing his. "Well," she said, glancing down at the manuscript on his desk, "I did interrupt your reading of something important, judging by the look on your face when I came in."

Jonathan raised his eyebrows and stood, walking back behind his desk. "Um, yes. Quite interesting." He longed to tell her about the mysterious manuscript, but in the midst of his swimming emotions, he was still able to hold on to some sort of stable judgment. "Thanks for your interest in Ms. Wilkes's work. I'll take a serious look at the book."

Sydney straightened her posture and stiffened her demeanor, and suddenly, in a mere instant, they were two professionals again.

Sydney nodded and moved to the door. "You're welcome. Have a good day, Mr. Harper."

"You too," Jonathan said, but he was already longing for whatever form of intimacy they had just shared two minutes before. Suddenly the formalities that he once had gotten such a kick out of were not enough.

But all that became a blur when he looked back down at the manuscript. His soul was troubled again. Who was writing this? And how did they know? Had his father written this before he died and had it sent years later? Never! His father would've never thought of such a thing.

But who, then? Jonathan had always been in control of his life, and something like this was enough to make him crazy. Of course, he always had the option to *not* read it. He could just toss it in the wastebasket and move on with life.

No, that was not an option for him. He would face this mystery and face it with courage, no matter how eerie it got. And not only that, he would find the person writing it.

Jonathan ran his fingers through his thinning hair and drew in a deep breath to help him think. He needed someone to bounce ideas off of, someone who could think logically about this situation.

Kathy? Not a chance. Besides, who knew what could be in the following pages? Many things existed in his past that he would never care to discuss with her, especially right now, with their present circumstances.

Sydney? No, he didn't know her well enough. Although he suspected he could trust her, he wasn't about to gamble. He was never a gambling man.

He could maybe pull a few of his fellow editors into it, but he'd never formed much of a friendship with any of his colleagues, except Carl.

Perhaps . . . Clyde? Could he trust Clyde? Would Clyde think he was absolutely insane? Of course not. He had the manuscript to prove it. But the gamble was not knowing what was ahead. What facts of his life would this manuscript produce?

Jonathan walked out of his office to go fix himself his nine A.M. cup of Earl Grey. As he walked over to the lounge he hoped he would see Sydney, but she was nowhere around.

He sighed, poured boiling water over his tea bag, and steeped his tea for a few minutes. He loved the smell. It reminded him of some time he spent over in London as a young man. It also tended to clear his head.

Yes, he would call Clyde to meet him for lunch. But before he met him, he'd have to get caught up on his manuscript. Clyde wouldn't let him off easy, and besides, Jonathan was quite intrigued by the story so far.

He poured a touch of cream into his mug, stirred it carefully, and walked to his office, shutting the door behind him. Yes. Clyde could help him. He was sure of it. He dialed Clyde's number and left a message for him to call.

C H A P T E R 5

Jonathan sank into his office chair and turned toward the window. He adjusted himself, propping his feet up onto the windowsill. Outside his door he could hear the soft hum of the office coming to life. He switched his phone to "Do Not Disturb" and picked up Clyde's manuscript. Flipping through the pages, he tried to remember where he'd left off. There it was . . . Keaton Spade was just about to see Dietrich Donomar in his cell.

Donomar came into view immediately, and I let out a short, definitive breath, thankful Donomar wasn't facing the glass. I grabbed a nearby chair and slid it across the cement floor, causing Donomar to turn around, though I suspected he somehow already knew I was there.

"Agent Spade!" he exclaimed, clasping his hands together after setting down a book he'd been holding. "Thank you for coming."

"Been a long time, Dietrich," I said lightly, watching as Donomar organized a few things on his small desk and put away his crayons, the only writing tools he was allowed.

Donomar shrugged, smiled a little boyishly, and grabbed his own chair, pulling it in front of the large Plexiglas window. "Well, I've been keeping up with you in the papers. I saw the case you solved in Colorado—the girls disappearing? Caught that gentleman fairly rapidly."

I had to smile a little. It amused me that Donomar could discuss another serial killer as if he had no relation. "Yeah, well, we got lucky on that one."

I watched as Donomar twiddled his thumbs methodically, the only indication that inside that pretty head lurked a diabolical killer. Donomar was looking down, his light hazel eyes barely noticeable against the whites of his eyes. He soon picked up on the awkward silence and raised his head.

"Sorry," he apologized graciously, "I'm a little distracted today."

"Is that so?"

Donomar smiled knowingly at me. My hair stood on end. "Yes."

I casually adjusted myself in my seat. "I was pretty shocked that you wanted to see me."

"Why, Agent Spade? I like you."

My lips spontaneously pressed together. "Yes, well, Dietrich, I wish I could say the same about you."

Donomar sighed a bit and lifted his hands in a quiet, unassuming manner. "Keaton, I wish you wouldn't take everything so personally."

"It's my job," I said quickly, and then reminded myself to never let Dietrich Donomar in. Ever. His tongue was slick and deceptive. "Why did you want to see me?"

Donomar paused dramatically. "Why did you come?"

I felt my throat tighten. Donomar was turning the tables, but I felt no immediate danger, so I obliged. "Curiosity, I suppose."

Dietrich's eyes narrowed, making him look very intellectual. "Killed a cat once, I hear." He cracked his knuckles. "You've got cats, don't you, Keaton?" He grinned then and said, "That's a joke."

I smiled carefully. Donomar's attempt at humor rolled my stomach over. I made a deliberate glance at my watch. "Why did you want to see me, Dietrich?"

Donomar rose, a typical move he made when he wanted to dominate. He knew his height made an impression. "I've been thinking, Keaton. I have a lot of time to think in this place, as you know. I've been reflecting . . . on my life."

I sat perfectly still, not wishing to break his concentration in the least bit. As I listened, I could not remember Donomar ever making such a statement. He rarely talked about himself.

"I've taken the lives of so many innocent people. So many," he said, and I thought his voice seemed a little strange. I wished I'd brought a tape recorder. Jenkins would never believe this. He'd worked for years trying to find some sort of conscience in Donomar and had never been successful. I didn't know what was happening, but I did know that whatever it was wasn't normal.

Donomar paced briefly and then turned with a dull stare in his eyes. I wondered if I should respond, but my instincts and twenty-three years of experience told me to wait.

This, however, didn't seem to bother Donomar too much. He pivoted on his right foot and walked to his desk. He sat down and opened a file folder. "Some of the victims' families send me photographs regularly to remind me of what I took from them." Donomar held up the folder so I could see it more clearly. "It gets to me sometimes."

I instantly felt my whole body shake. It "gets to me sometimes"? I tried to hide any expression that might indicate I was about to explode inside. I had to admit I never saw this coming. This was monumental, and as frozen with shock as I was, I was still kicking myself for not bringing a tape recorder.

Donomar stood and walked close to the Plexiglas. He held up a picture and I recognized it immediately . . . Ashley Horton, one of Donomar's victims he'd killed in Texas. Horton was twenty-seven, found dead in her car after a jog at the park.

"Take Ashley, for example," Donomar said as he looked the picture over. "How could I have taken the life of such a beautiful, promising young woman?"

I could no longer contain myself. I leaned forward and in one breath said, "A lot of people are wondering that same thing."

Donomar looked up at me, as if surprised I had spoken. He held up another picture. "And this one. James Whitfield."

Whitfield had been a lawyer from Detroit, horribly tortured with fire and then left to die slowly. I looked away from the picture. Whitfield had probably disturbed me more than the others because of our own similarities . . . he was the same age, our mothers had the same name, and we both had light brown hair and a medium build.

Donomar slowly closed the folder and walked back to his desk to set it down.

"Why? Why am I such a horrible person?"

I felt my head spinning. Why hadn't I called for Jenkins to come? Why hadn't I brought the tape recorder? I silently justified it all inside my head. Never in a million years would I have seen this coming or ever expected it. The Dietrich Donomar I knew had no soul. The Dietrich Donomar sitting ten feet away from me had seemed to grow a conscience.

"Can I ever make this right, Keaton?"

I let out a heavy sigh and raised my eyebrows in dumbfounded astonishment. "Right? I, um . . . I . . . you've killed over 150 people, Dietrich. So can you make all of that right? I don't know if that's possible." I watched as he lowered his head a little, and I quickly added, "But it wouldn't hurt to try."

Donomar had a very sad look on his face, and I almost felt compassion for him. Almost.

Silence filled the still chamber, and for what seemed like forever, Donomar just sat and stared at the floor. I could hear my watch tick but wasn't at all interested in how much time was going by. I didn't know if Donomar had anything else to say, but I wasn't about to take the chance that he didn't by leaving prematurely.

Then Donomar looked up. "There are three men about to be executed on death row here, correct?"

I tried to think about that question and process the entire event as it unfolded all at once. I didn't keep up with the actual execution dates too much, but I thought that sounded about right. "I think so."

In that very instant I saw something remarkable. Donomar's hard features turned softer. His body, usually straight and strong, was hunched a bit. And I noticed one other thing that would stick in my mind more than anything else. He had stopped twiddling his thumbs.

He deliberately looked at me and said, "One of them is innocent."

I kept eye contact with him, something they'd trained us in the Academy to do at all costs, and tried to find something, anything, that would connect him to the old Donomar.

"One is innocent," I repeated.

"Yes. One is on death row for a murder I committed."

I couldn't even imagine what I should say next. My mind methodically searched through all the manuals and books and classes I'd been exposed to at the Academy. Nothing prepared me for this. I hoped Donomar would go on, and he did.

"I can't make things right. You are correct in that statement, Keaton. But perhaps I can keep a further wrong from happening."

"What are you saying?"

Donomar leaned back in his chair and let out a huge sigh. After a moment, he said, "The body of Manuel Roberts was supposedly found in the North Haven drainage ditch, near the river. But Roberts was actually killed on the other side of town in Bear Woods."

I scrambled to remember all this. I wasn't familiar with the Manuel Roberts case and immediately repeated the information back to myself silently. Donomar then stood and moved away from the front glass. He walked to the back of his cell, where a tiny barred window let in an ounce of light, and gazed out without saying another word.

After a little while, I decided to leave. I rushed down the small corridor and kept repeating Donomar's statement over and over in my head. As the gates opened, I pulled out my cell phone and dialed the number to my office.

"Janine," I said to my secretary through the static the thick cement walls caused. "Get ahold of Pierce for me. Tell him to meet me at the office as soon as he can. And get me the number to the DA's office."

"... wondered what time you wanted to meet."

Edie Darkoy's raspy voice abruptly interrupted the story. Jonathan set down the pages of Clyde's manuscript and looked up. "What?"

"Clyde's on the phone—said you called him," she said, chomping her gum. The stench of her cigarettes saturated her clothing. "What time you wanna meet him?"

Jonathan looked at his watch. "Tell him to meet me at the Sienna for an early lunch. Eleven-thirty."

Edie left and Jonathan closed Clyde's manuscript. He liked what he saw so far, though he was still skeptical Clyde could pull it off. At least he'd read some of the manuscript so Clyde wouldn't be disappointed. But the truth was, the last thing Jonathan wanted to discuss was Clyde's new story—though he was amazed he'd read so much already. All he wanted was for someone to tell him what was going on with the *other* manuscript in his life . . . the one *about* his life.

He glanced to the side of his desk, and there it sat, looking so ordinary, blending in with all the other stacks of stories around it. Jonathan wondered if he should read any more before his meeting with Clyde. He glanced over at the rest of the stack and wondered when in the world he would get any of *those* manuscripts read.

He sighed, shoved the mysterious manuscript away, and got to work.

———

Eleven o'clock came quickly, and Jonathan found himself fidgety. Anxiety filled him as he second-guessed himself on whether or not to tell Clyde about the manuscript. Although the Sienna was only a few minutes away, he hoped he could get out of the office a little early without raising any suspicions. Edie had been giving him a few looks that signaled if she had more information, she'd start talking in the break room. Although it was only eleven, he felt sure he could go ahead and leave without her noticing he was early for his eleven-thirty with Clyde.

Jonathan snatched his jacket off one of the chairs in his office, put it on, buttoned it, and grabbed his briefcase. He stuffed both Clyde's manuscript and the other manuscript in there, closed it, and walked out, trying to carry himself with authority.

"I'm gone to lunch with Clyde," Jonathan said smoothly.

Edie's fast-moving fingers never left the keyboard, but she said without hesitation, "It's only eleven."

Jonathan wasn't going to say anything to defend himself—why should he, to Edie Darkoy of all people?—until Sydney Kasdan walked by. It happened quickly, and if he'd been able to do it over, he would have played it out much better.

But either way, he'd already looked and smiled at Sydney before he realized Edie had caught the whole thing. And the clue that her little mind was churning came simply—her fingers stopped moving across the keyboard. Her eyes lingered on Sydney, then on Jonathan, then back on Sydney. She cleared her throat in a disapproving manner and pretended to be interested in the document in front of her.

"Dry cleaning."

"What?"

"I've got to pick up my dry cleaning. That's why I'm leaving early," he said strictly as he watched the elevator doors shut Sydney in. Jonathan stiffened and added, "If that's okay with you, Ms. Darkoy."

Jonathan always used *Ms. Darkoy* when he wanted to underline the authority he had over her. Edie never seemed to be phased by it but nevertheless backed off.

"Of course," she said and resumed typing as if the conversation had never taken place.

On his way down in the elevator, Jonathan wondered where Sydney was going. Yet why should he care?

As the elevator doors opened he saw her standing outside, her arms wrapped around her to block the cool fall breeze that always seemed to snap around the corner of the building. He swept his hair to one side and exited the building.

"Hi."

She turned around and, with a surprised look on her face, smiled.

"It's a little cold for you to be standing out here, isn't it?" He noticed how rosy her cheeks were, and the breeze caught her perfume and swept it into his nostrils.

She shrugged. "I'm a pretty tough cookie."

Jonathan wanted to resist the question, but the truth of the matter was, he never seemed to be able to resist much of anything when he was around her. "Waiting on someone?"

She nodded and shivered a bit. "Yes."

Don't ask who! Jonathan screamed inside. But at that moment he wanted to know if she was involved with anyone. And the sad part was, he couldn't justify that curiosity. It was none of his business, and he shouldn't care anyway. Still, it gnawed at him enough for him to manage to disguise it with a little humor. "Your knight in shining armor, I presume?"

She laughed and pulled a short wisp of hair up off her forehead. "Well, the armor's not quite as shiny as it used to be . . . just needs a little buffing." She smiled, then simply offered, "My fiancé."

Fiancé? He hadn't even noticed a ri—ah, there it was, right in front of him, glinting brilliantly in the sun. Perhaps he'd never cared to look.

"Congratulations," he managed, though rather dully. "You must be very happy."

She glanced down at her ring, as if a symbol of her happiness, then asked, "Where are you headed to?"

"I'm having lunch with Clyde Baxter."

"You two are good friends."

"Yes."

A Firebird suddenly pulled into the circle drive in front of the building and stopped with a screeching halt. Sydney seemed embarrassed by the display. She hastily threw her purse over her shoulder and gave Jonathan a quick smile.

"Don't forget, you owe me a date."

"A date?" Jonathan asked.

"With Naomi Yates." She glanced at the car and said, "I've got some new manuscripts for you. I'll bring them by after lunch."

Jonathan nodded and she quickly disappeared into the car. Jonathan sighed and realized what an idiot he'd been. How could he ever think someone as beautiful and young as Sydney Kasdan would be interested in him? She had her mind on younger men, and being engaged, she certainly wasn't looking.

As Jonathan made his way to his car, he reminded himself once again that he wasn't available anyway. But that was a fleeting thought, which quickly disappeared into a mind filled with everything but conviction.

CHAPTER 6

Jonathan watched Clyde play with the turquoise buttons on his favorite western shirt, the one that was so old it was practically see-through. With his free hand he moved a single olive around his plate.

"That's odd, if I do say so myself," Clyde said. Jonathan had the manuscript on the table but kept a protective hand on top of it. "Never heard of such a thang."

"No kidding," Jonathan sighed. "I'm not worried, I just thought it was strange," he said as he tapped his fingers rapidly against its white pages.

Clyde let out a short laugh. "Well, is it good?"

Jonathan smiled a little. "Haven't paid much attention to the writing style, frankly, but it's not great, no. It doesn't flow real well, though the description is pretty good." *Too good.* "I don't know, Clyde. I mean, I'm not counting the periods and commas or anything."

"How exact is it? The content, I mean. Does it follow your life exactly?"

Jonathan wavered back and forth in his honesty. He didn't want to reveal too much, just in case . . . in case of what, he didn't know, but he knew he had to keep his guard up.

"Oh, you know, it's fairly . . . vague."

"Then are you sure it's about your life?"

Good point. "Um, I think so. Yeah. I mean, Jason's name and my name . . . can't really discount that. And everything I've read so far has happened—not *exactly* like it depicts, but close." He paused. "Not close. Just sort of similar."

Clyde finally popped the lone olive in his mouth and narrowed his eyes. "Jonny, you're scared."

Jonathan's fingers stopped tapping and his defenses immediately rose up. But Clyde wouldn't let him speak. He waved a large hand. "I know, I know, you ain't gonna admit it. But I can see it in your eyes." Clyde's own eyes traveled down to the manuscript underneath Jonathan's hand. "And I have a feeling whatever's in there, it's very close."

Jonathan clenched his jaw and tried to suppress his anxiety. He could either dismiss all this in front of Clyde or tell him everything. He had to make a choice. He rubbed his hands over the stubbled, unshaven skin on his face. "I hadn't thought of Jason in years—not until this."

Clyde nodded. "What else?"

Jonathan swallowed hard. "After Jason died, a year or so, maybe more, I was in the barn with the horses one night and dropped the lantern and burned the barn down."

"That's in the book?"

"Manuscript. Yes."

"Anyone else there at the time?"

Jonathan paused. "My father."

"Who is dead," Clyde thought out loud. "And your mama?"

"Yeah, she was there." Jonathan ran his finger along the sides of the manuscript, giving himself several paper cuts he didn't even feel. "It's like they're speaking from the grave or something."

Clyde looked at him directly. "You know that ain't possible."

Jonathan's voice trembled with frustration. "Oh yeah? No one knew about what my father said in that barn but my father. He and I were the only ones there!"

"Only God knows everything." Clyde shook his head, obviously with no answer. "The whole conversation was in there?"

Jonathan felt his head was about to explode. "Yeah! I mean, I think it was. The conversation is real hazy, but I remember my dad asking me—" Jonathan stopped himself suddenly and stared into Clyde's concerned eyes. He quickly took a bite of cold food to do something with his mouth other than talk.

"Asking you what?" Clyde asked.

Jonathan swallowed the food slowly. "I just remember certain parts of the conversation, that's all. Certain parts were in there. As for the other parts of the conversation, they could've happened. I just don't remember."

Silence descended as the two men remained at a loss for words. Jonathan knew there were no easy answers, and he wasn't sure why he thought Clyde might have some. But the fact that Clyde had nothing told him this was serious. This was no game, no practical joke. Someone was messing with him. He just wondered how far it would go. And he wondered what it meant.

"So they just sent you three chapters?"

"Yes, I think. I haven't read it all." Clyde raised his eyebrows at that, and Jonathan explained, "I've been busy."

"Too busy to read the secrets of your life?"

"Look, it's probably just some stupid joke. I don't have time for this, really." Jonathan glanced up at Clyde, then away. "And besides, it's not like I have anything to hide. I mean, fine, write about my life. No big deal. It's not that interesting of a life anyway."

Clyde folded his napkin neatly on the table. "Well, looks like someone thinks it's worthy of writing."

Jonathan laughed at him, trying to keep it light. "Oh, come on, Clyde. You don't think it's a ghostwriter doing my biography for free, do you?"

Clyde's face grew solemn and he asked, "Jonny, seriously. Can you think of anyone who would do this to you? Is there anyone who knows everything about you, anyone who might want to get revenge—"

Jonathan held up his hands. "Wait a minute. Are you saying you think this is blackmail?"

"Is it?"

Jonathan stared hard at Clyde. "Why would you say that?"

"I'm just sayin', do you have any enemies?"

Jonathan laughed uneasily. "Yeah, just about every author I've ever rejected."

Clyde smiled a bit, but concern still flashed in his eyes, which made their way back down to the manuscript. "You should read that. All of it. You should know what's in it. That's your only defense."

Jonathan's heart raced, but he kept his cool with a light laugh. "Clyde, you're so serious! Come on! What could they possibly do? Write me to my death?"

Clyde sat silently for a moment and only stared at him with interest. "I'd just read it. That's all I'm sayin'."

Jonathan threw his napkin on the table and waved down the waiter for the check. "Clyde, I'm not going to turn into some paranoid freak because I'm reading some weird story about myself. Maybe that's what they want. Maybe they want me scared. Well, it's not going to happen." Clyde started to say something, but Jonathan cut him off. "Case closed. That's it."

Clyde sighed and his heavy body slumped back into his seat. "Then why'd you call me here, Jonny? If you ain't worried."

Jonathan swept up the ticket the waiter slid onto the table. "To discuss your manuscript, actually. I'm not finished by any means, but I like what I see so far. Interesting characters, especially this Donomar fellow. A serial killer? Never knew you had it in you."

Clyde's eyes lit up. "I'm glad you're reading it!"

"I'll let you know," Jonathan said as he threw some money on the table. "Thanks for meeting with me. I'm sorry, I've got to get back to the office."

"Sure," Clyde said and rose with Jonathan. "I'll get you the rest of my manuscript as I finish it."

As they left the Sienna, Jonathan stopped Clyde suddenly. "Um . . . Kathy doesn't know about this." He paused as Clyde's eyebrows rose. "I don't want to tell her because she'd worry. You know how she worries."

Clyde put a heavy hand on Jonathan's shoulder. "You should tell her. She's your wife."

Clyde walked down the sidewalk to his old, dented Chevy

pickup. Jonathan watched as he pulled his heavy frame into it, tried to start it twice, and took off in the other direction, leaving a heavy smell of exhaust behind.

Jonathan returned to the office with a chill in his bones. Though he'd brushed it off in front of Clyde, he was growing horribly concerned. Was this blackmail? If so, who? And why? Clyde was right. He had to read it. He had to know what was in it.

Jonathan returned to his office with ease, glad not to run into any fellow editors or Edie Darkoy. He closed the door behind him and walked immediately to his desk. Whatever it took, he'd find the author. But he would need more information, and that information, right now anyway, would come from the information about him. He picked it up and started reading where he'd left off.

>*The years following the barn burning down proved tumultuous between Jonathan and his father. His father had moved his family to a suburb and taken a job as an insurance salesman. His mother, forced to carry a job now, worked at a local ice-cream shop. Jonathan spent his days at school, joining as many activities as he could in order to stay longer. His nights were spent locked in his room in solitude, playing by himself and entering into worlds he created with his imagination.*
>
>*Summers were the hardest, as days were spent at home, until one summer his mother took him to the local library, where Jonathan discovered books. At first he found them difficult to read. His mom wasn't educated, and his dad never took the time to teach him to love books. But soon enough, he found that those books could create an imaginary world he never thought possible. At the age of ten, he discovered one of his favorites,* The Chronicles of Narnia.
>
>*He would curl up in his small bed, underneath a tattered old blanket, and read. He started with* The Magician's Nephew *and read through them all. C. S. Lewis had introduced him to a world he would grow to love with all his heart . . . the world of books. And when he stepped into the land of Narnia, he would step out of the cruel world to which he'd been born.*
>
>*The books consumed him, and soon enough his mother*

began to worry that she was losing her only son. She would try to reach him, but it was hard to pull him away from his books, and when she finally did get his attention, his distance was impenetrable.

But one night she entered his room without her usual excuse of laundry or dusting. Jonathan hardly looked up, his head barely visible over the large copy of The Catcher in the Rye. *His mother tidied up around the room, trying to get up the nerve to confront this eleven-year-old boy with eyes of stone.*

She finally managed to sit at the end of the bed, and for a few passing moments picked the fuzz balls off the blanket he had tucked underneath his feet. Jonathan never so much as glanced up at her, so she knew she would have to make the first move.

"Jon, honey?"

Jonathan's only response was to flip to the next page.

"Jon, honey, I wanted to talk to you."

Jonathan said something under his breath, something demeaning no doubt, and his mother blotted the tears that came with the ridicule.

"Jon! I am talking to you!"

Jonathan's cruel eyes eased up over the top of the book, and he glared at his mother with the fury that only a young boy could. His mother adjusted herself on the bed, trying to hold her demanding position, while also making sure she wasn't coming across too hard.

"Thank you," she said softly, and Jonathan lowered the book a little more, waiting for her to continue. "Jon, I wanted to tell you that . . . well, that I know things have been rough on you since your brother. . ." His mother's words trailed off with her own emotions, and she hated herself because she didn't want to start off that way.

Jonathan simply sat there, his eyes avoiding his mother's, anxiously fingering the pages of his book.

"I'm sorry, Jon," she said, wiping the tears away. "I know how difficult this is for you, and here I am blubbering away."

Jonathan had always had a little bit of a soft spot for his mom, and he said quietly, "It's okay."

She nodded and smiled at him, her small hand grabbing

his covered feet. 'I know things have been hard, and I know your daddy has been distant. But it's not because he hates you. He loves you"

"He hates me," Jonathan said in barely a whisper.

"No, that's not true. He just . . . he just has trouble expressing his emotions, that's all."

"He never did before," Jonathan pointed out.

His mother sighed and nodded in agreement. "True. But your daddy hasn't dealt with Jason's death too well. He feels a lot of guilt—like he could've stopped it somehow."

Jonathan clutched the sides of his book and said, "No, Mama. He hates me because he thinks I could've stopped it."

His mother looked away, and the tears ran down her face with a furious velocity. "No, baby. That's not true."

"It is! It is!" Jonathan said, his tiny teeth clenched together, extracting a small jaw muscle on either side of his face. "You don't know! That's what he thinks."

"Baby, he . . . he doesn't. He's having a hard time, he just is confused—"

"Mama! Don't lie! Daddy hates me and you know it! And that's why you're here, to try to make me feel better. But I know! I know he does!"

His mother shook her head and in a feeble attempt tried to soothe her son, but to no avail. Jonathan's emotions, the emotions he had quietly tucked away inside each story he engulfed himself in, now exploded inside the tiny room with a horrifying echo.

"Jon, that's not true . . ." she said over and over, but Jonathan could not stop himself. He knew the truth, and no matter how many times his mother tried to comfort him with her words, the truth still stung him like a killer bee.

Finally, though, like any eleven-year-old boy, his energy betrayed him, and his tear-swollen eyes grew heavy. He fell into his mother's warm lap, and before he knew it, he'd drifted off to sleep, to a safe world with dwarfs and goblins and fairies and brilliant colors that he had never before seen on this earth.

Jonathan gently set the last page of the chapter down. He gathered himself, quickly shoving his emotions aside and gently wiping the stray tear that had escaped his eye. He picked up a pen and a note pad and began to jot down a few notes.

1. Knows how to use some description, uses educated words, but has no sense of how a story should flow. Story is choppy, just a bunch of information, point-of-view problems.
2. Never referred to his mother's name, Mary.
3. He never called his mother "Mama" in real life.
4. This conversation did take place. Can't remember how old. Was reading *The Catcher in the Rye*.
5. Writer somehow knows my favorite books are *The Chronicles of Narnia*.

Jonathan tapped his pen against the edge of the desk, glancing up at his leather-bound collector's edition of *The Chronicles of Narnia* on the lowest shelf of his bookcase. He tried to stay unemotional about what he had just read, but he remembered the conversation with his mother as if it were yesterday. She had looked so tired, her long hair tied up into a tight knot on the top of her head, except for a few stray pieces that had fallen down around her face.

He remembered, though he had been distant and unapproachable, how very much he'd wanted his mother to talk to him and tell him everything was okay. And though he knew that his father still blamed him, the fact that he could lay his head in his mother's lap, even if just for that one night, brought about a childlike sleep he hadn't experienced since Jason's death.

Jonathan arose from his chair and stretched his back, deciding to step away from the story and take a break. He suddenly thought of Sydney and decided to give Naomi Yates a quick call to see if he could set something up with the three of them.

He dialed her number and the old woman answered the phone. After a few brief pleasantries, Jonathan explained the situation and asked if they could come see her sometime next week. Naomi was happy to oblige, and they set a date for the following Monday at noon.

Jonathan hung up the phone and hurriedly rushed out of his office to find Sydney. He first checked her cubicle, but she wasn't there. He walked the halls, hoping they'd run into each other, but couldn't find any trace of her.

Finally he went back to her cubicle and asked the department secretary.

"She called a little after lunch. Said she wouldn't be in for the rest of the day."

"Are you sure?" Jonathan asked.

The secretary nodded. "Yep. Didn't sound too good. Probably got the flu or something."

"I see."

Before Jonathan had a chance to inquire further, Carl Osburg grabbed him on the shoulder and steered him away from the secretary's desk. He guided him to the hallway, then walked with him in the direction of Carl's office. Though Jonathan didn't have many friends, Carl Osburg was probably the closest thing to a friend he had. Carl had been in the business a little longer, but he always treated Jonathan as an equal, and they'd had years of playing practical jokes on each other, a simple way of breaking up the monotony of the editorial business.

"Zippy come see you?" Carl asked, his accent heavy Brooklyn.

"Yes," Jonathan sighed as they dodged employees walking the opposite direction in the narrow hallway. "What am I supposed to tell him?"

"Your problem," Carl said with a grin. "You can tell him no and clean the snot off your carpet."

"Gee, thanks," Jonathan said solemnly. "Really, Carl. I mean, what am I supposed to do? Zippy can't write fiction. . . ." Jonathan looked around and then asked quietly, "Can he?"

Carl shrugged and laughed again, apparently very amused by the situation. "I don't know. Never read any of his work."

"Exactly. He's a nonfiction *ghostwriter*, and for *good reason*, as we all know," Jonathan said as they stepped into Carl's office. "Why in the world would he want to write fiction?"

Carl sat down at his desk and motioned for Jonathan to shut his door. "Like this is any surprise to you, Jonathan. We've seen ghostwriters decide to write under their names before."

"I know, I know," Jonathan said as he sat down on Carl's long leather couch, "but not do a crossover thing." He laid himself out as if he were at a shrink's office.

"Well, he does have a long list of nonfiction credits," Carl offered.

"I know that," Jonathan snapped impatiently, much to Carl's amusement. "But we're talking about gardening books and corporate know-how books . . . very dry stuff, no offense."

"Not if you're a gardener," Carl laughed and then tried to behave. "Hey, what about that book about how to entertain your children? What was it called?"

"I don't know, Carl," Jonathan said dully. "That's your department."

"At any rate, that was sort of creative."

"You're loving this, aren't you?" Jonathan finally turned his head to look at Carl. "Someone other than yourself having to deal with Zippy?"

Carl only smiled and winked.

"This is a nightmare, you know. Besides the fact I'm quite sure Zippy can't write fiction, he's a complete and total enemy of the very concept of sociability. If we published his book, could you imagine taking him to a book signing? Carl, you've got to see my dilemma here!"

Carl's chair squeaked as he rocked back and forth in it. "You betcha."

"Like I'm going to get any sympathy from you, right?" Jonathan stretched his arms over his head. "Where did Zippy get a crazy idea like writing fiction, anyway?" Jonathan heard Carl snicker and turned his head toward him. "What, Carl?"

Carl was now crying with laughter.

"*What*, Carl?"

Carl held out his hands as if hoping to catch his breath and answer, but instead he just kept laughing . . . howling, to be more accurate.

"Give me a break," Jonathan said, getting up off the couch to leave the office. But as he grabbed the doorknob, something occurred to him. He turned back around and glared at Carl, who was still trying to catch his breath. "Wait a minute." Jonathan walked toward Carl's desk. "You didn't . . ."

Carl finally opened his eyes and blinked desperately through tears of laughter. "I did . . ."

Jonathan crossed his arms. "*You* suggested Zippy write fiction?"

Carl whipped out a handkerchief and blotted his eyes and face. "Don't kill me," he said, still chuckling.

"You're unbelievable, Carl! Unbelievable! I don't have time for this!"

Carl finally regained control of himself, although he couldn't lose the prideful smile that seemed permanently spread across his lips. "Then just tell him no."

Jonathan shook his head, laughed at the absurdity of it all, and walked to the door. "I'll get you for this, Carl. You'll pay."

Carl started howling again and Jonathan shut the door behind him.

CHAPTER

7

The evening air had a bite, and the orange and yellow autumn leaves shone white underneath the full moon's light. Jonathan drove the long way home, taking the hilly roads that drove through the older neighborhoods, where everyone still had their own backyard and the houses didn't touch.

He'd decided to make a deliberate attempt to be home for dinner this evening and try his best to patch things up with Kathy. And the more he thought about what Clyde had said, the more he decided Kathy ought to know what was going on with the manuscript. At least partly. He had the option not to reveal everything to her, but she was, after all, his wife, as Clyde had so poignantly pointed out. She ought to know something.

Perhaps seeing Sydney with her fiancé today helped his wandering heart back into place, too. Was he really willing to throw everything away just for a young girl who tickled his fancy? He and Kathy weren't connecting, but every marriage has its ups and downs. Besides, his three daughters meant the world to him, and he wouldn't let them go for anything.

After a silent pep talk to himself, he headed home, determined to make things right with his wife, if only for tonight. As he pulled into his driveway, he was pleased to see the whole house lit up from the inside out, a sure sign everyone was home and active.

He didn't bother parking the car in the garage, and he hopped out and ran to the front door, shivering the whole way. He found the front door unlocked, and he entered with a smile and yelled, "Hello! Daddy's home!"

His heart gushed at the sound of squeals and footsteps tromping downstairs, and he suddenly found himself wrapped about by six little arms. Even Sophie had managed to keep up, though she could only reach as high as his thigh.

"Hi, girls," he said, hugging each of them individually.

"Hi, Daddy!" they all said in unison.

Jonathan noticed the Thanksgiving wreath and pumpkins were out and made a mental note to compliment Kathy. "Where's Mom?"

"In the kitchen," Meg said.

"I gotta picture I drew for you, Daddy!" Leesol said as she headed back upstairs.

"You *have* a picture," Jonathan corrected and smiled as he watched her nod and keep going.

He looked down at Sophie, who simply peered up at him with her big brown eyes. "Hi, kiddo."

"Hi, Daddy."

He ruffled her curly hair and moved to the kitchen, Meg right behind him. He found Kathy washing dishes and he approached her from behind. But before he could touch her, she turned around and stiffened her shoulders.

"Hi," he said and gave her a light kiss on the cheek, one she didn't make an effort to receive. He glanced at Meg, who took her cue to exit. "I wanted to make sure to be home in time for dinner."

Kathy's eyes narrowed, and she crossed her arms after tucking a stray gray hair behind her ear. "Is that so?" She made a deliberate scope of the room. "Do you see dinner here?"

Jonathan backed away a bit, and she continued. "No, Jonathan, I don't have dinner ready because I never know if you're going to be home and I'm tired of guessing. So I was going to fix sandwiches or something like that. I know that's nothing compared to the fancy meals you're used to having with your writer friends, but that's all that's around."

Jonathan probably should've expected the hostility, and his immediate response was defensive. However, he calmed himself and figured he deserved that for sleeping on the couch and leaving early in the morning.

"Honey, I'm sorry. I didn't mean to imply you had to have dinner waiting for me." He tucked his hands in his pockets and tried to soften his mannerisms in an effort to get her to relax. "I just know it's important to you for me to be here, so I wanted to make sure to be home early."

She didn't budge. "It *should* be important to you, Jonathan. This is your family. Those are your girls." Her whole expression turned drastically sharp. "I'm your wife."

"I know that," Jonathan snapped, trying his best to hide the edge in his voice. He turned and walked to a counter, so as to have something to brace himself against. "I'm sorry about last night."

Kathy didn't seem to have any insult or remark waiting for that one, so she busied herself by pulling out meat, lettuce, tomato, and other sandwich items from the fridge. Jonathan stopped her, stepping into her path from the fridge to the counter. "Honey, I'm sorry."

Kathy looked up at him and at that moment they were very close, closer than they had been in a long time. He could feel her breath on his face, and it was familiar and good. He'd forgotten how petite she was, but standing over her he realized she was a small woman. She certainly did not carry herself that way.

It would've been the perfect moment to kiss her, and he couldn't remember when he had kissed her as a husband kisses a wife. There was the occasional peck on the cheek and the brush of the lips when the kids were around, but nothing more than that. Nothing with passion.

And Kathy seemed to be expecting it. It was, of course, the next natural move. Her small eyes were wide with anticipation, and every vulnerability she ever had waved a white flag of surrender to him. Even her lips were turned up in a small, expectant smile. It was all set up so perfectly, and even the cold air from the open refrigerator added a nice exotic touch.

In one swift moment, though, he stepped around her and

simply shut the door to the refrigerator. Kathy covered well, moving forward with deliberate motion, unscrewing the jar to the mayo as she ran water over the lettuce.

"Ham okay?"

Jonathan, already kicking himself, wanted to make up for his error—and figured he knew exactly how.

"Hey!" he said, moving next to her by the counter. "Let's order a pizza. The girls would love it. We could watch old movies and—"

She opened the bread as if he had never suggested pizza. "Look, if sandwiches aren't good enough for you—"

"I didn't say that!" Jonathan said, throwing up his arms. "You're putting words in my mouth!"

"Am I? Well, that's because we never talk, so I've got to make up some sort of conversation between us, just to have an adult to converse with."

Jonathan's head was spinning. This was not how he had imagined the evening would go. "Keep your voice down," he said harshly. "The kids are in the other room."

Her stare could have cut steel in two. "Keep my voice down for the kids. Is that it? How do you know what the kids want or need? Maybe they'd like to see their parents interact, even if it is a fight."

"You have to be so melodramatic all the time, don't you?" Jonathan yelled. "I was just trying to do the right thing tonight! I was trying to apologize, to make things right. But you're going to make me earn my right back into the house, aren't you? Punish me until you feel like I've learned my lesson."

Kathy slammed the knife down on the counter. "No, Jonathan. That's what you do to children. You punish them so they know they've done wrong. You're an adult. I shouldn't have to punish you. You should just know."

"Just know what?!" he said, his voice a pitch higher than he was comfortable with. "It's like walking on eggshells with you. Everything I say, every move I make, is the wrong one."

"That's right," she said, peeling cheese from cellophane and avoiding his eyes. "That's exactly right. And you know why?" She glanced up at him to make sure he was listening. "Because you've left this family. We're not important to you anymore."

"Don't you dare imply that my children aren't important to me, Katherine. Ever." Jonathan's voice was as smooth as black ice, and he felt his entire face turn red with controlled anger.

"Fine," she said as she spread mustard furiously across a piece of white bread. "Maybe I should restate. *I'm* not important to you. And, unfortunately, I come with this family. Too bad for you."

"How can you say such things?" Jonathan said, beginning to pace the kitchen. "How can you say that?"

"Because it's true." Kathy was eerily calm.

"We're going through some tough times," Jonathan said angrily. "And from that you conclude that you're not important to me? That I don't care? Well, I hate to tell you this, but maybe I'm not the only one with the problem here."

Jonathan waited for Kathy to reply with something, but for a long time she only folded ham and laid lettuce neatly across it, placing a piece of white bread on top of her masterpiece. Finally she turned to him and looked him directly in the eye. "Why didn't you kiss me?"

Jonathan felt as if someone had unexpectedly punched him in the stomach. "What?"

"At the refrigerator. Why didn't you kiss me?"

Jonathan had no answers, and his loss for words was the only answer she needed. She walked to the doorway of the kitchen. "Meg, honey? Can you come here?"

Meg appeared instantly. "What, Mom?"

"Can you finish fixing the sandwiches? I'm not feeling too well. I think I'll go upstairs and run a bath. Yours is done. Fix Leesol's with extra ham and no cheese, and be sure to cut Sophie's up into small pieces. And no pepper on Sophie's."

"Sure, Mom," Meg said, eyeing both Kathy and Jonathan. "What about Dad?"

Kathy glanced at Jonathan and shrugged. "What about him?" She disappeared quickly.

Meg walked over to the counter and picked up where her mom had left off. Jonathan thought it odd that Kathy was now making it blatantly obvious to Meg, at least, that there were problems. Before, they'd always tried to hide any conflict between them.

"What do you want on your sandwich, Dad?"

Jonathan had lost his appetite, but he said, "Everything."

"Okay."

He could see the depression on Meg's face, so he tried to lighten things up a little. "Hey, what do you say you and I eat sandwiches, pop popcorn, and watch old movies all night?"

Meg smiled a little. "It's a school night, Dad."

"Oh." Jonathan watched as her little girl seemed to grow up before his eyes, doing tasks her mother did. She carefully sliced Sophie's into small squares. "Well, then Saturday. Is it a date?"

Meg finished the sandwich and turned to him. "Sure. If you'll go to church with me on Sunday."

Jonathan melted at her pleading eyes, and he could tell at this moment that was the most important thing in the world to her.

"Of course I will, Meg," he said softly.

"Good!" she said excitedly. "Be sure and get popcorn and Milk Duds, okay? It's gotta be Milk Duds. And maybe some chocolate milk."

"Got it," Jonathan said and watched as she left the room to deliver the sandwiches to her siblings. "*Has* to be Milk Duds," he said to no one but himself. He turned and looked at the empty kitchen, with its cold tile floor and stark clean cabinets. He was alone, and Kathy, though upstairs in the bath, was nowhere to be found.

———

Jonathan had made himself sleep in the bed that night, though he waited till nearly three A.M. to come up. He was tired when the alarm went off in the morning, and Kathy had already gotten up.

After brushing his teeth and dressing for work, he wandered downstairs, pleased to see the girls hadn't left for school yet. He sat at the breakfast table with them, and Leesol showed him the picture she'd drawn. Kathy quietly fixed oatmeal in the kitchen, and Jonathan was surprised when she set a bowl in front of him, too. The aroma of apples and cinnamon flooded his senses.

"Thanks," he said softly. She responded with a small, delicate smile. He wondered if just the fact that he'd come to bed had somehow lessened the intensity of the night before. It was a mystery to him, but he was glad that he wasn't being scraped over the coals at the moment.

The bus honked and the girls hopped up, grabbed their sack lunches off the counter, and kissed both their parents before running out the front door. The house grew silent suddenly, except for the sound of Sophie sucking her thumb. Kathy grabbed a brush off the counter and began to pull Sophie's hair back into a ponytail.

"Well, I'd better get to work," Jonathan said as he took his last bite of oatmeal. He picked his bowl up and obediently took it to the sink, running water in it and throwing his paper napkin away. If he couldn't do the big things, he at least had to keep up with the little things.

He slid his briefcase off the counter and then kissed both Kathy and Sophie lightly on their cheeks. "Thanks for breakfast."

Kathy pulled a band around Sophie's fine black hair. "Thanks for staying."

He nodded and headed out the front door for work.

On the way in he thought about the night before and how it had been such a disaster. He didn't know if there would ever be a good, comfortable time to tell Kathy about the manuscript. He supposed he would know when the time was right.

When he arrived at the office, things were already moving, and he reminded himself that for him, he was running late. Edie's questioning look reemphasized that. He walked into his office, set his briefcase down, took off his coat, and decided to go find Sydney and tell her about the lunch he'd set up with Naomi Yates. But before he could do that, he noticed it was nine o'clock. He had to go make his tea.

In the executive break room, he waited for the water to heat up in the electric teapot. Behind him, he suddenly heard the break room door shut quietly. He turned around, and there stood Sydney.

At first he thought a few small shadows were hitting her face, but the more he studied it, he realized she was black-and-blue, especially her left cheekbone, and her right eye was partly swollen shut. She even had a small cut across her lower lip.

"Hi," she said and walked closer to him. "Anna said you were looking for me yesterday."

"What happened to your face?"

She smiled, shaking her head and said, "May I?" She pointed to the teapot, which was now whistling. Jonathan never even heard it. She poured some water into his mug, then took one from the cabinet above them and poured hot water into hers. She shook a package of hot chocolate, tore it open, poured it in, and stirred it slowly. Jonathan eagerly waited for a reply.

"Car wreck, if you can believe that," she said, gently touching her right eye and wincing a little in pain.

Jonathan stepped forward to get a closer look. "Yeah. I can believe that, the way your . . . fiancé drives."

She shrugged, and he noticed she was steeping his tea for him. "Seriously," he said. "Are you all right?"

"Oh, I'm fine." She laughed, and her bright smile gleamed through all the bruises and cuts. "Makes me look tough."

"You should see a doctor. Did you hit the windshield or something?"

"Yeah. Cracked it, actually."

Jonathan then did something that he couldn't have stopped if he had wanted to. He reached out and touched her bruised cheek. She shyly looked down but didn't pull away. It was only for a couple of seconds, but he could feel her soft skin underneath his fingers, and he so badly wanted to move his hand down to her full lips. But he didn't.

"You should definitely see a doctor. Those are some bad bruises."

"I'll think about it," she said with a wink. "Your tea is ready."

"Thanks," he said. He took one more long look at her, then found the cream and busied himself by pouring it in.

"So what did you want to see me about?"

He'd almost forgotten! He stirred his tea for a moment and then looked up at her with an excited grin. "I called Naomi Yates yesterday. I have lunch set up with her next Monday. She's anticipating meeting you."

Sydney just about dropped her own mug. "What? Are you serious?"

"As a heart attack." He realized he'd just dated himself with that silly cliché.

"That is so wonderful!"

"So you're free?"

"If not, I'll cancel anything!" She stopped. "Oh . . . I'm supposed to go look at wedding invitations with Jeremy."

Jonathan cringed at the name. Jeremy. He even sounded young and attractive. Probably former captain of the football team or something. "Oh."

"I'll cancel, I'll cancel," she said with a wave of her left hand, and the harsh fluorescent lighting caught her engagement ring. "Really. This is so important. I can't miss it."

"It's about a forty-five-minute trip out to her house, so we'll leave around eleven-fifteen."

"Wonderful," she said, then moved toward the door. "Thank you, Mr. Harper."

"Will you stop calling me that?" he said with a short laugh. "It makes me sound so old!"

She nodded and said, "Thank you, Jonathan."

He loved how she said his name, as if it meant something important. "My pleasure."

She opened the door and disappeared, and for a moment, Jonathan could do nothing but stand there and sip his tea.

C H A P T E R

8

Jonathan felt distracted by about a hundred things, the least of which being the changing fall leaves that were framed perfectly by his large office window. For what seemed like an hour, he sat with his feet propped up on the window, gazing at the leaves as they helplessly floated one by one to the ground. With each falling leaf came a different thought about his life. He wondered what his future held with Kathy, and if there was any hope of ever feeling anything substantial for her again. He entertained thoughts about Sydney, then battled the guilt that soon followed. He thought about his girls, how much they'd grown, and how much he loved them. But perhaps overshadowing all of that was the manuscript he'd deliberately turned his back to.

He hated the power it had over him, the fact that he could not stop himself from reading it, the fact that it literally seemed to call his name. But he was determined to not let it control his life. If he was going to read it, it would be on his own time, his own terms.

The next few hours he spent reviewing manuscripts and writing rejection letters. And toward the end of the day, he took Clyde's manuscript out and continued reading it. Although the premise looked promising so far, he was sure at some point it would fall to pieces. Clyde couldn't write westerns all his life and then suddenly change to an entirely different genre without a hitch. Could he?

He settled into his chair, turned off his phone, and buried himself in this most unusual story. He tried to remember where he'd left off . . . oh yes. Donomar had just told Keaton Spade an innocent man was about to die for a crime he'd committed.

Pierce Jenkins pulled a cigarette from his shirt pocket and lit it with a match that sat on the table between us. I was one of the few agents who worked for the FBI who didn't smoke. Pierce's hands were shaking, and I attributed that to the fact that he had probably been trying to lay off the bottle . . . again.

"Talk to me, Pierce," I said anxiously. "I mean, this is bizarre, right?"

Pierce took a long drag on his cigarette, his eyes following the smoke as it rose toward the ceiling. Janine had gotten ahold of Pierce immediately after I'd called, and now we sat in an empty interrogation room, alone, the only place we could have some privacy.

He seemed highly disturbed by something, and after fiddling with his cigarette another long moment, he finally looked at me. "My job is over with Donomar, you know."

I sighed and tapped my fingers against the cold metal table. "Pierce, come on. I wouldn't come to you if I didn't think I had to. I can tell by the look on your face this is disturbing you, too."

Jenkins carelessly flicked an ash onto the floor. "You mean, besides the fact that I spent ten years trying to find some sort of stinkin' conscience in that monster, and now, suddenly, it blooms? Out of nowhere?" Pierce rubbed his rough beard with his left hand, and I noticed how gray it had turned over the years. He'd always been scruffy looking, wearing his hair long, below his ears, and his beard unruly and unkempt. Sometimes Pierce Jenkins looked more like a criminal than the ones he studied, especially someone like Donomar.

"So you think he's faking it?" I asked quickly. "This is all some sort of joke?" I wanted Pierce's opinion, though I'd already made up my mind.

Pierce's eyes narrowed in what I hoped was contemplation, and he stared at the white wall behind me. Then he laughed a little. "Joke? Interesting word, Keaton."

My pulse raced a little, and I wondered why Pierce had suddenly seemed so intent on playing games with me. "Pierce, what?"

Finally Pierce seemed to come back to the room, his tired, bloodshot eyes focusing on me with deliberate intention. "The joke was on the FBI, Keaton. The Manuel Roberts case."

I shook my head, not understanding.

Pierce continued talking as he smoked. "It was real hush-hush. Manuel Roberts was missing, and of course everyone assumed it was murder. His buddy, Jerome Mitchner, had the motive. They'd had a fight over some gun exchange, and three witnesses came forward stating that Mitchner had told them he would kill Roberts. Problem was, they couldn't find a body. So they did, at that time, the unthinkable. They hired a psychic. The psychic was sure the body would be found in the North Haven drainage ditch, somewhere near the river."

I leaned forward. "Yeah?"

"The media made a big deal about it, since the psychic was used. Not only that, the location made sense. A witness had seen Mitchner around the area the night Roberts disappeared. By this time, the FBI was under fire for not being able to find Roberts." At this moment, Pierce Jenkins paused. The butt of his cigarette was flush against his fingers, but he didn't seem to notice.

"And?" I urged him to continue.

Pierce's face reddened a little. "An off-duty FBI agent, fishing by himself, found a body in . . . Bear Woods." He swallowed smoke and threw his cigarette to the cement floor, grinding it under his old leather boot. "It was none other than Manuel Roberts. So the FBI did the unthinkable again. They moved the body to the drainage ditch, called the media out on a lead, and pulled Roberts from the water."

"A cover-up?" I asked, astonished. "But why? They were sure this Mitchner fellow did it?"

Pierce smiled and lit another cigarette. "Sure. Mitchner had the motive. But the FBI looked bad, and that was unacceptable. So they moved the body, just to show everyone they knew exactly what they were doing the whole time. Sickening."

"How'd you know about that? Did you work on the case?"

"Naw. Just had a little inside information, that's all." Jenkins took in a deep breath, as if he'd just confessed to a murder himself. "You know, I read the 'official' files later, and though Mitchner confessed to the murder, he always said he was never near North Haven."

"So how deeply was this covered up? Who knows about the move?"

Pierce glanced nervously at me. "Nobody. Nobody knows but the few agents involved in the transfer. And the agent who found him. It was an unbelievable cover-up. I only know of about ten guys who know the story, and their lips are sealed. It was in their best interests not to talk."

I sighed, thinking hard and trying to pull all of this into focus. Pierce wasn't silent for long, though. "There's only one person in the world, other than those few men, who would know where Roberts's body was originally found." He paused and looked his cigarette over, twirling it carelessly in his fingers. "The man who murdered him."

"Donomar," I whispered to myself.

Pierce only acknowledged the answer by making eye contact with me. He punched his cigarette out on the table and stood. "The FBI isn't going to let this happen, Keaton."

"You mean, they'd rather let an innocent man die than admit to wrongdoing?"

"You haven't been in this business long enough to know that?" Pierce sneered. He ran his fingers through his hair. "I'd go around the FBI—go straight to the DA." He smiled a little as he found his keys in his pocket. "Esther Caladaras. She never cared for the FBI much anyway."

"I have no intention of smearing the FBI, Pierce. It's not in *my* best interest. But I can't let an innocent man die, either."

"I understand."

"So I do this quietly."

"If you can."

"Caladaras has to cooperate."

Pierce nodded, and his whole body seemed to suddenly slump in fatigue. "Maybe you oughta become a profiler, Keaton. You made a coldhearted killer confess to his diabolical ways. Doesn't really get any better than that."

I stood. "Pierce, I didn't do a thing. I just listened. He'd already made up his mind to confess."

Pierce looked away, then quietly started to exit. He turned

around one more time as he opened the door and said, "Keaton, make sure you know."

"Know what?"

Pierce's mind seemed to be sifting through words. "Make sure you know this isn't a hoax."

I nodded and understood the statement completely. With a little pride I said, "I know it isn't. I watched his thumbs."

"His thumbs?"

"Yeah. Donomar was trying to act as if he had it together, playing it off real cool in the beginning . . . basically just the same old Donomar. But the one thing that gave him away was his thumbs. He kept twiddling his thumbs. You know how he always did that. Sort of a silent indication that there's this crazed killer in there, you know?" Pierce nodded as I continued. "So when he started in on this weird confession episode, his thumbs stopped twiddling. His whole body changed. It was like he was . . . insecure."

Pierce listened intently to all I had to say. Then he opened the door to exit. "I'll keep you posted," I said.

"No thanks," he replied quietly and left.

Jonathan rubbed his eyes and tried to focus on the story but felt he should probably stop. He'd been reading all day, and this was a good place to finish. He was very intrigued by the story and admittedly quite impressed with it so far. He was drawn to its mystery, and he knew he would have no problem finishing it. But today he would have to stop.

He checked his watch, astonished to find it was nearly five-thirty P.M. He left his office and checked Edie's desk for messages for him. Just a few, nothing that couldn't wait until Monday.

As he walked to his car, he remembered the "date" he had with Meg and looked forward to spending Saturday night with her. But this was Friday night, and he wondered if he shouldn't take Kathy out. He couldn't remember the last time they'd done something together.

On his way to his car, he noticed Sydney's fiancé's Firebird parked a few cars away. Although the windows were slightly tinted, he could tell no one was in there. As he passed it, he noticed something very peculiar, something that stuck out without his having to look very hard. He turned back around to double-check.

There was no crack in the windshield.

Their evening might have been perfect if Jonathan had been able to concentrate. Kathy sat across from him at the small, familiar table of the Redwood Crest Restaurant. The mood was set with a single votive candle lit in the center of the table and the soft, haunting music of violins in the background.

Kathy had even made an attempt at looking presentable. She wore a flattering brick-colored silk dress, had combed her hair and pulled it back on both sides with barrettes, and even dabbed on a little mascara and lipstick. The candlelight on her skin drew out a translucent illumination, and even her eyes danced with the slightest bit of anticipation.

They ordered their favorites, a silent signal to them both that familiarity is always so comfortable. The conversation mostly consisted of talk about the girls, thankfully. Jonathan could follow that with only half interest, pretty sure he came off as intrigued and captive.

His mind, though, was being pulled away by a single thing he *didn't* see upon leaving work . . . the crack in the windshield. Over and over he played it out in his mind. Had he misunderstood Sydney? Had she been joking when she mentioned her head hitting the windshield?

As he watched Kathy's mouth move, hearing about every other word, all his mind could see were the bruises and the cuts on Sydney. And those images festered up even more disturbing images, especially one in particular: When he had stated how happy she must be to be engaged, she had simply looked at her ring and moved the conversation along.

His conscience kept avoiding the obvious, until Kathy's words startled him from his reverie.

"—beating her up." The words followed by the silence rang in his ears like a bell. "Jonathan?"

"W-what? Sorry?"

Kathy tilted her head to the side and gave him one of those

looks that no husband could miss—the look of disappointment. But Jonathan tried to quickly recover. He smiled, winked at her, and said in his softest, most soothing voice, "I was just thinking about this vinaigrette."

"The salad dressing?" she asked with deliberate blandness in her voice.

"Yes. I think I had this exact same dressing our very first night here."

Kathy folded her hands together on top of the table, and for a moment, Jonathan couldn't read her. He pretended to be obsessively interested in the vinaigrette as he waited out the grueling silence from the other side of the table.

"I'm surprised you remember that," she said softly, and Jonathan could tell by her tone that he had her. He looked up at her with an intentionally surprised expression.

"Why is that, dear?"

She simply shrugged and continued eating her own salad.

"So—what were you saying?"

Kathy resumed the conversation without missing a beat, explaining that math was, in Meg's own words, "beating her up," and Kathy was wondering if they should get a tutor. Jonathan tried his best to keep up, all the while entertaining disturbing thoughts of Sydney and the fact that perhaps her knight in shining armor was beating her to a bloody pulp.

Relying completely on what little self-control he had left these days, Jonathan managed to finally stick the thoughts of Sydney in the back of his mind and finish dinner with his wife.

Afterward, as the waiter took the dishes away and asked for their dessert orders, Jonathan resigned himself to tell Kathy about the manuscript. The mood was right, the night had been light and cheerful. Kathy was in a good mood.

Jonathan uncharacteristically ordered dessert and coffee, which prompted Kathy to do the same. He noticed she almost had a dreamy look in her eyes. Almost. It was as if she wanted to surrender but couldn't quite find the courage. For some strange reason he understood. He felt the same way.

Still, there was a peace at the table, and Jonathan was relaxed enough to bring up the topic of the manuscript.

"Honey," he said after the waiter brought out their coffees, "there's something I've been wanting to talk to you about."

The waiter appeared out of nowhere with two pieces of cheesecake, and as he placed the dessert in front of each of them, the pause seemed almost too much for Kathy to bear. She picked up her fork as if she wanted to do anything with it but eat, and she must have folded her napkin five times, twice in her lap and three times on the table.

Jonathan waited for the waiter to leave, then continued. "I should've told you about this a long time ago. I just . . . we've just . . . there have just been some problems between us, and I wanted it to be the right time. It's nothing big," he said as he watched her face turn pale. "Seriously, nothing alarming. But I thought you should know."

"Know what?" she asked stiffly.

Jonathan took a bite of his cheesecake and pointed to hers with his fork. "Aren't you going to—"

"Know *what?*"

Jonathan was a little surprised at her tone. He wondered if he should indeed tell her, but it was too late. He had to tell her *something*. He took one more bite of his cheesecake, so as to appear relaxed, sipped his coffee, and said, "Well, there's this little mystery going on in my life."

He chuckled a bit, hoping to lift the sudden fifty-pound weight that had apparently dropped in the middle of the table. Kathy didn't so much as blink.

"It's the oddest thing," he said again cheerfully, "but a few days ago I received this strange manuscript in the mail, addressed to my boyhood address, of all places, and when I opened it, it didn't have an author's name." He sipped his coffee again, this time feeling a little nervous and fidgety. Kathy was stone-cold. "Anyway, long story short, it's sort of similar to my life." He paused and looked up at her, hoping for a response.

The waiter returned and warmed his coffee. Kathy's cheesecake and coffee were untouched. "Um, the story starts out with these two young kids, and one kid gets killed by this tractor and plow.

Anyway, they're brothers, and their names are Jonathan and Jason."
He paused to try to stop any emotions that might want to creep
up. Nothing was coming, so he continued. "I think I told you that
Jason, my brother, died."

"Barely."

"Yes, well, the story was so similar it really caught my attention.
And the more I read, the more similar the story became about my
life."

Kathy stopped him, holding up her hands. "Wait a minute. Are
you trying to tell me that you're reading a story about your own
life?"

"Well, honey, it's nothing big. It's *similar*. Key word there.
There are a lot of discrepancies—"

"How similar?"

Jonathan swallowed and scraped the side of his cheesecake
with his fork. "You know, just sort of generalizations. I mean, it
doesn't record every bathroom break I took in elementary school."

Kathy leaned forward a bit. "Jonathan, what are you saying, exactly?"

"I'm just saying that—and there's nothing to be alarmed about,
I assure you—that it may be some practical joke or something, but
it appears that someone is sending me my life's story. Anonymously."

Kathy's face turned worried. "Do you know who?"

"Honey, if I knew that, it wouldn't be anonymous," Jonathan
said smoothly, trying very hard to keep his voice steady and calm.

"Who would do such a thing?"

"I don't know. I'm sure it's just a joke or something."

Kathy finally picked up her cup of coffee and sipped it. "You're
not worried?"

"No, no. Not in the least bit. I mean, it's weird. But it's not dangerous. And it's only been three chapters, just about my childhood—vague, very vague descriptions of my childhood—and that's
it. There's nothing in there about you and the kids. Nothing to
worry about. I just told you because I thought you should know."

Kathy set down her coffee cup, picked up her fork, twirled it in her fingers, and looked directly in his eyes. "So is that what this dinner was about?"

Jonathan's whole body went limp with relaxation. He'd done it. He'd told her, with few questions asked. And it seemed as if the evening would go on as normal. His appetite furiously rushed back, and he took two or three more bites of cheesecake with barely a breath in between. "Yes, honey. I wanted to tell you."

But before he could finish his third bite, the table shook as Kathy laid both of her hands down onto it with a thump. Jonathan looked up in surprise.

"So this wasn't about us? About you and me?"

Jonathan felt his head begin to spin. He hated being lost in a conversation in which he had no idea the direction it was about to take. "What?"

"This whole night was what? A prompting for this big news you had to break to me?"

"Kathy, I—"

"I get it," she said, throwing down her napkin and almost knocking her coffee over.

"Get what?" Jonathan demanded, setting his own fork down.

"This night. This wasn't about you and me. This wasn't a date. This wasn't *you* wanting to spend time with your wife. This was an attempt to relax me so you could tell me about some dumb manuscript about your life."

Jonathan was so caught off guard that he didn't know what to say. He flung his body back into his chair, opened his wallet, took out a credit card, and looked for the waiter. "I guess I can assume the evening's over," he stated harshly, avoiding her heated eyes.

"Apparently it never began," she blurted out. Shoving her chair back, she grabbed her sweater off the back, turned toward the door, and then stopped. Without turning around, she said quietly, "I just wish you knew how much I wanted this night to be about you and me." She then quietly walked out of the restaurant.

Jonathan slumped in exhaustion, and when the waiter arrived to take his credit card, all he could do was slide it slowly across the top of the table. Nothing was simple. Nothing could be enjoyed anymore. He felt as desperate as he ever had.

CHAPTER 9

Jonathan vowed to not let Kathy ruin his entire weekend. Although he would've rather subjected himself to acupuncture needles than stay home, he remembered his date with Meg Saturday evening. And so he and Meg went to the video store and rented some movie Kathy would never have let her watch and stayed up late eating junk food.

He waited till Meg was absorbed in the movie to slide the mysterious manuscript out of his briefcase, all the while participating by grabbing obnoxious handfuls of their famous popcorn-and-Milk-Dud mix, something they'd accidentally created when Meg was seven and both discovered they loved.

Kathy kept herself busy upstairs with the two other children, making enough noise to let everyone in the house know she was around. Jonathan deliberately left the movie case on the kitchen table, daring her to say something about the movie choice he'd made. But neither of them spoke, and though Jonathan knew the silence was more grueling for her than him, he remained silent and unapproachable the whole day and evening.

The manuscript, its pages still not crumpled from many readings, its white paper not smudged and stained with tea, as others usually were, had seemed to call his name Friday when he left. He had intended to keep it at the office, to not let it interfere with his weekend. But it nagged at him until he finally gave in and threw it in his briefcase.

He only had a few pages left to finish what had been sent. The chapters had been short and stopped and started with no apparent logic. Another mark of an amateur. He took out a note pad; it somehow eased his soul to approach it methodically. He found his place and began reading.

> *Jonathan continued to read and love books, though he remained a poor student all the way through high school. In college—*

Jonathan stopped reading and quickly picked up his pen. He couldn't believe it. The writer had left off with a young, anguished boy lying in his mother's lap—all of which happened, from what he could remember—to college?! Jonathan scribbled feverishly. This was his first big clue. There was what, maybe ten years missing? The person writing this didn't know what had happened in those ten years! If he had, he certainly would've written them down.

Jonathan tapped his pen against his chin, loud enough to make Meg glance over, even during a violent scene. "Sorry," he smiled.

She drew her soft eyebrows together. "Are you watching, Daddy?"

"Of course," he said, pointing at the TV. "You'd better watch, too. I think this is going to be an important part to the plot."

Meg whipped back around and Jonathan was thankful he'd seen the movie before. He was right, and Meg gasped as the attractive actor delivered a clincher line.

Jonathan tried to think about those ten years. What, of significance, had happened? He and his father had grown more distant, but Jonathan was growing more into a man and didn't need his father's approval for much of anything. Instead of a desperate puppy dog, Jonathan was now independent and as cruel and cold as his father had ever been to him.

He'd joined varsity basketball, and though he never made first string, he saw some significant playing time. He'd had a few insignificant girlfriends, but no one he would later brag about to any-body. There were no prom queens. He mostly dated bookworms, and most of those types had long, stringy hair down to their waist and glasses that always looked outdated. He mostly referred to those girls as friends, and only they knew he'd kissed a few along the way.

College had been different, though, and he wondered if this ghostwriter would know anything about those days. Before he con-tinued, though, he took the page of the manuscript and made a huge star by the sentence he'd just read. He'd never dared to write on the manuscript before; it held some sort of strange power over him, a power that he silently revered by respecting its neat white pages. But now he'd found a weakness, and he pressed his pen hard against the page. Then he continued.

> *During college at the University of North Carolina, Char-lotte, Jonathan Harper seemed to fit in perfectly. He joined all the appropriate clubs and associations for his particular inter-ests and made his way to the head of his class with ease. He was a hit with all the professors, and a few of them often asked him to join them for coffee at the Student Union.*
>
> *Perhaps it was all the coldness and hardness of his child-hood that had molded him into the kind of man everyone wanted to be around. He had a certain unapproachable atti-tude, the kind that made people want to approach him more. He always chose his words carefully, and if he smiled or paid interest to a particular person, it meant they were special. It was just how he worked. He demanded attention, because for the most part, he never wanted it.*

Jonathan flipped the page of his pad for more room, noting that this person knew his personality and maybe knew him in college, though no specific details had been given yet.

> *It was a cold winter morning when he decided to go to the campus library. He was working on one of his first term pa-pers, and though he'd already done his research, he always felt at home and comfortable surrounded by books and silence. And it was there, that morning, in the silence of the library,*

that she first caught his eye. Her name was Katherine Williby.

Jonathan tried hard to not let that affect him, but one never does have much control over emotional reactions inside the body. His heart stung and then pounded hard against his chest, and even his skin began to crawl with a strange sort of itch. Now his family was involved. And not only that, whoever wrote this had the details right. He'd gone to work on a term paper in the library when Kathy had first caught his eye. He jotted down a couple of notes, though without enthusiasm. He hoped the following details would be vague. But his hope soon vanished.

Her hair was long, brown, and shiny, and it swung against her back as she carried her books close to her chest. She hardly seemed to notice him as she sat at the same table as he, though at the other end. She was noticeably petite, and Jonathan wondered if he shouldn't help her with the books. But she'd dumped them on the table before he could offer. She glanced up once to find him staring at her, smiled briefly, and then opened her own book.

Jonathan couldn't concentrate. He could smell the light scent of her perfume from where he sat, and her left leg, crossed over her right, dangled to the side of the table in his perfect view. Her eyes sparkled, even under the dim light, and he guessed they must've been the most amazing shade of dark blue, almost navy, lined neatly with dark black lashes and framed with thin, neatly formed brows.

A certain energy penetrated from her, even as she read her book and took notes on a pad that looked brand-new. After a few moments, Jonathan—well aware of his sudden stardom status on campus—moved a few seats over toward her, making her look up with curiosity.

"Hi," he said in a deep voice that didn't seem to fit him.

Katherine smiled cautiously, gripping her pen a little too tightly. "Hello."

At that moment, Jonathan could think of nothing more to say, and the awkward silence seemed to resonate off the library walls. Her small mouth spread into a tolerant smile.

"Um . . . I'm Jonathan. Jonathan Harper."

"Well, Jonathan Harper, is there something I can help you with?"

He felt his heart flutter and only because he could not think of anything else to say, he blurted out, "Will you go out with me?"

At first her face seemed to indicate that she would not. She closed her book and her lips made a straight line across her face. "Go out with you?"

He nodded and felt so incredibly foolish that he wanted to sink below the table. The only way out of this was for her to say her polite "No thank you," and then for him to pretend he had finished his research, close his books, and leave with his head up.

"What did you have in mind?" she asked suddenly.

Jonathan twitched a little, blinked his eyes twice, and asked, "What?"

"Do you have an idea of what we're going to do? Because I like having a good time, and if you wanted to do something boring, I probably wouldn't go."

Jonathan smiled at her candidness. "Oh. Well, I tend to think I'm pretty good company, so how does dinner sound?"

She cocked her head to the side. "You think you can entertain me the entire evening?"

Jonathan's heart surged with anticipation. "Well, I'm buying, so you have nothing to lose if you try me."

"I am a very busy person," she said in a playfully serious voice.

"And I'm a pathetically bored person," he said, making her laugh. "Tell you what. Give me two hours. After that, you're free to leave."

She held out a small, dainty hand, and he took it. They shook hands and both said, "Deal."

It was the beginning of a love affair.

Jonathan held the last page of the manuscript in his hand and stared at the last three words: *a love affair*. It seemed so ironic as he heard Kathy continuing to slam things upstairs.

But his mind switched gears quickly, and he began analyzing. This person had to have known either him or Kathy in college, or maybe both of them. Jonathan tried to remember how many people he'd shared details with about the first time they'd met. He couldn't think of anyone specific and noted that was probably more of a female thing to do anyway.

However, what bothered him more was that the connection between a college acquaintance and his childhood didn't make sense. If the writer was a college acquaintance, then the details about him and Kathy made sense. But how could you factor in the childhood details? Not even Kathy knew much about his childhood, at least the things that were written in the manuscript.

Jonathan tried to rub away the tension in the back of his neck as his mind churned with a million different possibilities. Suddenly he heard a click and watched Meg jump off the couch and take the tape out of the VCR.

"Great movie, Dad!" she said and plopped back down on the couch to finish off the popcorn and Milk Duds.

"I knew you'd like it," he said, trying to scoot the manuscript subtly to the other side of himself. He checked his watch. "It's late, big girl. You probably should get to bed."

She nodded. "I know. But remember your promise?"

"Promise?"

"Yeah. You promised me you'd go to church with us in the morning."

Jonathan had almost forgotten. He tried to contain the huge sigh that attempted to escape. "Sure, honey. I'll go."

Meg smiled approvingly, grabbed one last handful of goodies, and sprang upstairs.

"Meg?"

"Yeah?" she called from the top.

"What time?" There was silence. "For church? What time do you leave?"

"Fifteen till ten, Daddy."

"Thanks. See you in the morning."

Jonathan released the sigh that had been building and sank back into the couch, crushing part of the manuscript underneath him.

Jonathan tossed and turned all night and awoke much earlier

than needed the next morning. To his surprise, Kathy was already up, too. He could hear her downstairs in the kitchen. He wasn't sure what time she got up on Sunday mornings. He was either asleep or working at the office when they would leave for church.

His body seemed unusually heavy as he rolled it out of bed. He guessed Kathy hadn't slept well either, a sign that they at least still cared enough to lose sleep over their heated, unresolved fights.

He had over an hour before he needed to get ready for church. He stretched his body, brushed his teeth, splashed some water on his face, and decided to read a few more pages of Clyde's manuscript. If he wasn't going to go to the office this morning, at least he could get a little work done before church.

He settled into the large upholstered chair in the corner of the bedroom, scooted the ottoman underneath his feet, and began to read.

"We got 122 men on this death row," the guard with a southern drawl said. "Only three are scheduled for execution in the next two months. Jerome's one of them." The guard glanced down at me. "I got to wonder what it's like to know the exact moment you're gonna die. Ever think about that?"

A thick sheet of Plexiglas separated me from where the prisoner would sit. Beside me a young Mexican woman cried to a man on the other side I assumed was her husband. Before I could do much else, Jerome Mitchner was seated in front of me, his large head holding a boyishly curious look. The guard next to me gave us our privacy.

"Who are you?"

"Keaton Spade," I replied steadily.

"I don't feel like talkin' to no one," Jerome said heavily. "Why you here? You look like some cop or somethin'. I couldn't do nothin' else from death row, could I? Get in trouble? Gonna arrest me, are ya? Can't be sentenced to death twice, can ya?"

"I'm from the FBI." I opened my briefcase and pulled out a pad and pen. "I want to talk to you about your case."

"What about it?" Jerome said defiantly. "I killed a man. I gonna die for it. What's there to talk about?"

"Did you kill that man?"

Jerome was silent.

"You confessed to it," I said after he didn't reply. "You said you killed him. Why did you say that?"

"You with the FBI, you say?" Jerome asked. I could tell by the unsteadiness of his voice that Jerome was very much caught off guard. "What you want? You tell me why you here, why you askin' these questions."

"You had no criminal record before this crime. But you certainly had the motive to kill the guy. And witnesses say you said several times you were going to kill Roberts. It's a simple question. Did you kill Manuel Roberts or not?"

I heard Jerome shuffle his feet against the cement, a sign he was agitated and nervous. "I want my lawyer. I gotta right to see my lawyer."

I cut him off quickly. "You can talk to your lawyer all you want, Mr. Mitchner. But I'm asking you this once. What harm is there in asking you this simple question? I'm two minutes from walking out that door. You either answer the question now or you don't. That'll be the end of it."

Jerome's heavy brow formed a scowl. He took in a deep breath and his fingers fiddled around methodically for a phantom cigarette. "I didn't kill Manuel." There was a long pause between us, and then Jerome kept talking. "It was a setup."

"A setup? Who?"

Jerome was talking fast and nervously, rambling. "I don't know, man. I mean, I got some enemies. Sure. Everybody does, don't they—"

"You confessed."

"I-I-I . . . they brainwashed me. I mean, they were in my face, you know? Tellin' me they had the evidence! Tellin' me it'd be worse if I didn't confess! What's worse than death row?"

"You didn't kill him?"

"Nah, man, I didn't kill Manuel. I didn't kill him. I'm an innocent man." Jerome moved his face close to the glass. "You gonna get me off death row? Clear my name, man?"

"I'll be back," I said and snapped my briefcase shut.

"Whooo-hoooo!" I heard Jerome squeal as I left the room. "You crazies hear that? Hear what that man just said? There's somethin' goin' on! I don't know what! But there's somethin' goin' on!"

The door opened to their bedroom, and a flushed, just awakened face peeked around it.

"You're up, Daddy!"

"Of course. Did you think I would miss this? We had a deal."

"You better get dressed!" Meg said and shut the door.

Jonathan glanced down at his watch. It wasn't quite time, but it was a good place to stop in Clyde's book. He picked out a nice dark suit from his closet, shaved, got dressed, and headed downstairs.

A heavy aroma of homemade waffles filled the kitchen, and Jonathan laughed as even the birds on the windowsill seemed to greet him with a morning song. Sophie was on the floor playing with some pots and pans.

"Good morning," he said cheerfully. Kathy turned around and froze for a moment. She then looked him up and down.

"A suit?" she asked in a not-so-friendly tone.

Jonathan looked down at himself. "I didn't know. I mean, I thought I'd try to look nice."

Kathy whirled back around and started distributing butter and syrup on the waffles. "A little dressed up just to be doing some weekend work at the office, aren't you, Jonathan?" she said with what he was sure was a sneer on her face.

Jonathan moved forward a bit. "I'm not going to the office. I'm . . . going to church with you."

Kathy turned back around, still holding the butter and the syrup. "You are?"

He smiled. "Yes. Is that okay?"

She softened immediately and set down the butter and syrup. "Really?"

He picked Sophie up off the floor and kissed her on the cheek. "Really. Meg and I had a deal."

"Jonathan, I can't believe . . . I mean, I just assumed you were going to the office—"

Her gentle words and the tender moment were abruptly cut short with the shrill ringing of the telephone.

"I'll get it," Jonathan said. Kathy just stared wide-eyed at it and then looked back at Jonathan. "It's okay, honey. I'll get it. Go fix the waffles."

He watched as Kathy slowly turned around, and then he answered the phone.

"Hello?"

"Jonny, it's Clyde."

"Good morning, Clyde! How are—"

"Listen. Meet me at your office in ten minutes."

Jonathan's heart sank suddenly. Clyde sounded panicked, yet all he could do was watch Kathy and remember how soft her words had been just minutes before, how her face had brightened when he told her he was going to church with them.

"Clyde, what's the—"

"Jonny, ten minutes."

He watched as Kathy walked two plates to the kitchen table and arranged the napkins and silverware with a delight that could only come from a mother and wife.

"Can't this wait?"

"Jonny, it's urgent. Hurry."

CHAPTER 10

Clyde was waiting in front of the office building, leaning up against the brick wall. Before he was even able to get out of his car, Jonathan immediately noticed the manila envelope tucked under his arm. His heart raced with apprehension and paranoia. He looked around the near-empty parking lot for anyone suspicious. But the truth of the matter was that the only person in his view was Clyde.

Jonathan turned the ignition off in his car and slowly got out. Clyde quickly walked up the sidewalk to greet him. His face was solemn. Jonathan stiffened and waited for Clyde to approach.

"Jonny, I . . . I swear I didn't know what it was. I guess it came in the mail yesterday, but I didn't check my mail till this mornin'. It was addressed to me." He flipped it over to show him the front. "I didn't know—I mean, I just started readin', and then I figured it out."

Jonathan stared hard at Clyde, whose eyes were wide and voice was trembling. He slowly reached out and took the envelope from Clyde.

"How much did you read, Clyde?" Jonathan asked, his jaw muscles tight as his teeth clenched together.

Clyde dug his hands deep into the pockets of his Wranglers. "Enough."

Jonathan backed away from Clyde, down the sidewalk, and toward his car. Though two stamps were stuck to the upper right corner of the envelope, it didn't have an ink stamp indicating it had gone through the mail system. Jonathan's eyes lingered a bit longer on that, then he looked back at Clyde with narrow eyes.

"How long did you think you were going to get away with all of this, Clyde?"

Clyde took a step forward but Jonathan backed up more. Clyde stopped and held out his hand. "Wait a minute. You don't think . . . Jonny, I didn't. . . . You don't think I'm sendin' that stuff to you?" Clyde swallowed.

Jonathan felt his throat swell and his eyes sting. "I don't know what to think."

Clyde fumbled over his words. "I'm sorry I read it, Jonny. I didn't know it was for you. I wasn't expectin' to get anything like that at my house." He shuffled his large boots. "And why didn't you tell me you and Kathy were havin' troubles?"

Jonathan felt like someone just squeezed all the air out of his chest. "Excuse me?"

"Well, the book said that—" Clyde stopped and seemed to crawl inside himself when he looked up at Jonathan. "I'm sure that's just a bunch of garbage, right? 'Course it is."

Jonathan was completely unaware that his shaking hand had moved itself up and over his mouth. His only indication that he might be as white as a ghost was Clyde's sudden move toward him. Clyde grabbed his elbow.

"Jonny, for heaven's sake, sit down."

Jonathan yanked his arm away from Clyde. He opened the door to his vehicle and grabbed the lighter. Before he could stop himself, the envelope and its contents were on fire. He threw it to the cement ground and sucked the smoke through his nostrils as if it were a pleasant fragrance. In some ways, he felt a sudden surge of power over the situation. But his emotions contradicted one another, because in that same instant, he felt he might have just thrown away his only real clue.

Clyde stood silently by his side and watched with him as the fire quickly engulfed it until all that was left were a few charred pieces. Clyde moved away a dry leaf that the fire had hoped to attach itself to, and without anything else to burn, the flames disappeared.

Clyde raised his heavy body to a tall stature. "You know I ain't writin' this, Jonny."

"Do I? *Do I?*" Jonathan turned and walked to his vehicle.

As he lifted himself up and into his SUV, Clyde called after him. "I think you and your family might be in—"

Jonathan never heard the rest of it. He had rolled up his window and driven off.

———

Jonathan felt sick inside. He was disappointing his family—Meg had cried when he left the house to see Clyde this morning—and now he was battling an invisible enemy. As he'd watched the flames engulf the pages of that manuscript, a sense of danger had overwhelmed him. The fact that they revealed he and Kathy had been having trouble meant that whoever the writer was had walked the halls of their house. And Clyde had walked the halls of their house hundreds of times.

Chills crawled his spine and the hair on his arms stood straight up as he meticulously checked every lock in his house. Could it be possible someone was watching every move he made? He had talked himself in and out of the idea that Clyde was the author. Clyde knew them better than anyone, yet why would he write something so brutally eerie? He knew Clyde too well to believe he would want to harm his family. Yet if it wasn't Clyde, then who? No one knew them better.

He unscrewed every telephone receiver and checked it for a tiny microphone or something. He saw nothing that looked out of place. As he descended the stairs of his basement, his pulse raced with fear. If someone had been in their house, perhaps they stayed in the basement. Predictably, the single light bulb that hung from the ceiling midway down the stairs popped and went out when he flipped the light switch. Nevertheless, there was enough illumination from the small window in the back of the basement to allow him to search. Nothing seemed out of the ordinary. A pad of dust lined nearly everything; boxes piled to the ceiling crowded every corner. Still, though everything looked in place, Jonathan found a hammer and nailed the tiny window—barely big enough for a child to fit through—shut.

"What are you doing?"

Jonathan's foot slipped, and he tumbled off the ladder and hit the cement floor with a *thud*. He heard two feet scurry toward him, and when he rolled over and opened his eyes, Kathy was bent over him.

"Jonathan! Are you okay?"

Jonathan moaned and slowly tried to move each of his limbs. Everything seemed to be functioning normally, though his back felt as if someone had hit him with a two-by-four.

"I'm okay. You scared me to death."

Kathy grabbed his face, still worried. "What were you doing up there?"

Jonathan tried to get up, but his body seemed to weigh a ton. "Kathy . . ."

"What?"

Jonathan let his head drop back onto the floor and he closed his eyes. Everything was spinning, and it wasn't because of the fall he'd just taken.

"What are you doing down here in the basement on a ladder?"

He wanted to tell her everything. He wanted to grab her and hold her and make her hold him. His body trembled. But his instincts kicked in and told him not to frighten Kathy with the circumstances.

Kathy grabbed his hand. "Does this have to do with the phone call from Clyde this morning? You rushed out of here so quickly, honey."

Jonathan swallowed. Though Meg had begged him not to leave, Kathy seemed more understanding. And even now her voice was concerned, not angry. Maybe things were changing between the two of them. Maybe he needed to tell her everything.

After one final sigh, Jonathan managed to sit up with his wife's help. He looked into her concerned eyes and said, "Yes."

"Is Clyde okay?"

"Remember the manuscript I told you about?"

"Yes . . ."

"Remember I told you that the manuscript never mentioned you and the kids? Well—" Jonathan could hardly get the words out. "It mentions you, Kathy. The whole event surrounding how we met was in there."

Kathy stood, her eyes never leaving Jonathan's, and dusted herself off. "The library?"

"Yeah."

"Why isn't the light working in here?"

"The bulb burned out."

Kathy walked up the stairs toward the light from the kitchen, then sat down on a step, facing Jonathan. Her hands were clasped together as if in prayer.

Jonathan stood slowly and took a few steps up toward her. "Kathy, have you told anyone about . . . about the problems we've been having?"

Kathy frowned. "What do you mean?"

"I mean exactly what I said. Have you told anyone we're having problems?"

Her eyes narrowed. "What you're meaning to say is, have I gone around blabbing our problems all over town?"

"Have you told Clyde?"

"No!"

Jonathan took a few more steps toward her. "Kathy, I'm not angry. I just need to know. Have you told anyone?"

Kathy looked him in the eye. "Is it in that stupid book?"

Jonathan pressed his lips together. "I'm not sure. I burned the pages this morning without reading them." Kathy looked at him curiously. "That's why he called this morning. Clyde supposedly received more pages at his house, but I never opened the package."

"Then why are you asking who I've told about our problems?"

Jonathan reluctantly said, "Because Clyde read a few of the pages and . . ." Jonathan couldn't even finish. He suddenly felt intense frustration building inside him, and the very thought of having to explain it all exhausted him to the point that he couldn't say another word. He stood and walked past Kathy.

As he reached the top step, Kathy said, "I told Pastor Gregory."

Jonathan didn't turn around. He didn't have the energy. "You told him what?"

"I told him we'd been having some problems. That it seemed our marriage was falling apart right before our eyes. I asked him to pray for us."

"He's the only one you've told?"

"Yes." She paused, then said, "He told me not to give up."

Jonathan turned around. "Give up?"

She had tears in her eyes. "He said you were worth fighting for, and that I should do everything in my power to save our marriage. If I did that, God would take care of the rest." Kathy didn't even bother wiping the tears that now flowed from her eyes. Her eyes searched him intensely.

Jonathan smiled a little. "Well, I guess I'll have to go see if Pastor Gregory has written any books lately."

He started to leave, but he heard Kathy say, "Jonathan, I'm scared."

"Honey, I'm taking care of this. I'm going to go see Clyde this afternoon and find how much he read of those pages and what was in them. Then I'm going to go see Pastor Gregory. I swear to you I'll find out who is writing this."

Kathy stood. "That's not what I'm talking about."

Jonathan shook his head, not understanding.

"I'm scared you're going to walk out the front door one day and not come back."

Jonathan lowered his head, wanting to say something, but instead he continued out of her sight.

Jonathan played everything over and over in his head. If Clyde had really received the manuscript in the mail, it would've been metered. But there was the chance someone had stuck it in his mailbox after his mail had arrived. Either way, Clyde was a suspect.

Even so, he knew he had to find out what those burned pages

contained. What was in there could hold the only clue to who was writing this, whether it was Clyde or someone else. The problem was, the only person who knew what was in those pages was Clyde.

"Can I get you some tea?" Clyde asked precariously as they stood on his back porch. "I promise I won't poison it."

Jonathan looked up at him, gave an uneasy smile, and declined the offer. He leaned against the wood railing that circled the back porch and took in the view. The sun's bottom just touched the horizon, setting the land on fire with an orange light. Its warmth glowed on his face, but a soft, cold wind tickled his back and threatened to grow stronger as night approached. So many times he'd sat on this porch, relaxing in the swing or sitting in the wicker chairs, talking to Clyde about books or many other things, watching the kids swim in the small lake a couple hundred feet away. But now the tall, lovable teddy bear of a man he'd come to think of as a father seemed as much a stranger to him as his real father. A wall of uneasiness separated them, and Jonathan could do nothing to change that. Clyde was a suspect, and he had every reason to believe he was sending those pages. Jonathan just didn't know why.

Clyde had disappeared into the house to fix himself iced tea, then emerged again wearing an old ragged cardigan that his wife had knitted for him when he was fifty pounds lighter. Jonathan smiled a little at the sight of the poor sweater stretched to its maximum, buttons missing and holes starting underneath each armpit.

Clyde joined him at the railing, and for a while they just appreciated the picture Mother Nature was painting before their eyes, though it was doubtful either one of them was really thinking of that at all. Clyde finally spoke up.

"I don't think you're here to shoot the breeze with me, are ya, Jonny?"

Jonathan shook his head without looking at him.

"And you think I'm the one sendin' you those pages of that manuscript." Clyde said that statement definitively, and Jonathan didn't feel the need to add anything to it. After drinking his tea, Clyde continued. "Then why are you here?"

Jonathan turned his head to look at Clyde. "I want to know what was in those pages."

"Why?" Clyde moved to a wicker chair as if he was too tired to stand any longer. He carefully lowered himself down and slowly bent his knees into position, wincing in pain at the arthritis that always flared up in the fall. "I mean, Jonny, if I'm the writer and you've found your man, why do you care what was in there?"

Jonathan looked down and rubbed his temples. "Clyde, I swear if you're doing this . . ." Jonathan looked into his eyes. "I want to believe you're not. It's just that things aren't adding up, and now my family is involved."

Clyde set his tea down and pointed for Jonathan to sit across from him. "Whoever it is that's writin' this, Jonny, is messin' with you. You understand that? They're involvin' people you know so you don't know who it is, and you're suspectin' everyone, includin' me." Clyde wiped the condensation off his glass with his sleeve. "First it comes in the mail, and now it's hand delivered to my mailbox. Don't you get it? They're hidin' their tracks."

"Maybe that's what you want me to believe. Make you an obvious suspect so I don't suspect you."

Clyde cocked his head sideways. "Well, I suppose you can psychoanalyze this all ya want, Jonny, but the fact of the matter is that you got some real trouble on your hands. Someone knows everything about you, and they're going to make sure you know it."

Jonathan stiffened. "They don't know everything." Clyde raised his eyebrows questioningly. "Whoever it is." The fact that years were missing in the manuscript was the only clue Jonathan had that the writer wasn't some supernatural, omnipresent being. Someone had a lot of information, but not all of it.

"Well, they got enough."

Jonathan crossed his legs and tried to get comfortable in a wicker chair that seemed to warn with every little movement that it could collapse at any moment. "How many pages were there?"

Clyde held up his pointer finger and thumb a half inch apart. "About that many."

"Where did it start? With what event in my life?"

Clyde thought for a moment. "Well, it seems to me there was

the story of your daughter's birth—"

"Which one?"

"Meg's. Said in there what hospital she was born at, what time—"

"All public record," Jonathan thought out loud.

"And how blown away you were by the birth, that it radically changed your life."

"Shot in the dark."

"What?"

Jonathan looked up at Clyde, almost forgetting anyone else was around. "Nothing. Continue."

"Anyway, then it went into some vague descriptions about your life between children. Kathy's attempt to return to work. Your big break with Bromahn & Hutch. Basically just a lot of info."

Jonathan eyed Clyde carefully. "A lot of info. You said you were sorry to hear we were having trouble. That was in there."

"Yeah, toward the end. It seemed to all move chronologically, like someone was just outlinin' your life. There was some detail, but I gotta tell ya, Jonny, the writin' isn't that good."

Jonathan smiled tolerantly at Clyde. "Yeah, well, maybe a really good writer is disguising that very fact."

Clyde pressed his lips together. "Maybe."

"Continue, please."

"I don't know. I mean, I wasn't payin' close attention to detail, 'cause I wasn't expectin' you to burn it."

Jonathan sighed. "Clyde, just tell me what was in there about Kathy."

"Well, if I recall correctly, the story started with your weddin'—"

"I thought you said it started with my child's birth."

Clyde paused. "Nope, it definitely started with your weddin'. I remember there was a nice description in there about it and how there were hundreds of lilies everywhere. Lilies are my favorite flower."

"How convenient," Jonathan sighed. "Clyde, let me get this straight. Basically the first few pages outlined my marriage to Kathy, the kids' births, and our careers."

Clyde thought about it. "Yep."

"So where does it start in with our troubles?" Jonathan asked, embarrassed to even have to discuss it with anyone.

Clyde circled his ice cubes around in his tea. "Well, I think it just sort of implied throughout the story that you two were growin' apart. I mean, it never really gave details in that area, but it was apparent that trouble was brewin'."

Jonathan placed his head in his hands and scratched his face. "So was it past trouble or present trouble?"

"Well, like I said, it implied about it in the past, though there wasn't anything specific. But it seemed the more toward the present it got, it started givin' more details, specific fights—"

"What fights?"

"It talked about a fight you and Kathy had about three years ago, right after Sophie was born. You ended up cancelin' a vacation or somethin' because you had to work with a writer on her deadline."

Jonathan nodded. "That happened."

"And then another time when you forgot Kathy's birthday."

Jonathan smiled a bit. "Yeah, that was a killer."

"And the time you forgot to pick Meg up from the baby-sitter's—"

Jonathan threw up his hands. "Okay, I get it. We had a lot of fights."

"Fascinatin' readin'," Clyde chuckled. "A real page-turner."

"Very funny," Jonathan said and sighed heavily.

"And that's about it."

Jonathan frowned and looked up at Clyde. "That's all? Just a bunch of fights?"

"Well, there was a lot in there 'bout your career as an editor and all, but it certainly emphasized that you two don't exactly have a fairy-tale marriage."

Jonathan winced at that statement. If only they knew. Then his stomach churned. He wondered if they really did know.

"So—it stopped where in my life?"

"Mmm, from what I could tell, anywhere from a year to a few months ago." Clyde tapped his fingers against his glass.

Jonathan stood and stretched, walking over to the edge of the porch. The stars were now lit on top of a darkening blue sky. The white moon's reflection bobbed up and down in the waters of the lake.

"Well, I guess when it's all lined up one after another for someone to read, it seems like a divorce waiting to happen. But when it's your life, you hardly seem to notice until—" Jonathan stopped himself and buttoned the top button of his knit shirt to hold in the little warmth he still had. "They just don't seem that blatant, that's all."

Clyde joined him at the railing. "I lied earlier when I said I didn't know you and Kathy were having troubles." He looked at Jonathan. "I love you and your family. You know that. You've been my family ever since my wife died. Quite frankly, I've been worried about you."

Jonathan didn't so much as glance at Clyde. "What in the world would make you worry about me?" he asked dryly.

"Well, for one thing, you've been drinkin' a lot lately."

"I'm not a drunk."

"No, but you're also not facin' your problems with a steady head on your shoulders."

"Look, I'm under a lot of pressure at work right now, and Kathy doesn't seem to understand that I've got to put in extra hours—" He stopped and stepped away from the rail. "Why am I telling you all this? So you can write another seven chapters about how my life is right now?"

Clyde shook his head and didn't turn around. "You want to believe I'm writin' that stuff, you go right ahead, Jonny. I can't say anything that would convince you otherwise."

Jonathan suddenly felt very alone. Clyde had been the one solid rock in his life, and now he couldn't trust him. He couldn't trust anyone, for that matter. At the same time, he felt sad that Clyde wouldn't even turn around to face him. He noticed for the first time how old Clyde looked. The back of his hair was completely white. He had started to hunch. Even his hands were a little shaky.

Jonathan opened the screen door, walked through the house, and went out the front door to where his car was parked. Something told him Clyde was not the person he should be accusing, but he wasn't about to let his guard down. Not yet. He had one more person to confront . . . someone he hadn't seen or spoken to in over a year, but someone who knew about him and Kathy. Someone who probably knew too much.

The wooden doors of the study opened, and Pastor Gregory slid an old silk robe over his pajamas as he entered. He dropped the large glasses that rested on his forehead down onto his nose.

"Jonathan Harper."

"Hello, Pastor Gregory," Jonathan said, shaking the hand that was offered to him. "I'm sorry to come so late."

"Our home is always open, day or night."

Jonathan sat down in the leather chair and waited for Pastor Gregory to situate himself on the other side of his desk. "Your girls are sure growing fast, aren't they? Meg especially."

"Yes," Jonathan said in a rather short tone, hoping to move past the chitchat.

"I have to say, I'm quite surprised to see you."

Jonathan rubbed his hands together. "I have a few things I need to talk to you about."

"Please, don't hesitate."

"I noticed all your books. You like to read."

"Yes. I'm an avid reader. I must admit I envy your job, getting to read all day long."

Jonathan smiled a little. "Yes, well, I wish I could say all the reading was good." Jonathan cracked his knuckles. "Do you do much writing?"

"Oh, I've tried my hand at it a few times. Every pastor wants to leave a legacy, as I'm sure you know." He shrugged. "I'm sure I'm an editor's nightmare."

Jonathan bit his lip at that statement. The question was if he was *this* editor's nightmare. Jonathan stood, unable to remain pleasant and personable. His skin itched with curiosity. "Pastor Gregory, I'll cut right to the chase here. My wife apparently talked to you about our marriage."

Pastor Gregory carefully formed his words. "Yes, that is true."

"I didn't know about that."

"Well, she was very concerned about you. She felt you two were growing apart."

"Yes, she mentioned that was why she talked to you." Jonathan paused and studied the man's face. He seemed so innocent, an older pastor who'd spent his years devoted to ministry and people. The gray hair on his head and deep lines in his face accounted for all the tragedy and suffering he'd allowed himself to feel along with his congregation. Now he simply sat quietly behind his desk, his hands folded neatly against his chest, with a questioning look across his gentle face. "Anyway, I wanted to talk to you about that."

"You're angry she confided in me?"

Jonathan, not expecting a question so direct, cleared his throat with a predictable, nervous cough. "Um, that's part of it."

"Everything anyone says to me in a counseling session is confidential, Jonathan, if that's what you're worried about."

"No, sir, what I'm worried about is . . ." Jonathan looked him in the eyes.

"Is what?"

"When did she come and see you?" Jonathan felt an immediate necessity to shift gears. If this man wasn't the author, he would feel horribly foolish trying to explain what was happening, and the less people who knew about the manuscript, the better.

"About six months ago, when it was obvious you had lost interest in church and God."

Jonathan narrowed his eyes. "Sir, I'm not here to talk about my spiritual life."

"Maybe you should be."

Jonathan laughed out of sheer frustration. "So I'm the bad guy, is that it? I don't come to church and suddenly all the marriage issues are my fault!"

The pastor seemed only distantly disturbed by Jonathan's explosion. He adjusted a nearby book on his desk. "No one said that."

Jonathan opened the shutters to a window, but since it was dark outside and light inside, he had only his reflection to look at. He quickly shut them. "Look, Pastor Gregory, if there's something you want to tell me, say it to my face."

"What do you mean?" he asked in a tone that seemed genuinely concerned.

"I mean, there have been some things happening in my life . . . some . . . some things, and I want to know if you're involved." Jonathan gripped the back of the leather chair. "If you've got something to say about me and my life, I want you to say it now!"

The pastor was silent. He wasn't fearful or shocked. He was peaceful. His eyes radiated a strange compassion that made Jonathan feel all the more uncomfortable. "No, I don't believe there's anything I need to say to you. It seems as though your convictions have reared their ugly head, so to speak." He smiled a bit at that statement.

Jonathan thought his fingers might just squeeze right through the leather. "What?" he asked with irritation.

"You're frustrated with your life. You're angry. You're confused and even a little regretful, I sense. But there's nothing I can say that you don't already know." The pastor stood and walked to the side of his desk, tying his robe tight around his belly. "I'm sorry if Kathy confiding in me has upset you. But I don't think she felt she had anyone else to talk to."

"Yeah, so I'm the jerk who can't communicate. The wayward husband with emotional issues."

The pastor only stood silently.

"What?" Jonathan felt his blood boiling. "That's right, isn't it? It's my fault that we've grown apart. It's my fault we don't talk anymore. Every fight is the result of something *I* did. I can't ever do *anything* right."

The pastor again said nothing.

"You don't have to say it," Jonathan fumed. "I know that's what you're thinking. You're standing there watching me lose my temper, quite certain that I'm failing at running my household and failing at loving my wife."

The pastor took a deep breath, a breath that seemed to clear the air, though only for a moment.

"Well, maybe what Kathy *didn't* tell you is she has turned cold as ice! Maybe what she *failed* to mention is that her fuse is so short it barely lights! I apologize for my screw-ups, but that's never good enough. I'm not good enough. Did she tell you that? Did she?"

The pastor's lips squeezed together in pity.

"Oh, please . . . please, for pete's sake, don't look at me like that. Don't pity me. I understand what's going on here. I understand everything, and let me tell you that I have tried . . . I have tried to reach her! I have tried to understand, but she has not given me that same grace! And now we're distant and cold and fragile, and it's everything I can do to keep my household from exploding, not to mention the fact that I'm in love with anoth—"

Jonathan held his breath and felt as if he might pass out. Surely he didn't just say . . . did he? Did he just say he was in love with . . .

The pastor hung his head, stepped around his desk, and sat back down. Jonathan was frozen in the middle of the room, unable to speak another word. Unable to move. The pastor cleared his throat, then looked Jonathan deeply in the eyes.

"You know what people who interrogate criminals are taught?"

Jonathan couldn't so much as shake his head as he tried to process the question.

"The television depicts interrogations as this big, bad cop standing over a frightened criminal, bullying him into confessing. But in reality, interrogators are mostly silent when they are trying to get someone to confess. Do you know why? It's because they've found that if they just let people talk, eventually they will convict themselves."

Jonathan swallowed.

"It's the funny thing about the tongue. It just never seems to know when to stop," the pastor said delicately. "If you let someone talk long enough, they'll always reveal the truth."

Jonathan watched as the pastor rose again and walked to the doors he'd shut. Before he opened them, he said, "Jonathan, I'm not sure why you came to see me here tonight. But I sense you are searching for something. And my advice to you, though you haven't asked for it, is that if you listen more than you talk, eventually you'll be able to hear your answer."

The pastor opened the doors and walked silently down a dark hallway, leaving Jonathan to let himself out of the house. Though his feet felt like lead, he managed to make his way out of the study and toward the front door. As he turned the doorknob, he felt someone behind him. As he turned around, he saw the pastor again.

"Everything said here tonight will be kept confidential, Jonathan. It's a policy of mine I strictly enforce. If you need to talk again—"

"No," Jonathan snapped. "No."

He walked out the front door. The cold breeze took his breath away, and he wrapped his arms around himself as he walked to the car. He wondered if his answer to this mystery in his life was as simple as listening to everyone talk.

C H A P T E R

11

"I went to see Clyde and Reverend Gregory."

Kathy drew the blanket she'd wrapped around herself up toward her face. The night air of the house was cold. Two single lamps dimly lit the living room.

"What'd you find out?"

Jonathan fell into the chair opposite the couch. His body ached with fatigue. "I found out I should listen more than I speak." Kathy stayed silent in her curiosity. Jonathan smiled a little. "Obviously you've already learned that lesson."

Kathy smiled and warmed her hands against a steaming cup of coffee. "Want some?"

Jonathan shook his head and leaned back. "Kathy, I'm sorry this is happening. I'm doing everything I can to find out what's going on here. But I'm hitting dead ends. No one fits the profile and everyone seems suspicious."

Kathy sat up and dropped her feet to the ground. "Sounds like a bestselling novel."

Jonathan agreed with a tired laugh. He looked at his wife, her hair swept up on top of her head, her face freshly washed. She looked beautiful suddenly. He wished a fire were going and he could grab her and they could sit in front of it and talk until the early-morning hours. "Kathy, I don't know what to say. I'm scared to death."

Kathy rose, walked to her husband, and knelt at his feet. "Of what?"

"Of what?" He lightly stroked her hair. "You have to ask? My whole life is being played out in the pages of some eerie manuscript, and I don't know what's going to happen next."

Kathy grabbed his hand. Jonathan looked down at her. "You know me, Kathy. I don't like to talk about my personal life. I mean, it took me years to even tell you about Jason's death. And even then, I didn't tell you what happened." Jonathan's hand tore through his own hair. "It doesn't make sense. There are holes in the story, but they don't follow a pattern. At least not one I've picked up on."

Kathy wrapped her hands around his knees and laid her head in his lap. "Did Clyde tell you what was in the pages he received? About me? Us?"

Jonathan's nostrils flared from the deep, anxious breaths he took. "Whoever is doing this, I swear I will find them and they will pay. No one does this to me and my family."

Kathy lifted her head up.

"I've got to think." He stood and stepped around Kathy. "There has to be *something*. One thing this person has neglected to hide. One track they haven't covered. I've just got to find it." Jonathan's body begged for a strong drink, but all the alcohol in the house had been done away with a long time ago.

"I don't want you involved, Kathy. I want you to talk to the children, though, especially Leesol and Meg. I want you to tell them, under no circumstances will they go with *anyone* other than you and me, no matter who they say they are. Can you do that? Make them understand that, Kathy. Please."

Kathy nodded, then stood, neatly folded the blanket, and placed it on the back of the couch. She walked toward Jonathan, stood next to him, and without any words, lightly kissed him on the cheek. Jonathan felt confused. His confession to Reverend Gregory came surging back through his head as the feeling of Kathy's soft lips lingered on his cheek.

"I'll pray for us tonight, Jonathan," she said and ascended the stairs and out of sight.

Jonathan turned and placed his head against the mantel of the fireplace. He might pray for help, too, if he wasn't so sure God himself might not be writing down his life and sending him pages through the mail. He laughed at the absurdity.

Whoever it was, they knew more about him than anyone, which, in the late hours of the night, Jonathan felt was ironic— since most of the time he didn't even know that much about himself.

───────

The morning came early. Jonathan awoke and asked for a large mug of coffee to at least get him to work. Kathy put the exact right amount of cream and sugar in it, something only a wife could know. The girls kissed him and followed him out the door.

On the way to work, Jonathan made a mental list of the events that had occurred so far, hoping to find something that would clue him in to who this writer was. The first set of pages had arrived in a manila envelope, mailed to his boyhood home. Why, then, were the other pages delivered to Clyde's house, apparently by hand?

He noted that as important, then moved on to the story itself. The first part, the story of his brother's death and the childhood events of his life after that, were perhaps the most chilling of all the passages in the manuscript. Absolutely no one other than his dead parents knew what happened. How could anyone else know? And who would his parents tell? They were private people and would never air their dirty laundry.

Jonathan thought it particularly odd that the story had jumped from a boy's painful childhood to his college days, where he met his wife and began what the manuscript called "a love affair." He pondered that phrase for a bit. Maybe it once was. But the words "love" and "affair" had too many ambiguous meanings in his life right now—and were attached to one too many people.

Although he regretted having burned the next set of pages that arrived, he felt he had a pretty good understanding of what was in there. Basically someone had attempted to summarize nearly twenty years of marriage by highlighting a few negative incidents in his life. Though Clyde had mentioned the story also followed his career quite extensively, he guessed that most of it was personal. The balance of the two really didn't matter. Whoever it was knew his career and family well.

The elevator doors opened to a busy Monday morning. Fax machines and computers were already up and running. Though it wasn't even eight o'clock yet, the office buzzed with life. Jonathan scooted through a busy hallway and toward Edie's desk.

"Good morning, Jonathan," she said, unusually jolly.

"Good morning." Jonathan stopped at her desk. "Hold all my phone calls this morning, please, Edie."

Edie nodded and said, "What about visitors?"

"I'm not expecting any appointments."

"Yes, I know, but what about—"

"Use your discretion."

"Yes, but—"

"Edie, I trust you."

Edie sighed and watched Jonathan as he headed into his office. As he opened the door, which he couldn't remember having closed on Friday when he left, he found the sight before him more than he could handle.

He froze in the doorway as Edie called, "I tried to warn you."

"Well, it's your office, Jonathan. Come in," Francis Flowers said, his little mousy nose twitching with delight.

"Get out of my chair," Jonathan demanded with irritation.

"Just keeping it warm for you, my friend," he charmed, scooting out of it and around the desk. "Quite nippy this morning, isn't it?"

"It just got colder," Jonathan mumbled and sat down behind his desk. "Francis, what are you doing here?"

Zippy folded his arms together and tried to stand as straight as he could. "What do you think I'm doing here, Jonathan? Do you think I'm here to get you coffee? Or discuss why everyone in marketing should be shot? Or why gardening book sales are up on the East Coast and down on the West Coast?" Jonathan glanced up. "You think I don't know your disrespect for my kind, Jonathan? You laugh behind closed doors. You sneer. You make jokes at my expense because I ghostwrite gardening books."

Jonathan sighed heavily. "Francis, has there ever been a day in your life when you weren't bitter?"

Zippy didn't miss a beat. He pointed a finger at Jonathan's desk. Jonathan hadn't even noticed, but right there on top, in plain view, sat a crisp manila envelope with something inside. His heart cramped.

Jonathan could barely look up at Zippy. Zippy seemed to grow irritated. "You can't tell me you don't have the time. I know you do." He pointed his finger at Jonathan's face. "Don't you lie to me, Jonathan Harper, big, bad editor of high-and-mighty fiction." He paused and then quipped, "Jiminy Christmas, Jonathan. It's not going to kill you."

Jonathan lightly touched the manila envelope. "Did you read this?"

Zippy's eyes scrunched together and he cocked his head to the side. "Hello? McFly? Hello? Maybe I do need to get you that cup of coffee!" Zippy grabbed the envelope off the desk and began slipping the pages out. Jonathan practically jumped over the top of the desk.

"Give me that!" he yelled at Zippy, who was so startled he dropped the envelope and the pages to the floor. Zippy stepped back a couple of feet as Jonathan dropped to the ground and scrambled to pick up all the pages as fast as he could. As he did, though, he realized something dreadful. This was not the mysterious manuscript. This was Zippy's proposal for his novel.

Jonathan quickly snapped his head up to look at Zippy, whose eyes were wide and whose hand was moving toward the inside pocket of his jacket, presumably for a Ziploc bag.

"Francis, please, calm down. I didn't mean to . . . I was just . . . this is a big misunder—"

Zippy's eyes were watering and his nose was reddening, twitching and scrunching like he'd just sniffed pepper. Jonathan watched as Zippy pulled out a single tissue.

"Aaahhhchhhooo!" The velocity of the sneeze tore the tissue in two and managed to miss everything that was supposed to catch it. Zippy removed his glasses and blotted his eyes.

"Um, you okay, Francis?" Jonathan asked carefully.

"F-f-fine . . . aachhooo!" And then, one right after another, sneezes so powerful his eyes looked as if they might pop out. And unfortunately, the two small pieces of tissue were doing nothing but blowing in the breeze. Jonathan looked around for a box of tissues but didn't see one.

"Edie! Edie! Get some Kleenex in here! *Now!*"

Two eternities passed before Edie came in, holding a stack of tissues. Jonathan snatched them from her hands and threw them at Zippy, who managed to catch a couple between sneezes.

"Aaaahhhhhchhhhooooo! Aaaaahhhhhchhhhoooo!" On and on it went. It was like a chain reaction. A few people had gathered in the doorway to gawk.

"Breathe, breathe, breathe," Jonathan chanted, and Zippy seemed to calm a bit. A sneeze inadvertently slipped out here and there.

A few moments passed as Zippy continued to breathe in and out, holding a damp tissue to his bright red nose. Edie stood at a safe distance in the doorway. Jonathan was breathing in and out himself, trying to stop his racing heart and calm himself down.

Finally, everything seemed to stop and Zippy blotted his eyes, put his glasses back on, folded his Ziploc bag, and stuffed it in his shirt. He then looked at Jonathan.

Jonathan played with the edges of the manuscript, careful not to make any sudden move that would cause Zippy to feel in the least bit insecure or frightened.

"Well. You're quite the grizzly in the morning, aren't you?" Zippy said as he straightened his shirt and wiped off his mouth. "So the rumors are true."

"Rum—?" Jonathan stopped himself. He didn't want to know. Zippy was probably making it up anyway. "I'm sorry. It was a misunderstanding. I thought this was . . . was something else."

Zippy's eyes, the rims red and puffy, narrowed into cutting slits. "Like what?"

Jonathan tried to recover quickly. "Um . . . a proposal from an author who, um, wants to remain anonymous. She's using a pen name, but her real name is on the, um, proposal. So that's why I reacted like that."

Zippy hardly bought the story but, in his crudely annoying way, changed the subject toward himself. "Well, no, that's actually *my* proposal. You think you might read it without biting my head, arm, or leg off?"

Jonathan wanted to punch Zippy, but the next best thing he could do would be to get rid of him. "Sure. Of course. I'll get to it as soon as I can."

"Don't give me that 'as soon as you can' lie, Jonathan. I've been in this business long enough to know an editor saying, 'I'll get to it as soon as I can' is the same thing as a church member saying, 'I'll be praying for you.' Neither one is true."

Jonathan frowned and laughed a little. "Francis, how do you know about church members?"

Zippy looked at him as if he were the dumbest person on earth. "Hello? McFly? I go to church!"

"*You* go to church?"

Zippy crossed his arms against his chest. "Of course I do. I'm the most morally sound person in this company, Jonathan. When all you people go out for your smokes and drinks and chews and women, do you ever see me coming along?"

Jonathan bit his lip to try not to laugh as he thought, *No one ever invites you, Zippy.* But he remained silent.

"In fact," he said quite snidely, "if I didn't know better, Jonathan, I might suspect that your previous reaction to what was in that envelope was due to the fact that you read those steamy romance novels we publish and don't want anyone to know." Zippy tipped his head forward and lifted his eyebrows as his voice quieted to a hush, the few people who had gathered taking their cue to exit. "You know those things are as addicting as porn, don't you, Jonathan? If you need help, I've got a 1–800 number for a support group that helps men—"

"Francis!" Jonathan barked. "What in the world are you talking about?!"

Zippy simply held up his hands and smiled. "I know it's embarrassing, but if you change your mind, let me know."

"About what?"

Zippy backed out of the office in almost a bow. "Denial is the first hump to overcome. . . ."

Jonathan was about to scream at Zippy down the hallway when Sydney suddenly appeared in the doorway.

"Sydney . . . hi. I wasn't expecting to . . . I mean, I thought . . ." Jonathan fumbled over his words until he finally stopped himself and drew in some air. "Sorry. I've just had a very exhausting morning and it's barely past eight."

Jonathan watched as Sydney entered, dressed in a short but conservative dark skirt and a white silk shirt. Her short black hair was slicked back. She was striking.

"I can come back," she offered.

"No—please, no," he begged and motioned for her to sit, noticing her face was still bruised. "You're the first good thing I've seen all morning."

Sydney blushed at that statement and Jonathan did, too. His emotions swirled, suddenly, and he remembered his words to Reverend Gregory. As she took a seat and smoothed out her skirt, Jonathan wondered if he was, indeed, in love with this young woman.

"What can I do for you?" Jonathan asked, smoothing his own tie and pants as he sat down.

Sydney paused, looked at him curiously, and then said, "Aren't we still on to see Naomi Yates today? To have lunch with her?"

Jonathan realized he had completely forgotten. "Yes, of course, of course. I'm sorry, I've just been a little swamped this morning. I simply forgot the day. Yes. We'll depart at eleven-fifteen."

Sydney nodded and stood. "I'll meet you downstairs then."

"Great."

"I hope your day gets better."

"Thank you."

Sydney was about out the door when Jonathan said, "Sydney?" She turned. "Your face . . . how are you recovering from your . . . car wreck?"

Sydney lightly touched the bruise on her cheek, smiled sweetly, and said, "I'm fine. Thanks for asking."

Jonathan nodded and watched her leave, only to be met with a disapproving scowl on Edie's face. Jonathan ignored her by turning around and throwing Zippy's proposal on top of his pile of unread manuscripts. He knew if he didn't read Zippy's proposal soon, he would pay. He vowed to give it a quick read and get the rejection over with. The longer he drew it out, the more painful it would be for everyone.

He rubbed his forehead to try to push away the headache that had suddenly crept into his brain. He was still startled by the way he'd reacted to that manila envelope sitting on his desk. All of this was certainly beginning to affect him, and if he wasn't careful he was going to expose everything to all the wrong people.

He circled his head around on his neck and decided to distract himself by reading more of Clyde's novel. He had tried earlier, but too many distractions kept him from reading more than a couple of chapters. Whether or not Clyde was the author of the other manuscript was yet to be seen, but Jonathan couldn't deny that he was still very intrigued by the new story Clyde was writing, and if it ended as well as it started, he hoped to propose it to the committee soon. Nellie would be thrilled that Clyde had one last novel, and since Jonathan had presented a few bombs in the past few months, this could only help. He also hoped that while he read, his mind would clear of any thoughts he might have of Sydney. He had a forty-five-minute car ride alone with her. He was scared to even think of what feelings might make their way into that car.

He found where he had left off and began to read.

Esther Caladaras, with her big position, her big office, and her big mouth, was actually a rather small person, I assumed, when she wasn't wearing her three-inch heels. On this morning she was dressed in a fitted two-piece gray suit that accentuated every single curve of her body. Somehow, though a feminist who believed women have gotten the short end of the stick since the beginning of time, she didn't mind using her femininity to help her in all sorts of ways.

"You *what?*" she asked directly, raising her black eyebrows at me.

Esther Caladaras was famous for being a DA who was always mad about something. It made her great at her job but terrible to be around. However, I knew she was my only hope.

"Look, you were busy when I called," I said, throwing up my hands innocently and smiling.

"I told you to talk to me first," she said harshly.

"I know, I know," I sighed and looked at her with sincerity. "But time is short, Esther, and I had to make a move."

Esther pressed her lips together. "I'd be upset about this, but I just think you're crazy. Suddenly someone on death row is innocent? Hardly a first." She picked up a lit cigarette and tapped it against the ashtray. "Keaton, I must say, you seem to be on quite a crusade."

I tried to hide my anxiousness, though I knew I had a tremendous battle ahead of me. "Yes, I suppose that's true."

"Do you know how many hundreds of calls I get every time someone is about to be executed, Keaton?" She had the ability to smoke and talk and never miss a word or a puff. "The religious right wing calling me the spawn of Satan or a liberal— take your pick. The definition's the same. The left wing calling me a gutless conservative and a hater of humanity. And the friends and family, you know, the people who haven't seen him in years and are probably the reason he has ended up where he is, calling to let me know I'm about to destroy their lives." Esther Caladaras laid her cigarette gently in the ashtray. "So, Agent Keaton Spade, I've got to believe you're here to do something other than condemn me to hell for doing my job."

Her eyes were as dark as black steel. Esther was a very hard woman. Sure, she wore lipstick and earrings and skirts and long hair, but behind all that was nothing short of a relentless machine who made it her job to convict people in their sins and make sure they got the harshest of punishments.

I finally spoke, keeping my voice low and soft. "Esther, I appreciate your seeing me about this. I wouldn't be here if I didn't think—"

"He was innocent," she said, laughing. "Save the speech for the press, okay? Give me the facts. That's all I care about."

I swallowed and nodded all at once. "Yes, well, you are familiar with Dietrich Donomar—"

Esther slid off her desk to go sit in her chair. "Of course I am! I put that crazy pig behind bars. You know that." Her hands balled up into fists all at once. "And may I remind you, Agent

Spade, that it was *your* profiler who insisted he not sizzle. The FBI makes my stomach turn," she said with agitation, seeming to forget I was in the room.

"Yes, well, perhaps keeping Donomar alive was ordained by some higher power," I said, hoping to pique her interest. "Someone innocent has been blamed for one of Donomar's murders."

"Jerome Mitchner."

"As I mentioned, yes."

Esther Caladaras opened a file on her desk. "With all due respect, Keaton, I prosecuted Mitchner. I know all the facts of the case."

"Which are . . . ?" I said, hoping to set all this up in her own words.

Esther paused but then obliged. "Which are that Mr. Mitchner killed Manuel Roberts over a faulty gun exchange. Everyone was there when they pulled Roberts out of the North Haven drainage ditch. He had the motive, three witnesses testified to Mitchner's threats of killing Roberts," she said, reading some piece of paper from the file, "and, oh yes . . . he confessed."

I braced myself. "There have been cases in which innocent men have confessed to crimes they didn't commit."

Esther leaned forward on her desk. "Not on my watch."

And now for my trump card. "Well, Donomar has a different version of that story."

"Oh yeah?" she said, mildly amused.

"Yes." I, too, leaned forward for dramatic emphasis.

"And what version does that nut job tell?"

I smiled a little. "According to Donomar, Manuel Roberts was killed in Bear Woods, not in the North Haven drainage ditch."

Esther played along. "Really? And how does he know that?"

"Because he killed him."

Esther paused. I had her . . . at least I had her interest. But it was going to take a lot more than interest to get this DA to budge. "As easy as it would be for me to believe Donomar is responsible for every murder in the state, this file here on my desk says otherwise." She closed it. "And I'm not seeing any evidence of proof on your end, Agent."

"Let me finish," I urged.

"Please, don't let me stop you." She stood and began filing the folder away.

"I hadn't seen Donomar in months. I was surprised when he called me to come see him." Esther's back was toward me as she filed. "Esther, I'm telling you, what happened in there was remarkable."

She turned. "Well, don't make me guess, Keaton."

I hurriedly continued. "Donomar seemed regretful for what he'd done." Esther laughed out loud, but I tried not to let that affect me. "He started saying he was remorseful, and that all the pictures and hate letters the families had sent him were starting to take effect." She laughed again, but this time it wasn't as harsh. "And then he started talking about trying to right a wrong."

Esther turned around. "Right a wrong? *A* wrong?" Her whole body shook. "You worked the case, Keaton! You saw what he did to those people! He is a diabolical killer. He has no conscience!"

"Maybe. But he apparently has some regrets."

Esther rolled her eyes.

"Esther, please hear me out on this. Please." She softened a bit and I continued. "Donomar said that there was a man on death row who was innocent, who was there for a crime he committed."

Esther cocked her head upward, her defenses high but her mind reeling.

"And then he proceeded to tell me simply this: that Manuel Roberts was killed in Bear Woods, not North Haven."

Esther stopped me by throwing up her hands. "Keaton, this is fine and everything, but it's not making sense to me. Roberts's body was pulled from the drainage ditch at North Haven. I mean, so what if Donomar says differently. So what?"

I chose my words carefully. "Esther, I did some investigating. I found some things out, some things that legitimize Donomar's claim."

Esther raised her eyebrows and crossed her arms. "What?"

"I found out through a source that Roberts really was killed in Bear Woods. But the FBI moved the body to North Haven."

"Why would they do that?"

"According to my source, the FBI had come up short in their

investigation. They didn't have any leads, and since it was such a high-profile case, we were starting to look bad. They hired a psychic, something taboo back then, who was sure the body would be found in North Haven. The bureau came under a lot of heat for that decision, so when the body was found elsewhere, they moved it to cover it up." I paused, letting the DA process all this. "This was also around the time Joseph Beyers was charged with selling secret information to the Russians."

Esther had sat down. She didn't look up as she spoke. "Beyers . . . he was a supervisor and former counterintelligence officer for the FBI, right?"

"Yes. If you'll remember, it was horrible publicity for us. We were so desperate and uninformed about it all that we ended up having to use a Russian official to set up a false spy operation just to catch him."

Esther still didn't look up. I was glad. That meant she was thinking hard.

"In the end, even Beyers' own wife helped in the investigation. It was a mess of a nightmare for us."

"So what you're trying to tell me is that the FBI, still reeling from bad publicity due to the Beyers incident, hired a psychic in order to try to overcome another botched investigation, and when she failed to come through, they *moved a body* so they wouldn't look bad?" Esther looked up at me.

"That's what I'm saying. According to my source, the agents involved covered it up so drastically that only a few people inside the department know about it. A handful. No more."

Esther looked me in the eyes. "Well, apparently one more."

She was catching on quickly. "Yes. Only one other person would know where Roberts was actually killed."

Esther thought for a long moment. I didn't want to interrupt her. I knew this was all making sense. Finally, she spoke. "Who's your source?"

My heart stopped. My source? I couldn't identify my source. "Esther, you know I can't—"

"Oh, but you can, Agent," she said with a small smile. "You have to."

"I can't! It could jeopardize his career!"

Esther Caladaras stood, placed her hands on her desk, and looked at me fiercely. "You expect me to turn a conviction when I don't have a source? A name?"

I had nothing to say. Of course I couldn't. "Esther, there is an innocent man on death row! He is going to die in three weeks if we don't do something."

She turned to stare out the window. "You're convinced. I'm not."

I quickly joined her there. "But you have to admit that the only other person who could know that is the killer!"

She shrugged silently.

I turned her toward me. "Esther, please. You're a tough DA. Everyone knows that. But I also know your convictions run deep enough that you couldn't let an innocent man die for a crime he didn't commit!"

Esther broke free of me, walked to the door of her office, and opened it. "Give me the name of your source. Then we'll talk."

I rubbed my eyes tiredly. "You ask the impossible. My source would ruin everything for himself if he were exposed."

I walked past her out the door, and as I did she added, "Well, Keaton, have you ever considered the fact that your career could be in jeopardy, too?"

I stopped and turned around. There was one thing that would drive this woman to my side. And I had to know where this thing came from. "Esther, why do you hate the FBI so much?"

Esther paused. She looked hard and soft all at once. She started to answer several times and then stopped herself. Finally, in a trembling voice I'd never heard from her, she said, "My brother was killed in a stakeout that went bad. He was a field agent. Virginia."

She closed the door, and I prayed that man's untimely death would be the key to setting Jerome Mitchner free.

C H A P T E R

12

The leaves rustled in the slight northern wind as Jonathan Harper and Sydney Kasdan drove north to Naomi Yates's house, a small but beautiful cottage home in an exclusive neighborhood. The drive took a little over half an hour with no traffic, but it was worth every minute, especially with the leaves turning colors.

They had rolled the windows down, though it made it a little chilly. Still, the air was cleaner and fresher the farther north they went, a nice addition to a wonderful fall morning.

They chatted on their way out of town about business. Jonathan rambled about his morning's events, which included a disgruntled author's threat to sue the house, another author's relentless pursuit to change the cover of her book, and a third author's agent pressing for more money. A typical day, minus the Zippy incident.

But in the back of Jonathan's mind, all he could think about were the bruises on Sydney's face. As she was getting into his SUV, he also noticed a rather large one on the underside of her left arm. Sydney seemed unaffected, continuing to discuss the house, the authors she admired, and her dream of becoming a fiction editor like him.

As they turned onto Conwell, a narrow winding road that

would take them ten minutes to drive, Jonathan couldn't contain himself any longer. He had to know the truth about those bruises.

"So how's your fiancé's . . . car?"

Sydney kept her eyes forward. "It's okay. A little damage in the back."

"What exactly happened?"

Sydney tugged at her sleeves and pulled each one down over her hands to try to stay warm. "Oh, just a little fender bender."

Jonathan rolled up his window. "No kidding? You're awfully banged up to have just been in a fender bender."

"Yeah, well, I wasn't wearing my seat belt." She smiled and glanced at him. "There's a reason those things are in cars."

"Hmm. So you hit your head on the windshield and cracked it?"

"Yep," Sydney said, fiddling with the side of the door.

Jonathan paused. He didn't want to sound confrontational, but at the same time, he knew she was lying. The windshield had not been cracked. And whether or not something else was happening was yet to be seen. But he had to know why she was lying to him.

"Sydney," he said slowly, but in a tone that made her look over at him, "I walked by your boyfriend's—your fiancé's—car on Friday. There was no crack in the windshield."

Sydney stared at him for a moment, then stared out the window in silence. Jonathan had hoped she would just offer the real explanation, but she seemed to be withdrawing instead.

"Sydney, listen, I don't mean to put you on the spot here. Honestly. But I've been around long enough to know that those bruises look like something else."

"Like what?" she said, her tone bland, her eyes distant.

"I know it's none of my business—"

"Then why are you asking?"

Jonathan stopped. He knew the reason he was asking. But did she? "Because . . . because I care about you, Sydney. I don't want you to be in a relationship that might harm you—" He cut his words off, fully aware of the irony that danced in the words he just spoke. "In a relationship that could bring physical harm to you."

Tears formed in her eyes, and she turned to look back outside. "Jeremy never means to hurt me. He just . . . he just loses his temper sometimes. He doesn't mean to. I probably provoke it." Jonathan couldn't believe what he was hearing. "You don't understand. He's trying to change. He had a rough childhood."

"Those are all excuses. None of them valid." Jonathan reached for her hand. "You deserve better."

She continued to weep. "The whole office knows. All the secretaries. They talk about it in the break room. I walk in and everyone gets real quiet. I'm embarrassed. I don't know what to say."

"You need to get out of the relationship," Jonathan urged.

"You don't understand. We've been together for eight years. He's everything I know. He's my whole life." She fiddled with the engagement ring on her left hand. "He's comfortable."

Jonathan understood that statement. More than she knew. "Yes, but you could end up dying." Jonathan spoke slowly. "Sydney, he could lose his temper and get so out of control that he could kill you." He tried to drive and look at her at the same time. "I mean, from the looks of it, he came real close last time."

Sydney touched her face delicately and said, "I guess I'm just afraid of being alone."

Jonathan fought every urge inside of him to tell her he would not let that happen. He wanted to help her, but he also knew he was inching closer and closer to a very dangerous line that begged him to cross over. He wasn't sure how Sydney felt about him, but he was very sure of how he felt about her. He cared for her enough to insert himself into her life and help her out of a situation she shouldn't be in. He cared enough to think about her outside the workplace. He simply cared too much.

He turned into Naomi's neighborhood. Sydney looked out her open window again. "What beautiful houses," she said, gazing at each of them as they passed by.

Jonathan loved it, too. He'd been here a few times working on books with Naomi, and he always marveled at the unique architecture and lush landscape that seemed to paint a perfect picture. Each house sat on more than four acres, and there were no fences dividing neighbors' yards. Every home was unique but inviting. People still sat out on their front porches in the evenings. Children played in the streets. Smoke swirled above tall brick chimneys as soon as it turned fall. It was like something out of a children's book.

Jonathan was a little relieved himself that the conversation had switched gears. He'd gotten the information he'd wanted. He'd said what he needed to say. Now it was time to back away and let her deal with her problem. He just hoped his heart would obey his mind.

"You're going to love Naomi's home," Jonathan said. "She has the most unbelievable gardens you have ever seen."

"She seems like that type," Sydney said softly. "People who garden are nice people."

Jonathan laughed. "Is that so?"

"Definitely. My grandmother gardened. And so did my uncle. They were both nice. They both had a fine appreciation for Mother Nature. They always treated me like I was a delicate flower, which needed the perfect amount of water and sun and air to flourish."

"Apparently they were good gardeners," Jonathan said quietly, pulling into Naomi's driveway.

The front of the cottagelike house was brick, and Boston ivy climbed up the sides with elegance. On the red front door hung a wooden sign that said "Welcome to my Fairy Tale." Two rocking chairs and a small table barely fit on the tiny porch, which was neatly swept and tidied as if it were part of the inside. A few potted plants with colorful flowers lined the sidewalk, and a small flower bed filled with ferns sat neatly against the house.

"It's darling!" Sydney said as she got out of the car. "It's exactly how I imagined she lived!"

Jonathan laughed, wondering how much time Sydney spent thinking about what kind of house Naomi Yates lived in. Sydney waited for Jonathan and followed him up the brick sidewalk. Jonathan said, "We won't make it to the front door before—"

"My Jonathan, my Jonathan!" Naomi Yates exclaimed with delight, beckoning him to move faster as she came out her door. She was hunched and wrinkled, feeble and little. Her hair was perfectly white and soft, cut chin-length and straight as a bone.

"I'm 'her Jonathan.' Don't ask questions," he said with a chuckle. He stepped up onto the porch and leaned down to give her a hug.

"You precious angel, you're so handsome!" she said and patted him on the cheek. Then she peeked around him at Sydney. "And this must be Sydney?"

Sydney stepped forward gracefully. "Sydney Kasdan. It's such an honor to meet—"

"Oh, enough of that, enough of that," Naomi said, pulling them both into her house. "I'm just glad to have some company. I get lonely, you know. It's just me and the flowers and books most of the time." She eyed Jonathan's old briefcase. "Dear, do you ever leave your work at the office?" Jonathan simply smiled and followed her in.

The inside of the house was as cozy as imaginable. A small fire was going and wherever there was space, a book filled it. Thousands of books decorated her home. And Jonathan had always found it interesting that none of those books were hers. She didn't have a single copy of any of her own books in her house. He'd once asked her why and she said, "My Jonathan, they're in my heart. I don't need them taking up space here."

Naomi ushered them into the kitchen, where a large glass window framed a wonderful garden of flowers in her backyard. Sydney gasped.

"How beautiful!"

Naomi smiled and turned on the stove to make tea. "A little bit of heaven before I get there," she said. "And that's probably not going to be too long," she added with a tiny snicker.

Sydney turned to her. "You've done all this?"

"Yes, dear. It's my hobby. I love flowers."

"If you'll notice on every single one of Naomi's books, there is a flower somewhere on the cover."

"You're kidding!" Sydney said. "I've never noticed that. I've read all your books, Mrs. Yates. I'm a big fan."

Naomi smiled and took teacups from the pantry. "I made some chicken salad for lunch, and I have fresh mint from my garden for the tea I made you, my Jonathan."

Jonathan wrapped an arm around her small shoulder. "That's my girl." Then he said, "Mind if I give Sydney a tour of your home?"

"Oh, this dusty old thing?"

"Yes, this dusty old thing. It's quite a treasure."

"Fine, fine, but my housekeeper doesn't come till Wednesday, so you'll have to excuse the messes."

"We'll be right back."

Jonathan gave Sydney the grand tour, which included the marble bathroom, the third-story study where Naomi used to write, and, of course, the library, which was even featured in *Architectural Digest* and held an unbelievable collection of classic literature. Naomi's husband, Ira, who had died ten years before, was an architect who had designed this house for her after reading her children's book *Cottage in the Woods*. The story went that her illustrator had spent days just trying to design the cottage Naomi had in her head. He finally got it, and as a surprise for their fiftieth wedding anniversary, Ira had designed this house for her, which was exactly like the cottage in her story.

Murals covered the walls of her home. Over her fireplace was a mural from *Alice in Wonderland*, and on the ceiling of her bedroom was another one from *Peter Rabbit*. Her house was one big celebration of stories.

Lunch was perfect, too, as Sydney and Naomi chatted lightly and Jonathan told stories from their nearly fifteen-year relationship as editor and writer. Afterward, Sydney helped Naomi clear the table. Then Naomi said, "Dear, wouldn't you like to go look at my garden? You've been staring at it since you arrived."

"May I?" Sydney asked anxiously.

"Of course. It's there for admiration." Naomi put a few dishes in the sink. "I'll join you after I finish up here."

Jonathan moved to the back door to follow Sydney, but Naomi said, "My Jonathan, why don't you help me with the dishes? My hands are getting weak."

"Of course," Jonathan said and let Sydney go on without him. "Your arthritis—how is it?"

Naomi filled the sink with warm water and soap. "Oh, good days and bad. I can predict the weather better than those fancy computers on the TV screen."

"You're taking your medicine?"

Naomi waved her hand. "Does no good. Does no good." Naomi

sat at the table as Jonathan washed each plate by hand. "Dry with the green towel, my Jonathan."

"Yes, ma'am," Jonathan said, laughing at the fact that Naomi Yates loved to play his mother. "And they go in the left side of the cupboard, right?"

"Yes, yes," she said. "Are you still writing?"

Jonathan laughed as he washed and dried. "Oh, Naomi, that was so long ago."

"I'm ninety, you know. Fifty or sixty years ago is long ago. It hasn't been that long. You were quite good."

"No, I wasn't," Jonathan insisted. "It was just a hobby. You're the only one I let read my work anyway."

"You wrote with passion!"

Jonathan smiled. "I'm glad you think so."

"It is true. You should write again."

Jonathan shook his head and added more soap to the water. "Maybe when I find something to be passionate about, Naomi."

Jonathan continued to wash dishes, and for a while Naomi watched Sydney make her way around all the flowers and trees outside. Then she said, "You're looking good, my Jonathan."

"As are you," Jonathan replied.

"You look young."

"I feel young." Jonathan said, though that wasn't completely true. He was in good health, but the circumstances of his life were beginning to take their toll.

Naomi tapped her fingers against her small kitchen table. "So . . . revisiting your youth by flirting with one?"

Jonathan turned around. "Excuse me?"

Naomi glanced outside. "I'm old, but I'm not naive, my Jonathan."

Jonathan about dropped the china he was holding. "Naomi, what are you—"

"Talking about?" Naomi smiled, stood with much effort, and walked to the window. "She is quite pretty. What is she, about thirty?"

"T-t-twenty something . . ." Jonathan felt his head spinning a little. "Seven. Or eight."

Naomi turned. "My Jonathan, I have known and loved you for so long. You are like a son to me." She joined him at the kitchen counter. "You are walking down a destructive path."

Jonathan gripped the edge of the counter. "Look, Naomi, I don't know what you think is going on here, but—"

"Oh, please do not try to convince me you are not, in the very least, flirting with this young woman. I see it in your eyes. In her eyes. The way you two stand close together when you're looking at something. The way you look at her when I'm the one speaking." Naomi patted him on the cheek. "I'm not blind yet."

Jonathan stepped away from her. "Naomi, please, you don't know what you're talking about," he said hastily and with too much anxiety in his voice.

Naomi laughed and moved herself along the counter with her hands, arriving at the sink to finish the dishes. She washed them, and Jonathan felt an urgency to try to convince her there was nothing going on.

"You must believe me. I mean, I like Sydney. She's bright and nice and fun, but we're not having an affair."

"I didn't say you were having an affair."

"But you said—"

"You were walking down a road that leads to destruction."

Jonathan couldn't think of anything to say, but Naomi wasn't finished anyway.

"You know, I have walked that same path." She turned to him. "Yes. It was 1940, and I had been married for one year. I met a young man, a delivery boy who worked in our neighborhood. My husband was away a lot, and I grew lonely. This boy started coming around more and more, and before I knew it I was in love with him."

"*You* had an affair, Naomi?"

"Yes, I did," she said sadly. "It was devastating. I couldn't believe I had actually kissed him. Twice."

"All you did was kiss him?"

Naomi shook her head. "Things were so different long ago. A kiss was everything. It meant intimacy. A kiss betrayed everything sacred in my marriage."

Jonathan listened and watched Sydney smell the roses outside. "But Ira forgave you." A deep, solemn silence hovered in the room. "Right?"

Naomi shook her head and continued to wash dishes. "Jonathan, Ira was my second husband."

Jonathan frowned. "What? I didn't know you had been married twice."

"Well, dear, it isn't something we older people are proud of. These days marriages and divorces come a dime a dozen." She sighed. "My first husband left me. His name was Wilton."

Jonathan crossed his arms over his chest. "Well, look, Naomi, I appreciate the advice. I really do. But nothing is going on. We're not having an affair. I haven't *kissed* her," he said with emphasis. "She's just in some trouble. I'm trying to *help* her."

Naomi dried the counter. "What kind of trouble?"

"Did you see the bruises on her face?" Naomi nodded. "She's in a relationship with a very violent man. His name is Jeremy. And she just can't seem to realize the danger she's in."

"Poor girl," Naomi said as she folded her towel.

"I'm simply trying to help her get out of that. That's all."

Naomi looked at him questioningly.

"That's *all*."

Naomi put everything in order on her counter, closed all the doors on her cupboard, sat down at the table, and said, "My Jonathan, if you're going to be her savior, who's going to be yours?"

C H A P T E R

13

Naomi Yates had let the conversation drop and joined Sydney out in the gardens. On the way back to the office, three hours later, Sydney was rambling on about how wonderful Naomi was, but Jonathan remained unusually quiet, listening, nodding . . . but far, far away.

Back at the office, Jonathan stopped by Edie's desk to get any messages.

"Long lunch," she commented, handing him a neat stack of handwritten messages.

Jonathan looked up at her, then quickly passed through each message to see which ones needed his immediate attention. The last one grabbed his attention. He looked up at Edie.

"Kathy . . . Kathy stopped by?"

Edie seemed to sneer and smile all at once. "Why, yes."

Jonathan casually leaned against her desk, trying to hide the fact that his pulse had just shot up to a level that caused his ears to turn red and burn. "No kidding? What, uh, what time?"

Edie was filing her nails. "Oh, a while after you left."

"What for?"

"What for?" Edie's face swirled with questions.

"I mean, why did she come by? Did she say?"

145

"She was hoping to take you to lunch." Edie took her concentration off the long pinky nail she was shaping. "Are you okay? You look a little—"

"I'm fine." Jonathan pretended to look at his other messages. "You told her I was . . . ?"

"Gone."

"So she left?"

"No, she waited for a while."

Jonathan was about to bite through his own tongue. Of course, nothing happened between him and Sydney, but knowing Edie, she wasn't about to shed a positive light on the situation.

"Why didn't you tell her I was at lunch? How long did she wait?"

"I did tell her you were at lunch. She decided to wait anyhow. She left about an hour ago."

Jonathan stuck his hands deep down into his pockets, trying to hide the fact that his hands, among other limbs, were shaking. "I see. Well, she'll be happy to know that I went to see Naomi Yates. She's a big fan."

"I bet," Edie said, flipping her file and starting on her left hand.

"I'll have to call her."

Edie didn't respond, and Jonathan figured she wasn't about to volunteer any information. He walked briskly to his office, shut the door, and dialed home. As the phone rang, he reminded himself, between deep breaths, that nothing had happened or was going to happen between him and Sydney. He'd act like everything was fine . . . which it *was* . . . and tell Kathy he was sorry he'd missed her.

He thought it was a little strange, as the phone continued to ring, that Kathy had come to his office for lunch. She used to do that all the time, but in the last year, she hadn't even been by once.

The answering machine picked up, which he thought strange, since the girls should have been home from school by now, so he left a message he hoped sounded sincere.

"Kathy, hi, it's me . . . of course you know it's me . . . um, sorry I missed you. Maybe we can go to lunch later in the week. Okay, I'll see you at home tonight . . . bye . . . I'll be home early . . . bye."

As he hung up the phone, he replayed everything in his head, wondering if he sounded too worried, too shocked, too . . . guilty.

His time for pondering was cut short, however, by the stack of unread manuscripts that seemed to sort of lean to the right, as if threatening to tumble if some weight wasn't taken off soon.

He definitely had to tackle Zippy's proposal sooner than later, but he decided to go ahead and continue to read Clyde's story. Though it contained the errors typical of Clyde's first rough drafts, he saw amazing potential.

Pierce Jenkins threw his fishing line out as far as he could into the pond in front of us. His waist-high rubber suit was covered in dried mud, and my being one who never quite "got" the whole fishing thing, I couldn't quite feel comfortable next to the large box of night crawlers.

"You're not here to hear my fishing stories, are you, Keaton?" he said, watching his line bob up and down in the water. "You went and talked to Esther Caladaras?"

"Yes. This morning." I paused. "I also talked to Jerome Mitchner. I—"

Pierce held up his free hand, took a drag from his cigarette, then took the cigarette out, exhaling slowly. "Keaton, I know why you're here."

"You do?"

"Yeah. I do." Pierce looked at me again. "You need me to go talk to Esther."

I nodded, a little thankful I didn't actually have to come out and say it. But I felt the urge to explain. "Yes. I think she's interested. You were right when you said she hates the FBI. The whole idea that the FBI would *move* a body to save their reputation really ruffled her feathers."

Pierce plucked at his beard. "Funny. I always saw Caladaras as more of a bulldog myself."

I laughed. "She's a little hardcore. But her hate for the FBI may help me get Mitchner off. I mean, Pierce, I'm haunted by the fact that an innocent man could die for something Dietrich Donomar did. He's already had enough victims."

"You don't have to convince me," Pierce said, though in a rather shallow tone.

"So you will talk to Esther? Tell her what you know?" I

asked. Pierce was silent. "Look, I know she can protect your identity. That's not going to be a problem. She'll guarantee that. And besides, when this story breaks, it will expose a really ugly side of the FBI, a side I suspected always existed but never really knew for sure."

Pierce drew in his line. "You're willing to stake your whole career on this, Keaton? The FBI won't just lie down and take this, you know."

He was right. I didn't know what would happen to me, but I did know that I couldn't let Donomar have one more victim. "I know."

Pierce hooked another worm on top of the one already on the hook. "These fish are pigs. Sometimes it takes three or four of these night crawlers to get them to bite."

I couldn't even pretend to sound interested.

He threw his line back out. "So, Esther never asked about your source, how I knew the information?"

I shrugged. "She said she wanted to talk to you, of course. But that's it."

"She never asked why your source saw the file?"

I paused. "Well, no."

Pierce looked at me with hard eyes. "Didn't *you* ever wonder, Keaton?"

I shook my head, not really following. "What do you mean?"

"I mean, did you ever wonder how I know this?"

"You said it was top secret, that no one knew, but that you had some inside info on it."

Pierce laughed suddenly, very hard. I smiled a little myself, wondering what the big joke was. "Boy, did I get you," he said, using his index finger to pull on the inside of his cheek like a fish caught on a hook.

"I'm sorry, I'm not—"

"I found the body."

I stopped everything . . . breathing, thinking, talking. I then processed those four words slowly. I guess Pierce read my puzzled expression, because he then said, "I was fishing on my day off. The body had floated onto land not more than twenty feet away from me."

I could hardly speak. "*You* were the agent who found the body?"

"Yep," he said, not looking at me. "I called my supervisor from my truck. I told them who I suspected it was. They asked if I was in an isolated location. I said I was. They told me to stay put. And then four men arrived, three of whom I didn't know. The fourth was my supervisor."

I couldn't believe what I was hearing. "Pierce, you were involved in this?"

Pierce laughed a little. "Well, actually, they paid me not to be involved."

I couldn't keep my mouth from hanging open. "You were paid off?"

Pierce puffed on his cigarette, keeping his eyes forward. "Yeah. It was a nice down payment on this house behind us."

I stood up. I couldn't believe what I was hearing. "Pierce!"

"What?" he said calmly. "Like you wouldn't have done the same thing?"

"No, I wouldn't have!"

Pierce shrugged, and his line went straight. "Got one!" he yelled and reeled in a small fish that did acrobatics in the air as it came onto shore. "Tiny thing."

"Pierce, what—"

"Look, Keaton, you may have looked that temptation right in the eye and walked away. I couldn't. Not on the salary they were paying me. Lucy had just had our son. Bills were piling up."

I took a deep breath and grabbed him on the shoulder. "Fine. What's done is done. I still need you."

Pierce flicked his cigarette into the water. "Funny how things come back to haunt you." He took the fish off the hook. "I thought that was history. I thought it was buried."

"But now it's what I need to help an innocent man. Will you help me?"

Pierce's bottom lip trembled a bit. He watched the fish he had just caught flop around helplessly on the wet grass next to him. He stared at it a long time. When it was just about dead, he gently picked it up, unhooked it, and threw it back in the water. "You would think fifteen years would sort of squelch some of the guilt. But it hasn't." His hands trembled as he rolled a new, unlit cigarette back and forth between his lips. "I thought it was harmless. I mean, I knew it wasn't exactly ethical, but I couldn't really see the harm in it. We all were sure Mitchner did it."

I didn't know what to say. Pierce was my only chance, but I couldn't ask again. He knew what I needed. I just hoped he would make the right choice.

Pierce closed his tackle box and lifted the collar of his jacket up around his neck. "I wonder what the FBI does to men who are paid for their silence and then 15 years later come forward with the truth?" He stood and stuffed his hands in his pockets. "I know what the Mafia would do."

I quickly stood, too. "Pierce, this isn't the Mafia. And besides, Esther promises full protection of your identity."

Pierce turned to me. "Come on, Keaton. We both know what a joke that is."

I nodded reluctantly.

He sighed and looked toward his house. "My son's fifteen now. Charlie's a good boy, you know? I mean, he drinks occasionally and hangs out with the wrong crowd sometimes, but I think he's going to turn out okay." His eyes lingered there. "I want him to be proud of his old man. That's what I want most. I want him to make the right choices because I did." He then looked at me. "Let me know when and where."

I wanted to let all the air I was holding inside out in one long sigh, but instead I just grabbed his shoulder and squeezed tightly. He nodded, shuffled his feet in the dirt, and then said, "Well, I'd better get inside. I've got a lot of explaining to do to the wife and kid."

I watched as Pierce slowly made his way up toward his house. He was just a silhouette against it as the lights from the windows created a bright glow in the inky night. I felt good inside. I was on the path to saving a man's life. I just hoped everything else would fall into place like I expected.

Jonathan finished the chapter just as Carl Osburg rapped lightly on his door.

"Come in," Jonathan said as he tapped the edges of the manuscript, trying to line up each page to form a neat stack. He wrapped a large rubber band around it and placed it on the edge of his desk.

Carl sauntered in, his tie loosened and the top button of his dress shirt undone, a sure sign the end of the day was near.

"Hey, Carl," Jonathan said. "If you're wondering about Zippy's manuscript, I haven't read it."

Carl ran his finger along the side of Jonathan's large bookcase, shook his head, and then pulled out a book, flipping through it nonchalantly. Jonathan tidied up his desk and asked, "Carl, is there a reason you're just hanging out in my office?" Jonathan looked at his watch. "It's five o'clock. Shouldn't you be going home?"

Carl smiled but avoided eye contact. "Been a long time since I left at five."

"Staying late to see how you can terrorize your fellow editors with a certain dysfunctional nonfiction ghostwriter?"

Carl smiled again, this time closing the book he had in his hand and returning it to the shelf. He walked to the door and shut it, causing Jonathan to sit up a little taller in his chair. "What is it, Carl?"

Carl sat down in the chair across from him. "I consider you a friend, Jonathan. And I hope you consider me one, too."

Jonathan loosened his tie as well. "Sure."

"I don't want you to take this the wrong way. I mean, I'm here because I care."

Jonathan swallowed hard and decided to remove his tie altogether. "Okay . . ."

Carl leaned forward. "There's been talk, Jonathan."

"Talk?" Jonathan repeated slowly. His mind reeled faster than he could control. A thousand scenarios passed through his brain in a few short seconds. "Look, it's just gossip." Jonathan's shirt stuck to his back as he suddenly began to perspire profusely. He wondered how much Carl knew about him and Sydney. And who else knew? Obviously enough people that Carl felt he had to come and confront him.

Carl bit his lip and said, "It's more than just gossip. The evidence is pretty clear."

Jonathan stood and popped the two top buttons of his shirt open. He turned his back to Carl and leaned on the windowsill. How could he save face now? People were talking. He reminded himself that nothing had happened. People could talk all they wanted and it was just gossip. But he also reminded himself that gossip had a way of making itself very real.

"Carl, just tell me what you know. I can assure you nothing is happening."

Although Jonathan couldn't see Carl's expression, the silence coming from him was enough to make him turn around. Carl was frowning, rubbing his forehead, and clearing his throat all at once. Jonathan moved around his desk, grabbing a paper clip so he would have something to do with his hands. "Seriously, Carl. I appreciate the concern, but nothing is happening."

Carl chuckled out of nervousness. "Yeah, I know. That's why I'm here. I mean, I'm sure you're just in a dry spell. It happens to the best of us."

Jonathan twisted his paper clip into a triangle, trying to follow the conversation without revealing too much information. "Dry spell?" He and Kathy had been having problems, but was it known these days as a . . . dry spell? He thought that was kind of crude.

"Look, it's nothing to be embarrassed about. I remember back in 1986, I had five bombs right in a row. It was a nightmare. I thought I'd lost it." Jonathan blinked as Carl stood and put a hand on his shoulder. "I just thought you should know what's being said. Just so you can prepare for it."

Jonathan nodded, though completely lost in the conversation. Carl let go of his shoulder and scratched his head, the way one does right before saying something uncomfortable. "Okay, look, I'm just going to come right out and say it, okay?"

"Please," Jonathan urged.

"All right. I heard Nellie on the phone a couple of days ago. Who knows who she was talking to? Could've been her husband. Could've been her dog. Could've been—"

"The point, Carl?" Jonathan said, impatience escaping in the form of a nervous foot tapping against the carpet. Nellie Benson, the editorial director of the fiction department and his boss since he'd been with Bromahn & Hutch, was one of the best in the business, mainly because she never hesitated to fire anyone who wasn't performing to her rather high expectations. Fortunately, Jonathan had always been a favorite.

"Yeah . . . well, she was telling *whomever* that she was concerned about you. I mean, Jonathan, the fact of the matter is that the last six books you've pushed through have, well, you know . . ."

Jonathan fell into his chair, poking an end of the paper clip deep into his finger. "What? What's that supposed to mean? I've had how many successes, Carl? And the last six is what everyone is looking at?"

Carl held up his hands. "Don't shoot the messenger, okay?"

Jonathan's eyes narrowed. "You were sent."

Carl looked away, glanced back at Jonathan, looked away again, then nodded slightly. Jonathan growled in anger, and Carl quickly tried to put out the fire. "Look, Nellie's concerned. I mean, no offense, but you haven't exactly been yourself lately. And with *Shining Dusk* getting all these horrible reviews—"

Jonathan slammed his hands down on his desk. "Since when have we listened to reviews? Huh? The critics hated Clyde, but the readers loved him."

Carl nodded but said, "I know, I know. But Clyde's books were bestsellers. *Shining Dusk* has only sold forty thousand copies, Jonathan. We've lost money . . . again." Carl shuffled his feet. "And, well, there's talk that you're a one-author editor. I mean, yeah, Clyde's been big for you, but he's retired now. He's not going to be 'it' for you forever."

"I know that," Jonathan snapped. He threw the paper clip aside. "Nellie cannot fairly say that my last six books have failed. *Red Wings* took off like a rocket."

Carl cocked his head to the side, curiously looking at Jonathan. "Sure, but . . . um, haven't you seen the latest figures?" Carl paused. "It's not doing well at all. It sold fifty-eight thousand copies the first two weeks because Hattie Emerson wrote it. Three months later we're only at sixty-five thousand." Carl didn't wait for Jonathan to explode again. Instead he continued in a soothing tone. "You used to always follow the sales. It shocks me you don't know this."

Jonathan glared at Carl, but his anger was distributed to many more people and things than just Carl. "So suddenly I'm incompetent!" Jonathan exploded, though in the back of his mind he scolded himself for not being on top of this. It was true. He had always followed his books closely, almost to a fault. He knew the market so well that it made it easy to accept and reject manuscripts. He could almost do it in his sleep. A few years ago he had turned away Elton Megan, one of the top mystery writers ever. Nellie had almost had a heart attack, but Jonathan stood in her office and said, "Trust me." A few months later, after a rival publishing company, Stubach House, had signed a five-book contract with him, Nellie came into his office and told him she would never question him again. Elton's first three books were such bombs that Stubach House was considering just paying him off for the rest of his contract and letting him go.

"No one is saying that you're incompetent." Carl stepped forward and braced himself with his hands on top of Jonathan's desk. "Nellie's just concerned. I am, too. You haven't been yourself. At last week's editorial meeting, it was like you weren't even there."

Jonathan calmed himself so he could think straight. He rolled up his sleeves in an attempt to seem at ease. "Carl, listen . . . I'm sorry I got upset. I'm okay. Kathy and I are having some . . . some issues at home that are distracting me a bit. But it's nothing that anyone should be concerned about."

"Are you divorcing?" Carl asked with wide eyes.

Jonathan shook his head and quickly said, "No, no, nothing like that. Just a twenty-year itch, you know? I mean, I've been putting in a few thousand hours here. Kathy's probably going through a mid-life crisis. That sort of thing. A distraction at the most." Jonathan punctuated all this with a firm smile.

Carl, in barely a whisper, said, "Man, get her on some hormone pills, Jonathan. I'm not kidding. Susan went through that and I thought death couldn't come too soon. Crying like a baby. Barking like a dog. I couldn't win. It was a nightmare. I swear I—"

"I get the point," Jonathan interrupted, trying to sound as polite as he could. "We're fine."

Carl nodded and an uncomfortable silence suffocated them both. They exchanged a few cordial smiles, then Jonathan said, "Look, Carl, I'll go talk to Nellie. I've got a few aces up my sleeve."

"I knew you would." Carl moved to the door and opened it. "Don't be too hard on Nellie. She was just concerned. She didn't want to upset you by coming herself."

"She should have. Sending you was low. No offense."

Carl quietly shut the door behind him. Jonathan glanced down at Clyde's manuscript and thumped it a couple of times with his fingers. He had no doubt in the power of this ace.

CHAPTER 14

Jonathan had hoped to find Nellie after his discussion with Carl, but she had left for the day. He spent two more needless hours at the office working, just to prove to himself that he hadn't "lost it."

He reviewed Zippy's proposal and sample chapters, and to his astonishment, it was quite good. The story revolved around a pharmaceutical company being paid off to destroy a cure for cancer because cancer care was such a big money-maker. He would talk to Zippy tomorrow.

After writing a few rejection letters and emailing three house authors, he decided to head home. When he turned into the driveway, Clyde's old truck was parked there, blocking him from pulling his vehicle into the garage.

Jonathan opened the front door of his house, and Clyde and Kathy, sitting at the dining room table, both stood to greet him.

"Clyde, what are you doing here?"

Kathy piped in. "I invited him for dinner. You're just in time. The lasagna is nearly done." Kathy paused, as if she were going to say something more, then excused herself to the kitchen.

"Been a long time since I had a home-cooked meal," Clyde said, sitting back down at the table. He sipped his iced tea as Jonathan took off his jacket and set his briefcase in the corner.

"So Kathy just called you out of the blue to come over for dinner?" Jonathan said, not covering up his suspicious tone in any way.

Clyde looked him the eye. "I called to check on you. The both of you. To see what you found out 'bout that story."

Jonathan sat down at the table. "Where are the girls?"

Kathy appeared from nowhere with a large pan of lasagna. "Meg's at Alexandra's. Leesol is next door at the Chamberlains'. Sophie's in bed." She set the pan in the middle of the table. "Let me get the bread."

Jonathan unfolded his napkin and set it in his lap. Clyde, distracted by the lasagna, finally looked up at Jonathan, only to be met with a relentless stare. "Still your star suspect, Jonny?" he asked casually.

"Why not?" Jonathan replied, pouring himself a glass of water. "Everyone is."

Kathy set the bread down and joined them at the table. "We were discussing the manuscript, Jonathan. Clyde is very worried." She cut the lasagna and served each of them. "Are you?"

Jonathan took a piece of bread and passed the basket. "I haven't received more pages. So I guess I'm not worried," he lied. He took a large bite of lasagna and washed it down with his water.

Kathy lightly touched his hand and said, "Shall we bless it?"

Jonathan looked around with embarrassment. "Of course. Clyde, why don't you?"

They bowed their heads and Clyde said a short prayer. Clyde then continued. "Jonathan, what more do you know?"

Jonathan stared at his plate. He pondered whether or not he should go into detail with Clyde, not to mention Kathy. However, both were staring and wondering, and he figured at this stage in the game, he didn't have much to lose. Besides, there wasn't much to report.

"I don't know, I don't know," he said as he dug his fork into his lasagna. He looked up at Kathy, whose gentle eyes watched him with concern. "Whoever it is, they're going to make a mistake. I'll be there when it happens."

Clyde had already gulped down half of his lasagna. "Jonathan, maybe instead of lookin' at the actual manuscript, you should concentrate on *why* someone would be doin' this."

Jonathan watched as Kathy looked at him for a reply. He was nervous. He didn't want to say anything that would upset Kathy, and she was already starting to look worried. "I have no idea who would want to do this."

Clyde kept shoveling food in while he thought out loud. "I mean, why would someone want you to read about your own life? What harm or good could come from that?"

Jonathan set his utensils down. Kathy gulped her water. "Perhaps to scare me. Make me think they know everything about me."

Clyde emphasized his point by holding his fork up in the air. "Yes, but *why*? I mean, what point would someone want to make by tellin' you everything you already know about your own life?"

Kathy had set her utensils down, too, apparently concentrating very hard on the conversation. Jonathan tried to ease the tension a little. "I don't know. To let me know what a moron I've been all these years?" He laughed, but Kathy and Clyde didn't.

Kathy poured herself another glass of water. "Maybe . . . maybe like a reflection. Maybe this person wants you to review your life."

Clyde buttered a piece of bread. "Good point. But again, we have to ask *why*." Clyde wiped his mouth after taking a bite of bread. "It's like when I create my characters. For instance, Bart Callahan. My audience was first introduced to him when he was twenty-nine. But I knew him long before that. I had to write down his past so I could create his present character." Clyde heavily salted his piece of lasagna. "Maybe that's what's going on here. Maybe someone wants you to look back at yourself for some reason."

Jonathan pushed his plate away. He'd lost his appetite. "Fine. So maybe someone does, Clyde. Why? Why would someone care what is in my past?"

"Well," Clyde continued, "maybe it somehow links you to something they're going to do in the future. I don't know. It's a wacky thing, but it sure seems to have a purpose. And they sure seem to know a lot about you."

Kathy had also seemed to lose her appetite. Her plate was still full of food.

Jonathan took her hand. "We're fine, Kathy. I don't want you to worry. I don't think whoever is doing this is going to be a danger to us." Jonathan glanced away, hoping that statement was true. "But Clyde's right. Someone definitely wants to make some sort of statement."

Kathy began clearing the table. "I guess what Clyde's saying, then, is instead of looking at what's in the manuscript, we should be trying to figure out why it exists at all."

"Just a thought," Clyde said as he scraped the last bit of lasagna off his plate and handed it to Kathy. "Wonderful cookin', Kathy."

"Thank you," she said and patted him on the back. "You should come over more often."

Kathy went to the kitchen and Jonathan leaned back in his chair. "I swear, Clyde, if you're doing this, I'm going to kill you."

Clyde chuckled a little. "Well, maybe I'm writin' in my sleep, but I don't think it's me. I got my hands full with my own story right now. By the way, what do you think of it so far?"

Jonathan twirled his fork from finger to finger. "I'm very pleased. A real work . . . so far."

Clyde winked at him. "Well, I'm workin' hard. I should have some more chapters to you next week."

"I plan on presenting it to committee. I'd like to have as much as possible when I do."

"Sure, sure. But I don't want to tell you the endin'. Not yet. I want it to be a surprise."

Jonathan laughed and felt good inside. It felt like old times with Clyde. He threw his napkin on the table and said, "Yeah, fine. But I need a complete proposal when I present it." He looked up at Clyde. "In your case, an outline. I know you don't do synopses."

Clyde winked and called to Kathy, "You got any cobbler in there, honey?"

Kathy returned with a dish full of peach cobbler. "I'm trying my new recipe out on you, Clyde. It's my turn to do dessert at Thanksgiving this year, and I want it to be good."

Clyde watched with delight as Kathy cut him a big piece and placed it on the dessert plate she'd brought in. Clyde took a big bite and grinned widely. "Darlin', it'll be a hit."

Kathy glowed with pride and served Jonathan a smaller piece. "That reminds me, Jonathan. Your aunt Eleanor called and wanted to know when we were planning on coming. She hoped a few days before Thanksgiving. She and Earl want to see the girls so badly."

Eleanor was his mother's oldest sister, still alive and doing well. Her husband, Earl, a retired naval officer, was the girls' favorite uncle. "Is it going to be a big gathering?" Jonathan said in pretend disgust.

Kathy waited for him to take a bite of cobbler. He did and indicated it was the best he'd ever had with a big thumbs-up. She continued. "I think just our family."

Clyde and Jonathan raced to see who could finish their cobbler first, but unfortunately, Jonathan had to skip a bite to respond to Kathy. "I'll let you know in a couple of weeks. I should know more then what my work schedule will be."

Kathy raised her eyebrows. "Jonathan . . . Thanksgiving is next Thursday."

Clyde paused as Jonathan shook his head in amazement. "Good grief. You're right. I'm sorry, honey. I've really lost track of time, haven't I?" He gently grabbed her hand. "I will let you know after work tomorrow."

She smiled, stood, and said, "I have fresh coffee. We can light a fire and move to the living room."

Clyde took his finger, swiped the side of his dessert plate, licked it, and then held up his hands. "Thank ya, but I need to be gettin' home. I have trouble drivin' at night and it takes me a while 'cause I drive so darn slow." He lifted his large body out of the chair, folded his napkin neatly, and placed it on his plate. He then gave Kathy a hug. "Sweet of you to invite me."

Kathy kissed him on the cheek. "Our home is always open to you."

Clyde moved to the front door and Jonathan followed him, opening it up for him. Clyde slid his old coat on and buttoned it tightly. "I love the cold weather. I remember cuddling up next to my wife, wrapping the large blankets around us, and listening to some Louis Armstrong and Miles Davis on the record player." He patted Jonathan on the shoulder. "I miss those nights. Don't take your life for granted." He walked down the front steps of their home. "And, Jonny, don't waste your time investigatin' me for all this weird stuff goin' on. It ain't me."

Jonathan's body chilled quickly and he stepped inside, shutting the door behind him. He heard Clyde's muffler backfire and his loud engine become softer as it backed out of the drive. He went to the kitchen, where Kathy was pouring them both large cups of coffee.

"Should I go get Meg?"

"She's spending the night. So is Leesol."

Jonathan took the mug from Kathy. "Do we know the Chamberlains that well? I mean, I don't think I've even talked to Mr. Chamberlain."

"Joel. He's away on business a lot. Leesol and their daughter are only a year apart. And you know how Leesol has trouble making friends as it is. She really seems to like it over there."

"Did you have the talk with them? Did you tell Meg not to go with anyone other than us? Anywhere? For any reason whatso—"

"Yes, yes." Kathy stirred her coffee. "Meg and Leesol both asked questions. I played it off pretty well, I think. I told them there had been a kidnapping in the next town over and I just wanted to be sure they remembered the rules." She looked up at Jonathan. "Honey, one minute you say everything is fine and not to worry. The next you're checking all the locks twice and worried the girls are going to get kidnapped. Which is it?"

Jonathan didn't know, truthfully. He suspected his family wasn't in danger, but how could he really know? With each new page he read from this manuscript, the more mysterious and startling it became. "Honey, I'm just taking precautions. I mean, we need to regularly review these types of things with our girls anyway. There are plenty of other wackos if this writer isn't one." He smiled and sipped his coffee, all the while trying to remember if he'd locked the dead bolt on the front door.

———

Jonathan fell into bed early that evening, completely exhausted and barely able to keep his eyes open. Though his body was motionless, his mind was alive with activity, a circus of fears, anxieties, anger, and guilt.

He had sensed Kathy had wanted him to stay up and talk, but he didn't have the energy. He lamely apologized, took a shower, and went to bed before she did.

In the morning, he was awakened by Sophie throwing a temper tantrum and a car pulling out of the drive, presumably Alexandra's parents dropping Meg off. He dozed on and off for another thirty minutes before all the commotion downstairs began echoing off his bedroom walls.

He checked his clock. It was 7:30 A.M. He decided to go with a more casual look this morning—khakis and a long-sleeved, heavy knit sweater. The chill in the air indicated maybe some snow had fallen overnight, and as he looked out the window to his backyard, he was thrilled to see a soft layer tickling the tops of the grass and brightly reflecting the morning sun. He warmed his hands underneath the faucet, did a quick shave, then thundered down the stairs to join his family.

Meg was busily talking about her evening with Alexandra while Leesol was teaching Sophie how to butter her toast. Kathy was fixing oatmeal, a different flavor according to each child's preference.

"Dad, I have a boyfriend!" Meg exclaimed as she hopped out of her chair to greet him with a hug.

Kathy followed right behind her with a fresh cup of coffee for him. "You're going to need this."

Meg pulled out a chair at the table and insisted he sit down. She sat right next to him. "His name is Damion, and he's fourteen. Dad, don't freak out. Dad!"

Jonathan realized he must've had a bewildered look on his face, because so far he hadn't said a word.

"He's Alexandra's older brother's best friend. He plays football. The quarterback. He reads a lot. I thought you'd like that. His last name is Barker, which rhymes with Harper, which is sort of how we met. It was this whole confusing thing on the phone when he called for Chad, and I ended up getting on the phone and well, we started talking. He actually knows who I am! For like, two hours, Dad. He's really sweet. And very cute. He said I reminded him of

Meg Ryan, and not just because of my name. He said I looked like her, too. . . ."

Jonathan held up his hands and shot Kathy a look, which was returned with a little chuckle and a shrug of the shoulders. "Meg, good grief. Slow down. You can't have a boyfriend. You're too young. You're only . . . how old are you again?"

"*Daaaadddddd*," Meg moaned, her eyes already tearing up. "*Moommmmm?*"

Kathy approached the table. "Honey, your dad's right. You're not going on any dates, so get that through your head right now."

"I'm not a baby!" Meg sniffled.

Jonathan brushed her hair out of her face. "Sweetheart, I know that. But you're also not ready to date. I'm glad Chad thinks you're—"

"*Damion.*"

"—Damion thinks you're cute. You are cute. You're adorable. But you're absolutely not going on any dates."

"Dad! You're being mean! This is the most popular guy at school!"

Jonathan broke his toast in two. "That makes it even worse."

"Mom!" Tears flowed from Meg's eyes.

"Honey, you know you can't date until you're fifteen. We've talked about this."

"But Alexandra's already had *two* boyfriends! I haven't had any!"

Jonathan glanced up at Kathy. "And you say Alexandra's okay to hang out with?"

Meg slid her chair back. "Great! Now I can't hang with Alex, either? What's next? You're going to keep me out of school so I don't look at any boys?" Meg dramatically shoved her chair back underneath the table and stomped upstairs. "You're sooo mean!"

Jonathan blinked, not sure he'd had an opportunity to yet, and Kathy brought him a warm bowl of apple cinnamon oatmeal. Leesol, who had managed to somehow get toast in Sophie's hair, said, "Daddy, he is cute. I've seen him."

Kathy quickly ushered Leesol upstairs. "Go get ready for school. The bus will be here in ten minutes."

Jonathan swirled his oatmeal with a spoon, his head already pounding. "What in the world just happened?"

Kathy picked pieces of toast out of Sophie's hair while Sophie made crumbs with the piece she had left. "She's at that age. We knew it would happen."

Jonathan sighed and poured himself a glass of orange juice. "Yeah, but shouldn't she be out of diapers first?"

Kathy joined him at the table for a glass of juice. "Hard to believe she's not a baby anymore, isn't it?" She buttered a piece of toast and Jonathan checked his watch.

He walked to the kitchen, put his dishes in the sink, and picked up his briefcase from the dining room where he'd left it the night before. "Thanks for breakfast," he said and kissed both Sophie and Kathy on the cheeks. He glanced upstairs and said, "I've got to run. I guess I'll do damage control when I get home this evening."

Kathy nodded and opened the front door for him. "You want a coat? There's snow on the ground."

Jonathan shook his head and grabbed a scarf off the coatrack. "This will be fine."

He kissed Kathy one more time on the cheek and then walked out the front door, remembering he had been unable to get into the garage because Clyde had been parked in the driveway. Kathy shut the door behind him and he stood on the porch for a moment and took in the view. It was perfect. The autumn leaves hadn't completely died and fallen off yet, so a few still remained on the trees, capped with tiny bits of snow and ice, which were beginning to melt, though the sun barely emitted any heat yet. The ground was as smooth as white silk, and not even a dog's prints had ruined the perfect layer of snow in his front yard.

He checked his watch and decided he had better get going. His commute to work would likely be slow this morning. He wrapped the scarf around his neck and stepped carefully along the sidewalk, watching for any spots of ice. When he got to his car, he fumbled around for his keys, which he was sure he'd put in his pocket. Finding them, he dusted off the keyhole and then saw the one thing that he dreaded the most. A manila envelope was tucked underneath the windshield wiper on the driver's side. Jonathan's keys fell out of his hand and he immediately grabbed the envelope, dusted off the light bit of snow on it, and stared at it without breathing.

His mind froze without any thoughts at all, and his body was unaware of the cold wind that was chapping his skin. In the background he heard the roar of the school bus turning the corner onto his street, and without hesitation he quickly threw the envelope in his SUV, picked his keys up off the ground, and got in. He turned the ignition on and violently tapped his hands against the steering wheel as he waited for the defroster to work.

The bus honked and the front door opened, and Leesol and Meg rushed out into the snow, through the front yard toward the bus stop. Kathy waited at the door, watching them run and yelling what Jonathan presumed were warnings about the ice on the road. She shivered, waved at them, gave Jonathan a short wave, and then disappeared into the house.

Jonathan closed his eyes, told himself not to panic, and backed out of his driveway with a full sheet of ice on his back window.

CHAPTER 15

The fight the night before had been one of their worst. Kathy, in her usual, overly emotional way, had declared their marriage over due to Jonathan's long hours at the office. Jonathan, in his usual underemotional way, had agreed by not disagreeing. The explosion between them was monumental. Jonathan screamed that he couldn't tell what she was feeling anymore. Kathy retorted, crying and yelling, "If you read me as carefully as you read all those stupid books, maybe you would know what's going on inside me!" Jonathan had thrown a few things off the kitchen counter and stomped upstairs. Kathy cried hysterically and locked herself in the downstairs bathroom.

The next day, at the office, Jonathan felt empty. He covered this up by working, but in his mind he knew, out of the last six months, this one had been the worst. The progression had been slow. A few side comments here. A couple of small arguments there. Nothing, standing alone, that would indicate a twenty-year marriage was on the rocks.

Though the argument had been over Jonathan's long work hours, that was simply a mask for what was really going on. They had grown apart, plain and simple. Their lives, though lived under the same roof, were separated by emotional distance. And it seemed with each passing day, their marriage crumbled even more.

The day after the big argument, Kathy had called several times, but Jonathan refused to return her phone calls. Little did he know that on that day, one piece of mail would change his life forever.

Jonathan breathed shallowly, unaware that his hand was covering both his mouth and nose. Dare he turn the page? When he first began reading, he wasn't sure at what point in his life the story picked up. Since he'd burned the previous section, it seemed as if he were picking up on the story right in the middle. It spoke of a monumental argument, but these days, he could pick and choose. Though the last few days had seemed better between him and Kathy, he attributed that mostly to the fact that he was so consumed with guilt over Sydney that he was making extra efforts toward Kathy.

The last sentence on the page, though, the one about a piece of mail that would change his life, made him chew off the ends of each one of his fingernails on both hands. He sat and stared at the page as if it might turn by itself. The stark reality was that whoever was writing this was in a process. The author was writing his life as it happened.

Jonathan tried to think logically, trying to remember the day the first pages of this manuscript had arrived. It had been a busy morning, as he recalled. The more he thought about it, the more he remembered he and Kathy having a fight the night before, over his work hours, just as the manuscript had said. He felt completely violated—as if someone had been in his house, listening to his life and writing down every detail of it.

He quickly reminded himself, as he snapped back into the present situation, that whoever it was did not know *everything*. He had to keep telling himself that. Some details were wrong. Others were left out. Whole sections of his life were missing.

But overshadowing those facts, as comforting as he tried to make them, was the reality of the details that *were* written down, many of which no one knew but him. And now this writer was not only writing about Jonathan but had also entered the story himself, with the mention of the manuscript. And whoever it was correctly stated that that single piece of mail had changed his life. What was on the next page was anyone's guess.

At first it blended in with all the other manuscripts that crossed his desk every day. It was in the typical yellow manila envelope, and it was marked "Requested Material." But when he began reading, to his astonishment, it was about his own life, starting with the death of his brother.

This was quite shocking, because no one knew about this incident except him and his parents, who were now both dead. At first he wrote it off as coincidence. After all, there were some differences. But the more he read, the more he knew that this was no coincidence. Someone was indeed sending him a story about his own life.

The story continued with the barn fire, a time Jonathan would have rather forgotten, and also a conversation he had had with his mother in his bedroom. As he sat and read the story in his office, his hands trembled and his heart raced.

All these memories rushing back to him were more than he could handle, especially as he dealt with the usual business of the day. By the end of the day he was exhausted, too exhausted to face his wife. Luckily he had a dinner appointment with one of his favorite people, Clyde Baxter. But dinner could only last so long and eventually he had to come home.

Still reeling from the night before, Kathy greeted him with disdain. He'd missed dinner due to his appointment with Clyde, which he knew would upset Kathy. The night was a disaster, like so many other nights.

Jonathan quickly ripped a piece of paper off his yellow pad and grabbed a pencil.

"Think, think, think," he said, trying to remember the day he'd received the manuscript. How much of this was accurate? What details were in and what details were left out?

He reread the first part slowly and wrote notes to himself. Yes, he and Kathy had had a fight, and it had been over his work hours. The author had presumptuously, as before, written down how Jonathan might have felt about the situation. The author also assumed that their problems went deeper than arguments over his work hours.

Jonathan tapped his pencil against the edge of the desk. His eyes scanned his notes and lingered on the words *presumptuous* and *assumed*. As he scratched the end of the eraser with his thumbnail, he made a mental note that the author was right on. Jonathan did feel empty inside. And the problems, though he didn't wish to admit it, were deeper than simply about long work hours. The trouble was, he didn't even know how deep they went or from where they came.

He continued and reread the line about Kathy calling several times that day. Jonathan tried to remember that day as best he could. He remembered the fight the night before . . . who could forget it? And the next morning seemed to be the usual. He had begun his morning looking at manuscripts and somehow had stumbled upon this particular one.

Jonathan started to write down a note and then paused. "Wait a minute," he said out loud. Sydney had brought in the manuscript. Yes! Sydney had brought it in and they had discussed . . . Embeth Wilkes! That's right! And then Zippy had come in and wanted to talk about his new book. Jonathan wrote as fast as he could. Things were missing! Perhaps the author just didn't deem them important, but nevertheless, those details weren't in there. That could be vital.

He thought harder. Whoever it was knew that Kathy had called but presumably not that Sydney or Zippy had come in. Jonathan drew a line down the middle of his page. On the left-hand side he wrote *actual*. On the right-hand side he wrote *story*.

He took a deep breath and began to think of and catalog that whole day, every detail that he could remember. He scribbled thoughts down as more ideas piled on top.

Two pages filled with notes. He broke his pencil lead twice, and at the very end stabbed his pencil into the page to make a deep period. He looked over his notes for a minute or so, the proud smile on his face slowly fading as he realized that this small clue brought him no closer to knowing who was doing this or why or even *how*.

As he nervously scratched the dry skin off his lips, he silently encouraged himself to continue to find clues. As he thought some more, he noticed something in particular. In the first chapters that were sent, the author seemed attentive to detail. It had been more like a work of fiction. There had been much more detail. The story's flow was smoother.

Now, though, it seemed as if it were just a list of things that happened. Sure, a few sentences were thrown in, trying to describe how he *might have* felt in a circumstance, but it read more like an outline than a story. He wrote that thought down at the end of the page and put a star by it.

He traced the star with his pencil as one single, overwhelming thought pounded inside the walls of his mind. It was a thought that he had refused to entertain all morning. Now, though he didn't want to, he had to address it.

The writer had been to his house.

Jonathan gently folded his hands together and pressed his index fingers against his lips. Had he walked right up to their house in the middle of the night? Jonathan had not thought to look in the snow for footprints, though he did remember it being a soft sheet of white. By now the snow was gone, anyway.

His whole body seemed to go numb at the sickening thought that whoever this person was knew a great deal about him, including where he lived. Had he peeked in the windows in the middle of the night? Did he know the layout of the house? Had he been in the house, as the evidence seemed to indicate?

"No," Jonathan said out loud. The house was locked and there was no evidence of intrusion. But someone knew what went on inside the house.

His head ached with anxiety and fear. Was his family in danger? He quickly dialed his home number, but the machine picked up. He hung up without leaving a message.

On his desk, a few more pages lay waiting to be read, waiting to invade his life. He picked up his pencil, which felt as if it weighed a ton, and turned the page to continue to read about his life.

Perhaps the next night could've been saved. Jonathan had

*come home early, hoping to smooth things over from the day
before. However, Kathy wasn't receptive. The night ended in a
harsh fight, which was no surprise to either of them. Even
their attempt at a date the next evening was disastrous.*

But Jonathan always did have poor timing.

*He'd decided to tell Kathy about the manuscript. He tried
to act unaffected by it, play it off as mildly annoying, but the
truth of the matter was he was extremely worried. Unfortunately, Kathy had hoped the date was an attempt to start over,
a way to wave the white flag without speaking it. The date
ended with Kathy getting up and leaving.*

Jonathan pushed the lump in his throat back down. How could
anyone know this? How could someone know what went on in his
office, out of the office, in his home, and everywhere else? Was he
going insane? Was this writer trying to make him insane? Had someone been watching at a nearby table as he and Kathy had dinner?
Close enough to hear their conversation and know he had spoken
to her about this manuscript? He feebly wrote a few notes down,
then continued.

*The weekend was filled with silence between them until
Sunday morning, when Jonathan announced he would go to
church with the family. It had been nearly a year since he'd
gone, and Kathy and his daughters were delighted. After all,
at one time he had faithfully attended, but the more Jonathan
got buried in his work, the less time he spent at church, until
he wasn't going at all. Had Jonathan forgotten his God, or
maybe never known him at all?*

Jonathan set the pages down, his eyebrows rising while he reread the last sentence. It startled him, for more than one reason.
He read the last part out loud.

" 'Had Jonathan forgotten his God, or maybe never known him
at all?' "

His fingers painfully underlined each word. His jaw muscles
tightened in reaction to the word *God*. Resting his head against the
back of his chair, his body slumped and he looked up, as if expecting to see God himself hanging from the ceiling. He did believe in

172

God. But more in an abstract way. Kathy always talked of God as if He were in the room. To Jonathan, He was something far, far away, a star in the night that had watched his brother die and done nothing to stop it. And maybe more than that—blamed Jonathan for it. If He noticed at all.

"Are you writing this, God?" he said with a short, disturbed laugh. He traced his eyebrows with his fingers as he wondered what all this meant. First his childhood. Then his marriage. And now his spiritual life? Sure, Kathy and even the girls had been harping on him to go to church, and every Sunday he had good intentions. But when Saturdays are filled up with work, Sundays are precious. Most of the time he was too tired. And when he did have the energy, the lawn needed mowing, among other things. Besides, church didn't have much meaning to him. He mostly did it out of family duty. Kathy expected it of him.

Several months back, Kathy had wanted them to pray together, especially about their marriage. But Jonathan had never felt comfortable praying and instead assured Kathy he would do it on his own time . . . which he had not. He didn't even know how to pray.

He jotted down the word *God* in his notes, and then thought about who might be concerned about his spiritual life. Pastor Gregory was the obvious choice, though he didn't have enough evidence to prove he would be the writer. Clyde, however, was a different story. Clyde always seemed concerned about his spiritual life and was quite the Christian advocate. And, Jonathan wrote swiftly, *Clyde is always concerned about my drinking.* He had made several comments about it the last few times they were together. And Kathy. He wrote her name down slowly. Kathy.

Jonathan stood and looked out his window. Clyde had been at his house the night before. But did he really have enough guts to leave the manuscript right on his windshield? As Jonathan rolled up his sleeves, the thought came to him that maybe Clyde knew he was close to being caught. After all, he had been confronted. Maybe he knew Jonathan was closing in.

"Maybe he *wants* me to figure out it's him," Jonathan thought out loud. Why? And how did he know so much?

Jonathan shook his head, doubt right on the heels of every

hopeful thought. Clyde wouldn't do something like this. And besides, as good of a writer as he was, he couldn't know so many details about him. Even if Kathy had felt the need to confide in Clyde, how would Clyde know about his brother's death, the incident in the barn, and his conversation with his mother? His parents had died before he ever met Clyde. Still, it was odd that he happened to be at the house the night these pages turned up. And the time before they had *mysteriously* landed in Clyde's mailbox.

Jonathan decided to read on, hoping that with a few more slip-ups or clues, he would discover who the writer was.

> *That weekend he woke up early enough to go to church with the family. Unfortunately, a call from Clyde shattered that possibility. Clyde had insisted that Jonathan meet him right away at Jonathan's office.*
>
> *When Jonathan arrived, Clyde was there with a manila envelope in his hand. He didn't have to say what it was. Jonathan knew. It was more pages to the manuscript.*
>
> *In a thoughtless rage, Jonathan burned the envelope right then and there. He then drove in a complete panic to his house where he checked all his doors and windows to make sure everything was locked. He went to the basement to see if he could find evidence that someone had been there. He was startled when his wife came downstairs to find him.*
>
> *As painful as it was, Jonathan had to tell her the truth. The truth, according to Clyde, was that apparently the story depicted their marriage as rocky, which it was. Unfortunately, it also meant that now Kathy was even more involved, and Jonathan had to tell her that she was in the story, too. Obviously concerned, Kathy then admitted that she had told Charles Gregory, the pastor of their church, about their problems.*
>
> *Jonathan immediately went to confront Pastor Gregory, but ended up empty-handed, without much more evidence to prove who was writing this. He then went to Clyde's house to try to find out more information about the pages he had burned, though in the back of his mind, Clyde was just as much a suspect as anyone else.*

"Yes!" Jonathan exclaimed. The writer had gotten another fact wrong. He had visited Clyde first, then Pastor Gregory. Jonathan marked his notes, underlined them twice for emphasis, and continued.

> *After finding out more about what was in those pages, Jonathan was more on edge than ever. This came through when a house author, Francis Flowers, was waiting in Jonathan's office the next morning. Jonathan saw a manila envelope on the desk and with utter trepidation, caused quite a panic when he snatched the envelope out of Francis's hand with such fierceness, the poor man was about scared to death. This was when Jonathan knew all of this chaos was about to send him over the edge.*
>
> *But little did he know that his roaming heart would do more damage than the mysterious story. His infatuation with a young woman named Sydney was pushing him closer to the ledge. Though he couldn't see the drop-off, he seemed willing to jump anyway.*

The pencil in Jonathan's hand snapped in two. Staring down at the pages, he could hardly believe what he was reading. The writer knew about Sydney? How? He had told absolutely *no one* about her. Sure, he figured Edie had her suspicions, but they were just suspicions, because nothing had happened between them. Only some harmless flirting. How could someone look into his heart and know how close he had been to falling for her?

Jonathan stood, paced his office, stopped, closed his eyes, and made himself sit back down in his chair and read the rest of it. Somewhere in all of this mess was his clue as to how this writer knew so much.

> *He spent the day with her at Naomi Yates's house, a famous children's author. There, though, Jonathan was confronted by the old woman on this deadly infatuation. She told him about an affair she had in 1940 and how it destroyed her marriage. Jonathan denied anything was going on. In fact, he played it off as simply trying to help Sydney, as he suspected she was being beaten by her fiancé, a suspicion that was underlined by an awkward confrontation he had with her in the car on the way over to Naomi's house.*
>
> *But Naomi knew better and asked him a simple question*

that Jonathan had no choice but to ponder. "If you're going to be her savior, who is going to be yours?"

While away from the office with Sydney, Kathy had stopped by to take Jonathan to lunch in an attempted peace offering. Unfortunately, he wasn't there and Kathy left disappointed.

Jonathan's day was further complicated when a fellow editor and friend, Carl Osburg, stopped by his office to break the news to him that their boss, Nellie, was beginning to worry about Jonathan. His last few books had hardly sold, and the choices he was bringing to the conference table weren't the usual superstars. As Carl put it, "You haven't been yourself lately."

Jonathan dismissed his seeming incapability by sharing with Carl that he and Kathy had been having a few minor problems, but it wasn't anything to be alarmed about, and it certainly wasn't the reason he wasn't doing well at work. Although angry, he assured Carl that he would talk with Nellie and put her fears to rest.

When he arrived home that evening, Clyde Baxter was waiting for him inside his home. Kathy had cooked a lasagna, and Jonathan sat down just as it was being served. They discussed the manuscript together and tried to come up with reasons why someone would write all this about him. Clyde commented that perhaps the writer was showing him his past for some reason; there was something the writer wanted Jonathan to know.

When Kathy left the table to go get cobbler, Jonathan threatened Clyde. "I swear, Clyde, if you're doing this I'm going to kill you." Clyde, in his usual mild-mannered way, simply denied it.

Jonathan slept restlessly that night, and the next morning, as he walked out to his car to go to work, his nightmare resurrected itself in the form of another manila envelope located on the driver's-side windshield, underneath the wiper.

Jonathan was breathing hard as he finished the last page. He carefully clipped the pages together and slid them back into the envelope. A million questions flowed in and out of his mind, his racing heart trying to keep pace. Thought after thought knocked him dizzy. The writer knew of his conversation with Sydney in the car. The writer knew of his conversation with Naomi Yates at her house. The writer knew of his conversation with Carl in his office. How?!

The manuscript had *almost* accurately depicted the events of the last few days in his life. There was no set pattern to the knowledge. Sometimes it gave great detail, even accurately quoting people. Other times it gave rather vague descriptions.

But perhaps what was most startling was the fact that it told the story all the way up to that very morning. Jonathan couldn't understand how all this was playing out. He stood and walked circles in his office to try to get the blood flowing back to his brain.

That morning he had, as the manuscript indicated, walked to his car and found it on his windshield. But the more Jonathan remembered, the more he realized that the writer had not described his morning completely accurately. Though part of his morning played out as it said, he realized that the writer could only guess what would happen, for it had to have been written the night before. Of course he would go out and find it on the car, where the writer had left it. That wasn't hard to predict. But it made no further mention of the morning's happenings or his fight with Meg over her new boyfriend.

Jonathan's dark cloud of insanity revisited him, though, when he thought of all the events the manuscript *had* accurately described—nearly everything of significance that had happened to him in the past few days, including his relationship with Sydney.

Jonathan stopped walking and stared at the walls in his office, wondering if they talked. As silly as that thought was, it led him to the idea that perhaps he was being recorded. Had someone sneaked into his office and placed a camcorder somewhere?

It didn't explain how the author knew everything else, but it was a start. Before he could stop himself, he was pulling books off his shelf. First, one at a time, but the more the thought of someone spying on him overwhelmed him, the more furious he became, grabbing books by the handful and throwing them from their shelves. He rolled his chair over and climbed onto it so he could reach the top shelves. One by one, books came toppling down to the floor, as Jonathan tried to keep his balance on a chair with wheels. A cloud of dust hovered near the ceiling.

"Are you watching me?!" Jonathan said loudly, scooting himself along the bookshelves, tossing books left and right. "Is that it? Spying on me? Watching my every move? I'll catch you! I swear I will—"

"Jonathan?"

Jonathan turned around quickly, causing a book to drop onto his head with a thud and then fall, hitting his shoulder and hand before crashing to the ground.

"Nellie . . ." Jonathan's voice was barely audible.

Nellie Benson, in her dark navy tailored suit and high heels, carefully stepped around a few books near the door, eyeing both the books and Jonathan carefully. "Is everything okay here?"

Jonathan wobbled a bit on the chair before stumbling off it and falling onto the ground. He hopped up and, still choking on the dust, managed to get out, "Sure. Why?"

Nellie stooped to pick up a book bent backward at the spine. "Well, the floor in your office is covered in books and your bookshelves are left with just dust." She poked her fingers into her French twist. "You want to tell me what's going on?"

Jonathan leaned casually on his desk. "Just doing some rearranging. That's all. I've been needing to get rid of some of these books for a while." Jonathan glanced down at the book-ridden carpet and stooped down to grab one. "Would you look at that! *Moby Dick.* I've been looking for that."

Nellie tried to clear the air of dust by waving her hands. "Yes— well, next time maybe you should dust first."

Jonathan laughed lightly, brushed the dust off *Moby Dick*, and returned his chair to his desk. "What can I do for you, Nellie?"

Nellie picked a book off one of the chairs in front of his desk, unbuttoned her jacket, and sat down. "Well, Jonathan, don't be so surprised to see me here. Carl told me he came and talked to you."

Jonathan threw *Moby Dick* aside and sat down. "Yeah, that was low, Nellie. Why not just come here yourself?"

She adjusted the watch on her wrist, avoiding his eyes. "I don't know. You've been acting so strange lately, I thought maybe the problem was personal. I didn't want to pry, but I thought you and Carl were close. Maybe he could find out." She glanced up at him. "You and Kathy okay?"

Jonathan sneezed, his allergies ignited by all the dust. "Fine, fine," he said, grabbing for a tissue.

"You're sure?" She looked around the room for emphasis. "You're sure this isn't affecting you?"

Jonathan blew his nose and nodded.

Nellie fiddled with her left earring. "You can talk to me, you know. I mean, maybe it's not your marriage. Maybe it's something else."

Jonathan, between sneezes, questioned her with a tilt of his head.

"I'm just saying, your editorial choices have left something to be desired lately, and I'm thinking maybe you should take a break. A sabbatical or something. Hmm?"

"Nellie, please. I'm in a slump. You're acting as if this is something uncommon. It happens."

"Sure it happens, Jonathan. But your behavior lately has been so weird, I just thought maybe it was—"

Jonathan held up his Kleenex, waving it like a white flag. "Nellie, please. Give me a break. I've got two sure winners for next month's editorial meeting."

Nellie raised her eyebrows, impressed. "Good. I'm glad to hear it. We'll meet the week after Thanksgiving."

Jonathan stood and leaned forward on his desk, trying to muster up as much confidence as he could. "Trust me."

Nellie stood, and they exchanged knowing smiles. "All right, Jonathan. Well, I'll let you get back to . . . whatever it was you were doing."

Jonathan walked her to the door. Nellie scoped the office one more time, gave Jonathan an awkward glance, then headed off down the hall. Jonathan was then met by Edie's persistent, disapproving stare, to which he slammed the door.

The hundreds of books on the ground and the empty bookcases above him were exhausting just to look at. His eyes were swelling with his allergies, and he felt drained. There was obviously no camcorder. He walked to his desk, his chest tight with anxiety. Before he could stop himself, he was unscrewing the receiver of his phone. As he was screwing the phone back together, Edie's voice roared over the speaker. "It's Kathy. You want it or should I take a message?"

"I'll take it," Jonathan said. "Hold all my other calls, though." Jonathan collapsed into his chair and hit line one. "Hey."

"Jonathan? You sound so tired," she responded. Strangely, her voice soothed him.

"I'm . . . okay. What's going on?"

Kathy paused. "Nothing, really. I just wanted . . . I just wanted to check on you. With all these weird things happening, I just wanted to make sure you were okay."

Jonathan wiped his nose. "I'm fine. I don't want you to worry about me."

"How can I not?"

Jonathan's mind swirled with so many thoughts he could hardly think at all. But one thing he knew was that he had to get Kathy and the girls away from this. He didn't know what danger lurked ahead in the "story," but the very fact that the writer knew about Sydney was risk enough. "Listen, honey, I need to talk to you about something."

Kathy's voice lowered with concern. "What is it?"

"I can't talk to you about it here," Jonathan said, feeling underneath his desk for any sort of small mike or recording device.

"Jonathan, what—"

"Let's meet at eleven." Jonathan pulled each of his drawers out, feeling the sides and bottoms. "For coffee. At the Coffee Bean." That was a favorite spot of theirs, a quaint little coffeehouse filled with thousands of books and a cozy fireplace in the corner. He hoped that might make it sound a little more . . . social.

"Jonathan, why not tell me now? What is it?"

"Look, it's nothing to worry about. I just . . . want to see you. There are some things we need to discuss, but I don't want to do it over the phone. Can you make it by eleven?"

There was a pause, then Kathy said, "Yes."

"Seriously, honey, there's nothing to worry about. Please don't get worried. Everything's fine."

"Are you sure?"

"Positive. See you at eleven." Jonathan hung up the phone, then ordered Edie to call maintenance and order him new locks for his office door.

C H A P T E R 16

After Jonathan did a halfhearted job of dusting and returning all his books to his shelf, the morning was still early. He took three different antihistamines that Edie had hunted down for him, fixed himself a cup of Earl Grey, and holed himself up in his office, hoping to read more of Clyde's manuscript before he met with Kathy. Just as he was about to find where he left off, a light tap came at the door, and then it slowly opened. Sydney peeked in and smiled softly.

"Sydney!" Jonathan leaped out of his seat as if he'd been caught naked. Sydney slipped in and closed the door behind her. "What are you doing here?"

She approached him at his desk. "Edie went to the bathroom, so I snuck in. She's always giving me looks."

As she stepped into the light streaming through the window, Jonathan could see her eye was blackened. Touching it self-consciously, she looked away and stared curiously at his bookshelves, which, though put back together, weren't as neat or tidy as before. His picture frames and knickknacks were still out of their obvious places. "I wanted to talk to you."

Jonathan suddenly felt as if he had an audience of ten thousand. "Listen, Sydney, I think we should—"

Sydney cut him off. "You were right."

"Right?" Jonathan tried to follow her while also wondering if someone was hearing every word of their conversation.

"About Jeremy," she said and instinctively began arranging the rest of Jonathan's bookshelf. "It's hard to admit. I've always been a strong woman. But I have a weakness for him. You understand?" She glanced over her shoulder at him.

"Um, yeah, but I—"

"I'm tired of making excuses about why I've got bruises all over my body. You can only be in so many car wrecks. You can only get hit by the softball so many times." She laughed a little. "You can only lie so long before you get caught."

The white collar of his dress shirt soaked up the sweat that was beginning to collect around his neck. "True. Listen, why don't we—"

"Jonathan," she said, her lips curving into a small, sweet smile, "I'm here to thank you. And to apologize." Jonathan stood silently as she approached him. "I was rude in the car and it was uncalled for. And because you called me on it, so to speak, I've been thinking a little more clearly."

"That's . . . that's good. . . ." Jonathan said, taking a couple of steps backward as he pretended to tidy his desk. Sydney was only inches from him, a light floral scent floating in the air around them.

She tucked her short hair behind her ears and sat on the corner of his desk, watching him. "I've never been able to open up to anyone about this. I don't know why you're so easy to talk to."

Jonathan laughed nervously, blotting his forehead with the cuff of his shirt and wondering if he'd indeed put on deodorant this morning. "Yes, well—"

"I mean, I have girlfriends that I can't even talk to about this. You're special, Jonathan. I knew that when I met you."

Jonathan unlatched his window and opened it up two feet, the cold air filling his lungs and drying his skin.

Sydney looked at him with curiosity. "It's certainly cold out there. Like, below freezing . . ."

"Yes, well, I'm just going to let the room air out for a moment.

There's a lot of dust in here. Sort of seems foggy, wouldn't you say?"

Sydney shrugged and crossed her thin legs. "Anyway, I wanted to thank you. Thanks for being so perceptive. Thanks for having the guts to confront me." She paused long enough for Jonathan to look up at her from his place at the window. "Thanks for caring."

The cold air against Jonathan's back cooled him off enough so he could think a little more clearly. He had so many questions for her, but every one seemed inappropriate if it were typed out on a white page in the form of a story. It would make him look . . . guilty. He searched his mind for words that at the very most seemed ambiguous and at the very least seemed filled with innocent concern. "You're quite welcome, Sydney," he began carefully, looking up and noticing his ceiling light. He made a mental note to check it later. "I hope for your sake you will take all this seriously." He winced at every word.

"Seriously?" she laughed. "Of course I am."

"I didn't mean seriously," he said, crossing his arms across his chest only to discover his armpits were wet with perspiration. "I mean, you will take all that I said into . . . consideration."

Sydney slid off the desk and adjusted her skirt. "I have. I don't know exactly what I'm going to do, but just talking about it makes me feel better."

"You don't know what you're going to do?" Jonathan blurted. "Sydney, you must leave him!"

His tone startled both him and Sydney. Suddenly the room was overly chilled. Sydney rubbed her hands up and down her arms, and Jonathan shivered. "It's harder than you might expect," Sydney said as she hung her head.

Jonathan sighed, loosened his tie, and shut the window. "I'm sorry. You're a grown-up. You can handle this."

She touched her black eye. "Apparently not very well." She rubbed her hands together and then turned to walk to the door. "Anyway, thanks."

Jonathan followed her, and as she started to open the door he put his hand over her head to keep it shut. "Sydney," he said, barely whispering. "Have you told anyone about . . . about us?"

Sydney stared into his eyes and frowned. "Us?"

Jonathan swallowed. His perspiration turned cold from the chill, causing him to become abnormally rigid. "I mean . . . that we talk. Have you told anyone about our conversations?"

Sydney backed up a little against the door, and Jonathan sensed he should step back to give her breathing room. "No."

Jonathan loosened his tie further. "No one? Not even a friend?"

Sydney's hand found the doorknob behind her. "What are you talking about?"

Jonathan's teeth ground against each other. He had to know if Sydney was talking, even if it meant upsetting her. "Maybe a friend at a bar one night? You talked about me? About us?"

She turned the doorknob slightly. "No. I've never mentioned you to anyone. Why are you acting like this?"

Jonathan tried to smile to soothe her nerves and his. "Listen, Sydney, I just want to make sure. This office is full of gossip and people think they see things. You know what I mean? People might . . . misunderstand."

Sydney's head cocked upward with mustered confidence. "Misunderstand *what*, exactly? You invited me to go have lunch with Naomi Yates. I'm just a fellow editor, low-ranking as I may be. I bring you manuscripts. We talk business. That's it." She eyed him carefully. "Is that what you want me to say?" she asked snidely. "Just in case someone asks?"

"Sydney, please don't be upset. This isn't what you think—"

"Look," she said, holding her hands up as Jonathan took a step forward. "I get it. Okay? I'm smart. I'll leave you alone."

She opened the door and quietly excused herself, closing it softly. Jonathan leaned against it, his head hitting the wood with a *thud*. Everything in his life was so complicated. If he could just get two minutes without anything to think about, maybe he could think straight, figure out all this mess, and get on with his life. He turned around and leaned his back against the door, glancing up at the wall clock, which read 10:34. He wondered if, literally, for two minutes his life would stop and he could do absolutely nothing. He started counting and just as he was hitting fifteen seconds, his door unexpectedly opened, knocking him to the ground.

"Jonathan?"

Jonathan rolled over and looked up to behold none other than Zippy. "Oh, dear God . . ."

Zippy stood over him, enjoying the dominance. "One shouldn't take the Lord's name in vain, my friend. And I seriously doubt you were getting ready to pray, though in the Bible men did pray prostrate."

Jonathan rolled his eyes and managed to peel himself off the carpet. "Don't you knock?"

"Well, I just saw a lovely young lady exit, so I figured it was a free-for-all." He smiled and sniffed. "Why all the dust?" He received Jonathan's quizzical expression with, "I have sensitive nasal passages. My sinuses can pick up any sort of disturbance in the atmosphere. If I sneeze twice in two minutes it means it's going to storm. If I sneeze less than once during the day, there's a ninety-percent chance it will snow tomorrow."

Jonathan tore off his tie and fell into his chair. "What can I do for you, Francis?"

"Well, I'm not here to discuss my meteorological genius, Jonathan. Have you read my proposal?"

Jonathan had read it and, though he wouldn't completely admit it to Zippy, was extremely impressed with not only his writing style, but the story line and even his dialogue—which was incomprehensible, since Jonathan had never had a normal adult conversation with Zippy once in his life. Nevertheless, this could be his sure shot at the next editorial meeting.

"Not bad, not bad," Jonathan said smoothly. "With a great editor like myself, it certainly has potential."

Zippy whipped himself into a chair. "Am I correct in understanding it met your editorial approval?"

Jonathan smiled and nodded, eager to see a side of Zippy he wasn't sure existed . . . a bright side. "Yes. It was quite good. I'll be wanting to see more."

Zippy leaned forward, his face tight with excitement. "Jonathan, don't lie to me. Are you taking this to committee?"

Jonathan wondered for a moment if he should tell Zippy or not, but then decided there wasn't much to lose. He'd have to tell him eventually. Plus, Jonathan wanted to talk to him about using a pen name anyway. "Yes."

Zippy leaped up from his chair and shouted, "Praise God!"

Praise God? Jonathan watched as Zippy danced around excitedly. "Glad you're happy, Francis."

Zippy rushed over to his desk, placed both hands on it, leaned in close to Jonathan, and placed a finger at his tear duct. "I'm tearing up. And this time it's not allergies."

Jonathan laughed nervously. "Yes, well, before I take it to committee, Francis, I would like to talk to you about your name."

Zippy calmed down enough to sit back down, though he did blot his eyes with a handkerchief. "My name?"

"Yes, we'll need to think of a good pen name."

"A pen name? What are you talking about? I'm a ghostwriter. I don't have a pen name. I'll be using my real name."

Jonathan frowned, not sure Zippy was following him. "What I mean is, we need to find a more *appropriate* name."

"A more appropriate name for *what?*"

Jonathan blinked twice. "For . . . for your book."

Zippy started tying his handkerchief into knots.

Jonathan's heart sank. Francis didn't get it. He didn't get the fact that he didn't have a good writer's name. Not only was it not good, but it sounded feminine. Only one other time in his career did Jonathan have to talk to a writer about changing his name. The writer's last name had sixteen letters. The typesetter couldn't even figure out how to fit it on the front cover of the book without making the font size too small. The writer was so offended that he left the house after the book was released. To this day, he's never seen the writer's name anywhere.

"Francis, this isn't a big deal. Writers do it all the time. It protects your identity, for one thing," he offered.

Zippy threw his handkerchief to the ground. "Jonathan! Do you think I've worked all this time as a ghostwriter to finally make it into fiction and then have to change my name so no one will know who I am? Absolutely not! I want the whole world to know who I am! I'm tired of writing things only to have someone else's name on the cover!"

Jonathan bit his thumbnail. "I understand, Francis. I really do. But I think we need to look at the fact that the name Francis can be male or female, and then add the last name Flowers and you're likely to be mistaken for a woman." Jonathan laughed lightly and added, "You wouldn't want that . . . would you?"

Zippy paced the floor behind his chair. "I don't care. If people think I'm a woman, then fine. I'm not changing my name!"

Jonathan stood, afraid that Zippy might be getting too agitated. "Listen, I think we just want a good, strong name, that's all. This is an excellent book, and I want the author's name to stand out. How about changing your name to Frank? Hmm? A version of Francis? A little more masculine sounding?"

Zippy stopped and pushed his glasses up his nose, his face red with fury. "I come from a long line of Francis Flowerses. Do you understand? I'm the thirteenth in my family to be named Francis Flowers, and not once . . . *not once, do you hear me* . . . has anyone gone by the name Frank! Don't insult me!"

Jonathan's sweaty hands found their way into his pockets. "All right . . . maybe we can keep Francis and change your last name. From Flowers to . . . say . . . Mann, with two *n*s? Francis Mann. That has a ring to it."

"You think this is funny?" Zippy said with disdain. He scooped his handkerchief up and proceeded to tie it into more knots. "I can't believe this! I work all this time to come out of the ghostwriting closet to be met with the idea that I need to change my name!" Zippy's nose was twitching.

Jonathan kept a safe distance. "Francis, look, please don't be insulted. It's not that you don't have a good name. Your name is fine. But it just doesn't work with the type of book you're writing. Francis Flowers seems like it might belong to, say, a romance novelist."

Zippy's eyes lit up with anger. "Well that's not *my* problem. Sounds like a problem for *marketing* to me, Jonathan. I am *not* changing my name!" With that, and two small sneezes, Zippy turned and stomped out the door.

Jonathan sighed, wondering when Zippy was ever going to get a life and not be so picky and sensitive about things. He decided it was time he left to go meet Kathy for coffee. He grabbed his brief-case and on his way out, his phone rang. He thought twice about answering it, but then decided to go ahead.

"Hello?"

The reception was fuzzy. "Jonathan? It's Kathy. Can you hear me?"

"Barely. We need to get new batteries for your car phone, I think."

"Yeah, well, I'm running a little late. I'll be there as soon as I can."

"Okay. I'll see you then."

Jonathan hung up the phone and stopped at Edie's desk for messages.

"Early lunch?" she inquired, sporting a cunningly curious ex-pression.

"Yes."

One haughty eyebrow rose. "When should I expect you back? Around five?"

Jonathan growled, "I'm going to meet my wife. I'll be back at noon." He straightened his collar. "Anyone important call?"

Edie handed him a few messages. "Nothing too important, ex-cept Clyde said he would like to talk with you." She smiled and, mimicking his accent, said, " 'Tell that Jonny to give me a holler.' It did sound urgent."

Jonathan shuffled through his messages as he headed for the elevator. "I wish he wouldn't call me that. It's so annoying. When is he going to learn my name is Jonathan and that's what I like to be called?"

———

Jonathan arrived fifteen minutes early at the Coffee Bean and was delighted that a small table near the fireplace was open. Since Kathy said she was running a few minutes late, he decided he might read a few more pages of Clyde's manuscript while waiting. He took the pages out of his briefcase and set the briefcase in the chair across from him to save it for Kathy.

"How's your family about this?" I asked Pierce outside Esther's office. He'd been in there twenty minutes, presumably telling his story.

He looked me deeply in the eyes, as he had never done before, and without hesitation he said, "They're fine. Charlie gave me"—he choked up—"gave me a hug and told me he was . . . proud of me."

"I'm proud of you, too." I peeked in Esther's office to make sure she hadn't sneaked out a back door and then said to Pierce, "You two got everything squared away in there?"

"I just told her everything I know and told her I'd make myself available whenever she needs me." He zipped his jacket up and said, "Well, I'd better get going."

"Where are you going?"

"Going to see Stewart—give him my resignation." He nodded at his decision. "It's the best thing."

"Well, don't be a stranger."

He nodded again, smiled pleasantly at the secretary, who'd decided she didn't like me too much, and then headed out of the office. I didn't waste any time getting into Esther's office. I shut the door behind me.

"So?" I asked anxiously. Esther didn't respond. Instead she continued looking through a file on her desk. "Come on, Esther. Don't leave me hanging here. Did you get what you need?"

She looked very serious, and for a moment I thought maybe Pierce hadn't convinced her. But after a few dreadful seconds, she finally looked up at me. "Brave thing that man did today."

I approached her desk. "Yes. Now, are you going to be able to use it? Are we going to get Mitchner off?"

Esther was obviously choosing her words carefully, as she began to speak several times and then stopped herself. Finally, she said, "There is no DNA evidence for this case. All the evidence was destroyed . . . for obvious reasons," she said with a sharp lift of her dark brows.

I loosened my cheap tie. "Come on, Esther. What more do you need? Pierce just confirmed what Donomar said. Donomar is the killer! All the pieces to the puzzle fit!"

Esther straightened her tailored suit. "Keaton, I'm not the district attorney of this town because I believed every story every person told over the years. People lie."

My stomach flip-flopped and I felt angry. "Why would Pierce make up a story like that? His career is ruined! He'll probably lose all his benefits at the bureau. His life as he knows it is over. Why would he lie?"

Esther closed the file and stood, towering over me in her three-inch heels. "I'm not talking about Pierce. I'm talking about Donomar."

I was a bit surprised but didn't lose steam. "Donomar? If he is lying, why are all the pieces fitting here?"

"I don't know that he is lying. I'm just saying that I check things out, Keaton. I check all my facts. I do my research. I look people in the eye and make them lie to me that way."

I felt exhausted suddenly. I didn't know where Esther was going with all this. "Esther, what do you want?"

She had found her makeup bag and was just about to apply lipstick, a deep bloodred color that made her eyes darker and skin paler. "I'm going to go see Dietrich Donomar myself. Ask him the questions. Look him in the eye."

"You? You're going to go see Donomar?" I couldn't hold in a surprised laugh.

She carefully lined her thin lips with lipstick. "Of course I am, Keaton. Do you really expect me to file a motion to release a convicted killer on death row because a couple of people have told me some good stories? You know better than that." She snapped her compact shut.

I guess I did. I just thought Pierce's story would be convincing enough. I sighed and ran my fingers through my hair, hoping I had as much as I did yesterday, which wasn't that much. "Fine. I'll set something up."

"Sooner than later, Spade."

"Tomorrow. First thing." I headed to the door. "You want me there?"

"You think I'm scared of that sick excuse for a human being?"

I loved the irony of how Caladaras, a lifelong prosecutor, lived her life on the defensive. It made her more of a woman than she cared to admit. "No, Esther," I said smoothly. "I just thought you might want a second opinion of the interview. And for some reason, Donomar likes me. He opened up to me once. It might make it easier if I were there."

Esther clicked her nails against her hard cherrywood desk. "Fine. Be there. But I do the talking."

I smiled and, as I opened the door to leave, said loud enough for her to hear, "You always do, Caladaras."

Esther Caladaras didn't mess around. She even dressed for the occasion . . . an all-black, tightly tailored pantsuit that made her look like a man. Her hair was pulled tightly back, not a stray hair to be seen. A crisp stark blue shirt, visible only at the collar, was the only color on her clothing, and her lips seemed to have an extra dark layer of red on them. Her heels made her an inch taller than I am, not to mention that she carried herself tall anyway. I felt a little out of place in my faded khakis and short-sleeved white shirt. Then I remembered we weren't going to some social event. We were going to see the most notorious serial killer our nation had ever known.

As the guard opened the final steel door, I found myself picking lint out of my pockets and wondering if Caladaras was dating anyone. She'd been divorced twice. Go figure. As we stepped into the corridor, she looked a little nervous. Though she was prepared to lead the way, she glanced back to see if I was behind her.

"Last cell on the left," I said gently.

"Thank you."

She walked slowly, confidently, and pretended not to notice the obscenities that were being yelled at her by the other prisoners, not because she was most likely the prosecutor that put them behind bars, but because she was a woman. I had called the afternoon before to try to arrange another way to see Donomar, stating to the warden that I didn't feel it was a good idea for the state prosecutor to walk down the corridor by some of the most notorious killers around. The warden, not a fan of Caladaras's, denied my request.

I hurried up a little and walked beside her, staring at all the men as hard as I could. The walk seemed endless, but finally we were at the end, a few cells away from the other prisoners. Donomar had his back turned to the front reinforced-glass window. He was tearing an article out of a newspaper.

Caladaras carefully studied him, and after a few seconds,

though I knew Donomar knew we were there, I announced our arrival. "Dietrich."

He turned around in his chair, a small smile on his face, his eyes never meeting mine. He was looking at Esther. "Hello, Counselor," he said, setting his work down and standing as if he were greeting a dinner date. He tucked the shirttail of his prison uniform in.

Esther's chin lifted and she folded her arms together. "Looks like you're stirring up trouble again, Donomar."

His smile remained and he approached the glass. "Well, if that's what you want to call it. I'm assuming you're here because of my conversation with Keaton."

"I'm here, Donomar, because I want to know what you're up to." She sat down in a small plastic chair near the glass. I grabbed one next to the wall and sat, too. "I'm here because I don't believe a word you're saying."

Donomar seemed distressed. His eyes fell to the floor and he shook his head in a moment of private thought. Esther looked at me questioningly, to which I just shrugged and continued to watch Donomar. He never looked at Esther as he said, "I know. I'm not exactly sure how I can convince you. I just know that I've got to try."

Esther swallowed and straightened her back. "Yes, well, you're going to have to do a heck of a lot of convincing. You're a liar by trade, Donomar. You confessed only when you were caught, and then, I suspect, only to brag about your killings."

Donomar finally looked up, first glancing at me, and then her. "I was sorry to hear about your brother." Esther started to say something, her face tense with anger, but Donomar continued. "I read about it in the papers a few years ago. A real tragedy. Should've never happened." He paced along the glass. "Neither should this prosecution against Jerome Mitchner. The FBI can really screw things up, can't they? No offense, Keaton."

Esther drew in a tense breath. "Maybe since you can't do any harm locked away in here, since you can't kill anyone anymore, you've decided to make up some stories. Maybe this is your sick way of trying to get more attention. Or maybe in your delirious mind, you really *want* to be Roberts's killer. But someone else did it and that made you mad. Which is it?"

I was watching Donomar carefully, hoping to see more signs

of the breakdown I'd seen before. When we first arrived, I watched his thumbs. His notorious thumb twiddling was not to be seen. Now he looked sad as Esther listed off the possible scenarios surrounding his strange confession. He just watched her, and when she ended, he seemed speechless.

"Well?" she breathed after a minute or so of silence. "Don't you have anything to say?"

Donomar went to his desk and sat down, his head lowered and his body slumped. Finally, he looked up at Esther, and for the first time I thought I saw a real flicker of humanity in him. It startled Esther so much she glanced at me with wide eyes. "Esther, if you don't want to believe me, I can understand that. But there's more than what you think about me at stake here. I can't change your opinion about me. I know that. I'm not trying to. All I know is that there's an innocent man on death row. That's all I know."

Esther buttoned her jacket, flattened the flaps on her pockets, bit her bottom lip, and then stood, indicating with a dart of her eyes toward me that I should stand also.

"Thanks for coming," Donomar said as Esther began to leave. "I hope you can see what an error the FBI made."

Esther had taken a few steps back down the corridor, but then she turned around, about knocking me over, and walked straight back to his cell. Pointing her finger at him, she said, "The thing I regret about the FBI is that they persuaded a weak group of people to keep you alive. That's the biggest mistake they ever made."

I swallowed hard and closed my eyes, unsure of what Esther was thinking. It sounded as if Donomar had not convinced her that Mitchner was innocent. As the guard unlocked all the doors, and as we passed through each one, I tried to study her, get some sort of clue to what she was thinking. At that moment, Donomar was easier to read than she was.

When we reached the lobby, a stale mix of cement, cheap tile, and an endless stench of cigarette smoke, Esther let out an enormous sigh toward the ceiling, reached in her jacket pocket for her cigarettes and lighter, and with trembling hands managed to light the end and suck in all at once. She swallowed the smoke and took another puff before eyeing me.

"What are you staring at, Spade?"

"You all right?" I asked, making a deliberate glance at her trembling hand.

Smoke escaped from her nostrils. "I get irritated when people talk about Glen. They don't know. They say, 'Sorry to hear about your brother.' They just don't know what it's like to lose . . ." Her words trailed off in a soft echo against the cement walls, and she flicked her ash onto the ground. "Anyway, I think I got what I needed."

"You believe him?" I asked anxiously.

Her eyes deliberately narrowed as the smoke rose from her cigarette and hovered in front of her face. I felt short of breath, but it seemed to calm her more. "No. I don't. But I think we've got enough evidence without him. The FBI obviously covered up here. We've got someone to testify to that. And we've got someone, although not someone reliable, saying he's the killer." She moved the cigarette between her fingers with her thumb. "I wish we had some of that evidence left. We could do some DNA tests—maybe come up with something definitive."

I grabbed her at the elbow and leaned in closer to her. "Esther, just shoot straight with me. Is this enough?"

Esther pressed her lips together and then threw her cigarette to the floor, smashing it underneath her heel. "Every person I've ever gotten a conviction on I thought to be guilty. Do you understand that? I thought Mitchner was guilty."

I looked her square in the face. "This can't be about pride. We're talking the life of a man here."

She nodded in a rare humbleness. "Let's go to my office. I'd like to look over the details one more time, discuss this with Jack, and then I'll make my decision."

"Let me go get the car."

We'd parked out back, in a secured area, but I told her I would drive around and meet her on the front steps. She'd agreed it would be less of a walk. As I pulled around the corner, I was astonished to see a crowd of photographers on the front step, and Esther pushing her way through.

Flashing light bulbs mixed with what sounded like hundreds of voices yelling out questions. I saw Esther curse under her breath and shove through bodies twice as big as her. I was thankful the windows in her car were tinted, but I cracked the passenger's-side window so I could hear what was going on.

"Is Jerome Mitchner really innocent?"

"What evidence do you have to support this?"

"Is it true that you're reopening this case because of the cases in Oklahoma and Texas where they executed three innocent men?"

"How deeply involved is the FBI in this?"

"No comment! No comment!" Esther growled as she pushed her way through more reporters. I saw her actually elbow a skinny photographer in the ribs when he tried to jump in front of her and take her picture. Esther had always had problems with the press. They'd never placed her in a favorable light, especially since she seemed determined to put every killer to death and usually got her way. She was portrayed as icy and inhumane and had had more than her share of death threats, though she refused a bodyguard. It never helped that she always seemed to have an unkind word for any reporter who might dare get in her way or question her decisions. "You animals! Don't you have a life?" She jumped in the car and I took off, our tires squealing against the pavement.

She pounded her hand against the inside of the door, then looked at me, her eyes wide with fire. "Would you like to tell me where that came from?"

"Me?" I glanced back to see the crowd of reporters starting to disperse from in front of the prison. "What do I have to do with it?"

"Well someone leaked *something*, and I haven't told anyone about this."

"It wasn't me, Esther. I swear. I hate the press."

"Then Pierce—"

"No, no. He'd never do that. There's got to be someone else."

Esther didn't say another word as we drove to her office. Inside, she flipped on the TV and paced her office. "This is all I need!"

I didn't have anything to say, so I just stared at the TV, hoping the noon news wouldn't report anything, at least on the front end of the newscast. We weren't so lucky, however. It was Channel Seven's leading story. The blonde in the pink suit, who didn't look smart enough to know all fifty states, led the hour with a "report that District Attorney Esther Caladaras may be looking to get a ruling overturned on convicted killer Jerome Mitchner. The preliminary information we're getting right now is that Mitchner may be innocent of the killing of Manuel Roberts in 1989, for which he was sentenced to death, a sentence all too familiar to those who follow DA Caladaras's track record."

"Oh, shut up, you stupid bimbo," Esther snapped at the TV.

The gentleman with short, dark, outdated hair continued the report. "It has also been reported that this may be a result of three recent executions, two in Oklahoma and one in Texas, where DNA evidence later showed the men to be innocent of their crimes."

Esther threw a pen across the room. "Why don't you quote a source? How about that? Anyone do that anymore? Actually check their sources? You idiots!"

I listened to several more reporters give their opinion about the case, one from the steps of the prison where Donomar was. No one had actually mentioned Donomar yet, and one reporter stated they did not know why DA Caladaras had been at the federal prison, since Mitchner was, of course, in the state prison.

Esther took off her shoe and threw it at the TV set, her aim remarkably hitting the Power button and turning it off just as the weather report was about to get its plug.

With one shoe missing, Esther sat down at her desk, her jaw muscles protruding in anger, and said slowly, "Let's look at the facts, shall we?"

"Sorry I'm late," Kathy said, just as Jonathan wrapped up another chapter in Clyde's manuscript. "Traffic was crazy."

She adjusted the pale yellow sweater she wore and smoothed out the wrinkles in her long floral skirt. She looked stunning, a spring flower in the midst of a dark winter. Jonathan took his briefcase off the chair and pulled it out for her. "Are you going somewhere after this?"

She brushed her hair off her shoulders. "No. Why? Have you ordered coffee yet?"

Jonathan got the attention of a waitress and said, "You just look like you're dressed up for something."

"I am. You." She smiled warmly as the waiter approached.

Jonathan blushed a little and, cocking his head to the side, said, "I'm assuming a regular caramel latte with skim milk and a dash of cinnamon?"

She twirled her hair with one finger. "Uh-huh. And you, of course, will be having an espresso."

The waitress jotted down their order as Kathy gazed into the fireplace. "We loved coffees long before they were ever popular, didn't we?"

Jonathan laughed and looked around. "We probably need coffee more than most."

She laughed and said, "You haven't told me how your lunch with Naomi was yesterday."

Jonathan paused. Had he told her he went to see Naomi? They hadn't even discussed his day, had they? Not that he recalled. Was Edie lying when she pretended not to know where he was? Had Edie told her? "Um . . . Edie told you I went to see Naomi?"

Kathy pulled sugar packets from the holder. "Who else could take you away from the office for so long?" She glanced up at him with a smile. "Plus, I saw it on your desk calendar."

"Ah." He breathed out. "It was nice. She looks great."

"I hope you told her hello for me." She sighed and propped her head up with her hand, her elbow resting on the table. "Sophie had a terrible night last night. I was up and down all night with her. She even threw up once. She seemed great this morning, but I'm exhausted. Susie came by to take Sophie for an hour, to give me a break, so I could come have coffee with you."

Jonathan suddenly became very aware of the situation. Kathy had made a special effort to get dressed and look nice for this meeting. Yet she had been up with Sophie several times during the night, so maybe she saw something. Jonathan had obviously slept like a rock. But maybe she had heard something. Dare he ask? Now? As she sat across from him, her full attention fixed on him, her face as delicate as a dandelion?

Luckily the waitress returned with their coffee to fill in the awkward silence left by Jonathan's reluctant pondering. All Jonathan could think about, though, was that he had to get Kathy and the girls out of the house. As much as he wished he could embrace this time together and have a wonderful lunch with Kathy, he knew more important things stood in the way. He would have to be direct with her from the beginning.

She sipped her latte. "Mmm. Perfect for a cold day like today." She peeked at him over the rim of her mug. "Brings back good memories, being here. Doesn't it?"

Pouring the espresso down his throat, only half aware of how hot it was, he nodded and gulped it all at once. Then, just out of nervousness, he flagged down the waitress for another one.

"Boy, you must really be tired," Kathy said, taking another sip. Her flat tone reflected a bit of suspicion.

Jonathan pretended to be interested in a couple standing nearby, but then resolved himself to the fact that he wasn't getting out of this one, no matter how smoothly he played it. He shut his eyes for a moment of clarity before turning to look directly at her.

"What is it?" she asked immediately.

"Kathy, I don't want to mislead you, here. I would love to have lunch with you. You look absolutely stunning. But when I called, I needed to talk to you about something. I told you that."

She traced the rim of her glass with her index finger, watching the steam rise. "I know. But it is good to see you." She paused, then looked up at him with a small, warm smile that deflated all the tension in his body.

The waitress returned with his espresso as Jonathan grabbed Kathy's hand from across the table. "Honey, I want you to take the girls and go to Eleanor's."

"What?" Her forehead crinkled in surprise.

"I know the girls still have a few more days in school before the break, but I don't feel comfortable leaving you at the house during the day."

Kathy removed her hand from his. "Why?"

Jonathan drew in a deep breath, filling his lungs with the stark aroma of his espresso. His nostrils flared as he exhaled. "All right. This freak writer of my so-called biography has been to our house."

Kathy sat completely still.

"*To* our house, not *in* our house," Jonathan said slowly and with emphasis. "I found more pages on the windshield of my car this morning." He downed his second espresso and then asked, "When you were up with Sophie last night, did you hear anything? Maybe a car? Or a strange noise?"

Kathy swallowed hard and shook her head, her eyes staring at him.

"Nothing, honey? Think hard."

She shook her head again.

Jonathan scratched his head to give his shaky hands something to do. The espresso wasn't helping to calm his frazzled nerves. "Okay . . . well, whatever. I still want you to go to Eleanor's. I mean it, Kathy," he said as she started a rebuttal. "I don't know who this crazy is. And now we know he knows where we live, which shouldn't be a surprise, since he knows every other thing about—" He stopped and looked up at Kathy. "Anyway, I think it's best."

Kathy's fingers circled her temples with hard pressure. "Fine, fine. I'll talk to their teachers. See what I can arrange. But," she added, her eyes flashing up at him defiantly, "I'm staying."

"What?"

"I mean just what I said. I'll send the girls to Eleanor's. I'll drive them myself. But I'm not leaving you alone."

Jonathan grabbed her hand again, though she resisted at first. "Listen to me, Kathy. I appreciate your concern. I really do. But this involves you now, too. You and the girls. And I would feel better if I knew you were all away from here. Just for a little while. I'll join you next week for Thanksgiving, and I'm sure I'll have it all cleared up by then." Kathy started to say something, but Jonathan added, "I can take care of myself."

"As can I." Kathy's back was straight as a board, and her chin was lifted so high she was looking down her nose at him. "I'm not scared. And I'm not leaving you here by yourself. That's final."

Jonathan paused, hoping she might show a little weakness and back off her stubbornness, but she sat erect like a statue, her body not so much as offering a slight nervous twitch.

"All right. Fine. Fine. Stay," Jonathan said with an irritation they both knew was not directed toward her. "But we're getting a gun."

"A *gun*?" Kathy's voice rose in astonishment. "A gun, Jonathan?"

Absolutely not! We talked about this years ago. We agreed to never have a weapon in the house."

"Yeah, well, that was before we had a stalker. Things have changed."

Kathy set her cup aside and leaned across the table. "Jonathan, do you really think your life is in danger?" she whispered.

"How should I know?" Jonathan whispered back, suddenly aware that this "stalker" might be sitting at the table next to them. A gentleman with long red hair sat to their left, drinking coffee and reading a David Mamet play. To their right were two college-aged girls working on homework. Kathy noticed him looking around and did the same. "He could be in here, you know. Watching us. Close enough to hear our every word."

Obviously frustrated, Kathy twisted her lower lip between two fingers. Then she bit it and said, "Jonathan, do you think you're overreacting?"

"Am I?" he said in a loud voice that made a few heads turn. He hushed himself as he continued. "The last pages I received depicted my life this last week with remarkable accuracy, Kathy. Meetings with authors. Conversations with co-workers. Conversations we've had in *our own home*." Jonathan's voice was so strained it sounded as if he might begin to cry. Kathy's whole expression changed and this time she grabbed his hand.

"Okay, okay. I get it. This is . . . this is serious. Um, let's just be careful. Let's have our conversations about this in public places. Let's go through our house tonight and check for . . . for . . . I don't know. Just check it. Okay? But no guns. Promise me, Jonathan, no guns."

Jonathan wanted to scream at the top of his lungs that it didn't matter where they went or how careful they were. The writer knew everything. He was everywhere, with no apparent explanation. But there was no sense in scaring Kathy. If she felt she had some control by "being careful," as she put it, then that was fine. There was no need for both of them to be in hysterics.

"Good idea," he managed.

She smiled and brushed the hair away from her face. "It's going to be okay, honey. We'll take the girls to a safe place, and we'll figure out what's going on here. And why. Like Clyde said. Maybe *why* is the more important question."

"Maybe," he said with a forced smile. "Well, I'd better get back to the office."

As he stood, Kathy said, "Jonathan, what . . . um, what were in the last pages that you received?"

Jonathan fumbled around for a few loose dollars and some change in his pocket. He tried not to act as if that were the one question he was dreading. "Just some more details about my day-to-day life."

Kathy grabbed her purse and stood as well. "Like what?"

Finally looking her in the eye, Jonathan said forcefully, "Just stupid details about meetings with authors and co-workers and things like that."

"Things like that? That's it? Just a bunch of details? Nothing significant?"

Jonathan shook his head, his heart stinging with guilt. "That's it. No 'big twist,'" he said in a dry, joking manner. "Truthfully, this writer is just downright bad. Boring characters. A weak plot. Horrible dialogue. An editor's worst nightmare."

"No kidding," she said in response to his shallow laugh.

"Yeah . . . well, talk to the girls when they get home this afternoon. And call Eleanor. I'm sure she won't mind. And, Kathy, please reconsider going."

"Not a chance."

Jonathan sighed, threw a few dollars on the table, and began to move toward the door. His mind swam deliriously. His stomach felt as if acid were eating holes through it. As he scooted past a neighboring table, Kathy grabbed his arm.

"Are you okay?"

"Yes, why?"

"You seem very preoccupied. Very distant."

"I'm fine," he said with a short smile. "Really. Cool as a cucumber."

"Yeah, well, don't forget your briefcase," she said, pointing back to their table, where his briefcase sat underneath.

"Good grief!" He quickly retrieved it. "I guess I'm just tired," he said, rejoining her to escort her outside.

The cold north wind stung the warm skin on their faces, and they both shivered and gave a quick kiss before heading in opposite directions. Jonathan glanced back once to make sure Kathy had made it to her car. She was unlocking it as he rounded the corner to where his was parked.

He hadn't prayed in a long time. A very long time . . . since he was a child. And he hated to think he was a man who only prayed in desperation, but he hoped as the wind passed by him, it would pick up his softly spoken prayer and carry it to wherever God was at that moment. If doubt didn't carry it away first.

"Keep her safe," he said and then briskly walked twenty more yards to his car. He pulled out of the parking lot without letting his car warm up and headed east on Markson, where he was certain he'd seen a gun shop once before.

CHAPTER 17

It took Jonathan an hour and a half to finally find someone who would sell him a gun without going through the mandatory two-week background check. A small pawnshop forty minutes from work sold him a 9-mm for a hefty price that would be worth their risk of doing an illegal gun sale.

He watched his rearview mirror perhaps more than he watched the road, but he never saw anyone tailing him. Since this writer knew practically everything else, he figured the fact that he purchased a gun wouldn't be hidden information, and he actually found comfort in the idea that whoever was writing this knew he wasn't playing around anymore. Jonathan never imagined he would actually shoot anyone, however. So far the writer had remained harmless, in a sense, but the fact that he had the guts to show up at his house was more than enough reason for Jonathan to be on high alert.

A dark cloud of despair quickly chased away his thoughts of security. A gun was useless to him and yet another reminder of how over the edge he was. This "writer" was changing him. He had never owned a gun in his entire life. He had never wanted to. And now the cold, shiny metal of the weapon was inches from his fingers. The entire thought sickened him.

On the way back to the office, he turned the radio to his favorite talk show. He tried to rid his mind of the tremendous guilt he was feeling over purchasing the gun, and even more so the guilt he was still feeling over Sydney.

His thoughts bounced back and forth between Kathy and Sydney. He couldn't stop thinking about how beautiful Kathy had looked at lunch and the amazing peace she brought in the familiarity they shared from their twenty years of marriage. That was something Sydney, with all her attributes, could never offer. He thought it so odd that it was that very familiarity that made him run from and to Kathy at the same time.

The more he thought about the predicament he was in, the more Jonathan realized how much he was risking with Sydney, though he'd never "technically" done anything wrong. He wondered where all the guilt came from if he could justify that he hadn't done anything wrong. The entire battle had been in his head, yet if he had to confess, he might as well have cheated on Kathy. His feelings had been so strong for Sydney, and his thoughts had been so consumed by her. Yet, when laid wide open for him to read, he realized what a high price he was paying for feeding his desires. The writer, however he knew, was planning on exposing his relationship with Sydney, and though Jonathan felt sure he could keep the information away from Kathy, just the fact that he would have to read about it was enough motivation for him to end whatever he did or didn't have with Sydney.

As he exited off the highway and turned onto Kryer Street, he decided that the best thing he could do would be to talk to Sydney and be honest with her. He hated the way their conversation had ended today, and he hoped there would be no ill feelings after he talked with her. The truth was he did care for her, and whether that emotion came from pure infatuation or a little sincerity, he wanted things to end well between them.

The decision he made about Sydney lifted a large weight off his shoulders, and though he and Kathy were having problems, he felt they had a better chance of working things out if his mind was on the right track.

Jonathan pulled into his reserved parking place, grabbed his briefcase, and walked briskly into the building and right into an open elevator. He checked his watch. His "lunch" had taken almost two hours and he loathed facing Edie's questioning expression when he arrived at his office. Luckily he had gone to lunch with Kathy, so there wasn't too much for Edie to be suspicious of.

Just as the elevator doors opened on the tenth floor, Jonathan caught a glimpse of Sydney passing by in a nearby hallway and decided it best to take care of the situation immediately, before he lost his nerve.

He rounded the corner and passed five or six cubicles before he came to hers. She was there, her back to the opening, filing something away. Jonathan waited a moment, hoping she would turn around and find him there but then felt self-conscious just standing and staring at her, so he tapped lightly on the metal frame and cleared his throat.

Sydney turned around and immediately greeted him with a stiff posture and narrowed eyes. "What do you want? Aren't you afraid of being seen with me?"

Jonathan stepped in a couple of feet and said, "Is there someplace we can talk? I really want to clear some things up from before. I hated the way our conversation ended."

Sydney paused, lowered her eyes, and walked to her desk. She sat down and swiveled back and forth in her chair a few times before saying, "I'm the only one here today. Alice is at the doctor. Maria is sick. Joe's on an errand. Nobody's around but me. This is about as private as we'll get."

Jonathan held his briefcase tightly across his chest to try to hide the fact that his heart might actually be pounding hard enough to be seen through his shirt. He inched toward a plastic chair sitting in the corner and set his briefcase down, too nervous to sit himself. Sydney carefully watched him with her red lips in a defiant pout. Even though the copiers, fax machines, and computers buzzed loudly enough to keep their conversation private, Jonathan still spoke softly.

"Sydney, I want to apologize—"

"For what?" she snapped.

"For . . . for how I acted. I didn't mean to upset you, and it was

... it was completely unfair of me to, in a roundabout way, accuse you of saying things. I'm just . . . I just, well, it's that—" Jonathan stumbled mercilessly over his words, trying to say everything he meant without actually having to come out and say it. After a few more fumbled attempts, he stopped himself and finally looked at her. "Can I just be honest with you?"

She toyed with two paper clips on her desk. "I think that's probably best."

Jonathan removed his briefcase from the chair and sat down, his body too big for the seat. He brushed his hair to one side and then began. "I'm so sorry for how I acted earlier. It was wrong of me to do that, and I want you to know I'm truly sorry."

Sydney offered a small smile of reassurance, but small enough that it was clear he should continue.

"I . . . um, I didn't mean to sound accusatory. I just . . ." He took a deep breath while listening to see if anyone was around. "I, well, I . . . I have some feelings for you, Sydney. Some strong feelings. Inappropriate feelings. You're young and beautiful, and we sort of clicked the first time we met. I never intended to have these feelings for you, but nevertheless, they sort of just appeared. I know this is probably shocking to you, and that's why I wanted to—"

Sydney held up her hand and Jonathan stopped midsentence. She leaned forward on her desk, tossing the paper clips aside. "Well, I wasn't very honest with you, either."

"What?"

She lowered her voice and eyes all at once. "Before, in your office, when I got upset. I wasn't honest then."

Jonathan scooted his chair closer to the desk as he asked, "So you have told someone? Who? I won't be mad. I just need to know."

She paused, looked curiously at him, and said, "No, that's not what I mean. I acted as if I had no idea what you were talking about when you mentioned 'us.' But the truth is that I've been having the same feelings."

Jonathan felt his Adam's apple swell. "Oh. I, uh . . . well . . ."

"I felt it from the beginning, too, Jonathan. That day I knocked over that whole stack of manuscripts in your office. I felt so silly, but you put me at ease. And then the more I got to know you, the more I liked you. And the more I got to know you, the more I realized I didn't have to put up with someone like Jeremy. He treats me horribly. Tries to control me. When I don't act the way he wants, he hits me. I guess I thought that was the best I was ever going to get. You showed me otherwise."

An awkward silence resounded around them, and Jonathan noticed that the small smile on Sydney's lips never left, nor did she ever break eye contact with him. She continued after a moment. "The other thing I wasn't honest about was that I have already ended it with Jeremy. I don't know why I didn't tell you before. It was just awkward for me. But I think I was pretty clear with him, and thankfully I was bold enough to mention there was another, *better* man in my life." She grinned. "You."

Jonathan's body shot out of his seat. "You . . . you mentioned me?"

"Well, yes. I mean, you *are* the reason I had the nerve to break it off with Jeremy. And you can't tell me now that those feelings we're both experiencing weren't real. You just said they were. I told Jeremy I'd met someone who wanted to treat me right. I really thought he was going to kill me right there. Luckily I had enough sense to do it in a public place. I've gotten all the locks changed on the doors at my apartment, and my roommate's boyfriend has offered to stay over for a couple of weeks just to make sure he doesn't try to break in. I'll probably have to get a restraining order."

"You mentioned my *name*?" Jonathan's voice rose with every word.

She thought for a moment. "Well, I think I may have once or twice. I can't remember. But the important thing is that I did it. And I did it because of you. I feel great."

Jonathan could hardly believe what he was hearing. He sat breathless until finally Sydney said, "Are you okay?"

"Okay? No, I mean . . . I'm fine, it's just that . . . you actually used my name? Did you go into detail? Like how we've been spending time together? Did you tell him we went to Naomi's house?"

Sydney crossed her arms. "I can't remember, Jonathan," she said forcefully. "Does it matter?"

Jonathan shook his head to try to clear a thought path. "I guess not. I just wasn't expecting you to do that."

"Well, you told me to," she stated bluntly.

Sydney's tone demanded immediate damage control. "Yes, yes, I know. That was a very brave thing you did. I'm happy that you're out of that horrible relationship."

She frowned. "You don't seem too happy."

Jonathan attempted to pace in her small cubicle. "I am. Really. I feel a lot better knowing you're going to be okay."

"I'm great," she said with a big smile. "And I'm even better knowing how you really feel about me. I mean, I took a risk breaking up with Jeremy, not knowing for sure if you really wanted to be in a relationship with me. But I definitely did the right—"

"R-relation . . ." Jonathan couldn't even finish the word..

"Yes," Sydney said slowly. "That's what you wanted, right? I mean, you've been coming on to me for weeks now. And I think I know you better than to think it was just for some cheap thrill."

Jonathan held his hands up. "Whoa, now, Sydney. I never said anything about a relationship. Yes, I cared for you. But I'm married."

Sydney stood and said, "Well, apparently not very happily."

"Excuse me?"

"Excuse me?!" Sydney said, her voice rising. "Don't stand there and pretend like nothing has happened between us."

"Nothing *has* happened," Jonathan said in a harsh whisper.

"Well, I know *that*," Sydney retorted, "but you've already admitted you have feelings for me. And I have feelings for you. So what's the hesitation?"

"The hesitation?"

Sydney walked around her small desk toward him. "We're meant to be together. We can talk about anything. You make me laugh. You cared enough to make me realize that my relationship with Jeremy should be ended. Now that I've done that, you're not just going to leave me alone, are you?"

Her dark eyes, wide with wonder, blinked several times and then stared at him. Jonathan's knees felt so weak he had to sit back down. His voice was barely audible above all the clamor of the office. "Sydney, I didn't mean for this to go this far. I never meant—"

"To hurt me?" she demanded loudly, never thinking twice about who could hear.

"I just wasn't thinking. I knew you were in a bad relationship, and I cared for you—or I thought I cared for you—enough that I knew you should get out of it."

"And I did," she exclaimed dramatically. "Because of you!"

Jonathan gazed up at her. "Because of me."

Sydney towered over him for a moment longer, then crouched next to him, putting her hand on his knee. "Jonathan, what's so hard for you to understand? I'm in love with you. I want us to be together."

Jonathan shook his head in disbelief. "No, Sydney. I'm married."

"You already said that," she said flatly. "So leave your wife. Get a divorce. It's no big deal."

Barely conscious of his surroundings, Jonathan shook his dizzy head.

"Fine. Then don't get a divorce. It still doesn't mean we can't be together."

Jonathan's eyes looked at her hand on his knee, then at her face. It was all he could do to contain his fear. He never imagined he would be in this situation.

"I can't, Sydney. I just can't be with you."

Her response was surprisingly soft. "Why?"

Jonathan hung his head and realized he couldn't answer the simple question of *why*. He knew he'd had strong feelings for her. He knew his marriage was rocky. He knew men did this all the time, and some were applauded for it. He knew divorce wasn't taboo and that he would still get to see his kids regularly. But with all of those elements, there was still something deeper that kept him in his place. He couldn't put his finger on it, but he knew at that moment all he wanted in the whole world was to be at home with Kathy and his girls. Whatever problems they had, he felt sure he could overcome them. Still, this mystery of why he couldn't follow his desires perplexed him to the point of being utterly speechless, even as Sydney's pleading eyes burned through him.

But before he had any longer to think through an answer, Clyde Baxter appeared in the entrance of Sydney's cubicle. His questioning expression and darting eyes made Jonathan's body shudder. Sydney's hand slipped off his knee and she stood up, quietly returning to the other side of her desk.

"I was just on the way back from the bathroom," Clyde nervously explained, "and I saw your briefcase sittin' here in the doorway, so I came in and—" He cut himself off and shoved his hands into his pockets. "I was just in the neighborhood and decided to stop by to see you, Jonny. You're busy. I'll—"

Jonathan snatched his briefcase up and moved swiftly past Clyde. "I'm not. I was just on my way to my office."

"Wait," Sydney demanded, and Jonathan motioned for Clyde to move on to his office. Then he looked at Sydney. Her eyes narrowed as her fingers dug into his forearm. "I won't be hurt again. I'll expose you. Everything about you."

A deep anger welled up inside him, and he stared Sydney down until she backed away and said, "I didn't mean that. I'm just a wreck. I didn't mean that." She turned away from him and wept.

Jonathan straightened the sleeve of his shirt and headed for his office, where Clyde was waiting for him. Jonathan hardly acknowledged he was there as he snatched his messages off Edie's desk. Clyde barely escaped Jonathan's office door shutting on him.

"What do you want, Clyde?" Jonathan snapped.

Clyde didn't bother sitting down. "I was just here to discuss my book with you. I'll talk to you another time."

Clyde quietly opened the door, and Jonathan said, "It's not what you think."

Clyde paused and met Jonathan's eyes. Jonathan felt a burning anger swelling within himself, an anger he hoped wouldn't be directed toward anyone—but that was reaching an unstoppable boiling point.

"How long were you standing there?"

Clyde looked away. "Long enough."

"It's not what you think," he said again, this time with clenched teeth.

The sting of Clyde leaving without saying another word was

more than Jonathan could bear. His knuckles turned white as he gripped the edge of his desk with uncontrollable force. His body shuddered in an attempt to suppress the rage that was about to escape, the type of rage that can change the entire direction of a person's life in an unlucky instant.

His hands slid underneath his desk and he was standing in an effort to try to topple it over when Nellie walked in, saying, "What's your excuse this time?"

Jonathan hadn't another word left on his tongue, and to his silence, Nellie's hands dramatically rose above her head in question. "What, Jonathan? You missed our vision meeting. It's been on the calendar for months! You've gotten three memos about it!"

Jonathan's hand swiped his desk, pushing everything off onto the floor. "I don't care about a stupid meeting! Do you understand, Nellie! I just don't care!"

Nellie gasped and slammed the door to his office, shutting them both in. She approached his desk as Jonathan's quivering hands ran through his hair. "For heaven's sake, Jonathan, what is going on?"

Jonathan couldn't even look up at her. And he had nothing to say at that moment. All he wanted to do was cry.

Nellie waited a few seconds, then began picking up his stapler and desk calendar from off the carpet. She placed them gently on his desk. "Why don't you take the rest of the month off—"

"No! No, I'm fine!"

Nellie deliberately bent down and rose again with his pencil sharpener. "No, Jonathan, you are not fine."

Jonathan fell into his chair. "I'll be all right. The editorial meeting is the week after next. I want to be there."

"I don't think that's a good idea."

Jonathan's voice was sharp with irritation. "Nellie, please. I'm fine. I've got two good proposals I want to bring. Sure winners."

Nellie's hands found her hips. "I just don't think you're ready. You can't seem to make important meetings, and you're an absolute basket case. I think you need some time off."

"I don't need any time off," Jonathan said harshly, and then calmed down enough to say, "I was going to save this for the meeting, but I'll tell you now that Clyde is coming out of retirement for one final book, and it's going to be a good one. It's not a western. It stands alone. But I'm confident it will be a bestseller."

Nellie then picked up two pencils and a pen, laid them on his desk, and, after an intentionally long pause, said, "Fine. But I think you'd better come out of whatever denial you're in. I don't know what's going on with you, but you're only fooling yourself if you don't go get some help. If you need to get into AA or something, we'll work it out."

"AA?"

"Something is definitely going on, and it's affecting your work. Now, I care deeply for you. You've always been a top editor here. But lately your choices have been less than something to be desired, as I've said before, and now your mental state seems a little shaky. For the sake of the house, Jonathan, you're either going to have to get yourself together and perform like you used to, or I'm going to have to let you go. I know that's hard, but someone's got to be tough with you, because you're obviously not going to go get help without the proper incentive."

"You're firing me?" Jonathan said with a delirious laugh.

"That's not what I said," Nellie replied firmly. "But you're real close to losing your job here. Let us get you some help. That's what I'm saying."

Jonathan's body sank into his chair. "You can't help me." His hands rubbed his face furiously. "I'm okay. I'm sorry I missed the meeting." As his eyes rolled back into his head he realized that even now he couldn't recall having a meeting.

Nellie took one more long look at Jonathan and said, "Fine. Have it your way. But don't expect any more favors. Any more tolerance. Get it together or you're fired." She walked to the door. "Don't be too proud to ask for help." She left and with another swipe of his hand, Jonathan cleared his desk again.

"I called Eleanor," Kathy said after dinner as Jonathan helped her clear the table. The girls had scattered and they were alone in the kitchen. Jonathan had worked for the rest of the day digging through slush piles and writing rejection letters to proposals that on any other day might have gotten some consideration. But Jonathan could write a rejection letter in his sleep, and all he was capable of doing this day was work that took no mental effort at all.

At five o'clock sharp he left the office and returned home to his family. All were happy to see him, and he wished that everything were as normal as it seemed when he opened the front door to his home.

The lump in his throat had lingered all the way home, and after kisses from his daughters, he collapsed on the living room sofa and remained unconscious for over two hours until Kathy had come to wake him around seven-thirty.

The dinner table was full of chatter from the girls, Meg discussing her wish to become a cheerleader, Leesol lecturing all of them on how despicable boys are, and Sophie showing everyone how to mash peas so they're easier to eat. Kathy, unusually quiet, listened and smiled, as did Jonathan, who felt as if he had just awoken with a hangover.

With dinner over and the girls out of sight, Kathy must've felt it was time to talk about the trip to Eleanor's. Jonathan scraped Sophie's mashed peas into the disposal as he said, "Is it all right for the girls to go early?"

Kathy nodded and wiped the counter. Jonathan studied her for a bit, waiting for her to add something, then said, "Honey, you're quiet. Are you okay?"

She looked up at him, her eyes moist and shiny, a sign that tears were soon to follow. She looked away and Jonathan approached and put his arm around her. "Kathy, I know you're scared about this writer. It's going to be okay. But I wish you would go to Eleanor's."

Kathy shook her head, wiped a lone tear away, and continued to busy herself in the kitchen. Jonathan followed closely behind, picking up the loose crumbs she'd missed. "I'm going to figure this out. I'm going to figure out who is doing this. I promise you."

Kathy threw her sponge in the sink and loaded the dishwasher, still wiping tears away. Jonathan finally made her stop. He turned her around and tilted her chin up so he could look in her eyes. "Are you okay?"

A stream of tears flowed from her eyes, but she managed to look back at him. "Jonathan, I love you. I always have. I would do anything for you. Anything at all to make you happy."

Jonathan laughed a little at the odd statement and said, "You do make me happy, Kathy." He guided her gently to the kitchen table and pulled a chair out for her. "I know we're having some problems. I don't think either of us can deny that. But we'll work them out—"

"I want us to pray," Kathy said suddenly. She cut him off and stared diligently at him.

"Excuse me?"

"I think you and I need to start praying. Every night."

"Okay . . ." Jonathan was confused but decided to go along with her.

"That's the only way it's going to work." She gazed at him. "God's our only hope."

Jonathan felt uncomfortable with this sudden talk of God. He went to the cabinet to get a glass and filled it with tap water. "Don't worry about this writer, okay? Whoever it is, is going to make a mistake, and I'll be on top of it when it happens. Promise me you won't worry?" Kathy nodded a little and Jonathan said, "The only person that makes sense is Clyde."

Kathy looked up. "Clyde?"

"Yes, Clyde," Jonathan said in an angry but thoughtful tone. "He just seems suspicious."

"But how could Clyde know all—"

"I don't know. All the pieces to the puzzle don't fit yet. But they will. I don't trust Clyde with a ten-foot pole right now, though I do need his manuscript in a desperate way. I've got to be careful right now. For my sake."

"Jonathan, I don't think Clyde—"

"I don't want you talking to him. Got it? Not at all." Jonathan set his glass down on the counter and shook his head. "Honey, you don't worry about this. I'm going to take care of it." He peeked in the freezer for ice cream as he asked, "So you'll go to Eleanor's with the girls tomorrow?"

"Tomorrow's too soon," Kathy said in a tired voice. She rose to finish cleaning up the kitchen, her body language lifeless, her eyes strained and distant. "Meg has a test she can't miss. We'll leave Saturday morning." Her body slumped against the counter.

"Kathy, honey? Are you sure you're okay?"

"Fine." She closed a cabinet and said, "Maybe you could help me drive the girls to her house Saturday morning. It might be nice, just the two of us, on the way home. A nice time to talk."

Jonathan studied her for a moment. Her eyes never met his, and he sensed there was some deliberate reason she wanted him with her. He didn't really want to go, but he thought twice about saying no.

"If you really want me to go."

"Only if you really want to," she said. Though she smiled and pecked him on the cheek, she seemed sad. As she finished up the kitchen, he imagined that all this weird business about the manuscript was finally taking a toll on her. She had tried to remain strong and at times even seemed indifferent, but it was catching up with her. He could tell.

"Honey, why don't you let me finish up here?" he said. "Go upstairs, run yourself a bath. You look tired."

"Do I?" she said, seemingly on the verge of tears again. "I feel a little tired."

He grabbed her around the shoulder and steered her in the direction of the stairwell. "I'll worry about the girls for an hour, okay?"

She nodded and as she walked out of the kitchen said, "Can you take out the trash? It's overflowing."

Jonathan glanced over at the garbage, glad that Kathy didn't bite his head off about it but simply asked him. He nodded and smiled and pointed in the direction of the stairs as a silent order for her to go on up. As she disappeared at the top, Jonathan pulled the garbage out of the basket and tied it together, trying to stuff everything inside the plastic bag. He laughed to himself and wondered why it was so hard for him to remember to do the little things.

As he tried to juggle the trash and open the front door, he reminded himself that he had been home for dinner, and that seemed to make an impression on everyone. He wondered if he should grab a coat to run the trash out but decided it was too much trouble and went ahead and stepped outside onto the porch. His foot slid a little and he almost fell. The doormat felt different, and he guessed one of the kids had turned it upside down. Trying to maneuver the trash bag, he reached down to flip it over and realized that he had not stepped on the doormat, but on a single manila envelope where the doormat should've been.

CHAPTER 18

Jonathan climbed the stairs as fast as he could and then at the top listened carefully for sounds indicating Kathy was in her bath. After a couple of moments, he heard the sound of splashing and classical music, a sure sign Kathy was reclining in the tub, listening to Beethoven, her favorite. He could hear Sophie and Leesol in Leesol's room, a few key words like *frogs* and *snakes* making it to his ears, something ordinarily he might be alarmed about. Now, though, he was glad it sounded like a conversation that might keep them preoccupied for a while. Meg was listening to music in her room.

Just as he was about to turn around and go downstairs, Meg appeared in her bedroom doorway. "What are you doing?" Her thin arms were crossed, and she shifted her weight onto one leg.

"What do you mean?" Jonathan smiled.

"You're peeking in your bedroom. You're acting all weird."

"Weird?" Jonathan chuckled and tried to act casual. "I'm not either. Why . . . what are you doing?"

Meg took a few steps out of her bedroom, enough to look into their bedroom and see the bathroom door was closed. She looked up at her dad. "What's going on? I want to know," she demanded in a whisper.

"Going on?"

"I'm not stupid, Dad. You and Mom have been acting weird lately. She's cried practically every night for a month. You're up here snooping around. And now we have to go to Eleanor's and miss school next week."

"It's only three days of school, and you love Eleanor and Earl."

"That's not the point. I want to know what's happening. You and Mom are getting a divorce, aren't you?"

"A divorce?" Jonathan said loudly, then steered her directly back into her room. "Where did you get a crazy idea like that?" he said after shutting her door behind them.

"What am I supposed to think? You guys fight *all* the time, and now we're being shipped off to Eleanor's. Come on."

Jonathan sat next to her on her bed. "Meg, we're not getting a divorce. I promise. It's nothing like that."

"Then what?"

Jonathan sighed, wondering how he was going to explain this one. He didn't have any explanation, and he had hoped that Kathy had come up with some reason they were going to Eleanor's early. Apparently not. "You know how Eleanor loves to see you. It's just extra time with her."

Meg stood and walked to her desk, rearranging her figurines. "Fine, don't tell me. But I'll find out. Kids always find out."

After a moment of silence, Meg turned around. Jonathan felt very old at that moment, as if Meg must be seeing a hunched-over, gray-haired, wrinkly old man. He looked up at the ceiling, wondering what in the world he should tell his oldest daughter. He didn't want to scare her, but she was right. She would find out. And maybe if she had some information, it would help protect her. He stood, smoothed out the wrinkle he had made on her bed, and stuffed his hands deep within his pockets.

"Okay, Meg." He stopped and found his nerve again. "Remember when your mom talked to you about not going with strangers?"

Meg frowned and sat down in the chair in front of her desk. "Sure."

"Well, some things have been happening. Some strange things. Um . . ." He watched her for a moment to see how she was reacting so far. Her eyes were bright with curiosity. "Okay, it's like this. My work as an editor is wonderful. But sometimes I can make people very mad."

"Because you don't like their books."

"Yes. I have to reject a lot of people's work and sometimes that makes people mad, because creative people get very attached to what they write. It's like a child to them. Understand?"

Meg nodded solemnly.

"Well, with that in mind, someone is apparently very upset with your dad. I don't know who, but they are . . . they are . . ." Jonathan's tongue felt as if it were swelling right in his mouth. Could he say "threatening" him? That was untruthful. No one had threatened him. But he couldn't very well tell his daughter that someone was exposing all the dark secrets in his life, could he? She'd want to know more. That would be deadly. What could he say? Time ticked loudly in his ear as Meg fidgeted at his uncanny silence. "What I'm trying to say is that there is evidence that someone might be wanting to harm Daddy—"

"Dad! No!"

Jonathan rushed over to her, and she grabbed onto his waist. "Listen to me, Meg. It's nothing serious . . . yet. Okay? It's just that someone has been toying with me. Understand? Trying to play mind games with me. And I just want to make sure you girls are safe. Understand?"

Meg looked up at him with tears in his eyes. "Daddy, what kind of games?"

"It's not important," he said, stroking her hair. "But what is important is that you are protected. Nothing is likely to happen. Someone is probably just trying to scare me. Understand? But I don't want to take any chances."

"What about you?" she said through sniffles. "Aren't you coming?"

"Your mom and I are going to stay here and try to figure some things out, okay? So not a word to your sisters, all right? This is just between you and me, Meg. Got it?"

"Got it, got it, Daddy," she said, flopping onto her bed.

"Okay. I've got to go do some things downstairs. Listen and

make sure your sisters aren't getting into trouble."

"Okay."

Jonathan opened the door, and just as he was about to shut it, Meg said, "Daddy?"

"Yes, sweetheart?"

"Um, I know I'm not supposed to tell Leesol and Sophie, but shouldn't we tell them not to go with strangers, too?"

Jonathan paused and then stepped back into her room. "What?"

"I'm just saying that we should probably tell them not to go with strangers. Just in case? Right?"

Jonathan walked farther into her room. "Didn't your mom talk to all three of you at once?"

Meg frowned and sat up on her bed. "Well, Dad, I was, like, four years old, so they weren't even born yet."

———

The steam from the bathroom moistened his skin immediately as he opened the door. As it cleared he found Kathy in the midst of a bubble bath, her hair tied on top of her head, her back resting against the end of the tub. She was startled by the door opening so fast and reacted by grabbing for a towel. As soon as she saw Jonathan she asked, "What's wrong?"

Jonathan tried to calm his nerves and sound rational all at once. The thought of the envelope downstairs was more than enough to send him over the edge, but he had to confront Kathy about why she hadn't told the girls not to go with strangers. He had asked her about it twice, and once she even responded by saying that she had lied about some kidnapping so they wouldn't ask questions.

He sat on the edge of the tub and in a firm voice said, "I just talked to Meg. You never told her not to go with strangers, did you?"

Kathy stared wide-eyed at him, as if she'd seen a ghost.

"Well?"

Her lips pressed together and she closed her eyes. "No."

Jonathan felt himself losing his temper. He stood and almost slipped on the wet floor. As he recovered he said, "Why? Why, Kathy?"

Kathy wiped the steam from her own face and avoided his eyes. "Because . . ."

"Because *why*?" Jonathan's nerves felt like they were on fire. "Is it because you know something, Kathy? Huh?!?" He leaned closer to her.

Suddenly, though, Kathy's eyes intensified, and she met Jonathan's harsh stare with one that made him blink and back away a little. The muscles in her jaw flinched. "Because all you can talk about is that Clyde is doing this, and quite frankly, Jonathan, I don't think Clyde would harm the children. I *know* he wouldn't."

Jonathan stood up and crossed his arms tightly across his chest. "I have my suspicions about Clyde. But it could be someone else."

Kathy's eyes darkened as she stared at her bath water. "I also thought . . . maybe this was all just . . ."

"Just what?"

Kathy met Jonathan's questioning stare. "I thought you might be . . . having an affair. Are you?"

Jonathan gripped the edge of the sink. The steam in the bathroom suddenly felt suffocating.

"You work late. You've been distant. Our relationship is crumbling," she said, sadness now replacing the rage in her voice.

Jonathan swallowed hard. A part of him wanted to confess everything. Even though he hadn't had an affair, he knew he had wandered into off-limits territory. Should he tell her? Should he tell her everything?

"No." He seemed to answer her question and his all at once.

Kathy's eyes lowered and she stared into her bath water. "Then, to answer your question, the reason I didn't tell the girls not to go with strangers is because there was a part of me that didn't believe you. A part of me that thought . . . maybe this was just a way to get us out of here . . . an excuse to be alone." A silence was followed by Kathy's eyes meeting Jonathan's as she said, "You should know, Jonathan, that jealousy can make women do strange things."

He shook his head, relief bathing him as he realized the issue was over. "Okay, then." He wiped the moisture from his face. "I told Meg everything. She was beginning to have suspicions anyway."

"Fine."

Jonathan smiled slightly, then left Kathy to her bath. But he knew that downstairs, waiting in a plain manila envelope, could be the truth he was unwilling to tell.

———

Downstairs, he took the envelope out from underneath a couch cushion and went to his study, turning on only a reading light. Their bedroom was directly over his study, so he could hear Kathy upstairs, going to the closet in the bathroom, near the armoire. He kept an alert ear as he opened the package and pulled out the pages, of which there were only two.

He listened as water ran in the bath again. She was finishing up. Enough time to read the pages.

> *Jonathan raced immediately to his office, where he opened the manuscript to find, to his surprise, accurate details of his day-to-day life, not to mention a few secrets he thought he'd covered well. Reading about his life, knowing someone knew everything about him, was more than Jonathan could take. He wondered if someone was watching him at that moment. He yelled, "Are you watching me? Are you?" and then proceeded to pull every book from his office bookshelves onto the floor. He was on quite a roll until his boss, Nellie Benson, opened the door and caught him mid-act. Jonathan fell to the ground and tried to act casual, but Nellie already had her suspicions about Jonathan and this wasn't helping.*
>
> *Nellie tried to reason with him, but of course Jonathan attempted to explain it all away. Still, Nellie suggested that maybe Jonathan take a sabbatical, but Jonathan again tried to convince her he was fine. The conversation ended with Jonathan telling Nellie that he had two sure winners for the next editorial meeting.*
>
> *Jonathan called his wife and asked her to meet him for lunch, telling her he needed to "talk to her about something," but not "to worry." Before he could get out the door to lunch, though, Sydney came into his office, shutting the door and—*

Kathy's footsteps left the bedroom and went down the hall toward Sophie's room. He heard a hall cabinet open and figured she might be putting some towels away or getting toilet paper. His heart raced with every word he read.

—approaching him. She came in to "thank" him for helping her get out of her abusive relationship. Jonathan was nervous, opened a window, and continued to let her talk. Sydney went on about how it was hard for her, being such a strong woman, to imagine that she had let herself get to this place in her relationship with Jeremy. But because Jonathan "cared" so much for her, she had decided to end the relationship with Jeremy once and for all.

Kathy was back in the bedroom, near the armoire, probably still putting some laundry away. Thank goodness. He took out a pen and noted something that, although subtle, seemed very apparent to him. Sarcasm. There was a hint of it, though nothing he could for sure put his finger on. The word "cared" in quotes was the obvious one. It wasn't anything tangible, but hopefully it would help him find out who was doing this. He thougt for a moment and then wrote *Sydney* in the margin. The water in the bathroom was running again, and Jonathan continued.

But because the writer had exposed him and Sydney in previous pages, Jonathan had to know if Sydney had talked to anyone. He confronted her about it, but Sydney said she had no idea what he was talking about and acted a little "uncomfortable" at his insinuation that they were having some sort of relationship. After denying she had talked to anyone, she quickly left his office.

Before he even had time to breathe, an author he disliked very much, Francis Flowers, appeared in his office. Jonathan had to tell Francis that his name would have to be changed if his book were published, and Francis was very irate about it. The conversation ended with Francis stomping out the door in a rage.

By now it was time for Jonathan to meet his wife for lunch. They met at the Coffee Bean, one of their old hangouts. Though Jonathan had the urge to try to make the lunch "light and cheerful," he also had ulterior motives. He told Kathy he wanted her and the girls to go to his aunt Eleanor's house a few days before Thanksgiving, for their protection from the "writer." Although Jonathan tried to sound as if it were just a precaution, Kathy knew from his tone that he was very scared. He told her that the writer had been to their house, and now that the writer knew where he lived, he didn't feel they were safe.

Kathy was astonished and agreed to drive the children to Eleanor's, though she was adamant about staying home herself. Jonathan objected, but she wouldn't budge. Jonathan told her he was thinking about getting a gun, but Kathy reminded him that they'd agreed years ago never to have a weapon in the house. He promised her he wouldn't buy one, and then they left the Coffee Bean.

After running a few errands, Jonathan returned to the office, where he—

Jonathan slammed his hands down onto the desk. He couldn't believe it. He didn't know whether to jump for joy or cry. The writer had left out the fact that he went and got a gun! This was so important! He wrote that note down as fast as he could, his hand trembling with every word. However, his teeth bit into the pencil he was holding as he realized his buying a gun was the one thing he *wanted* this writer to know! And here it was, missing from his "biography" that seemed to have every other detail of his day listed in less-than-poignant accuracy. Did the writer not know he had bought a gun?

Jonathan pulled his desk drawer out and trembled at the sight of the gun, then pushed the drawer back in and locked it with the key he kept underneath his desk. He stuck the key in his pocket, just in case someone was watching where he took the key from. He would find a hiding place later.

Upstairs was quiet, and Jonathan wondered what Kathy was doing. He knew he would hear her if she came downstairs, so he continued reading.

—decided to go talk to Sydney. Their conversation began with Jonathan apologizing for how he had acted in his office before.

"No . . ." Jonathan said weakly, his hands trembling as he turned the page. "Not this . . ."

Jonathan asked if he could be honest with her, then proceeded to tell her that he had had "some strong feelings. Inappropriate feelings." He told her, "You're young and beautiful, and we sort of clicked the first time we met. I never intended to have these feelings for you, but nevertheless, they sort of just appeared. I know this is probably shocking to you."

Sydney stopped him and told him that she had not been honest with him, and that she had already broken up with Jeremy because she wanted to be in a relationship with him.

All the air left his lungs. Someone had heard this whole conversation with Sydney. Someone heard him tell her he had feelings for her. Jonathan squeezed the back of his neck with his hand to try to relieve the building stress in his muscles. He cautiously read on.

Sydney then told Jonathan that she had a new, better man in her life. Him. Jonathan was horrified to think that Sydney had mentioned his name to her fiancé. He questioned her about it, what exactly she had told him, and she became upset. After Jonathan assured her he was happy that she'd left Jeremy, Sydney said, "I took a big risk breaking up with Jeremy, not knowing for sure if you really wanted to be in a relationship with me. You've been coming on to me for weeks, and I think I know you well enough to know it wasn't for some cheap thrill."

Jonathan said he never mentioned being in a relationship. He was married, after all.

"Apparently not very happily," Sydney said and then told him not to stand there and pretend like nothing had happened between them. She reminded him that he had already admitted having feelings for her, and she had feelings for him. She asked what his hesitation was. They were meant to be together. He cared enough to make sure her relationship with Jeremy ended. After all that, is he really going to leave her alone?

Jonathan told her he never meant for it to go this far, and that he simply cared for her and wanted her to get out of a bad relationship. Sydney told him that she loved him and she wanted them to be together. She wanted him to leave his wife and get a divorce. Or if he couldn't, to know that they could still be together.

Jonathan told her he couldn't be with her, but when Sydney asked why, he could not answer. Did he no longer love his wife?

The page ended and Jonathan's eyes filled with tears. The horror of reading this whole thing was more than he could bear. What a horrible mistake he had made with Sydney, but it was the last two sentences that haunted him the most. When Sydney had asked him why he couldn't leave his wife, what the writer couldn't possibly know is that he wasn't silent because he questioned his love for his wife or was having second thoughts about getting divorced. He was silent because he couldn't explain the innermost conviction that plagued him both then and now.

As Jonathan threw his pencil down and brushed away the stray tears on his cheeks, he couldn't decide whether or not he found comfort in the fact that the writer couldn't read his mind. The picture the writer had painted was of a man torn between two women. In reality, his intentions were to set things straight with Sydney and make sure she understood that he *did not* want to be in a relationship. But when the conversation was played back in the form of a written page, it sounded as if he couldn't make up his mind.

Another page followed, and he felt he barely had enough strength to read it. He just wished this was all over . . . his "fling" with Sydney, his troubles with Kathy, this mysterious manuscript. He wanted it all to end. But he knew his wishes weren't about to come true. He reluctantly turned the page and continued to read.

His talk with Sydney was interrupted when Clyde Baxter showed up in Sydney's office. There was an uncomfortable silence and then Clyde explained he was on his way back from the bathroom and wanted to talk to Jonathan about his book.

Jonathan angrily left Sydney's office, furious Clyde had caught him and Sydney. Clyde offered to come back another time, and Jonathan insisted, "It's not what you think." He

asked how long Clyde had been standing there, and Clyde an-
swered, "Long enough." Jonathan told him again that it wasn't
what he thought and Clyde left.

Then Nellie came in, furious Jonathan had missed an im-
portant meeting. That was when Jonathan lost it. He threw
things to the ground, making matters with Nellie worse. Nellie
told him he needed to take some time off, but Jonathan in-
sisted he was okay and that he had two good book proposals
for the next editorial meeting. Though not convinced of his
well-being, Nellie decided to leave anyway, though she did tell
him not to be too proud to ask for help.

After his long day, with a few brief phone calls with au-
thors and agents, he came home and took a nap for two
hours. He ate dinner—chicken, carrots, peas, and salad—with
his family, and afterward Kathy asked him to take the trash
out. In doing so, he discovered these pages to his story.

Jonathan stood, his chair shooting backward and crashing into
the wall. Was he going insane? How in the world could someone
possibly know that he would go home, take a nap, eat chicken for
dinner, take out the trash, and find these pages? Was the writer
now predicting his future? Impossible! Yet, here it was, sitting in
front of him!

"There has to be a reasonable explanation," Jonathan said as he
leaned against the wall of his study. His knees buckled and he slid
down the wall onto the floor, a quiet heap of nerves and numbness.
The details of his evening—the nap, the dinner, the trash—were
too precise to be coincidence. Was the writer in his basement,
watching every move and typing it out as he lived it? He looked up
at the ceiling. Was the writer upstairs in their bedroom? He thought
hard about who might know his day's events. Maybe Kathy had
sneaked into his office and hidden somewhere . . . was is possible?
Or maybe she was just outside his office. Wait. No. She had called
on her cell phone. He'd heard traffic in the background. She had
definitely been on the road, far from the action in his office. What
about Edie? Had Edie turned on his speakerphone in his office without his knowing and listened quietly? He didn't know how it was
possible. The speakerphone beeped when someone turned it on

from another phone. He shook his head. Besides, neither of them could know everything that was in the manuscript. No suspect made complete sense.

Jonathan managed to gather himself up off the ground and stand long enough to push the pages back into the envelope. Just as he was deciding where to hide them until he could take them to his office in the morning, he heard footsteps coming down the stairs. Kathy rounded the corner to his office as he slid the envelope into an unlocked drawer of his desk. Jonathan switched his reading lamp off, making the room pitch-black other than the line of moonlight escaping through the curtains onto the floor.

Kathy crossed through the light, enough time for Jonathan to see she had changed into her gown and gotten ready for bed.

"Jonathan?" she said, her voice quietly concerned. "Is everything okay?"

"Just finishing up some work."

Kathy tightened the silk robe she had over her gown and self-consciously messed with her hair as they came into the moonlight. "Oh, okay."

"I've got to read more of Clyde's book. I'm behind." He went back to his desk and turned the light back on.

Kathy scratched her head for a moment and mumbled, "Um, okay." She took three steps back and turned. "I'll wait for you upstairs."

Jonathan swallowed and nodded, the most he could do since he felt as if he might collapse. Kathy headed on up, and Jonathan sat dumbfounded for thirty minutes, not moving a single muscle. His mind clicked through the events of his day as if taking inventory, but he got stuck on Nellie's untimely entrance into his office. He didn't feel like reading anything, but he still had a family and barely had a job, so he figured he should probably grind out a few more pages of Clyde's manuscript, though he'd managed to get some reading done at the office. He took it out of his briefcase and opened to where he'd left off. He found where the DA, Esther Caladaras, had decided that there was enough evidence to let Jerome Mitchner off of death row.

It had been four days since we had visited Donomar in jail. Esther had wanted some time alone, I suppose to get away from my relentless pleading. I spent my days at the office, hoping my name wouldn't be leaked to the press. We still had not discovered who had leaked the story initially. At nights, I watched the news coverage, which had now exploded as the top story on every station and even occasionally as "breaking news."

The media was having a heyday with the story, doing interviews with death-row inmates in Texas and Oklahoma, and profiling the district attorneys for both cities where the innocent men had been executed.

My prayer was that Esther wouldn't get caught up in the media's depiction of her as a heartless feminist whose convictions were as "deep as a puddle," but that she would look at the facts. The facts spoke for themselves.

It was noon on Thursday, and I was eating Chinese takeout, picking the little pieces of egg out of my fried rice and watching the news, when the anchor's lead line made me sit up in my chair.

"Today, we have new information on the case involving death-row inmate Jerome Mitchner, whose case is being reviewed by the DA's office. About ten minutes ago, District Attorney Esther Caladaras announced in a brief news conference outside the state courthouse that she would be filing a motion to have all charges against Jerome Mitchner dropped." I stood up, my Chinese tumbling onto the coffee table. The anchor cut to footage of Esther at the news conference.

"I believe there is significant evidence to indicate that Mr. Mitchner was wrongly convicted and that the true killer of Mr. Roberts is Dietrich Donomar, the notorious serial killer, who is now serving life without parole in the federal penitentiary. We have filed our motion and are awaiting word back from Judge Barry."

The press screamed questions, and Esther backed away from the microphone and was escorted away.

"Ms. Caladaras, do you feel the state owes Mr. Roberts an apology?"

"What evidence is there that Donomar is the killer?"

Esther never looked back and then the TV cut back to the anchor, who continued with the many unanswered questions, none of which I waited around to hear.

A month later, Judge Barry ruled that there was significant evidence to release Jerome Mitchner, and he walked out of prison a day before his scheduled execution.

Esther must've been expecting my visit, because I had no trouble getting to her office after being cleared by security. The door was open, and when I entered she had her feet propped up on her desk and was just finishing off a cigarette.

"I've been expecting you," she said with a smile and then slid her feet off her desk and punched out her cigarette into the ashtray.

"I heard it on the news," I said and walked straight up to her desk. "Thank you."

"Well, Keaton," she said, "it wasn't about you. It was about doing the right thing. Despite what the media might think of me, I am out for justice and that's it. When justice isn't served, I blame myself. Do you understand that?"

"Of course, Esther," I said and sat down. "We all feel that way." I crossed my legs and said, "Not all DAs would admit they were wrong, though."

She laughed at me and said, "I wasn't wrong, Keaton. The evidence at the time proved otherwise. A jury confirmed that. It's just that now evidence has emerged that requires additional attention."

I shook my head and said, "Right. Well, whatever the case may be, an innocent man is free. And that's what counts." I stretched my neck, trying to relieve it of the accumulated stress of over twenty years on the job, and said, "I wonder how long it will take for the rest of the story to leak. The details about the FBI's screw-up. You've kept a tight lid on all this, and so has the judge." Esther shrugged, and I continued with my questions. "So I suppose Mitchner was a pretty happy man today?"

Esther nodded, seemingly sad and peaceful all at once. "Yes. He walked out of that prison with only his shoes, jeans, and a shirt. Not even socks. But I guess freedom means more than possessions." She laughed a little. "He came up to me and shook my hand. He didn't seem angry. Amazing, isn't it?"

"Did he say anything?"

"Not really. He had a letter with him he wanted to give to

some Joseph James guy on death row. Don't know why he didn't just give it to him while he was in there, but my assistant assured him it would be taken care of. And that's all that was said. I called him a taxi, gave him twenty bucks, and that was it."

Just then an assistant DA tapped on the door and walked in with a white envelope in his hand. "Sorry to disturb you, Esther, but I thought you should take a look at this."

"What is it, Jack?" she said as he handed it to her.

"We're not exactly sure. It's from Dietrich Donomar. Addressed to you. It's been cleared of any harmful substances. It's perplexing, actually. We thought you might know what it meant."

Esther's eyes lingered on the ADA for a moment and then she pulled a single white sheet of paper out of the envelope and unfolded it. She stared at it, glanced at both of us, and then stared at it again.

"What is it?" I asked, throwing my hands up in the air in frustration over her silence.

Esther Caladaras, in her usual hard, unpredictable manner, lit another cigarette, never taking her eyes off the page again. Her eyes narrowed as the smoke rose between her and the paper. Finally Jack stepped forward.

"Do you know what it means?" he asked.

Esther again was quiet. Her face had hardened right in front of me, and then she looked up with eyes as hot as burning coals. Even Jack lowered his head and stepped back out of the way.

"What, Esther?" I demanded in an unusually stern tone. Curiosity was getting the best of me.

Esther simply handed me the sheet of paper as she continued to smoke. I took it from her, glanced at Jack, and then looked at it. Written, with crayon, in the center of the piece of paper was the name Special Agent Nathan Hall.

"Who is this?" I asked, handing the paper back to her. She laughed suddenly, very hard, making Jack and me shift uncomfortably. Finally she laid her cigarette down in the ashtray as gingerly as one would a baby and picked up the phone.

"What's Pierce's number?"

"Pierce's number?" I stepped closer. "What do you need that

for? Who is this Hall guy? I don't know him."

"I don't know him, either. But I have a feeling Pierce Jenkins knows him. What's his number, Keaton?" Her face was bright, but her eyes were dark and hateful. I paused and then reluctantly told her the number. She put the phone on speaker and after five long rings, the phone was answered.

"Hello?" It was Pierce. Esther nodded at me to do the talking.

"Um, hi . . . Pierce . . . it's Keaton."

"Keaton! Hi. I've been watching the news. Looks like it all worked out. Mitchner's out of jail."

"Yes." I wanted to be happy about that fact, but something in Esther's mood told me not to gloat. "Listen, I have a name of an agent here. Could be FBI. I wanted to see if you knew him."

"All right."

"Special Agent Nathan Hall?"

There was a long pause on the other end of the phone, enough of one for each of us to look at the other while waiting for a response.

"Pierce? You there?"

"Yeah. Why do you want to know?"

"It's just a name we've come across. You know him?"

"Yeah. I know him."

"Who is he?"

Another pause and then, "He was an agent I worked with."

"Is he still with the FBI?"

"Uh, no." A short pause with a nervous laugh preceded the next statement. "He's in jail."

I swallowed hard. Esther hung her head, and Jack just looked stunned and confused.

"For what?" I asked, pretty confused myself.

"Possession of narcotics."

I looked up at Esther, not knowing where this was leading and wondering what question I should ask next. Esther pressed her lips together and, while looking at me, said, "Pierce, it's Esther. What prison is he at?"

Pierce paused and then said, "The federal pen. Here."

I was still confused and didn't know why Donomar would send Esther that name. Esther smiled, a smile that would fit a demon, and never taking her eyes off of me, she said, "Pierce, let me ask you something. Please tell me the truth."

"Okay."

"Was Agent Hall involved in the Manuel Roberts case?"

A suffocating hesitation blared through the phone. Finally, Pierce said, "Yes. He was one of the agents who knew about it."

"Thank you, Pierce." Esther hung up the phone and then threw it across the room, nearly missing Jack.

"Esther, what the—" Jack said as he finished ducking.

"What's going on here?" I was angry that I wasn't following.

Esther stood and looked as if she could've used a good piece of tough leather to chew on. She finally turned to me and yelled, "You don't get it, Keaton? Can't you see what's happened here? Donomar didn't kill Roberts! He got his information from Nathan Hall! He knew we wouldn't figure out that Hall was there or make that connection! He *tricked* us! We released a guilty man!"

I stumbled back, trying to make sense of it all. Esther was pacing furiously behind her desk, cussing and screaming all at once as she—

A soft thud, coming from somewhere in the kitchen, startled Jonathan. He stood and switched off his reading lamp. He slowly walked into the kitchen, holding tightly on to the edge of the counter. The small light above the sink, the only light on in the kitchen, cast odd shadows across the walls and floor. Suddenly the darkness scared him. Chills ran up and down his spine. He noticed the door to the pantry was cracked, and he thought he saw the door open a little more. With an outstretched hand, he slid a couple of feet across to the pantry, held his breath, and threw open the door. A couple of packages of spaghetti hit the ground. He shrieked as he jumped three feet into the air.

Clutching his heart, he stooped down to get the spaghetti, then was sure he heard something in the garage, a thump and a shifting sound, like heavy shoes against cement. He thought of the gun in his office, but he was afraid if he went back to get it, whoever was there might go out the side door and be gone. His eyes focused on the doorknob. The door was unlocked, which was how they accidentally left it over half the time. He tried to remember if it had been locked earlier in the evening. His ears strained to listen for any other sound.

As he touched the doorknob he heard it again, a shifting sound like feet dragging against cement. He held his breath so he wouldn't make any sound, counted to three, and swung the door open into the dark garage. His trembling hand searched for the hard-to-reach light switch, and after two or three tries he finally flicked it on.

The single light bulb poorly illuminated the area, but it was lit well enough to see at first glance that nobody was standing where they could be seen. Jonathan's first instinct was to check the cars. He carefully stepped down the cement stairs, and with his right hand grabbed a hammer hanging on the tool wall. He tiptoed across the pavement to his SUV. The doors were locked, which he remembered doing, and since the windows were tinted, he carefully stooped down and looked under his car, then turned to look under Kathy's. He jumped up, his heart racing so fast it hurt, and peered into Kathy's car. Nothing.

Then he saw the door that led out into the backyard. It was open two feet. The air from outside helped him breathe a little easier. Though they never locked that door, it usually remained closed, unless the girls had been playing in the backyard and Kathy had locked the back patio door. Then they would come in through the garage, usually leaving the door open.

Jonathan's hand tightened around the hammer, and his eyes quickly scanned the garage for a flashlight. He kept a flashlight in every room of the house except the garage. He could see the backyard grass from where he was standing, and it was bright from the moonbeam. He decided he could proceed without a flashlight.

He moved against the wall of the garage, came to the door, opened it farther, and looked around what he could see of the yard. He thought he heard footsteps crunching in the leaves but decided it could just as well be the wind moving them, though the wind had to be low because the tops of the trees were quietly still.

He rounded the corner with his back against the outside of the house. Now he could see his entire backyard, and it was as if God had shone His own flashlight into the yard. It was fully illuminated by the moon's light, and after a few seconds, the wind picked up the leaves in a small whirlwind and shuffled them along the ground, as though God himself were strolling through their grass.

He stood still for a moment, listening for any sound out of the ordinary. Across his back fence he could hear his neighbors laughing and watching TV. In the distance the roar of the local highway sounded monotonous and soothing. The *L* shape of the house allowed him to see his bedroom from where he stood in the backyard. Kathy hadn't pulled the shades yet, and he could see her on the bed, reading something and glancing at the clock a few times.

He realized as he stood out in the open air of his backyard that for the first time in a long time he felt safe. He remembered as a young boy, a couple of years after his brother's death, he lay in a soft patch of grass long after the sun had gone to bed and the moon had risen with its light, looking up at the stars and feeling the presence of God looking down on him. He remembered that though he hadn't prayed a single word, he knew God heard his every thought and felt his innermost pain. No one had taught him specifically about God, but he knew of Him. His aunt Eleanor had taken him to church once or twice. But those were childish imaginations, to think God cared enough to look, or existed in the time and space he occupied.

Jonathan's back rested against the brick and he closed his eyes. He thought it impossible for God to come down and write a story about his life. But whoever was writing about his life knew so much that it seemed as though he were omnipresent. Someone listened to every word he spoke in his house, at his office, in restaurants, and anywhere else. It wasn't God, but it might as well have been.

Jonathan didn't speak a word to God that evening. He had nothing to say to someone he barely knew. He was ashamed of his life and of the story that was being told about it. But as he stood in the cold moonlight of the fall night, he allowed his soul to be naked. He didn't hide anything. How could he anymore? Everything was in the open. Someone knew everything about him and apparently could predict his every move as well.

He looked up in the trees and wondered if the shadows of the bare limbs hid a stranger. If they did, then they would see a broken man, scared and downtrodden, fleeing into the night as a safe haven for his soul.

Soon the cold temperature stifled his breathing and tingled his skin. Without a coat he knew he would have to go in soon. His eyes wandered back up to his bedroom, where Kathy appeared to be praying. He wondered what she was praying for—if she was praying for him. He closed his eyes, and for a moment a prayer danced on the tip of his own tongue, but it soon faded, and the guilt and despair that plagued his heart now shut his mouth and closed his mind.

The north wind picked up and this time swayed the tops of the trees, loosening a few stray leaves. They floated lightly to the ground, spotlighted by the moon as if performing on a stage. The tiny voices of two playful brothers echoed in his mind. He could see them splashing in the river together, trying to catch fish with their bare hands. If only his brother hadn't died, maybe life would be . . .

He walked back through the door to the garage, climbed four cement steps into his house, reached for the light switch, and hoped that a God he wasn't sure existed would help him, if only for Kathy's sake.

CHAPTER 19

"Jonathan! Jonathan! Get up! Jonathan!"

Jonathan rolled over and lifted his tired and heavy head out of his feather pillow. He managed to open his eyes enough to see Kathy peering over him, her hand on his shoulder, shaking him hard.

"What?" He sat up quickly.

Her eyes were wide. "It's nine o'clock!"

Jonathan squeezed his eyes shut and opened them back up, trying to wake up and assess what was happening. "It's nine?"

"Yes! Yes! Honey, I thought you were up. I'm sorry, I—"

Jonathan swung his feet over the side of the bed. "Sorry for—"

Kathy had walked briskly to their closet and emerged with a white shirt, tie, and slacks. "Do you need a blazer this morning?"

"What . . . ?" Jonathan stood and felt dizzy. He steadied himself against his bedside table.

Kathy threw the clothes on the bed, paused, and looked at him for a moment before saying, "Honey . . . the meeting? Don't you have a meeting this morning at nine?"

Jonathan almost fell over as his heart stopped mid-beat. Did he? Did he have a meeting? He couldn't remember, but Nellie had mentioned one, hadn't she? Had she?

His hands raced down the front of his pajama top, unbuttoning it as fast as he could. "Do I have a meeting?" he asked Kathy as she handed him his dress shirt and began knotting his tie.

"It's on your desk calendar in your study." She buttoned the lower buttons on his shirt while he did the top ones. He threw the tie over his head and grabbed his pants.

"What day is it?"

"Thursday." She handed him his socks. "I'm so sorry, Jonathan. I had to take Leesol and Meg to school early and I thought you were up when I left. I'm so sorry."

Jonathan ran to his closet and grabbed a belt. Kathy lifted his shoes off the floor and set them on the bed. "Brush your teeth and forget shaving. I'll go fix you a mug of coffee."

With his vision still blurry from a hard night's sleep, Jonathan made his way to the bathroom, tripping over his pant leg twice, and grabbed Kathy's toothbrush and toothpaste because it was sitting out on the counter. As he splashed water on his face with one hand and brushed his teeth with the other, he fought through the fogginess of his mind to try to remember if he really had a meeting.

His hair was sticking straight up on the left side of his head, an indication that he hadn't moved all night. He had apparently made the mistake of taking one too many over-the-counter sleeping pills. He felt like he might go back to sleep as he stood at the sink.

He ran back to the bed and slipped his shoes on, forgetting to tie them, and ran down the stairs as fast as he could, passing Sophie on the left and stumbling over the dolls she had managed to scatter all over the stairs.

Kathy was at the bottom of the stairs with his coat and a spill-proof mug of coffee. She helped him put his coat on, he buttoned the top button, and then she handed him his briefcase and keys that were on the dining room table. She opened the front door for him and asked, "Do you want a scarf?"

Jonathan shook his head, buttoned another button on his coat as the cold air snapped him awake, and realized he had parked his car in the garage. Kathy realized it, too, and said, "I'll get the garage door."

Jonathan hurried down the sidewalk, watchful for any patches of ice, and waited impatiently for the garage door to crawl open, as if it were as groggy as he'd been. After making an awful rattling noise that ordinarily would need his immediate attention, the door reached the top. Jonathan finally ran into the garage, started his car, and threw it into reverse.

Kathy waved and mouthed, "I'm sorry," again as Jonathan backed into the street without even looking for traffic and sped off in the direction of the highway.

It would normally take him twenty minutes to get to work, but since traffic was lighter at nine and he was driving eighty-five miles an hour, it took him fifteen. His eyes were on the car clock more than the road, and he nearly had a wreck three times before he got off on Patterson Street and took a left onto Hudson. He parked his car at 9:21 and managed to turn his car off, grab his briefcase, and get out of the car all in one motion. He then entered the building lobby and ran for the elevator that was shutting.

It closed without regard to him, but before he could knock a hole through the wall punching the Up button, another elevator opened its doors with a delightfully annoying *ding*.

Jonathan shoved past the traffic exiting and hit his floor and the Close Door button at the same time. The elevator crept up ten floors and then opened. Jonathan stumbled out and ran as fast as he could toward Conference Room B, their typical meeting place. He swung the door open, breathing heavily, to an empty room. Maybe they were in Conference Room C. He tore his coat off as he ran down the north hall, but when he arrived at that one, it was empty as well.

Jonathan caught his breath for a moment and then thought with horror that maybe they were meeting in Nellie's office. Meetings in Nellie's office always meant they were of utmost importance *and* personal. Missing a meeting in Nellie's office was like a personal insult to her.

As he took off toward Nellie's office, Jonathan tripped over his coat and plunged to the ground, his chin scraping the carpet and burning like someone had struck a match across it. He scrambled up and flew past Carl Osburg, who tried to stop him to tell him something. Jonathan dismissed him with a harried wave of his hand

and kept running until he got to Nellie's office.

The door was shut and Jonathan closed his eyes and tried to breathe. He brushed his hair down toward his scalp, tossed his coat nonchalantly over his arm, and opened the door.

"Sorry I'm late—"

Nellie looked up, looked around the otherwise empty office as Jonathan did the same thing, and tilted her head to the side questioningly. "Late?"

Jonathan cleared his throat and realized suddenly that he didn't have a meeting. He felt relief and embarrassment all at once. He tried to think of how to recover since Nellie already thought he had been irresponsible lately anyway.

He straightened out his coat on his arm. "Oh, Nellie, I'm sorry. I must've been looking at an old calendar or something. I . . ." He laughed lightly. "I thought we had an appointment. Sorry to bother you."

Jonathan was backing out of her office when she said, "Wait. I want to talk to you." Her tone sounded grave and concerned. Jonathan closed his eyes and turned back around with a smile on his face.

"Yes?"

Nellie pointed to a plush leather chair near her desk and Jonathan took his cue to sit down. He set his briefcase next to him.

"I've been thinking about your two book proposals for the meeting. I have to say I'm quite excited about Clyde's novel. What's the genre?"

Nellie's continual clicking of her pen was starting to grate on Jonathan's already shot nerves. "It's a drama . . . sort of thriller . . . serial killer mystery."

Nellie's pen hit the desk. "A serial killer?"

Jonathan gave a short smile. "Yes. I couldn't believe it myself. But it's good so far."

Nellie messed with her French twist, a mannerism that always indicated either disapproval or apprehension. "Clyde doesn't write that kind of novel. He's spent twenty years writing westerns. There's probably a reason for that."

Jonathan nodded in agreement. "I thought the same thing, but he has a passion for this thing. He says he's got to write it. It's something he said he had to 'get out' before he dies."

Nellie laughed a little. "Well, let's hope our friend Clyde Baxter isn't a serial killer and this is a deathbed confession of some sort."

Jonathan couldn't even pretend to smile at that.

"Jonathan . . . that was a joke." Nellie's pen began clicking again.

"Yes. Sorry. I'm just . . . thinking."

"What about your other proposal. A no-name?"

Jonathan had hoped this wouldn't come up. He wanted to pitch the book to committee before revealing the author so no one would have any preconceived biases toward it. But he knew if he didn't tell Nellie when she asked he would be in trouble later.

"No, actually it's a house author."

"Really?" Nellie said in a satisfactory tone. "Who? Ebert Walton? I heard he was wanting to do another sci-fi soon."

"No. He's from nonfiction."

"Nonfiction?" Nellie's eyes stared at the ceiling in thought. "Don't tell me. James Underwood. That's it, isn't it? He's finally taken my advice and crossed over!"

"No."

Nellie's pen clicked faster. "Erika Soprano? She's so flowery with her words Carl says she's a nightmare nonfiction writer."

Jonathan shook his head.

"Fine, tell me. I could guess all day."

"Francis." Jonathan couldn't even get himself to say the last name.

"Francis?" Nellie leaned forward on her desk. "Francis . . . I don't recall having an author by that name. Has she been with the house long?"

"He."

"He . . . Francis . . ." Nellie rose from her desk and with wide eyes exclaimed, "Francis Flowers?!" Jonathan barely had time to nod when Nellie raced around her desk while laughing hysterically. "Are you saying Zippy's writing a novel?"

Jonathan swallowed before saying, "Yes."

Nellie couldn't hold back the tears. She hurriedly shut the door and said, "Jonathan, please tell me this is a joke."

Jonathan turned around in his chair to face her. "It's quite good, Nellie. You'll be surprised."

"To say the least," she said, blotting at the corner of her eyes to keep her mascara from running. "Jonathan, please. Zippy can't write fiction."

Jonathan's eyes followed Nellie back to her desk. "It's a great story. Better than decent writing. It's about a pharmaceutical company that's paid off to destroy a cure for cancer because—"

Nellie waved her hand. She wasn't laughing anymore. "Save it for the meeting, Jonathan. Please." She sat down at her desk, avoiding eye contact.

Jonathan stood. "What, Nellie? You're questioning my judgment? I know a good book when I see one."

Nellie nodded and stared at her desk.

"Nellie, for pete's sake, look at me! You can't even look at me!"

Nellie's eyes rose slowly until they met his. "I'm sorry, Jonathan. You're right. I am questioning your judgment. I mean, Zippy, for crying out loud. Zippy."

"Look, I know it sounds crazy. But it's really good. I was shocked."

Nellie's eyes fell onto her desk calendar and she made a deliberately long glance at her watch. "I'm about to be late for a meeting. I'm sorry, but you'll have to excuse me."

Nellie grabbed a black folder, punched her index finger through her French twist a couple of times, and moved past him and out of her office. Jonathan's head fell back and he stared at the ceiling, wondering if every part of his life were falling apart.

He finally picked his coat up off another chair, grabbed his briefcase, and headed right out of Nellie's office and toward his. As he approached Edie's desk, he noticed a tall, dark-haired, husky young man standing next to it. Edie's eyes were wide with anticipation as Jonathan came closer. She glanced at the young man several times and then said, "He wanted to see you, Mr. Harper."

Jonathan's whole body felt so tired he thought he needed to sit down at once, but there were no chairs around. The man looked familiar, and Jonathan was just about to decide he was a writer he'd met at a conference when the man said, "Yeah. I need to talk to you." His gruff voice fit well with the leather jacket, dirty five-o'clock shadow, and boots with chains.

Jonathan hung his coat on the coatrack nearby. "I'm sorry. I don't see writers without appointments."

The man moved closer. "I'm not a writer."

Jonathan turned, uncomfortable at how close the man was. He glanced at Edie, who couldn't stop herself from staring. "Then what do you need to see me for? I'm very busy." Jonathan kept his tone low and forceful as he met this man's angry green eyes.

"Yeah. Apparently you've been real busy with my fiancée."

Jonathan suddenly noticed how tall this man was, and before he could process the last sentence, the man said, "So busy that she's now too busy to marry me."

Jeremy. Sydney's fiancé. Edie was staring relentlessly, and this man's aggressive body language was drawing stares from the few people passing by.

"Let's go into my office, shall we?"

"Let's stay out here so I can beat you up in front of all your bookworm friends."

"Look, I don't want any trouble—"

"I know you don't. You're a coward. But you stole my girlfriend, and now you're gonna pay for it."

Jonathan pushed past him and headed for his office, hoping he could shut himself in or at least bring Jeremy into a secluded area.

"Should I call security?" Edie asked. No reply came. Jonathan didn't have an answer. He turned around in his office and Jeremy was right on his heels. As soon as he caught up with him, Jeremy shoved him enough to make him stumble backward and drop his briefcase.

"Yeah, Edie! Call security!" Jonathan locked eyes with Jeremy as he turned around and caught his balance. "You better back off."

Jeremy laughed and folded his arms together. "You think security is gonna protect you, you spineless coward? You don't think I'll be waiting out in the parking lot for you some late night when no one's around to save you?" Jeremy laughed again and glanced over his shoulder. Jonathan could see Edie on the phone, talking as fast as she could and pointing inside the office. A few of his colleagues were in the background trying to get a better view.

"Look, I don't know what you think happened between Sydney and me, but you're mistaken if you think we were . . ." Jonathan lowered his voice. ". . . involved."

Jeremy had taken two steps forward. "Then she wasn't talking about you when she said she'd found a better man who'd treat her right?"

Jonathan found his tongue heavy. "Well, maybe, but—"

"I treat her great! I buy her anything she wants! Have you seen the ring on her finger? Or did that just conveniently slip out of your sight?"

Edie was standing now, glancing down the hall as she waited for security to arrive. Jonathan clenched his jaw and felt anger rising inside him.

"You treat her great? Is that what you just said?" Jonathan managed to inch forward a little himself. "Then why does she show up here looking like a car wreck every week?"

Jeremy's eyes narrowed. "She plays sports. Things happen."

Jonathan nodded and tried to casually move behind his desk. "Yeah? Well, you could've fooled me. But you didn't fool her. I told her to get out of the relationship so she wouldn't end up dead. I could care less if you're upset about that. You don't deserve a woman like that."

Jeremy's face turned red and he was marching toward Jonathan's desk when two security officers bolted into his office. "Everything all right here, Mr. Harper?" Both men were eyeing Jeremy as they approached.

Jonathan could feel the perspiration soak through his shirt. "I think this young man could probably be shown the way out. Thanks for stopping by," he said with a forced smile on his face.

The security officers took Jeremy by either arm, but he shook them off as he headed to the door himself. Before leaving, he turned around, pointed his finger directly at Jonathan, and said, "You think she looks bad? Wait till I finish with you. You'll be dead."

"Let's go," the larger security guard said and pushed him out the door. They escorted him to the elevator as Jonathan breathed for what seemed like the first time since he came into his office. Edie rushed in.

"Are you okay, Mr. Harper?" she asked, glancing back at the elevator to see if he was still there. The doors were just closing.

"Yeah. Fine. Thanks for calling security." Jonathan avoided her eyes.

"Wow," Edie said as she smacked her gum. "I've never seen someone so mad in my life."

"Yeah, well, if you'll excuse me, I've got a lot of work to do." Edie hesitated a moment until Jonathan finally looked up at her. Then she left, shutting the door behind her.

Jonathan leaned against his window with both hands and wondered if it might be better for him to just jump and end it all now. It would probably only hurt for a second, but the mess his life was right now was painful every minute he was awake. He was still reeling from Nellie's obvious mistrust of his judgment, and now he was dealing with death threats from a violent ex-fiancé of a woman he now wished he'd never talked to. And then there was the spook writing down the facts of his life as if he were his shadow.

Jonathan's body ached for a drink, but he couldn't afford any more time away from the office. He had a lot more reading to do on both Zippy's and Clyde's manuscripts.

He scooted Clyde's across the desk, and as he did so, his mind wandered to the very real possibility that Clyde was behind the majority of his distress. After all, he was around a lot, enough to know at least some of the detail in the manuscript. He certainly had motive, as he'd shown disapproval more than once for the life-style Jonathan had found himself in. It didn't explain all of it, but it was the best explanation he had. Maybe if he broke into Clyde's house when he wasn't there, he could find evidence that Clyde was the writer. Jonathan's fingers drummed against his desk as he wondered if he could get away from the house tonight, see if Clyde was home, and maybe do it then.

Yes, he was certain Clyde was the writer. His only objective now was to find out why and to stop him before Kathy found out too much. But before he did that, he needed to read more of this manuscript. He had to make sure all the hype he was showing to

Nellie rang true in reality. He returned to the point in the book where the DA and the Keaton fellow had apparently been tricked somehow by the serial killer.

"What is it that you want?" Esther's teeth were clinched so tightly I thought they all might crumble.

Donomar rose, and my heart pounded heavily in my chest. He smiled at me, a smile that stung my soul. Then he looked at Esther. "Nothing. I'm done with you. In a practical sense, anyway."

"Oh, come on, Donomar. Don't you want to tell me what you're up to?" Esther pretended to smile. "Surely you can't just sit there in your cell and not gloat?"

Donomar shrugged, scraping the side of a red crayon with his thumbnail. I watched small pieces fall to the ground. "Well, I have to say both of you played into my hands perfectly. Keaton, you were the easiest." I swallowed hard, my nostrils flaring uncontrollably. He laughed. "You thought you had me figured out, didn't you?"

"I don't know what you mean," I said in my lowest, most confident voice.

Donomar laughed again, stared me square in the face, and then dropped the crayon. As I watched it fall, my attention was grabbed by his thumbs. They were twiddling. I slowly looked up at him, the smile across his face so sickening I thought I might puke.

"Wasn't this your big clue?" His twiddling thumbs stopped. "I wasn't twiddling my thumbs? A signature move that gave me away. Gave my humanity away." His laugh made my hair stand on end.

"Yeah, so, he's stupid. So what? So we let someone go that needs to be in prison. Worse things have happened. Your sick games are over, Donomar. And I hope you rot in this jail as slow as anyone ever has."

Esther turned to leave, but Donomar approached the glass. "Oh, Esther, I would hate for us to say good-bye just yet. And no, I'm not finished."

She turned around, her dark eyes cast at me and then him. "Oh yeah? What's the big finale, Donomar? You pull a rabbit out of your sleeve and then boil it alive for kicks?"

Donomar looked down, waiting patiently for her to finish. And then, without ever looking up, he said, "I told you there was an innocent man on death row. There are two prisoners scheduled to die. He's still there. I never told you that the man you released was the man that was innocent. I simply told you a story that you bought, and then you assumed this man was the innocent one, and you released him. But you were wrong."

Esther laughed hard. "Come on, Donomar! You still think we're going to fall for your nonsense? You think I'm going to believe there's actually an innocent man on death row? I've been burned once. I learn fast."

Donomar's eyes glowed with excitement. "Maybe. And whether or not you believe me is irrelevant. At some point, you're going to have to decide which one will die and which one will live. It will be your decision and your decision alone."

Esther's smile faded. "What do you mean by that?"

"Esther, I'm sad you're not following me as closely as I had hoped. But for your benefit and advantage, I will explain it to you." Donomar glanced at both of us. "You see what I've done? I picked you, Esther, because I knew that your decision would be based on emotion. You wanted the FBI to be wrong. You wanted a little justice, a little redemption in your life, didn't you? Even though Jerome Mitchner never once said he was innocent in his confession to the police, you still let him go." Esther stood so still I couldn't even see her breathing. "But it happened exactly as I knew it would, and now I will sit back and watch you in action. Watch you play the part I designed just for you."

Esther shook her head, trying to find words underneath all the anger I knew she was feeling. "I'm leaving in ten seconds. If you've got something to say, then say it."

Donomar lifted his chin, looking down his nose at her. "The truth is that there is an innocent man on death row who has been charged with a murder I committed."

"I don't believe you."

"You don't have to. The press is getting wind of this right now, and they're going to play you like a fiddle. Can't you see the headlines now? Caladaras Releases Wrong Prisoner. Refuses to Look into Who Is Innocent."

"What makes you think the media will believe you?"

He shrugged. "I tipped them off anonymously. They're a sucker for things like this, as you well know. But with the untimely and unfortunate deaths of three innocent men in Texas and Oklahoma, do you think they're going to let this go by without a hitch? It will be a national story, and you will be the center of it. Will you let your stubbornness and pride supercede your compassion for a man who may die unjustly? A man you prosecuted? Sure, you made a mistake once, and what a mistake it was. Will you make a second? Or will you swallow your pride and make a motion for the right man to be released?"

I couldn't hold in my curiousity any longer. "So what if the media backs you? Esther's never cared what anyone thought of her. But I know her well enough to know she wouldn't let an innocent man die. How can you prove he's there?"

Donomar laughed at me and said, "Well, I won't make it that easy." He looked at Esther. "No. You will have to make the decision yourself. But when the decision is made, I will be able to prove to you who was innocent and who was guilty." He turned and extended his arm out to his cell. "The clue that you need is in here. In this very cell. But you won't find it. Not until you've made your decision."

Esther turned and walked down the corridor. Donomar looked at me and said, "The men are scheduled to be executed three days from now, twenty four hours apart. But Esther already knows that, don't you, dear?"

Our bitter argument came to an abrupt hault as a heavy knock came at Esther's office door. She looked at me.

"We're using a forensic pyschologist, and that's final."

"That's ridiculous! A profiler can do just as good of a job."

"Not in my opinion," Esther said sternly, and then said, "Come in."

A tall, thin, well-groomed, and good-looking man entered, tucking his tie into his suit coat and smoothing out his shortly trimmed beard. "Sorry I'm late, Esther."

I stood as the man extended his hand toward me. "Dr. Alex Burrelson."

"Special Agent Spade," I said boldly, since he was keen on using titles.

"Ah," he said, as if my poor reputation preceded me.

"Please, Alex, sit down," Esther said, and we both took seats next to each other and across from Esther. Dr. Burrelson took a folder out of his shiny leather briefcase.

"Well, I've reviewed everything," he said with a predictable, intellectual sigh, as if only he could make any sense out of all that had happened. "I've also familiarized myself with some of the other studies done on Mr. Donomar."

"Don't call him Mister," Esther hissed. "He doesn't deserve the respect."

Dr. Burrelson eyed her for a moment and then continued. "At any rate, I've also put together a chart that compares Donomar's history of stories and lies, and cross-examined the evidence of—"

"Let's just cut through this egotistical nonsense, shall we?" Esther said, slamming her forearms down onto her desk. Her fingers were spread wide like the paws of a very mad cat. "Is the pond scum lying or not?"

Dr. Burrelson held himself together enough to offer a pause and a smile. He then answered. "It's only an opinion, as you know, but I believe he is telling the truth."

Esther lowered her head and closed her eyes. Dr. Burrelson continued. "I've looked back at serial killers of this sort, Esther, and they enjoy playing mind games. But the trick to all of them is that their mind games are centered around some truth. That gives them the upper hand and it also feeds their intellect." He paused and said, "It wouldn't be any fun for them if there wasn't something real for you to chase. The fight wouldn't be fair, so to speak."

Esther's eyes rolled back into her head, and with her eyes closed she snatched the lighter and cigarette off her desk. "They murder people and are concerned about fairness." Her tone was sharp and cutting. "This is just your opinion, of course."

"That's what they pay him the big bucks for," I chided. The flame on Esther's lighter shot up two inches.

Before Esther could get the cigarette out of her mouth, her assistant Jack entered without knocking. "Sorry to interrupt, but I've got the information you wanted."

Esther's silence commanded him to continue. "The two prisoners Donomar is referring to are Lincoln Smith and Joseph

James. Smith's in for killing his girlfriend, and James is in for killing a customer."

"A customer?" I asked.

"Yes. He apparently owned a furniture store or something. They found one of his customers, a young college girl, dead inside the store after it had been locked up."

Esther stood, the cigarette between her fingers noticeably trembling. "I suppose they're both proclaiming innocence?"

Jack's eyes fell as he nodded.

"Alright." Esther stood tall as if she were rallying the troops. "And the media? What's the damage assessment there?" I could not help but notice the tinge of sarcasm in her voice.

Jack's eyes were still lowered. "It's . . . it's about what we thought. They are playing this up really big. *Dateline*, *60 Minutes*, and *20/20* are all doing stories on it . . . interviews from the prison, courtroom analysis, stories about the families, documents—"

"I get it, Jack." The room stood still. "Thank you. I'll need the entire case file for each of those prisoners." Then she suddenly looked at me. "What about you, Keaton? Haven't you been fired yet or anything?"

"No one's said a word—" My beeper went off, making everyone in the room jump a little. I moved my love handle to the side so I could see the number. It was my supervisor's cell phone. "Yet."

Suddenly an assistant popped her head in and said, "This is bad. They're doing a 'breaking news' piece during a soap opera. Everyone knows not to do that unless it's some big story." Esther's glare moved her back out of the office quickly.

Her long fingernails scratched the skin on her forehead where her hairline started. She looked at Dr. Burrelson. "So this supposed 'clue' Donomar has in his cell . . . that's the truth, too?"

"Most definitely," Dr. Burrelson said, crossing his long legs as he lifted his note pad off his lap. "As you know, when he was finally captured, he bragged about owning something from every single one of his victims. At the time, they didn't even know how many people he had killed, so it was hard to assess what he had of his victims. Some things were recovered by victims' families, but there were also things that went unclaimed."

Dr. Burrelson closed his note pad. "Whatever it is, it will be his trophy when you choose the wrong person. If, I mean."

Esther lit another cigarette in her hand while the first one was still burning between her lips. "Alright. Then we just hit this head on. We're smart people. We can figure this out." She looked at me as she dropped the cigarette out of her mouth. "I want agents in his cell today. I want it torn apart. I want that evidence."

"You won't find it," Dr. Burrelson said in domineering confidence. Esther shot him an intolerant look. "He's smart, Esther. He's smarter than you."

"The sooner the better," she added as she stared at Dr. Burrelson.

We all stood and gathered our things. The assistant popped her head in again. "*Dateline* wants to know if they can do an interview with you—"

Jack was on top of it before Esther had a chance to scream. "Kerri, Esther doesn't do interviews, and secondly, I think we better work on your timing. . . ." His voice trailed off as they left the room.

"Alex, I'd like you to help me review these cases. I'd like your opinion on the innocence and guilt of these men." She then looked at me again. "Good luck with that page, Keaton. I'm assuming that wasn't a friendly one."

I swallowed and grabbed my jacket. No, it was not.

A light knock preceded the door opening, and before Jonathan could say, "I don't want to be disturbed," Sydney had slipped in and shut the door behind her. She was holding some manuscripts.

"Sydney, please, just—"

"I know what happened," she said, her back still against the door. "I'm sorry Jeremy did that. Now you see what I was dealing with."

Jonathan couldn't help but feel anger toward her, even though he was well aware that he had put himself in the present situation. He sighed heavily and leaned his body onto his desk. "Sydney, look, I can handle Jeremy, okay? But the time has come for me to be frank with you and just tell you that I am not interested in a relationship with you. At all. We need to sever whatever was there, if there was anything at all."

Tears swelled in her eyes and she wiped them away with frustration. "I can't believe you're doing this."

Jonathan stood where he was and said, "I'm not doing anything. I'm sorry if I led you to believe we had a future. But the most that's happened was that I found you attractive, I cared that you were in an abusive relationship, and I gave you advice to get out." Jonathan sat on the edge of his desk and continued. "And that's more than should've happened. I know better than that. I was just in a weak spot in my life. My wife and I are struggling and my job is rocky. You were a breath of fresh air meant for someone else. Not me."

Tears streamed down her face and for a long time she didn't say anything. Finally, though, she looked up at him, nodded a little, and said, "I understand. You're right." She opened the door a little and said, "But Jonathan, I want you to know that Jeremy . . . that he . . . just be careful, that's all."

She opened the door wider and was just about to leave when she turned around and said, "Oh. I almost forgot. I was in the mail room and this was on a shelf waiting to be delivered. I just thought I might as well bring it up." She laughed a little. "One final excuse to see you."

Jonathan smiled and reached out for the manila envelope. As Sydney was shutting the door behind her, Jonathan looked at the front of it. It only said *Jonathan Harper* in small, typed print on the front. Jonathan ripped the envelope open, pulled out a single page, and at a glance knew this was from his writer. Without even bothering to read it, he flung his door open and chased after Sydney, with Edie's disapproving look following him.

"Sydney! Wait! Wait!"

Sydney was near the elevator, about to turn down a hall, when she turned around, a happy expression filling her blotchy, tear-streaked face. "Yes?" she said with anticipation.

Jonathan caught up with her and caught his breath all at once. "I'm sorry, I just wanted to ask you something."

"Anything," she said as she straightened herself up.

"This envelope . . . it was just sitting in the mail room?"

Jonathan tried to ignore the obvious disappointment on Sydney's face. She looked at her feet, gathered herself, and said, "Yes, it was on top of a pile of mail that hadn't been sorted yet. Though I did notice it doesn't have postage on it."

Jonathan raced past her and took the stairs down four flights to the mail room. He rushed in and tried to find someone who looked friendly. A young man with buzzed hair and a goatee sat at a desk and didn't seem like he was doing too much.

"Hi," he said, and the young man looked up at him, yawned, and waited for more. "I received this envelope this morning from someone who picked it up from the mail room. This is very important. I need to know if you saw who brought this in. It doesn't have postage on it, so it had to be hand delivered."

"Dunno, dude," he said, and Jonathan realized he was making paper airplanes.

"Listen to me," Jonathan said in a stern tone. "You can't even imagine how important this is. Think. Was anyone here in the mail room this morning that doesn't work for the company? Someone that delivered a manila envelope?"

The kid looked at the envelope, looked at Jonathan, shrugged, and said, "Dunno, dude."

Jonathan felt his ears turn hot, which meant his blood pressure was rising. "Who is your supervisor?"

The kid continued to fold his paper. He thought for a moment and then said, "Dunno."

Jonathan was just about to grab the punk by his silk shirt when a better dressed, mild-mannered, familiar looking man approached him. "Mr. Harper, is it?"

Jonathan's chest felt so tight it might explode. "Yes," he managed.

"I'm Roger Tiddle. I'm the mail room supervisor."

"Yes," Jonathan started to feel a little better just by this man's demeanor.

Roger Tiddle looked at the kid and said, "Hank, don't you have some stamps to lick or something?" The kid rolled his eyes and Roger laughed at himself and then focused on Jonathan. "What can I do for you?"

Jonathan drew in a deep breath and said, "I received this envelope today. It was in the mail room, and it had to have been hand delivered because there is no postage. It's vital I find out who delivered it."

Roger smiled a little. "No kidding? A budding author on the horizon, I presume?"

"No, actually, it's my stalker," Jonathan admitted with little hesitation.

Roger's eyebrows raised and he took a small, instinctive step backward. "Goodness. Well, I'm not sure what we can do for you."

"Has everyone in this office been here all morning?"

"Yes. Except Hank. He's always thirty minutes late," he said with a glance over at the kid.

"You have how many people in here?"

"About five right now."

"Can I speak to them?"

Roger turned and waved his arms, getting the attention of everyone in the room. "Cody, Cindy, Larry, can you come over here?" Three people stopped what they were doing and approached. "Hank, you too. Where's Lizzy?"

"In the bathroom," Larry said. "What's the deal? We're going to be late for our mid-morning deliveries."

"This will only take a minute," Roger said. "This is Mr. Harper. He's a senior fiction editor for the house. He needs to know if you saw anyone bring this envelope into the mail room this morning." Jonathan lifted the envelope up for everyone to see.

They all thought for a moment and then Cindy said, "It's been so busy this morning. I don't remember." A young woman, presumably Lizzy, entered the circle.

Larry agreed. "Yeah, I remember seeing that but I don't know that I saw anyone bring it in."

"I haven't talked to anyone other than company people this morning," Cody said.

Roger's tone turned very serious. "Think, everyone, please. This is of the utmost importance."

"What's going on?" Hank asked.

Roger glanced at Jonathan, who hesitated but then said, "Can you remember anyone out of the ordinary in here? Someone who maybe just came in and didn't say anything to anyone?"

Cindy said, "I do remember someone, dressed in a real heavy coat, came in early this morning, around eight."

"With the dark hat?" Cody asked.

"Yes."

"That was Wilbur Porter, the maintenance man. The light bulb in our bathroom had burned out."

"I know Wilbur. That wasn't Wilbur."

"It was. He shaved his mustache. Looks like a totally different person."

"Dude, maybe he should grow a goatee like me," Hank said with interest.

"Look," Jonathan said, holding up his hands. "What about anyone else? What about Clyde Baxter?"

"The author?" Larry asked.

"Yes. Did he come in this morning?"

Roger shook his head, glancing at the group with perplexity. "I haven't seen Mr. Baxter."

"What about that lady that came in this morning?" Cindy said.

"Yeah, I saw her, too," Larry said.

"Dude, she was just asking for directions. She needed to be next door. She was at the wrong address."

"Oh," several of them said at once.

"Anyone else?" Jonathan asked anxiously. "Anyone dressed conspicuously?"

There was silence, and finally they shook their heads. Cindy added, "Mr. Harper, it's a nuthouse here in the morning. Someone could've come in and no one would notice. We don't have a receptionist, so people can wander in and out and we don't even pay attention."

"I understand," Jonathan said as pleasantly as possible. "Thank you for your time."

Everyone dispersed but Roger. "Mr. Harper, what can I do to help? A stalker is pretty serious business. Have you contacted the police?"

"Mr. Tiddle, if you could just please be on the lookout for anyone suspicious. Anyone at all. Carrying a manila envelope."

Roger laughed a little. "Do you know how many manila envelopes we see here every day?"

Jonathan placed his hand on his shoulder. "Please, just be on the lookout. I'm at extension 1042. Call me for anything. Okay?"

"Of course," Roger said, and they shook hands.

Jonathan left the mail room with his envelope, and in the terrace overlooking the lobby, he leaned against the rail and decided he had better take a look at what the writer had done now. He was curious that the writer was now down to only one page. He looked around to see if anyone was approaching him, then began to read.

Jonathan had finished the night in the study, reading the new pages left for him by the writer. His wife came downstairs and wondered when he was coming to bed. Jonathan said he would be up soon, but wasn't. Instead, he made his way outside, into the backyard, and stared up at the stars for awhile.

Jonathan made a mental note that the writer did not know why he had gone outside. In reality, he thought he'd heard something and gone outside to check it out. That was not in the story. Perhaps the writer was losing the power to know everything about him. He continued to read.

The next morning, his wife had woken him up quickly, fearful that he had missed a meeting that was written on his desk calendar downstairs. Unfortunately, Jonathan rushed out the door in such a hurry he forgot to take the pages the writer had left for him the night before. He had left them in an opened drawer in his study.

While he was at work discovering that he indeed did not have a meeting, his wife, while dusting his study, discovered the pages.

Jonathan's heart stopped beating. Hadn't he put those in his briefcase? Had he forgotten and left them in an open drawer?

Curiosity got the best of her, and she opened the envelope to read what was inside. Unfortunately, those pages would reveal to her that there was another woman in Jonathan's life.

Sydney. And the conversation she would read between the two of them, where Jonathan expressed feelings for her, and vice versa, would break her heart in two. But there was nothing Jonathan could do, because as he read this passage, she would be reading that one.

"No, no, no, no, no," Jonathan said in desperation. He raced down six more flights of stairs as fast as he could, knocking people over without even knowing it. "No, no, no . . . please, God," he said as he ran out of the building and to his car. He fumbled for his keys that he had luckily put in his pocket that morning.

Maybe the writer was wrong. Maybe. How could he predict his future? How? Impossible. This was just to scare him. Kathy probably didn't find the pages at all. His entire body was numb as he drove the fifteen long miles toward home.

Kathy's body hunched over their small, white kitchen table, her hair hanging over her face like a waterfall. He knew she'd heard him come in. Their front door always squeaked. Even through his tears, he could see the white pages on top of the table, spread out as if they had been studied with diligence.

Jonathan had no words and hoped that Kathy might say something first. After a moment of standing there, she finally looked up. There were no tears. Surprisingly, no anger either. Just a face full of sadness. A face that looked older and wiser. A face that reflected an unspeakable humiliation.

"You're home."

Jonathan nodded, his eyes darting back and forth from Kathy to the pages. She watched him carefully and he decided it was safe to sit down at the table with her. He tried to wipe his tears away, but they just never stopped flowing. He had hit his breaking point, and he knew it.

He disregarded his runny nose and fought the urge to hide his face in his hands. "I'm sorry. I'm so sorry."

Kathy's voice was eerily soft. She avoided his eyes and looked down at the pages when she said, "Do you love her?"

"No! No, honey. No! These pages . . . they . . . they don't really reflect what happened. Whoever wrote this didn't know . . . didn't know what was in my heart. They just wrote down this conversation."

"But you couldn't answer 'why,' Jonathan." Kathy's voice trembled. "When she asked you why . . ." Her voice trailed off.

Jonathan wanted to grab her hand, but his fear was that she would pull it away. He couldn't take that right now. So he folded his hands together and said, "Kathy, what the writer couldn't possibly know is that I couldn't answer that question not because I couldn't make up my mind. It was because . . . because . . ." Jonathan, who had made a career from the English language, could not explain what was inside him—now or then.

"What?" Kathy asked, her eyes beginning to glisten with her own tears.

Jonathan stood and paced, shaking his head and running his hands through his hair. "I can't explain it. It's weird. I mean, I was presented with this . . ." He glanced over at her. ". . . this temptation, I guess you could call it. And something inside held me back. I mean, men have affairs all the time. Bad and good men. And somehow they justify it. And I couldn't. I don't love her, Kathy. I don't. But at the time, when we were having so many problems, I thought she was the answer." Jonathan stopped and turned to her. "Do you understand?"

Kathy nodded a little, pushing her hair away from her face and tracing the arch of her eyebrows with a finger. "What does she look like?"

Jonathan slid into the chair next to her and this time did grab her hands. She didn't pull away, which gave him confidence to look her deeply in the eyes. "It doesn't matter what she looks like. Kathy, when I met you for coffee and you came in wearing that skirt and that yellow top, I don't think I'd ever seen anything so beautiful in my life. You glowed. I forgot all about the problems we were having. And that's when I knew I had to be straight with Sydney. Nothing had happened, but if we had continued down the path we were going, something might have. I didn't know what was going to happen to us, but I knew I didn't want to stop trying."

Kathy didn't resist his thumb moving up and down the back side of her hand, though she couldn't look at him. Jonathan waited as patiently as he could for her to say something, realizing that he could be a divorced man very soon. He had never imagined himself divorced before. Ever. But he had messed up. He had betrayed his wife, and that was enough to end a marriage that was already shaky. His mind wandered to an image of him alone in a small apartment with rented furniture, watching TV and holding a picture of his children.

Kathy pulled one hand away from his and touched her face lightly, her fingertips brushing the tops of her cheekbones as if she were concentrating on the texture of her skin.

For a moment their eyes met, and Jonathan said, "I love you. I do. I know I don't show it. And sometimes, Kathy, I don't feel it. But I know it's there. Buried sometimes. But it's there."

Kathy nodded and glanced away. "Don't you know I feel the same way about you? That's why I've been so upset that you've been working so much. You've been so distant. I thought it was me."

Jonathan hung his head. "I've felt empty inside. I don't know why."

Kathy squeezed his hand a little. "Don't you?"

Jonathan frowned with confusion. "Don't I what?"

"Know why?" Kathy stood, looking down at him. "Don't you know why you feel empty and why you couldn't have an affair? Don't you?"

Jonathan was perplexed by the question and wanted to answer, but he truthfully didn't know how. He just stared wide-eyed at her and wondered what would happen next. To his astonishment, a small smile crept onto her sad lips, and a single tear rolled down her face, around her lip, and dripped off her chin.

"I'm sorry, I—"

She cut him off with a wave of her hand. "It's okay. God's timing is perfect."

"What?" Jonathan couldn't begin to follow.

She sat back down in her chair. "I'm just . . . just so happy nothing really happened between you and this woman. I'm so glad."

"Me too," Jonathan said, touching her face. "I couldn't bear to lose you and this family." He cupped the side of her face. "We're going to get through this. We're going to make it."

Kathy laughed and cried all at once. "I know."

They sat together for a long moment, laughing and crying and holding each other, and then Jonathan said, "Don't you want to know why I'm home so early?"

Kathy wiped the tears off her face. Jonathan stood to get a glass of water. He opened the freezer to put ice in his glass. "Kathy, this whole manuscript about my life is getting spooky. Real spooky." He turned the faucet on. "I don't want to scare you, but . . ." He noticed his hands were shaking as he was trying to drink his water. He immediately set his glass on the counter. "But the reason I'm here early is because I received another page from the manuscript. And it said that . . . that you would be here, reading this, when I came home."

Kathy rose from the table, pages in hand. "Jonathan, I—"

Jonathan cut her off by grabbing her shoulders as gently as he knew how with the emotions that flooded his body. "I don't know how this is happening. I don't know. I've never been so scared in my life." Jonathan's eyes were wide and fearful. "How can someone know all of this about me? Is it a ghost? Is it God?"

Kathy shook her head, touched his face, and then laid her head on his shoulder. Jonathan held her tightly and before long they found themselves weeping. After a moment, Jonathan moved her a bit back so he could see her face. "It can't be a ghost. And it can't be God. God wouldn't come down here and open a life up like a book, would He?"

Kathy smiled a little. "Well, He did once. A couple of thousand years ago."

Jonathan moved away from her so he could think. He shook his head. "I've never heard of anything like this. Ever. It's not God. It can't be. So the next logical person is Clyde. He's got to be the writer. I'm going to go find him right now."

As Jonathan turned, Kathy grabbed his shoulder. "Wait."

"What is it?"

"Do you have to go now?"

"Now is as good a time as any. I've got to stop this madness. I feel like I'm going insane. Kathy, someone is predicting every move

I make, and they're right on. Right on! How is that possible?"

"Well, how could it be Clyde? He doesn't have any supernatural powers. He's just an old guy . . . and a good friend, I might add. Why are you so certain it's him?"

"Because he's the best shot I have." Jonathan threw up his hands and headed for the door.

Kathy stood a few feet away, her arms wrapped around herself to protect her from the blast of cold that would enter their house when he opened the front door.

"Kathy, I'm going to stop this once and for all."

Kathy touched him lightly before he opened the door, causing him to turn around. "Honey, don't be too hard on him."

Jonathan's head tilted to the side. "Why not? He's made my life miserable. He's acting like a psychopath. Why shouldn't I be hard on him?"

Kathy cleared her throat. "I'm just saying . . . I mean, it has helped us, hasn't it?" Jonathan's eyebrows raised in question. "Well, hasn't it? I mean, who knows what would've happened if you hadn't gotten those pages. Maybe you would've had an affair."

Jonathan opened the front door. "I don't know. But this is flat-out crazy. He's crazy for doing it."

Kathy reached for him. "You don't know it's him."

"I'm going to prove it today, if I have to tie him up and make him confess."

Kathy followed him out the door. "But . . . but . . ."

Jonathan turned around. "What, Kathy? Why are you sticking up for him?"

"I'm not," she said, shivering in the cold. "I'm just . . . it's just that . . . well, you really need his book, don't you?"

Jonathan sighed, so frustrated he wasn't even aware that a north wind had picked up and was blowing snow against him. "I don't know. I don't know what I need more. My sanity or another bestseller."

Kathy warmed her hands with her breath. "Just don't go crazy on him. That's all I'm saying."

Jonathan leaned forward and kissed her on the mouth, then continued to walk to the car as Kathy made her way back inside.

He was opening his car door when something suddenly dawned on him. He rushed back inside, meeting Kathy in the hallway.

"What is it?" she asked.

"This morning, you said that you thought I had a meeting. You said it was on my desk calendar in my study." Kathy nodded. "But I didn't have a meeting. With anyone."

Jonathan moved past her into the study. He moved a couple of books off the top of his calendar and then saw it. A large *9 a.m.* written on today's date and circled with bright blue ink.

Jonathan stumbled backward into Kathy, then turned toward her. His eyes stung with bitter, fierce anger as he whispered, "That's not my handwriting. He's been in our house."

CHAPTER 20

Jonathan took Kathy by the arm and rushed her to the kitchen. He grabbed her keys off the kitchen counter and opened the door leading to the garage.

"Jonathan—"

"Hush. You're leaving. We're leaving. You've got your car phone?"

"Yes, but—"

"Call the school. Go pick up the girls. Where's Sophie? At Susie's?"

"Yes, but—"

"Pick them all up. Meet me at the office, down in the parking lot. I'll call you to let you know what time." He opened her car door for her and all but pushed her inside.

"Jonathan, I think we should—"

Jonathan bent down to her level, and with eyes lit up with the fury of a frightened man, he said, "Kathy. I'm not going to tell you again. Get out of here. Now. Get the girls. Now. He's been in our house. Don't you understand what that means?"

Kathy started her car. "Where are you going?"

"Just go!"

Kathy's car slowly backed out of the garage, her eyes fearful and anxious. She continued to back down the driveway. "Don't speed!" Jonathan called after her, but he doubted that she heard him.

After he couldn't see her car any longer, Jonathan raced back into the house, rushed to his study, and unlocked the drawer in which he'd hidden his gun. His fingers trembled as he loaded it with the three additional bullets that lay at the back of the drawer. He wondered if he even remembered how to shoot a gun with any accuracy. He hadn't shot one in years, not since he was a boy out at the farm.

As he loaded the last bullet, he thought to himself that he wouldn't need to be that great of an aim. The person he was going to see was too old to run from him.

Jonathan felt sick. Paranoia had overtaken him. And he knew good and well he could never shoot Clyde Baxter.

The fifty-minute drive to Clyde's house could take less when the speed limit was exceeded but not pushed over ten more miles per hour. Twenty miles of that stretch of highway was known as "blue lights" for all the cops that set speed traps there. Jonathan thought it better to drive five miles per hour under since he had a loaded weapon in his possession.

He still didn't have all the pieces to the puzzle, and in a short moment of honesty, he managed to admit he barely had any pieces. He didn't know how Clyde could possibly know about his past. His parents were dead, so researching that part of his life would be useless. His present, though, was another situation. He didn't know how, but Clyde could definitely get most of that information if he worked hard enough. He was famous for his meticulous research on all of his novels. One *New York Times* review said, "His detail and accuracy is astonishingly readable. Maybe Ludlum and Clancy should take note." That was what Clyde did best . . . write smart enough to impress the critics, yet simple enough for most everyone to enjoy.

And Jonathan noted to himself that he wasn't just pulling Clyde as a suspect out of thin air. Too many coincidences pointed to him. For one, a manuscript just "happened" to appear in his mailbox.

And then Clyde just "accidentally" stumbled upon Jonathan's conversation in Sydney's cubicle. Not to mention the continuous hounding of his drinking, marriage, and life-style. How many times can a man tell you to go to church? Oh yes, and then there was the fact that he happened to be at the house the night another manila envelope showed up on his car.

Jonathan touched the gun next to him in the passenger's seat. Why did he even have the stupid thing? Maybe he would just use it as a threat. Was he crazy?

The gun's metal was cold against Jonathan's fingertips, and he suddenly realized he hadn't even turned the heat on in the car. His hands were like ice as he manipulated the knobs to get the heat going. For the first time he realized his teeth were chattering, but he didn't know if it was due to the cold air.

Jonathan was tucking the gun into the waistband of his pants as he turned onto the old dirt road that now had gravel on it in an attempt to keep the dust down. The tires of his SUV slipped a little due to his accelerated speed. He was trying to straighten out and pull his sun visor down all at once. The sun blinded him like a spotlight.

As he shaded his eyes and found the center of the road again, he came to a screeching halt all at once. The sight before him took his breath away. About a hundred yards down the gravel and dirt road that led straight to Clyde's old two-story house was a crowd of police cars, an ambulance, and a fire truck, their blue and red lights made brighter in the sun's white-hot backdrop.

Jonathan locked his hands around his steering wheel and hit the accelerator. As he approached, he remembered he had his gun on him. He reached and tried to open the glove compartment, but the sun blinded him again and the reach was too far, so he gave up quickly, before he crashed into a police vehicle. Instead, he took it out and placed it gently under the driver's-side seat.

Jonathan pulled onto the grass of Clyde's front yard and quickly got out of his car. A few photographers had gathered near a police car and seemed particularly interested in the new visitor. An officer approached and stopped Jonathan from going any farther.

"What's going on?"

"Who are you?"

"Jonathan Harper." Jonathan tried to peek around the large man to get a better view.

"A relative?"

"No." Jonathan finally looked the officer in the eyes. "I'm his editor."

The officer looked away, glancing around for any other officer nearby. "I'm sorry, sir."

"What's happened? Is he okay? Are you arresting him?"

The officer cocked his head and paused slightly before answering, "No. I'm sorry, but Mr. Baxter passed away during the night."

Jonathan's knees buckled, and the officer caught him under the arm and helped him to the hood of a nearby police car. Jonathan's stomach cramped so hard he winced in pain.

"Sir? Are you okay?"

Jonathan looked up at the officer. "How . . . how did he die?"

The officer was flagging down a paramedic for some water. "It's hard to say. Probably a heart attack." The paramedic brought a small cup over, and the officer handed it to Jonathan. "I've read every single one of his books. I was a big fan. It must've been an honor to be the man's editor."

Jonathan tossed the water aside and tried to stand upright. "I need to go in."

"Stay right here." The officer walked away for a few moments, disappearing behind the fire truck, then reemerging with another man dressed in a suit. "This is Mr. Baxter's editor," the officer told the man.

The man looked Jonathan up and down and said, "Do you have any identification on you?"

Jonathan felt for his wallet. He must've left it at the office. Jonathan sighed in frustration as he held out his empty hands. "Sir, I left in a hurry. I . . . I was supposed to be meeting with Clyde. I was running late."

The man in the suit dismissed the officer with a quick wave of his hand and then said, "Does Mr. Baxter have any living relatives?"

Jonathan held his stomach and tried to think. "He doesn't have any children. He's a widower. I think he might have a sister in

Oregon, but he doesn't speak of her much. I'm not sure." Jonathan waited for another painful cramp to pass, then said, "We were sort of Clyde's family."

"We?" the man asked.

"My wife. My children. I've been Clyde's editor . . . and friend"—he swallowed back a sour lump of guilt—"for twenty years."

The man glanced over at Jonathan's car. "How about an insurance verification card or something?"

Jonathan swallowed hard, remembering the gun under his seat. He carefully made his way to the passenger's side of the vehicle, thankful he had not put the weapon in the glove compartment. He opened it up, making sure his body blocked any view inside the vehicle, just in case his gun had slid out from underneath the seat. He found his registration and handed it over.

The man took a quick glance at it and then said, "Follow me."

Jonathan shut his car door and followed the man up the old back porch. He lingered a moment, looking out at the pond, touching the porch swing, smiling at the old battered wicker furniture that Clyde had been so proud of. The anger he had been feeling toward Clyde was pushed to the side by the good memories that surfaced.

The man in the suit glanced back as he held the screen door open.

"Give me a minute." Jonathan's voice choked into a whisper, and the man nodded and disappeared behind the rickety screen door.

Jonathan wasn't sure he wanted to go in. He wasn't sure what he would see. He had come here to confront Clyde about being the writer of the manuscript about his life, and now he had to confront the fact that his oldest, dearest friend was dead. Jonathan sat down in Clyde's favorite wicker rocker, buried his face in his hands, and wept uncontrollably. He didn't care who heard, and he never saw the occasional hand on his shoulder or pat on the back. All he wanted to do was cry.

So many questions emerged with every tear he shed. Why had Clyde written the manuscript in the first place? Why hadn't he just talked to him? Even with all the pain Jonathan was feeling, a sense of relief passed through his knotted muscles—relief that this nightmare was now over, sadly because Clyde was now dead.

Jonathan stuck the palms of his hands into his eyes to try to stop the tears, but it was useless. His whole body was crying. A lot had to get out, and he knew it. Grief, mixed with relief and confusion, swirled in and out of his mind with every breath he took.

"Mr. Harper?"

Jonathan looked up and the man in the suit was at the screen door again.

"I'm sorry to disturb you. The medical examiner needs to go ahead and move the body. Did you want to . . . to come in before . . . ?"

Jonathan nodded so the man didn't have to stumble over any more words. His heavy body almost didn't come out of the chair, and he felt his feet drag as he walked into the house. With each step was the familiar creak of the wooden floors, and the bold smell of pine caused Jonathan to close his eyes for a moment to let it penetrate his pores. It was like walking into a place where he had lived before. Ghosts from the past echoed in every room he passed. The kitchen rang with laughter and the clink of cold Cokes in glass bottles, the only way Clyde liked them. The living room almost seemed to emit a warmth as he remembered all the crackling fires they had enjoyed while talking about book ideas and drinking eggnog, a staple all year round in Clyde's refrigerator. They passed the dining room, which was on the left, and the sun presented a buffet of light across the top of the table.

The man guided Jonathan to the right, where a familiar hallway led them toward Clyde's bedroom. On the right, across from the small bathroom that always had a candle burning in it, was Clyde's study. It faced west, so it was darker than the other rooms, plus the shades were pulled. As he glanced in while passing, he saw no more than the shadows of a desk, a chair, and a bookcase. And, he noticed, the candle in the bathroom wasn't lit. His heart sank as he watched the man in the suit open Clyde's bedroom door.

Jonathan's feet felt heavy as lead, and it took him a moment to pick up each leg and move four feet forward into the doorway.

Inside, a tall, scholarly looking man with thin gray hair that hung over his ears was buttoning up a white lab coat he wore. When he stepped aside, Jonathan could see Clyde's lifeless body covered by a large gray sheet, lying on the left side of his double bed.

In a corner of the room, the man in the suit was speaking softly to the man in the white lab coat, and before long, the room was empty of all the people who had been there before. The man in the suit walked over to Jonathan and said, "We'll give you a couple of minutes alone, but then we really need to proceed."

Jonathan nodded thankfully, and soon the room was completely quiet. Only the soft milling sound of people on the other side of the house could be heard, but it sounded more like the hum of Clyde's old refrigerator, so it brought him a little comfort.

Jonathan had seen a few dead people in his life. He had viewed the bodies of both his mother and father when they had died. He had never seen Jason's body. His parents never allowed him in the viewing room at the mortuary. And once, while at lunch in the city, he saw a man get hit by a cab and die on the street.

But none of those experiences made looking at Clyde any easier. He knew he needed to do it. For closure. After all, several times as he sat on the bed, he swore he saw Clyde's chest move up and down.

To the left of Clyde's body, on the bedside table, sat a large framed picture of his wife, dressed in her best church clothes and glowing like light hitting a strand of pearls. Next to the picture were a neatly folded tissue, two small pills, and a glass of water. Jonathan picked up the picture of Clyde's wife and wondered what kind of woman she was. She looked so happy, as if she was the proudest woman in the world. Jonathan wondered if Kathy would look that way when she was that old. He figured Clyde had a lot to do with that woman's confidence. He knew a husband could make or break the whole identity of a woman.

Carefully setting the picture down, he now could hear some feet shuffling outside in the hallway and figured everyone would soon be back in. His heart beat faster as he moved a little closer to Clyde so he could grab the top of the sheet. With trembling fingers, he gently took the edges of the sheet and peeled them back over Clyde's chest.

Clyde looked peaceful. His color was paler than normal, but he still had a little color in his cheeks. His lips were arched upward, not quite into a smile, but enough to indicate his last thoughts in this life were good ones.

His pajamas were buttoned all the way to the top, and Jonathan figured it had been a cold night for him. The house's heater never worked well, and Clyde never seemed to care too much. *"You can always add layers,"* he would say as everyone complained about it.

Jonathan's throat was tight, and he clenched his jaw to try to find words and hold back tears all at the same time. Outside, he could hear the man in the suit's voice becoming louder. He knew he didn't have much time.

"Well," he managed, though the tears trickled with little control down his cheeks. "I came here for one final confrontation about the manuscript you've been sending me. You know which one I'm talking about. The story about my life." Jonathan paused to gather himself and his emotions. "I don't know how you did it. But I'll find out. I just wish you hadn't passed on—" His voice cracked. "I just wish you could answer me." Jonathan wept into his own hands as he continued. "Why? That's all I needed to know. Why, Clyde? Why?" He closed his eyes and let the tears dry a little before continuing. "The funny thing is, as crazy as this sounds, that stupid manuscript probably saved my marriage. Maybe even saved me. I don't know. I don't know what would've happened if I hadn't read my life as it unfolded." He laughed a little. "You were always good at research. Everyone knows that. But I still can't figure out how you knew all that about me. Some things, sure, I can understand how you might acquire that information. But others . . . others were private. And the people who would know are . . . dead."

Jonathan's hand moved to Clyde's shoulder. He was just about to say his good-byes—good-byes he had no idea how to say—when the door opened and several men entered the room, including the man in the suit.

"I'm sorry, Mr. Harper. We really should get to the morgue. I hope you'll understand."

"Of course," Jonathan said, standing up from the bed and moving out of the way of the crowd of people who were now gathering around Clyde's body.

Another man, a little less well dressed but authoritative looking, approached Jonathan. "A horde of reporters is out there. You're the editor, right?"

Jonathan nodded.

"You want to make a statement or something?"

Jonathan's eyes were swollen and heavy. "No," he said, giving them a good rub. "Tell them to contact Nellie Benson at the publishing house. She's the executive editor."

The man nodded, exited, and was quickly replaced by the man in the suit again. "Listen, let me escort you out."

Jonathan stepped into the hallway where it was quieter. "I was wondering. Clyde was in the middle of a manuscript that he was working on. I really need to go to his study and see exactly how many pages he has completed. We would have to come back and do that anyway, so I might as well do it now." The man in the suit hesitated. "I can have you call the house and confirm, if you would like. But a whole lot of people are going to be upset about this, and it might just be easier to take care of it now."

The man nodded and said, "All right. Go ahead. Let me know when you are finished." They walked a few feet to the study. "Where will all of his possessions go? He doesn't have any family, you say?"

Jonathan flipped on the light in the study. "Clyde probably has a will. He was organized in every part of his life except his writing. He has pages scattered all over the place in here. I may be a while."

"Take your time. We'll be here for another hour at least."

Jonathan excused himself into the study and quietly shut the door. It was true that he did need to find out how much of the manuscript was complete. He prayed all of it was and that Clyde just hadn't gotten around to sending the rest. But the real reason he wanted access to his study was to find out any information he could about why and how Clyde had written the story about his life. Though he was thankful he wouldn't be receiving any more pages, Jonathan knew it would haunt him until he had the answers he needed.

He slowly lowered the blinds to the windows as completely as they would go, which wasn't much further, and turned on the small lamp on the edge of the desk. He smiled at the old typewriter, partially covered with a sweater draped across the top, that sat on a small table next to his desk. Clyde had never learned to use the typewriter properly, and it frustrated him so much that he once pushed it off the table and it crashed into the ground. Ever since then the *w* had not worked and the manual return had to be pushed with two hands. But Clyde never gave it up, because there was one thing that he used the typewriter for, and that was for his title and dedication pages. For some odd reason, he insisted on typing out his own dedication page, an endearing quirk that made him who he was. No one ever questioned it.

He sat down in the chair, but as he did it tilted and he almost fell out. Jonathan remembered Clyde had mentioned he might need to get a new chair because a wheel had fallen off his and it was a little unstable. That had to have been six years ago.

He carefully scooted closer to the desk and began to try to figure out which piles he should be looking in. Clyde was notorious for his clutter, and when the photographer came to take the famous photo that now appeared on the back cover of every single one of his books, it had to be cropped so badly due to the mess surrounding him that they lost his shoulders on either side of the photo. Clyde always joked that it made him look thinner. But he had also demanded the photo be taken at the desk where he wrote, even though the photographer had desperately wanted him to pose in front of the pond as the sun set.

The desk was still a mess of pencils, rubber bands, erasers, and three different dictionaries. On top of the tallest pile was a Bible open to the book of John and written in as if he might have tried to write the book himself.

The pile closest to him consisted of a lot of white lined notebook paper, bound together with three thin rubber bands. Jonathan unwrapped it, one of the rubber bands snapping and stinging him on the hand, and thumbed through the pages. He realized that this pile was the handwritten version of the manuscript pages Jonathan already had. Years ago, the house finally convinced Clyde to hire someone to type out his work so it could be easily read by everyone involved. He did it, but not without kicking and screaming all the way. He finally found a nice young college student who typed one hundred ten words a minute and needed a little extra money, and everyone had joked through the years—she was now married with three children—that the only thing that had booted Clyde into this century was a pretty brunette who bleached her hair blond. The woman still typed his manuscripts to this day *and* was now his housekeeper.

"I'm a sucker for blondes," Clyde once told Jonathan when he had asked him why every lead female in his books was blond. Jonathan made a mental note to talk to her soon. He hadn't thought of it before, but it was likely she was the one typing out all the pages about him for Clyde.

Jonathan pushed that pile aside and chuckled a little at the fact that the wood on the edges of his desk was being held together with masking tape. This was certainly not a man who needed a beautiful environment to write in.

Jonathan thumbed through a few more piles, hoping to find any clue that would indicate Clyde was the writer. As he was wading through it all, he stumbled across a folder marked *Notes* written in Clyde's sloppy handwriting across three other headings that had been crossed out.

He opened the folder and several pieces of loose paper fell out and floated to the ground. Trying not to fall out of the chair, Jonathan gathered them all up and set them in front of him. He figured they were notes for the book he was writing currently, maybe some information on serial killers, the FBI, or district attorneys. But as Jonathan read closer, he realized that every single note within the folder was a piece of Scripture. One read, in shaky, arthritic handwriting, *1 John 2:2: He Himself is the propitiation for our sins.* Another, written on a yellow sticky note, said, *John 18:12: So the Roman cohort and the commander, and the officers of the Jews, arrested Jesus and bound Him.*

Jonathan thumbed through more notes, and every single one of them was a passage of Scripture. One, written in large handwriting and underlined, read, *John 19:10-11: Pilate therefore said to Him, "You do not speak to me? Do You not know that I have authority to release You, and I have authority to crucify You?" Jesus answered, "You would have no authority over Me, unless it had been given you from above; for this reason he who delivered Me up to you has the greater sin."*

Jonathan sighed, trying to make sense of it all. Why in the world would Clyde have a folder full of Scripture? Then Jonathan saw a piece of paper that made him set everything else down. It was white paper, and the Scripture was written neatly in the middle of the page in dark red ink. It read, *Isaiah 61:1: The Spirit of the Lord God is upon me, because the Lord has anointed me to bring good news to the afflicted; He has sent me to bind up the broken-hearted, to proclaim liberty to the captives, and freedom to prisoners.* The words *prisoners* and *freedom* were underlined with dark blue ink, and at the bottom of the page was a large star. Jonathan flipped the page over and was astonished to find many more Scriptures. *Luke 4:18: He has sent Me to proclaim release to the captives. Zechariah 9:11-12: As for you also, because of the blood of My covenant with you, I have set your prisoners free from the waterless pit. Return to the stronghold, O prisoners who have the hope; This very day I am declaring that I will restore double to you.*

Jonathan continued to sift through the notes, and every single piece of paper in there, from what he could tell, had Scripture on it. After a few minutes, he finally closed the folder, perplexed by what he had found. Why in the world would he have a folder full of verses from the Bible? Was this a clue he needed?

Jonathan set the folder aside carefully and continued to wade through the mess. The rest of the desk proved no more helpful. Scrap pieces of paper, notes from a book three years ago, and a sack of unopened fan mail was just about all he found.

"He hasn't finished the book," Jonathan said, hoping his words weren't true but unable to find anything that would indicate otherwise. Still, he had a lot more to go through: file drawers, cabinets, and several piles stacked on the floor near his desk. What was he going to do if it wasn't finished? Clyde's manuscript was all he was hanging on to, and since there was no synopsis it would be hard to find a ghostwriter to finish it. His job was at stake on this one.

Jonathan returned his focus to finding clues from the other manuscript. So far, nothing odd had turned up, other than the folder of notes from the Bible. Jonathan opened every drawer in the room. The door opened and the man in the suit peeked in.

"Mr. Harper, we're just about to wrap up here." Jonathan nodded. "Um, we did get ahold of Nellie Benson. She asked us to relay a message to you. She would like you to come to the office as soon as possible."

"Sure. Thank you."

"She was pretty torn up by the whole thing."

"I'll be right out."

The man shut the door and Jonathan stood in the middle of the room, scanning it with his tired eyes, trying to find something, anything, that would link Clyde with the manuscript about his life. After a few more moments of no luck, Jonathan decided he would leave and maybe come back the next day.

But just before he turned to open the door, something caught his eye. He didn't know why he missed it before. Perhaps he had been at a bad angle. But from where he stood now, he realized that underneath that heavy sweater on the typewriter was a single sheet of white paper.

He gently picked up the sweater, remembering how much that old thing meant to Clyde, and then sat down at the typewriter. He slowly pulled the paper out and read it.

> For Jonathan,
> may you find the light
> that has al ays shined for you
> and may it reveal itself
> in the pages that you have read
> and guide you to your first love.

Jonathan let out a breath that felt as if it had been held in for weeks. He read and reread the six simple lines, then laughed weakly as he read them one more time. This was it! This was his clue. This was what must be the dedication page for the manuscript he had been writing about Jonathan's life. It didn't answer a lot of questions, but it did answer one. Clyde was the author of that manuscript, and though many things remained unanswered, Jonathan knew one thing for sure. He would, thank God, never receive another manila envelope containing pages about his life again.

CHAPTER 21

Kathy's van sat idling near his assigned parking spot. She was out of her car before Jonathan could get out of his, and they met halfway on the sidewalk. Kathy rushed into his arms and Jonathan held her for a moment. Then Kathy looked up at him.

"What happened?" She held his hands. "Did anything bad happen?"

Jonathan couldn't keep his bottom lip from trembling, but he managed to keep the pool of tears in his eyes in check, at least for now.

"Jonathan?" She squeezed his hands as her eyes grew larger. "What happened? Please don't tell me that . . . that . . ."

"It's over."

"It's over?" Kathy barely managed.

"Yes. Clyde's the writer. I have proof."

"But—"

"Kathy," he said, holding up a finger to stop her from going on. "There's something very important I have to tell you. Something very sad."

By this point, Kathy couldn't even speak and she was holding her breath, so Jonathan thought he'd better continue quickly.

"Honey, when I got to Clyde's house, there were police cars, an ambulance and . . . a fire truck. . . ."

Kathy covered her mouth with her hands.

"Clyde . . . died in his sleep last night."

Her uncontrollable sobs were loud enough for everyone in the parking lot to hear. Jonathan grasped her around the shoulders and led her back toward her van where the kids were plastered to the windows, watching everything.

"I can't believe it," she said through loud sobs. "Clyde is dead?"

"Yes, honey. He died peacefully." He laughed a little to try to hold back the tears that were threatening to escape. "In his favorite pajamas."

Kathy shook her head. "What are we going to tell the girls? They'll be devastated."

Jonathan stopped her a few yards away from the van. "We just have to tell them the truth. But I don't want them to know Clyde was the one who . . . well, you know. They don't need to know that."

Kathy glanced back at the van and said, "But, honey, I need to—"

"Sweetheart, Nellie's a wreck, and I'm going to have to go upstairs and figure out what's going to happen with Clyde's book." Jonathan stuck his hands in his pockets to try to get the feeling back to them since he had left his coat at the office earlier. "I'm not sure he has finished his book. Maybe he was too busy on another piece of work."

Kathy didn't find that funny, but Jonathan was past the point of caring too much about what people were thinking of him. He'd stood on the edge of sanity and dangled one foot into the black hole.

"Please, honey. I know it's going to be hard, but I've got to get to the office. The press is going to be here any minute, and Nellie's going to need help trying to figure all this out."

Kathy wiped her nose on her sleeve and zipped her coat up as high as it would go. "The girls are going to be so upset."

"I know, I know." Jonathan hugged her again. "But you can go home now. It's safe. And I'll be home as soon as I can. Let's plan on still going to Eleanor's early, okay?"

Jonathan walked her the rest of the way to the van, avoiding the peering faces stuck to the slightly tinted glass. He opened the van door for her, but before she got in, she said, "What did you find that made you so sure Clyde was this writer?"

Jonathan took the piece of paper that had been in Clyde's type-writer from the pocket of his pants and, without unfolding it, handed it to her and said, "I'll be home soon."

Jonathan couldn't look back to see what was going on in the van. He figured Kathy would have to tell the girls right then and there, and he couldn't bear to see all four of them crying at once. Besides, his feelings for Clyde were mixed right now, and if he wasn't careful, he might say something he would regret.

As soon as the elevator doors opened to his floor, he knew everyone there had gotten word of Clyde's death. As he stepped out, a few people tried to act busy and not stare, but most everyone else had completely stopped what they were doing. Jonathan straightened himself up and pretended not to notice, which was pretty silly, but it was the best he could do at the moment. He was never so glad to see Edie in his life.

She stood at her desk and said, "Jonathan, I'm . . . I don't know what to say." She tossed her gum in the wastebasket as a sign of solemnness. "Nellie wanted to see you right away."

Jonathan acknowledged that with a nod and gently shut the door behind him. He stood there for a long moment, trying not to cry, trying to make sense of it all. He couldn't take his eyes off the large eight-by-ten photo of him and Clyde at a banquet in 1989 hon-oring Clyde as "American Writer of the Century."

He walked slowly to his window, his body as heavy as if there were two of him, and looked down at the parking lot. Kathy's van was gone, but now a swarm of media had gathered. Jonathan sighed, thankful he was already in the building.

He folded his fingers together and placed his hands gently to his mouth, as if he might pray. But instead, he felt the urgency to go see Nellie. He knew she would be a wreck. Five years ago her sister had died in a car accident, and she had to take three months off to recover.

Jonathan opened his door and quietly made his way down the

long hallway toward Nellie's office. A couple of people nodded at him as he passed, and he was nearly there when Carl Osburg came out of the bathroom, nearly knocking him over. His hand reached for Jonathan's shoulder.

"Jonathan . . ." The toe of Carl's shoe suddenly found something interesting on the floor to trace.

"I guess you heard."

"Yeah. Everyone here did. Nellie got a call from some guy from the medical examiner's office. She's not doing well."

"I know. I'm going to see her right now."

Carl nodded, still awfully interested in the green carpet underneath him. "That will help. You and Nellie were the closest to him." In rare, emotional boldness, Carl managed to look him in the eye. "I know he was like a father to you."

Carl patted Jonathan on the back and stepped aside so Jonathan could move down the hall. As he rounded the corner, several people were milling about outside Nellie's office. One of her assistant editors, Mark Stewart, glanced up to see Jonathan and got the attention of the others so they would move out of the way.

Jonathan shook his hand. "How is she?"

"She'll be better now that you're here. She's . . . she's pretty torn up." Jonathan looked at the crowd around him, and Mark added, "She wanted to be alone."

"Oh. Should I go in?"

"Most definitely," and he opened the door for him.

Inside, Nellie was collapsed on her desk, her head turned to the side with a tissue near her nose. As soon as her door opened, she sat up, saw Jonathan, and wailed hysterically. Jonathan moved nearer and offered open arms, which Nellie jumped into and wailed even harder.

"I can't believe it! I can't believe it!" she said, her mascara running down her face like a pen leaking ink.

"Well, Nellie, he was an old man." Jonathan grabbed another tissue and dabbed her eyes.

"But he was so healthy. It just came so suddenly." She blew her nose and returned to her chair. "I mean, I'm brokenhearted and scared to death."

Jonathan knew she was talking about the house. Clyde was their premier writer. They had tried to find bankable writers over the years, but no one matched Clyde. No one came close. And now they were without their money-maker. Even though he had already retired, this was very final.

Jonathan sat on the edge of her desk. "Well, we know his death will get a lot of publicity, so that will help boost sales for a while anyway." Jonathan hoped he didn't sound too callous.

Nellie cried harder. "Listen to me. How heartless. Thinking about the house!" She wiped her eyes, smearing her mascara up to her forehead and past her temples. "What about you? Are you okay? You seem okay. But I know Clyde was like . . . like a father to you."

Jonathan winced at that phrase. Why did everyone keep saying that? If only they had known what his father had been like. Besides, Clyde had been his nightmare, not a father, for a month now. "I've had some time to process it after I left his house. I took a slow drive here to the office."

Nellie nodded and propped her head up with her hands on her forehead, covering up her face, which wasn't that nice to look at right now anyway. But after a few seconds, she looked up at him. "Shoot me for asking this at this moment, but is the last book finished?"

"I'm still investigating," Jonathan said. "I need more time to figure out what's going on." Nellie shook her head and cried some more. "Nellie, listen, we can find a ghostwriter to finish the rest of it . . . if it's not finished." The sobs continued. "I'm sure it is, though."

"I know," she said between sobs, "but it's such a risk. I mean, releasing a new book from a dead bestselling author in a whole new genre? It could ruin everything we've built Clyde to be."

"Or it could work for us. It could work really well for us." *And I need this*, he said silently.

Nellie looked up. "I'll be very interested in hearing the proposal." Nellie buzzed Mark in and the door opened immediately. "Mark, when is the funeral?"

"Friday at ten A.M."

Nellie looked at Jonathan. "I had Mark and Tina work on the

283

memorial arrangements and contact *Publishers Weekly*. We all know Clyde doesn't have any family left." She wiped her eyes again. "He had mentioned to me before that he didn't have anyone who would even be able to plan a funeral for him. Family-wise. But his pastor's taking care of it."

She leaned back in her chair and let out a frustrated breath. "It's hard to believe, isn't it? He's got a million-reader following and hardly anyone to plan his funeral." The tears started running again, and Mark shifted uncomfortably. "Mark, let's order yellow roses for the funeral, too, okay? I think that's perfect, since *Little Woman of the West* had a big yellow rose on the front. Don't you?" She looked at Jonathan.

"Sure. Sounds wonderful."

"I'll take care of everything, Nellie. Don't worry," Mark said and left the office.

Jonathan waited for him to shut the door. "Nel, I need some time off." He always used "Nel" when he needed it to be very personal. "I'm going north to spend some time with my aunt."

Nellie grabbed for another tissue and threw the box to the ground when she came up empty-handed. She buzzed Mark again. "Mark. Bring me another box." Jonathan was amazed he would know what that meant. Then she turned back to him and said, "Of course. I know this is so hard for you. Take all the time you need." Her eyebrows rose as she poked at her falling French twist. "Are you *really* okay? No offense, but you were a little . . . off . . . before this happened. Now . . ." Her voice trailed off into more sobs.

"Really. I'm fine."

Mark entered with another box of Kleenex. "Anything else, Nellie?"

"No. Thank you. Wait. Order me a Reuben from Sammy's. Extra—"

"—kraut. I know." Mark quietly shut the door again.

"You've got him trained well," Jonathan said with a small smile.

Nellie laughed through her tears. "He's insecure and a kiss-up. I love him to death." She opened the day-planner on her desk. "Let's move our editorial meeting to Monday. Is that okay?"

"Fine."

Nellie buzzed out again. "Mark? Mark!"

A softer voice came over the speaker. "He's not here."

"Where is he?"

A short pause was followed by, "He went to get you a sandwich."

Nellie lowered her head and said, "Send him in when he gets back." She hit the button again with unneeded force.

"Maybe you should take some time off as well," Jonathan suggested in his softest, most reassuring voice, the one he used when Kathy was in hysterics over something that *might* be worth thinking twice about.

Nellie threw down her pencil. "What a Thanksgiving, hmm? Yeah, maybe I will. I hate Thanksgiving." She met Jonathan's questioning look with, "What? You want me to bow my head and thank whomever that Lester ran off with a blonde half his age and half my weight?" Jonathan laughed a little, and Nellie relaxed. "Don't forget Monday. We can't delay it any more than that."

"All right. I'll see you then."

Before Jonathan left, Nellie said, "Jonathan?" He turned around. "Are you still going to be presenting that manuscript from Zippy?" Her fingers found their way into her French twist, which was now not in a twist at all.

"Yes." He wasn't sure where the confidence came from, probably from the fact that he had nothing to lose now, but it was enough for Nellie to give him that reassuring smile he had missed for so long. He just hoped that was not the last time he would see it.

Winter had hit New York, and a soft blanket of snow showed itself near Newburgh. The children were buckled in their seat belts, trying to find creative ways to stay belted in—an unbendable family rule—and still be able to move as much as possible.

Jonathan and Kathy talked quietly in the front seat, discussing Clyde's death, what the funeral might be like, and Jonathan's ideas for how to save the manuscript. There were moments of silence, too, but it wasn't the kind of silence that had plagued their marriage for the last year. It was a silence of comfort and familiarity, underlined with occasional knowing glances when the girls would all giggle at once or a landmark would catch their eye.

In those quiet times, within his own personal thoughts, he thanked a God he wasn't sure was listening that he had his family together and that they were all okay. Over and over in his mind he replayed how close he had come to throwing his marriage away. He even allowed himself to think about what it might have been like without his three girls. It made his stomach hurt, but it was that sort of torture that he decided would keep him on the straight and narrow. Never again would he dance so close to temptation.

In the longer moments of silence, though he didn't want to entertain these particular thoughts, he couldn't stop thinking about why Clyde would do such a thing to him. Why would he have tormented him with that manuscript? Had he felt he had hit a dead end by just talking to him? There was so much about all of it that was still a mystery, it made his head hurt. And his heart, too. A man that he had once considered a father had betrayed him in a way that could well be unforgivable. Jonathan hadn't decided yet. Perhaps what he needed most was an understanding of his motivation. Clyde had loved him so much through the years. How could it all end like this?

"Think we'll have a white Christmas this year?" Kathy asked, breaking through his dark thoughts and making him concentrate hard on the road in front of him. The snow was heavier now.

He glanced over at her and smiled. "I hope so. It's been a long time since we haven't."

"I hate it when we don't." She turned the heater in the van up a notch and looked back to check on the children, who were now all asleep in awkward positions that their bodies would pay for later.

Jonathan tilted his rearview mirror down a little so he could see the girls, too. "They seem as if they're handling Clyde's death pretty well."

Kathy shrugged. "I guess. Meg took it the hardest. I think she's trying to be strong for you." Kathy glanced over at him. "She knows this is hitting you hard."

Jonathan kept his eyes on the road. "Not so hard."

Kathy held her hands in front of the vents. "Jonathan, he was like a fath—"

"Don't say it." Jonathan's stern voice stirred the children in the back. "I don't want to hear that phrase again."

Kathy kept her voice down but said, "It's true."

Large snowflakes started falling as they crossed into Kingston and melted instantly, the moisture disappearing with the movement of the wipers Jonathan had switched on. Sophie had woken up in the back and now sat quietly, gazing out at the snow with the wonder of a child. Kathy adjusted the heater again.

"I don't want to talk about Clyde," Jonathan continued. "I just don't."

Kathy paused, looking as though she wanted to say something more but patted him on the leg instead. "So have you figured out how close he was to finishing his book?"

"I think he was fairly close. He may have finished it, for all I know. You know what his office looks like. The rest of the book could be buried in a pile three feet high."

He slowed down to fifty-five miles an hour as the snow fell harder. The wonders of winter fell lightly onto the tops of the trees, and the gray skies seemed thick enough to stay for months.

"Turn your lights on," Kathy ordered, always a cautious backseat driver. Over the years Jonathan had learned to let it go and do as he was told.

"I just can't figure it out." Jonathan gripped the steering wheel as they passed a jackknifed truck in the ditch. "I can't figure out why Clyde would do that to me."

Kathy was picking balls off her sweater. She didn't seem to have any answers, either, and the rest of the drive was a quiet escape into white tranquility.

As soon as they turned into Eleanor and Earl's drive, Eleanor came running out of the house, wrapped in her wool coat, waving and carrying on like the very best aunts do. The girls had awoken twenty minutes outside Saratoga Springs and had fought and laughed the rest of the way. As soon as they saw Eleanor, their squeals were followed by the clicks of seat belts being undone.

"Put your coats on!" Kathy announced loudly, followed by Jonathan saying, "And be careful. It might be slick!"

Before Jonathan could turn off the car, the girls were out and running toward Eleanor, Sophie having trouble making it through the snow. Within seconds all three of them were in the arms of Eleanor, quite a feat for such a small woman. Kathy approached and Jonathan popped the back door to unload the suitcases.

"Jonathan!" Eleanor called. "Get in here! We can get the bags later! I've got hot chocolate and pumpkin bread waiting for everyone!" The girls laughed and cheered and made their way inside. Kathy turned around, waiting for Jonathan.

"I'll be right in," Jonathan called, barely making out their figures through the dense snow that had suddenly begun to fall. "Tell Earl to stay inside! He doesn't need to be out in this or carrying bags!"

Kathy ushered Eleanor inside, and Jonathan stood looking at the pile of suitcases in the back, wondering which ones absolutely needed to go in. But before he knew it, he was weeping, the tears on his cheeks barely noticeable to him because of the wet snow that clung to his skin. It was so hard for him to believe he would never see Clyde alive again. Even as the tears rolled, though, Jonathan wouldn't acknowledge his feelings. He brushed them away, along with the snow, and was glad it was cold outside, so his red cheeks and nose wouldn't seem out of place. He grabbed two suitcases and trudged up to the house through the snow.

The house had the aroma of a perfect Thanksgiving. The rich smell of sweet potato pie put everyone in a good mood, and all the girls were in the kitchen cutting up celery, onion, and other vegetables for the big feast the next day.

Jonathan had spent an hour or so with Earl, sitting by the fire and discussing books. Earl always loved to talk about the latest books he'd read and then pick Jonathan's brain about why he did or didn't think it should've made the bestseller list. Being a military man, Earl, as lovable as he was, tended to think he was an expert on everything. Jonathan always let him do the talking, agreed with him, and enjoyed the occasional brandy and Punch cigar that was offered.

After Eleanor had made her famous roast beef sandwiches for dinner that evening and had let the girls each taste the dessert of their choice before going to bed, Jonathan managed to find himself alone in the living room. The fire roared and crackled as if fighting to stay alive against the harsh winter weather that whistled through the chute. In the kitchen, he could hear Kathy telling Eleanor they would have to leave Thanksgiving afternoon to be home in time for Clyde's funeral. Earl had retired for the evening promptly at eight P.M. but had left the bottle of brandy out "just in case."

A large throw covered Jonathan's feet, and he sank into the plush leather recliner that was the perfect distance from the fire. He kept only the small reading lamp on next to him and pulled out Clyde's manuscript, hoping to get as much read as possible this evening. He found his place. The plot was moving fast in this story, and he couldn't wait to see if there was indeed an innocent man, and if the DA would figure out who it was.

I spent the rest of the day wandering the streets of the city. I grabbed a couple of hot dogs and prayed they wouldn't make my heartburn worse. As upset as I was about the prospect of losing my job, I was more concerned with the assessment Dr. Burrelson had made of the situation. I couldn't get the fact that there might be an innocent man on death row off my mind. Sure, I had been burned once. The man I thought was innocent had just been a lure for us all along. But what Dr. Burrelson had said made sense to me. That was the way Donomar worked. Surely it couldn't be that hard to figure out which of the two prisoners was innocent. With DNA evidence and more sophisticated crime labs, these types of cases could be more easily solved.

Esther had agreed to meet me for dinner, and I arrived at a restaurant by the name of Julio's twenty minutes early, since I had nothing else to do. The maître d' offered me a tie and confirmed the reservation that I assumed Esther had made after we hung up earlier in the day. I was seated at a corner table out of the way, but where I had a good view of the restaurant.

I drank an iced tea, and then she appeared in the doorway

and was shown to our table. I stood as her chair was pulled out for her.

"Well, Keaton, aren't you going to need something a little stronger than iced tea?" She took off her coat. "Nice tie."

"I'm not used to restaurants like this," I said, tucking in my tie. "I hope you'll order for both of us. And pay."

She laughed. "Well, since you are probably unemployed, I guess it's the only decent thing to do." The waiter approached the table, and Esther ordered some dish that sounded foreign and a strong drink for herself. She then pulled out a folder from the large bag she had set on the floor next to us.

"I've been looking over these cases all afternoon." Her expression suddenly went sour. "There's Governor Wallace. Let's see if he says 'hello.' "

I looked up as the governor passed a few feet from our table, glanced over at Esther, and moved on with no acknowledgment. "He hates my guts and I feel like a better person for it."

I didn't know how to respond to that, since it was true there were very few people who liked Esther and whom she liked, so I thought I'd better turn to business. "Did you find anything that would indicate either of these men are innocent?"

"Both proclaim innocence. That's about it." She sighed and moved the folder to the side as the waiter brought her drink. "Lincoln Smith claims he's being framed by some drug acquaintance. His story hasn't changed in ten years. His girlfriend's blood was found in the trunk of his car, and his car was found abandoned, with no tags, fifteen miles outside of town. His alibis don't add up. We prosecuted him on forensic evidence and the fact that he told his best friend he was going to kill her for sleeping with a guy by the name of Sandy."

"Sandy's a guy?"

She smiled. "I guess so."

"What about the other guy. James something?"

"Joseph James. Owned a custom furniture shop. When the police arrived they found a young college girl by the name of Christy Krennel dead next to a coffee table. James was standing over her with her blood on him."

"What was their connection? Lovers?"

"James says he doesn't know her. But he has no other alibi.

290

The guy's apparently sort of a loner. Friends say he's quiet but wouldn't hurt a mouse. No one could believe he would do it. Those are always the diabolical ones, eh?"

I shrugged. "I don't know."

"Both men have been on death row for ten years."

"What about prison records? Troublemakers?"

"Well, Lincoln Smith has been put in solitary three times. He's as mean as they come, but the warden says he got that way after coming to prison. He also says that in the last six months, he's been different. Acting . . . 'better,' " she said as she glanced down at her notes.

"Well, mean people aren't all murderers, after all," I said as an afterthought and then unintentionally glanced at her. "What about the other guy?"

Esther paused and then looked up at me. "Model prisoner. Absolutely nothing in his record. Was in no trouble before this came up." She had a strange look on her face as a frown crossed over her brow.

"What, Esther?"

She blinked a couple of times and then said, "The warden says he's the man everyone wants to see."

"What's that mean?"

"Before they're executed. He's like their chaplain or something."

"He's a preacher?"

"No. He makes furniture, like I said. But in prison, he's got a reputation of . . ." She shook her head. "I didn't get it." She drew in a stiff breath. "Michael Underwood requested he be a witness at his execution last year, and James was the last person he saw before they took him to be executed."

I raised my eyebrows. "You're kidding."

Esther took more than two sips of her drink. "And remember when we let Mitchner go? He wanted us to give a letter to one of the prisoners. That letter went to Joseph James."

"Esther, I think we—"

"Don't think anything yet," Esther said bluntly. "Last time you went with your feelings we released a guilty man. Why don't you leave the intuitions up to me, okay?"

I lowered my head, but my mind was moving fast. "What are their execution dates?"

"A week from yesterday."

I was aware my mouth was hanging wide open. "We have less than a week, Esther?"

She nodded. "And we have to make the right decision. When we ask the judge to delay the execution and review the case of the prisoner we think to be innocent, the other one will be executed on schedule. And that's *if* the judge even agrees to take a look. After the Mitchner episode, our chances are slim." The waiter appeared with our plates. "Tomorrow will be a busy day."

I looked at a plate full of buttered snails and said, "Why wait until tomorrow?"

Oliver Kittle, a small, stiff man with a thick mustache and puffy eyes, greeted me cordially as we entered his small, mildly decorated office. Esther had decided it would be best for me to go by myself. It would draw less attention, since the media was hounding her at every corner. He switched on a single light that hung overhead and sat down behind his metal desk.

"Warden Kittle, thank you for seeing me this evening."

He smiled and nodded. "What can I do for you, Agent Spade?" His accent was Deep South.

"Well, it may not be 'agent' for long. But that's neither here nor there."

Warden Kittle lifted up his chin. "They fired you for this whole mess, did they?"

"Not yet." I scooted forward in my seat. "But I'm not here about me. As you know, there is a debate as to whether or not one of the men on your death row is innocent."

The warden glanced up at his television set that was still on the news but turned down. "Hard to miss, Mr. Spade. The media's been callin' so much we had to put in a second phone line. I refuse to speak to any of them. It's not my job. But the DA's sure got herself in a mess this time, hasn't she?"

I scratched my nose. "Yes, well, I believe the person who is responsible for this mess is Dietrich Donomar."

"Yes, I heard that, too. That he's claimin' he killed one of the people that one of my prisoner's is accused of killin'. That he's had some sort of remorse for it all and doesn't want to see an innocent man die for what he did."

I folded my hands together to keep my fingers from shaking. "Well, sir, it isn't quite that noble. Donomar is a sick, cruel killer. But we do believe that he is telling the truth about this. He's trying to get us to choose the wrong man. Esther Caladaras, of course, wants to get to the bottom of this. That's why I'm here."

The warden stood, went to a file drawer, and pulled out two folders. He set them gently on his desk, found his glasses in his shirt pocket, put them on, and then looked at me. "Mr. Spade, I am responsible for the well-being of these prisoners. All of them. I am responsible for keeping the men on death row alive so they can be executed. Do you understand that?"

I hesitated. "I think so."

"So if you're going to sit here and ask me if I think one of them is innocent, I cannot answer that. I cannot afford to think of these men as guilty or innocent. I must think of them as guilty. All of them." He opened the folder. "This is the body of Mamie White, the girlfriend of Mr. Smith." He handed me the photo. It was hard to look at. She was horribly beaten and looked as if she had been strangled. Warden Kittle handed me another photo. "This is Christy Krennel, the young college student who was killed by Joseph James."

This photo was equally hard to look at. The body was naked and in an awkward position, bloody and bruised. I swallowed and held both pictures up.

"Warden Kittle, are you familiar with these cases?"

"As much as I need to be."

"Tell me about Miss White."

He glanced at the photo. "Drug user. Had a background in prostitution."

"What about this other woman? Christy Krennel?"

"Was majoring in nursing. Good student. Plenty of friends. Popular."

I looked at the photo. I noticed she had a belly button ring and a large tattooed heart on her left shoulder. "She looks a little rebellious to me."

The warden smiled. "From what I understand, Mr. Spade, that's just a trend for girls her age. From all accounts, she was a more-than-decent human being."

I nodded and handed the photos back to him. "Tell me about Mr. James. I hear he is a model prisoner."

The warden silently filed his folders away before turning back to me. "Yes. It is true."

"Tell me about him."

The warden shifted uncomfortably. "I don't know what more there is to say. He hasn't gotten into any trouble since he's been here. That's not unusual. Some men are like that."

I stiffened my posture. "Sir, there's something you're holding back." With twenty years in the FBI, I could tell when people were holding out.

The warden took off his glasses and brushed his mustache with two fingers. Then he said, "All right, Mr. Spade. I'll tell you about Mr. James. He's extraordinary."

I held my breath. "Extraordinary?"

"Yes. I've never met anyone like him. When I'm near him, there's just . . . just something about him. It's, well, it's unexplainable."

"Please try," I urged. "I understand that many of the prisoners on death row ask for him instead of the prison chaplain the day of their execution."

"It's true. And there hasn't been a man on my death row who hasn't been changed by him. At nights, sometimes, I hear them all singing old hymns . . . hymns I haven't heard in years. And when I walk down death row, there's a peace, even on the day of execution. There's a peace wherever he is."

I stood up, unable to sit any longer. "Has he been that way since the day you brought him in?"

"Yes, he has." The warden adjusted his shirt and tie. "It'll be a sorry day when I have to execute that fellow."

I turned to him. "But you must think he's the one who's innocent, Warden!"

The warden stared hard at me. "I don't have that luxury. If I thought about any one of those men being innocent, I would not be able to come to work every day. Do you understand that?" His tone was flat and hard.

"Not completely," I admitted.

"Of course you don't," he said, his voice growing anxious. "No one can understand that." He stood and pointed his finger at me. "It is not my job to decide who is guilty and innocent! It is that woman DA's job. And she's the one who put them here in the first place!"

I held my tongue for a moment and waited for the warden to catch his breath. He did and indicated he was better with a small, apologetic smile.

"Warden," I said carefully, "you must at least have some feelings toward Mr. James. Some . . . instincts."

The warden's hands made their way into the pockets of his cheap pants, and he said, "I know he was found standing over her body, covered in her blood. I also know he's an extraordinary man who I will be sad to see die. That is all I can tell you, Mr. Spade. Good night."

I shook his hand and then went to the door. As I turned the knob he stopped me by saying, "One more thing, Mr. Spade."

"Yes?"

"Mr. James has never said he was innocent."

I paused, a little taken back. "But I thought—"

"He's just never admitted being guilty."

"What does that mean?"

The warden's hands pressed down onto his desk. "Nothing to me. But maybe something to you."

The next day Esther and I walked through the prison gates and into the main waiting area. Behind us a horde of media had gathered and shouted questions at Esther. The guards let her through and kept them out.

"So we have one man who says he's not guilty and another man who doesn't say either way." Esther clicked her long fingernails together as we waited for the warden. "Why wouldn't you say either way?"

I shrugged. "I have no idea. Especially since he's the one who seems the more promising human being."

We watched as a prisoner was escorted in full chains past us. "I remember him, you know," Esther said softly.

"Who?"

"James." She stared down at the dull tile below us. "I remember he wouldn't take the stand, even though his lawyer proclaimed him innocent. Not too unusual. The story went that he had found the young girl late that night inside his furniture shop, half dead. He tried to give her CPR, and that was why he had her blood all over him."

I frowned. "Did he call the police?"

"No. The owner of the shop next door said he saw James's back door open and thought he'd check it out to make sure everything was okay. Inside he found James standing over her. She was dead."

"Did he try to flee?"

"No. He did nothing. He said nothing. Nothing at all in his own defense."

"Not exactly an argument for innocence."

Esther sighed. "He was just like what the warden said. I remember looking at him in the courtroom and there was just something . . ." She didn't finish her sentence. "Anyway, if you're innocent, you say you're innocent, and that's all there is to it."

Warden Kittle came around the corner and we stood. He shook my hand first. "Hello, Mr. Spade." He looked at Esther. "Ms. Caladaras."

"Are we ready to see Mr. James now?" Esther asked.

The warden shook his head. "Mr. James doesn't wish to see anyone. I'm sorry."

Esther and I looked at each other. Esther said, "Did you tell him that I am the DA and we're here to talk to him about his innocence—"

"I told him, Ms. Caladaras. He isn't interested."

I scratched my head and thought hard. Esther was at a loss. Then I asked, "What about Lincoln Smith? Can we talk with him now?"

The warden paused and then said, "Let me make a phone call. Please wait here."

After a few moments he returned and said, "Yes, Mr. Smith would like to see you."

We followed the warden down three long white corridors before we came to the visitors' area. We asked for a private room and the warden obliged. Before we were even seated, Lincoln Smith, a tall white man with no front teeth and long, oily hair was guided into the room, seated at the table, and chained to it.

I waited for Esther to begin. "Sir, you can have your attorney present. You know that, don't you?" Lincoln Smith sat silently. Esther pulled out a note pad and looked uneasy. "Mr. Smith, I'm Esther Caladaras and this is—"

"I know who you are," he said abruptly. "I seen both of ya on the television set." He looked at Esther. "I remember you in that courtroom."

Esther fueled her own confidence from somewhere inside. "That's right. I'm the district attorney. I prosecuted you for the murder of Mamie White."

"I didn't do it. I said that from da beginnin'." He looked at her note pad. "Write that down."

"So you say," Esther said smoothly. "You told Harley Waters you were going to kill her for cheating on you."

"People talk, missy. Don't ya'll know that?" He pulled at a piece of his hair.

"Her blood was found in the trunk of your car."

"I was set up. I didn't do it."

"You were a drug dealer, were you not, Mr. Smith?"

"Yeah. That don't mean I killed the woman."

"The woman? She was your girlfriend, Mr. Smith. Doesn't that mean something to you?"

Lincoln Smith looked around suddenly and then bit his fingernail. "I wasn't too sad she was gone, if that's what you mean. She was cheatin' on me. I knew it. She deserved it."

"She deserved to die for cheating on you? You must think awfully highly of yourself, Mr. Smith."

I smiled. Lincoln frowned, not completely following. "Don't know what you mean, missy. She's a prostitute. In the Bible, women—they were stoned to death for it. What's the big deal?"

Esther took more notes and then said, "You say you were set up. By whom?"

Lincoln Smith's face twisted into an expression of panic. His breath became shallow, and he looked us both in the eyes as he leaned forward. "I seen all this on the news. I know what's goin' on. And I tell ya somethin' else. That Donomar fella, he's the one that killed Mamie. I heard her talkin' 'bout him. She'd talk about some of her clients sometimes. I couldn't stand it, but she said it was her work. The night 'fore she was killed, she said she was with some creepy dude who was really tall. Ain't that Donomar? Ain't it?"

Esther glanced at me with disdain and then back at Lincoln. "Why didn't you mention this before, Mr. Smith?"

"Before? There wasn't nothin' to mention. She had a ton of clients. I hated all of them."

Esther stood. "Thank you. That is all."

"All? You don't believe me? Is that it? Is that it?" Two guards came in at the commotion. "I swear it's true! I swear on my mama's grave!"

Esther was closing her briefcase when I said, "I have one more question." I avoided Esther's stare and looked directly at Lincoln.

"That crazy serial killer killed Mamie and set me up. That's what happened!"

I leaned forward on the table and looked Lincoln Smith hard in the eyes, so hard he looked away twice. "Lincoln, do you think Joseph James is innocent of his crime?"

Lincoln's eyes widened with surprise and he looked over at Esther, his expression suddenly turning to worry. "What?"

"You know him, don't you?" I continued and Esther sat back down.

" 'Course I do. He's right next to my cell."

I nodded. "He's accused of killing a college girl. Do you think he did it?"

Lincoln's hands wrapped around his chains. "What's that got to do with me?"

I acted remarkably cool despite the pressure I was feeling in my chest. "Don't you know it's got everything to do with you, Lincoln? One of the two of you is innocent. Either you or him."

"Keaton, I don't think—"

I waved Esther off with a hand. Lincoln's eyes sparked with indecision. "It's quite simple. If you get off, Joseph James will lose his life next week. If he gets off, you will. Who deserves it?"

Lincoln's eyes shined with a trace of moisture. "I don't wanna die. I don't wanna die."

"That's not the question, Lincoln. The question is, do you think Joseph James is innocent of his crime?"

"He never said he was," Lincoln breathed quietly.

My tone tightened. "That's not what I asked you. Do *you* think he's innocent?"

Lincoln's eyes met mine. "He's a good man, that Joseph James. He's a good man." Lincoln glanced over at Esther. "He

. . . he taught me to read. Did you know that? I read an entire chapter from the Bible all by myself. In the King James."

I lowered my voice to keep things smooth. "Is a man like Joseph James capable of murdering a young woman, Lincoln?"

Lincoln didn't hear the question. "He's a good singer. Did you know that? The night that Mikey was executed we all sang 'Amazin' Grace' together. All of us."

"You're not answering my question. Did Joseph James kill that girl? Or is he going to be executed for someone else's crime? Dietrich Donomar's crime?"

I barely got the last word out when Lincoln slammed his fists down on the table. The guards rushed over to restrain him. Esther's chair slid back five feet, but for some reason I didn't even flinch.

"I don't wanna die!" he yelled. "I'm innocent! Donomar killed Mamie! I didn't do it! I swear! I swear on my mama's grave!"

The guards escorted Lincoln Smith out of the room as he continued to yell. I rubbed my eyes and turned to find Esther. She was standing above me.

"What in the world do you think you're doing?" she growled.

I stared up at her. "What do you mean?"

"You think I run some kind of crazy circus here, Keaton? You think anything Lincoln Smith tells us about Joseph James is in the least bit reliable?"

I stood so she wouldn't tower over me. "It was worth a shot. After all, these two men are dueling to see who will live."

"And pitting them against each other isn't going to move our case along any faster. Besides, the whole thing is tainted anyway."

"What?" I followed her out of the room.

"You heard him. He concocted the whole story off the media. Nothing he says can be reliable now. The same goes for James."

I grabbed at her as she rounded a corner. "Are you saying this is it? You're not going to do anything else?"

"My hands are tied," she said dryly and wiggled loose of my grip. I stood breathless as she exited out the doors without me.

The chapter ended and Jonathan set down the pages. The story was good. Very good. He couldn't imagine where in the world Clyde was going with all this, but he sure hoped he had finished it. Before he could read more, Eleanor and Kathy made their way into the living room. Eleanor carried a warm brownie on a plate.

"Working on a holiday!" she scolded, handing him his brownie.

"It's not a holiday for another"—he looked at his watch—"two hours." He set the pages down as Kathy nestled into the corner of the couch closest to the fire and Eleanor sat in a rocking chair farthest from it.

"I love this house, Eleanor," Kathy said warmly as Jonathan offered to pour her a brandy. She declined. "How long have you lived here?"

Eleanor picked up a blanket she was knitting from the basket beside the rocker. "Oh dear, I guess it's been . . . well, thirty or more years. I lose count, you know."

Jonathan smiled and pinched off a piece of the brownie. "The world's best, El. I swear it."

She waved her hand at him like he was being foolish while her face glowed at the compliment. "A lot of good memories," she said as she gathered her yarn. "Jon, your father used to love sitting in that very same chair. Drinking brandy and smoking those smelly cigars."

Jonathan lowered his head and smiled, feeling Kathy's eyes on him. He glanced up at both the women. "Dad liked brandy, did he?"

"Sure. Don't you remember? I can't believe you don't!" She laughed and began to knit. "Earl and your father would sit up until two in the morning discussing absolutely nothing of importance. You wouldn't know it listening to them," she said, her eyes focused on her knitting project. She glanced up at Jonathan. "That's why Earl leaves the bottle out for you, you know. It reminds him of those days with your father."

Jonathan swallowed. "Earl and Dad were close? I didn't realize."

"Oh, as close as two older men can be, I suppose. They were good company, anyway."

Jonathan then poured himself some brandy as Kathy looked on. They all listened to the fire for a little bit and watched Eleanor work yarn as if she were wrestling a rattlesnake. Jonathan doubted he'd ever seen anyone knit as intensely as Eleanor.

"I remember," Eleanor started after a bit more silence, "the last Thanksgiving my sister was alive. It snowed that morning, and we had both gotten up to put the turkey in the oven. We sat and watched the snow fall as the sun rose. Glorious."

Jonathan smiled. "Mom always liked coming here."

"Sure she did. I was always a better housekeeper than she." Eleanor laughed. "And she was so happy that you two had come with Meg and Leesol. Leesol had just been born, and we weren't sure Kathy was going to take her out in the cold. I'm glad you did, Kathy. None of us could possibly have known that would be her last Thanksgiving." She pointed a needle at Jonathan. "That's why you need to come visit me more! You never know when I might go stiff."

Jonathan and Kathy laughed quietly, trying not to wake the girls and Earl. "Eleanor, you always had a way of putting things."

She shrugged. "I'm just glad we all had that Thanksgiving together. It seemed like the whole week was just a blessing from God."

Kathy pulled her sweater around her and stared into the fire. Jonathan swirled his brandy around in his glass. But Eleanor wasn't mindful of what either of them were doing. "Jonathan, your mother was so proud of you going into books. She always bragged about what an avid reader you were. Remember that week she brought all those books you had edited and asked you to sign them?"

Jonathan laughed. He'd forgotten that. It seemed so absurd at the time. Editors never signed books. But his mother had insisted, and Jonathan figured it wasn't going to hurt anything. He didn't realize how much it meant to her until after she died. When he went to her house, he discovered she owned exactly three copies of every single book he'd ever edited in his entire career.

Jonathan took a long sip of brandy. "I miss her eggnog."

"Don't we all! Lord knows I can't make the stuff." Eleanor changed knitting needles. "That was the first year Kathy helped out in the kitchen, too."

Kathy looked up. "Well, I was so intimidated before. I'd have rather been in the kitchen with Martha Stewart!"

"Who, dear?" Eleanor asked, and Jonathan cracked up. "At any rate, I remember the three of us sitting up late, even after the men had gone to bed, and playing cards."

"Yes, I remember. . . ." Kathy's faint smile reflected a good memory.

"Boy, you two were the night owls! Talk, talk, talk!" Eleanor raised her yarn up into the light of the fire. "My sister always liked you, Kathy. She was glad Jonathan snagged you." She winked at Jonathan. "Anyway, I went on to bed, but I could hear the two of you jabbering on like a couple of schoolgirls!"

Kathy scooted to the edge of the couch. "Anyone want another brownie? I think I'll have one."

"No, thank you, dear. I always wondered what it was you two talked about. You must've stayed up two more hours after I'd gone to bed!"

"It's been a long time. It would be hard to say," Kathy said from in the kitchen. "Sure you don't want a brownie?"

The question was left unanswered, and the room grew quiet while Kathy was away. Eleanor stretched her arms up and set her knitting aside as Kathy re-entered.

"Boy, you two are quite the conversationalists without me, aren't you?"

Jonathan noticed she came back empty-handed. "Aren't you going to have a brownie?"

Kathy smiled and rubbed his shoulders from behind him. "Well, I didn't want to eat alone. Besides, I'm tired. I should get to bed." She kissed him on the cheek. "It's my turn to rise early with the turkey."

"This turkey ain't gettin' outta bed till noon!"

She playfully hit him. "You know what I mean."

Jonathan squeezed her hand, and then she walked up the stairs to the bedroom off the loft. The door squeaked as she closed it. Jonathan looked at Eleanor, whose old, wrinkled face grew younger next to the warm light of the fire. She pulled a single pin from on top of her head, and long, shiny gray hair fell down across her shoulders. "You've got a jewel in that woman and don't you forget it."

"Yes, ma'am," Jonathan said with a wink.

Eleanor walked to the fire and warmed her hands against it. "Family is so important. It's all you have when you have nothing."

"True." Jonathan's heart expanded with relief for the decision he'd made to stay with Kathy, and for the assurance that the frightening story he had been receiving had ended. He celebrated that thought by finishing off his brandy.

Eleanor had turned so her back was facing the fire. "You're far away, dear."

Jonathan smiled up at her. "Just thinking. Just thinking how . . . happy I am."

Eleanor nodded with approval. "You should be. You have a good life." Her eyes darted to his briefcase. "You're not overworking, are you? Couldn't you leave that at home just for the few days you were here?"

"I have an important meeting next week. I'm presenting two proposals."

Eleanor twisted her hair in her hand. "Proposals. Who cares? It's not as if these were your first two! This is what you do! This is what you're good at! When are you going to take the pressure off yourself?"

"Right now!" Jonathan reclined in the chair as the leg rest popped out. "Things are different now, El. My premier writer retired *and* died. I can't depend on him forever. Besides, if I'm ever going to be executive editor, I'm going to have to be better than the others."

"Well, being an executive anything isn't all there is in life." Jonathan smiled as she lectured him. "Your wife and kids need to see you."

"I know, I know," he said with a laugh, his hands held up in front of him in defense. "Believe me. I've changed a few things in my life, and I am going to spend more time at home."

Eleanor approached him and patted him on the shoulder. "Good, good. Sophie will be an old woman before you know it. I never imagined my life would go by so quickly. And so many things

I can only look back on with regret. I suppose if one could see the end of his life at the beginning of his life, one might measure his time differently."

"I've learned what's important. This family is everything to me." He looked up at her. "But thank you for caring."

Her sunken gray eyes peered down at him. "Are you taking your family to church, Jon?"

Jonathan's eyes darted to the fire. "Well . . . not . . . I'm going . . . no."

Eleanor moved around him so she could see him better. "My dear, have you forgotten that? Have you forgotten our Lord?"

Jonathan shook his head and muscled the leg rest back down into the chair. He stood and walked to the fire. "No, no. Of course not. It's just been . . . hectic. I'm tired when Sunday comes."

Eleanor laughed suddenly, so hard that Jonathan turned around to make sure she was okay. "What's so funny?"

Eleanor gathered herself and joined him at the fire. "Oh . . . I was just thinking back a few hundred years—"

"El . . ."

"Earl and I had gotten ourselves started in this fishing club. We were gone a lot on the weekends, making it to all the lakes nearby for fishing competitions and what not." She laughed again. "Anyway, we were traveling by camper on a Sunday, and I mean to tell you it was one disaster after another. First two tires blew. Then we ran out of gas. Then we left our fishing license back in a whole other county. And finally Earl broke three of his toes after he stumbled on a rock."

Jonathan glanced over at her. "I don't even like fishing."

"My point, dear, is that God made *His* point quite clear that he wanted Earl and me back at church. We'd been going once every two or three months. Boy, when God has a point to make, He sure knows how to make it! Earl doesn't even eat fish anymore." A log fell off the fire with a thud, sparks and tinder flying up into the smoke and then falling as lightly as feathers. "Well, I'd better head to bed." Eleanor moved past him and to the edge of the room.

"El?"

"Yes, dear?" She was only a ghostly silhouette against the light of the room behind her.

"Have . . . have you ever seen God?"

"Seen Him? No, dear. I've never seen God."

Jonathan cleared his throat, still warm from the brandy he'd consumed. "Do you think God . . . um, that He comes down here? Ever? To prove a point?"

Eleanor stepped back into the room enough so that the fire barely illuminated her thin face. "Sure. God has come down here once or twice." She smiled definitively.

"Recently . . . ?"

"Jon? What are you asking?"

Jonathan stared back into the fire. "Nothing."

"No. There's something on your mind. What is it?"

Jonathan's pause was filled with the crackle of the fire. "Maybe I've seen the writing on the wall. That's all. Except it wasn't on a wall." He looked up at Eleanor and then shrugged slightly.

The heat from the fire made him tired, and his mind was having trouble keeping up with his emotions. All he knew was that he would've rather believed God was writing that story than Clyde. God had the right. Clyde didn't.

Eleanor stood silently in the doorway, her hands clasped in front of her nightgown. "Well, dear," she finally said, "the last person who saw God's handwriting ended up dead." Jonathan's eyes shot up. "So let's hope you didn't." She smiled peacefully.

Jonathan rubbed his face in his hands and thought about pouring himself another brandy. Who was he kidding? Of course it was Clyde. How could he even imagine that God might be so personal as to send him pages for his salvation? He laughed to himself and took a deep breath that flared his nostrils. And the salvation part of it was questionable. It had been a nightmare above all else. A nightmare that he was glad was over.

"Good night, Jonathan," Eleanor said and flipped off the light in her bedroom, shutting the door quietly behind her.

"Good night," he said softly. No, he certainly hadn't seen God's handwriting. If God came down and wrote, it wasn't going to be legible to him. At one time in his life, God hadn't been quite as mysterious, but that was long ago when things were simpler and his brother was by his side.

"The last person who saw God's handwriting ended up dead." His ghostwriter was most definitely Clyde Baxter.

CHAPTER 22

"Honey, please, you don't have to drive," Jonathan argued as Kathy backed out of the driveway, all of them waving at Earl and Eleanor, who were standing on the front porch wrapped in their coats.

She turned on the wipers as the snow fell on the windshield. "You have work to do. I know that. This is a perfect time for you to read Clyde's manuscript."

"Yes, but—"

"And Clyde's funeral is tomorrow, so . . ." She lowered her voice and glanced back at the girls in the rearview mirror. "You probably won't feel like working."

Jonathan's hands ran over his two-day stubble. "I don't feel like working now."

Kathy patted him on the leg. "Honey, you've got to finish the manuscript."

Jonathan looked at her. "Why is it so important to you for me to finish it? You've never encouraged me to work before. You still don't believe it was Clyde sending me those pages, do you?"

Kathy kept her eyes steady on the road and switched on her lights. "I know you've got an important meeting Monday. You said Nellie's expecting something big from you."

Jonathan sighed and clicked open his briefcase. "I don't even know if it's finished. I mean, this is a nightmare. In more ways than one."

Kathy slowly passed a stalled vehicle. "I think you owe it to him to at least read what he did finish. This book was important to him." Kathy met his curious stare. "You said so yourself."

Jonathan pulled the papers out of his briefcase. "Girls, you have enough heat back there?"

"Yes!" they all sang in unison. Kathy and Jonathan smiled together.

"Get to reading," Kathy ordered and then smiled. "Nellie has nothing on me, baby," she winked.

Jonathan settled into his seat and tilted the seat back to a less upright position. She was right. Nellie was expecting something big, and regardless of how he was feeling about Clyde, his book had to be his ticket to getting Nellie's confidence in him back. He found his place.

The comment she had given the press sounded like a weather report on a dull weather day. "The two men were convicted of their crimes by a jury of their peers. We have found no significant evidence to release either one of them. We cannot and will not make a rash decision because we are coming under pressure from the media and from political agenda groups. The fact of the matter is that we have found nothing that would cause us to probe further into investigating either of these cases. Thank you."

I had listened to the broadcast on my car radio, followed by a bombardment of political opinions afterward.

"Obviously DA Caladaras has let her previous mistake of releasing a prisoner cloud her judgment in this. She doesn't want to make another mistake. And an innocent man will die for it."

"She's just covering her own behind. She won't admit she prosecuted an innocent man."

"Maybe Donomar is lying. But at least investigate it further than this!"

"Someone will answer if another innocent man is executed! Do we want to make it four in one year? Esther Caladaras will answer, and Governor Wallace, too!"

On and on the comments went, each more heated than the previous one. I felt helpless and angry with her, but I wasn't about to give up hope. Not yet.

I waited impatiently in a break room of the federal prison. I had at least persuaded Esther to let the FBI continue their investigation into Donomar's cell. Maybe, just maybe, they would turn up something that would link him to the death of one of those women.

Agent Lauttinghouse knocked on the door just as I was about to buy another Twinkie from the vending machine. "Keaton, there's nothing."

I sighed hard. "Are you sure, Gordon?" He nodded. I shook my head. "No. It's in there. That's part of the game. Don't you see that? He's laughing right now, knowing we can't find it. This is a game to him. The game has rules. He will follow those rules. He can't win if we're not all following the same rules."

"Keaton, my men have been at this for five hours. These men know what they're doing. Whatever it is we're looking for, it's not in there."

I was surprised Esther's secretary and guard let me through. I figured I'd been banned from seeing her, now that she had made up her mind. Four days had passed. Two days until Joseph James would be executed. He still would not return my calls or acknowledge in any way that I wanted to see him.

The national news's lead story every single night was the looming execution of these two men. Political agenda groups had made this story so big that even China and Europe were following it. The fact that three innocent men had been executed earlier in the year was fuel for their fire, and I hoped their fire would grow bigger.

The governor had been on every single national show that existed, hoping to help his campaign for the upcoming election but ending up answering question after question about the case. Even Lincoln Smith had found fame in his last days. He must've told his story a hundred different times, and it never changed one bit. I watched him carefully. The more I listened to him, the more I believed him. And so did the rest of the world. He had suddenly become the poster child for mistaken guilt.

Esther's door was cracked slightly. I didn't bother knocking. I figured someone had told her I was on my way in. When I entered, she was eating Chinese and almost seemed relieved as she waved me in.

"Keaton," she said after a large gulp, "you're the last person I expected to see. You fired yet?"

I smiled and took a seat. "The jury's still out on that one."

She pressed her lips into a smug smile. "Hate when that happens."

"What about you? I notice you still haven't given any interviews."

She closed her carton of Chinese. "So they can slaughter me with unfair, agenda-driven questions? I don't think so."

"Aren't you worried about what's happening to your reputation?"

"I don't care about my reputation. I do what I do because I'm good at what I do."

"But if you execute an innocent man, isn't that sort of a strike against your record?"

"I'm not going to execute an innocent man, Keaton," she said, leaning back into her chair. "They're both guilty. There's nothing but a crazed serial killer to say otherwise." Her forearms steadied her in her chair. "If Donomar hadn't said a single thing about this, would these cases have ever been reviewed again? No."

"But this is the evidence that makes these cases worth reviewing!" I threw up my arms but kept my tone light. She smiled graciously and sipped at her orange juice.

"In your opinion," she said in a low, assured tone. "By the way, what did your agents turn up at Donomar's cell?"

I cracked my knuckles in frustration. "Nothing. But," I said, before she could gloat, "I know it's there. It's just a matter of finding it. One single clue. That's it."

She laughed out loud and flicked the ash off her newly lit cigarette. "Well, good luck and good riddance, partner." Her western accent wasn't funny at all. "I'm sorry, Keaton. I'm offending you."

"How can you take this so lightly? An innocent man is going to die."

"I told you, Keaton. Not in my opinion."

Suddenly Jack entered. His expression was grim. "Esther, I'm afraid you may want to turn your TV on."

Esther hesitated and then hit her remote. Channel Seven came up, and Jack stepped in and closed the door. Governor Wallace was being interviewed by Jane Pauley.

"Well, Jane, I think that it's naturally the right thing to do."

"Are you in any way, Governor Wallace, being influenced by political pressure? Whether good or bad?"

"No, Jane. I believe that this case warrants a good look, and that's what I intend to do, even if DA Caladaras says otherwise."

"The majority of the people in your state are for capital punishment. However, more people have joined this crusade since the execution of the three innocent men in Oklahoma and Texas. Does that have any impact whatsoever on your decision to look into this case?"

"None whatsoever, Jane. I just want to do the right thing."

Esther punched off the TV and screamed, "He's lying! He's folding! I can't believe this!" She kicked her chair out of the way and it rolled three feet to the side. "The man has no guts! Everyone knows he's for capital punishment! What in the world is he doing?"

"Winning votes," Jack offered cautiously.

"I know that!" Esther fumed. "Get Marty on the phone. And get Ann Simon, too. And Steve Jarr."

Jack paused, as if wondering how he could do that all at once, then left the room quickly.

"Get out, Keaton. I've got to stop this madman."

I walked to the door and said, "You're going after the wrong one."

Two days later, in the late afternoon, the news broke. Governor William Wallace had made his decision. He called a news conference as the whole world seemed to be watching. I turned on the television in my apartment and sat breathlessly as the governor approached the microphone, obviously wearing a ton of makeup to cover his ruddy complexion.

"Ladies and gentlemen. Thank you all for coming. As all of you know, yesterday afternoon I decided to review the cases involving Joseph James and Lincoln Smith. I want all of you to rest assured I did not do this on my own. I brought in several experts from my own staff as well as men and women who are experts in this field. These are men and women from the FBI, from forensics, the sheriff's department, attorneys, and others who helped me review all of the facts.

"I want you to know that I approached this with the mind-set that both of these men were guilty. Two courts of law and a jury of their peers convicted both of these men of murder.

"But, as we all know, our system can be flawed, and as this new evidence has surfaced, I believe, unlike DA Caladaras, we have an obligation to look into this matter. However, I also would like to make it very clear that we do not intend to play games, as it was put, with Mr. Donomar, as he is wishing to play with us. No one from my investigation team has talked with him or had any contact with him.

"What we have done, however, is reviewed his case file and all the information we have on him in order to link him to either of these murders. So, with all of that said, we would now like to inform you that we have found overwhelming evidence linking Dietrich Donomar to the murder of Mamie White."

Applause and commotion caused the governor to pause and wait for silence. I fell to my knees in front of the TV. Joy and terror fought for control over my emotions. I couldn't believe it had happened. They had found a man innocent. I waited as the governor hushed everyone.

"Please, everyone, please. Calm down. Thank you. Yes, thank you." The governor situated his notes. "I do not have time to go into every detail of the investigation, but we will say that we do have evidence linking Mr. Donomar to that crime. We have evidence that he was in the city around the time Miss White was killed. And most importantly, we have testimony from a prisoner who will remain unnamed, confirming that Donomar was with Miss White the night she was killed."

More commotion. I reminded myself to breathe.

"We will be releasing Mr. Smith in exactly one hour. Mr. James will be executed according to schedule, for the murder of Christy Krennel, at six o'clock this evening. And now, my assistant, Ardon Howell, will answer any further questions. Thank you."

The governor backed away from the mikes and the assistant stepped up. As he was beginning to answer questions, I finally let out a sigh of relief. I had trusted my instincts for twenty years, but I also admitted when my instincts were wrong. I thought Lincoln Smith was lying. And maybe he was. Maybe he didn't know what Donomar knew. But regardless, I had to trust this team of investigators to make the right judgment call. Surely that many people couldn't make this big of a mistake.

I suddenly thought of Esther and quickly flipped through my small book of numbers for her direct line. I was amazed when she picked up the phone.

"Keaton. I knew it would be you."

I gripped the phone tightly. "You've been watching the television."

"Sure I have."

"You don't sound upset."

"Oh, I'm fine. Just fine. I love when the governor of our great state makes a fool of me in front of the national media. And boy, what confidence do I have in an investigation team made up by a man with an agenda. They probably sat around eating petits fours and drinking raspberry tea."

"Esther, are you okay?" I asked. The sarcasm in her voice was disturbingly light.

"He's going with the majority, you know. People who are for capital punishment are always scared of executing an innocent man. That's part of the risk of capital punishment. But I don't convict innocent men, Keaton. The governor is getting ready to release a murderer because the country's scared. But I hope they remember to lock their doors tomorrow night when Lincoln Smith is released. That's what they should be scared of."

A silence crossed the phone lines, and I suddenly felt very sorry for Esther. "You want to go grab something to eat?" I offered.

I could hear her laugh on the other end. "No, Keaton. I don't want to leave this office ever again. I've got to go." The line went dead.

I sat on my couch awhile longer, wondering what I should do. I wanted to go to Donomar. I wanted him to show me his evidence. But I doubted I could get in to the prison with all the hype. Still, my curiosity was overwhelming.

I grabbed my car keys and opened the front door, and there, on top of my welcome mat, was a clean white envelope, sealed

and addressed to "Keaton Spade." I sighed, tired of the endless
requests for interviews. I figured this was just another way of
asking. A mysterious envelope that I just had to open. Well, I
didn't have time for it, so I grabbed it, stuffed it into my coat
pocket, and ran down the steps of my apartment—

"We're home!!!" Megan squealed, and Jonathan looked up just
in time to see the moonlight accent the edge of their drive.

"That trip went by quickly," Jonathan said, stretching his back
as he put Clyde's manuscript back in his briefcase and turned off
the van's reading light.

Kathy smiled. "You fell asleep halfway home—Jonathan?"

Jonathan looked up as Kathy pulled the van into the driveway.
A small car sat in the driveway, and a shadowy figure stood in the
darkness of their front porch.

"Pull up slowly," Jonathan ordered and the girls grew quiet in
the backseat.

"Jonathan, what—"

"Shh," Jonathan said. "Stop the car here."

Kathy stopped the van midway down the drive. Jonathan
opened the door and Kathy grabbed his arm. "Wait. Jonathan,
please."

"It's okay, Kathy. Lock the doors. I'm going to go see who it is.
Stay put."

Jonathan shut the door, wishing the van lights were shining on
his front door. Instead, they cast shadows across it, and though he
could see someone moving, he couldn't see any more than that. He
walked up the sidewalk cautiously, his heart stinging with fear, as
he said, "Hello? May I help you?"

"Yes." The voice belonged to a woman. Jonathan stopped as she
stepped out into the moonlight. She appeared to be around thirty,
with blond hair and a smooth, pretty face. She rubbed her hands
together. "Are you Jonathan Harper?"

Jonathan immediately noticed a manila envelope tucked underneath her arm. His eyes darted to hers. "What do you want?"

She handed him the envelope and said, "I'm Penny Carmichael."

"Who?" Jonathan said, looking at the envelope. The cold air was not allowing the perspiration on his forehead to escape.

"I type Mr. Baxter's manuscripts for him."

The large breath Jonathan let out froze instantly in front of him. "I'm sorry. Of course." He shook her hand. "How are you?"

She sniffled and shrugged. "I'm so sad that Clyde is gone." She looked up at Jonathan. "I just wanted you to have that." She pointed to the envelope. "It's the rest of the story Clyde was writing."

Jonathan looked down at it. "Is it . . . ?"

"Finished? No. But that's as much as he wrote. He delivered me his handwritten copy the night he . . . he . . ." She dug her foot into the snowy grass.

Jonathan took her hand. "Thank you, Penny, for bringing this to me."

"You're welcome," she said in a choked voice. "If you'll excuse me, my children are waiting in the car."

"Of course."

Penny moved past him and then Jonathan said, "Penny?"

"Yes?" she said, blowing into her hands.

"Was Clyde . . . was he . . . working on another story at the time? Were you . . . typing something else out for him?"

"No," she said. "Have a good evening."

Penny got in her car and backed out of the driveway and into the street. Jonathan looked down at the familiar manila envelope and pulled the pages out, throwing the envelope to the ground. If he could make one thing happen, it would be to never see another manila envelope the rest of his life.

CHAPTER 23

The service was small and quiet, with a few select friends and three distant relatives of Clyde's attending. Most everyone else was from the publishing house. Arnold Avery, Clyde's pastor for forty-three years, identical in age to Clyde, led the service.

"Clyde was a man of honor, a man of integrity, a man whose own troubles he put behind himself in order to help others." The pastor continued, over Nellie's loud gasps and cries, to paint Clyde as a good friend, a creative genius, and a model Christian. Jonathan, Kathy, and the three girls sat in the front row.

Kathy was comforting Meg, but Jonathan could only stare blankly at the casket that held the body of his old friend. His former friend. He didn't know what else to call him now. Maybe simply . . . his writer. *In more ways than one*, Jonathan added in silent sarcasm.

Earlier that morning Pastor Avery had asked Jonathan to say a few words about Clyde, including his fondest memories, and then read from some of his favorite passages out of Clyde's novels.

"I don't think I can do that," Jonathan had replied. Pastor Avery cupped his hand on Jonathan's shoulder.

"This must be so hard for you, Jonathan. I completely understand."

Jonathan was glad the pastor hadn't pressed him. He didn't want to say the real reason he didn't want to deliver a eulogy. Instead, now he sat five feet from the coffin of a man he thought he knew but apparently never understood.

"And today we can do nothing but rejoice in the life of Clyde Baxter and in the death of Clyde Baxter." Pastor Avery gracefully paused as Nellie wept out loud and blew her nose with the fury of gale force winds. "We can rejoice because we know that right at this very moment Clyde is rejoicing as well. He is alive, you know. He is alive and in the presence of his Savior and Lord, Jesus Christ. And those of us who knew Clyde well knew that Clyde was more alive than most people. He was full of light and life—"

"I've never heard so much talk of being alive at a dead man's funeral," Jonathan whispered sarcastically in Kathy's ear.

"Shh," she ordered harshly, and Jonathan sighed and folded his arms over his chest.

"If you ever wondered why there was something different about Clyde, why his life seemed to shine a little brighter than other people's, it was because he had something inside to live for. He served a wonderful Savior, and he did it with boldness."

Yeah, Jonathan thought, *he was so bold he had to send pages anonymously.*

"And I must ask all of you today, because Clyde would want me to, if you died suddenly, just as he did, would you know where you would go? Would you go to heaven to meet your Maker? What would you say to Him once you got there?"

"What is this? A Billy Graham crusade?" Jonathan whispered again. Kathy shot him a look that quieted him immediately.

"Perhaps you go to church. Perhaps you're a model family man or a dedicated housewife. Perhaps you are a professional of integrity. All of those things are great, but the question still remains— are you certain where you will spend eternity?"

Jonathan's head pounded as hard as his heart. His chest cinched with tightness and the air around him seemed to vanish. He loosened his necktie, but it didn't seem to help.

"When you stand before almighty God, you will give an account of your life. All the good. All the bad."

Jonathan's jaws tingled and his neck felt weak. Kathy glanced over at him and touched his face. "Are you okay?" she asked softly.

"I need some air," he choked, then rose and made his way to the back of the room, passing Nellie's hideous wails and a few curious stares. He bolted out the doors and into the cold morning air.

"Ahhh," he said out loud, breathing the fresh air deeply into his lungs. He'd never felt that way before. He sat down on a cold stone bench and checked the pulse on his wrist to make sure his heart was still beating. He imagined this was what the beginning of a heart attack felt like.

After his lungs filled back up and the pressure in his chest relieved, he tried to hold back the mysterious tears that had so suddenly formed. Why was he crying? It certainly wasn't because he was missing Clyde so badly. Perhaps the mystery of why Clyde had written all those pages still loomed on the horizon of his heart. So many questions were still unanswered.

But if he were completely honest with himself, all the talk of death and eternity wasn't something he was comfortable with. The more he thought of eternity, the more he thought about his drinking and his feelings for Sydney. And, truth be known, all of eternity could be filled with the guilt he felt over those two things. Then add on to that the fact that he'd been an absentee husband and father over the last year. Eternity couldn't possibly hold the shortcomings of his life.

Jonathan thirsted for a strong drink, but he cared too much about what Kathy would think. Then he wondered why he needed the drink at all. What could be solved by drowning it in a drink? He had committed himself to being a better father and husband, and hitting the booze wouldn't take him any closer to either of those two things.

Through the heavy wood doors of the mortuary, the organ reverberated with Clyde's favorite hymn, "Blessed Assurance." The bird above him seemed to know it by heart and chirped in perfect rhythm with each verse. Before long, a few people were streaming out, walking across the sidewalk to the other building where the reception would be held. Jonathan stood and pretended to be interested in the ivy garden that lined the sidewalk.

When the crowd cleared a bit, he decided to go inside and find Kathy and the girls. Before he even had time to look, however, Nellie grabbed at his jacket and pressed her face into his chest.

"Ohhh, Jonnnn," she sobbed. Jonathan looked around to see how big a scene she was making. Only a few people glanced over, recognized it was Nellie, and moved on without another thought. Jonathan gently patted her on the back. She gathered herself and blotted her face with a handkerchief.

"Are you okay?" she asked with insistence.

"I'm fine."

She nodded. "I hate myself. I hate myself so much," she said with a loud sniffle. "I loved Clyde with all my heart, but all I could think of during the whole service was how fast we've got to replace him. We've banked on him being with us longer, Jonathan. Do you understand that?" She looked around and in a whisper added, "We've spent money he was supposed to bring in for the next five years." She folded her handkerchief five different ways before looking up at Jonathan with a tearful blink.

Jonathan frowned. "Nellie, you knew he retired. He wasn't going to be writing any more anyway."

"Yes," she said with heaviness, "but I had counted on him at least doing some final book tours. Some signings. We were thinking of selling the last three Bart Callahan novels as a set and sending him to Europe to promote them." Her hand swiped her nose. "The house is in real trouble unless we find a new bankable author. And quickly."

Jonathan sighed and bit his lower lip. "Nellie, I don't know what to—"

She held up her hands. "We'll be okay for a few months if this 'coming out of retirement' novel is as good as you say it is. We can send it out early with the spring catalog and hope his death is our best marketing bet." She covered her mouth. "I'm a hideous monster, aren't I?"

Jonathan smiled and turned her toward the outside door. "You're fine, Nellie, but let's not get caught discussing how we can make money off of Clyde's death at his funeral."

She looked over her shoulder at him. "Monday's meeting is

vital. You'll have the proposal ready?"

"Proposals," Jonathan reminded her. "I've got Zippy's, too."

She shot him a questionable look, then gathered herself into a tall posture and walked toward the doors, where her assistant, Mark, greeted her. Jonathan looked around the room to find Kathy, but the room was now empty, except for Clyde's coffin. He guessed he had missed her while talking to Nellie and decided to find her at the reception. But something wouldn't let him leave. Something drew him to Clyde's coffin.

His shoes tapped lightly against the shiny tile floor of the small chapel as he approached the coffin. A small stained-glass window that faced east spilled a gloriously colorful light onto the top of it, and the strong fragrance of over a hundred yellow roses ignited all of his senses. He was thankful they had decided to keep the coffin closed, but he ran his fingers along its dark, ornate wood.

"Why, Clyde?" he whispered softly, though even a whisper echoed off the marble walls and repeated itself in his ear. "Why did you leave me with so many questions? What could you have possibly been thinking, sending me pages like that?"

The echo was the only answer that came back, and his lip trembled at the silence that held so much mystery.

"He was quite a man, wasn't he?"

Jonathan whipped around and stumbled back, his hip bumping up against the coffin. Pastor Avery stood solemnly, his hands clasped in front of his black robe. The pastor joined him at the coffin and touched a yellow rose with an old, shaky hand. After a moment Jonathan said, "You and Clyde were close, weren't you?"

Pastor Avery nodded and smiled. "Clyde was my hero. Did you know that?"

Jonathan's surprise expressed itself through raised eyebrows. "Your hero? How is that?"

"I'm his pastor, but he was my shepherd. Whenever I would lose faith, or grow tired and weary, or be fed up with life in general, Clyde was always the one who steadied me and pointed me in the right direction." The pastor glanced over at him. "I presume he did the same for you."

Jonathan could only manage a weak smile.

321

"He talked of you often, you know." The pastor paused in thought. "He worried about you. Worried he was working you too hard."

Jonathan couldn't help but let a laugh slip out.

"His delight was those three beautiful daughters of yours."

"They loved him, too," Jonathan said to carry his part of the conversation.

The room was quiet, and after a while the silence had become more of an intrusion. "Well," Jonathan said, offering a gracious hand, "the service was just what Clyde would've wanted. Thank you."

The pastor's handshake was firm and gentle all at once. As Jonathan stepped around him toward the door, the pastor said, "Did he get a chance to write that book for you?"

Jonathan turned around. "Pardon me?"

"Well, Clyde rarely discussed anything he was working on, but he did mention he was working on something that he hoped would help you long after he was gone."

Jonathan swallowed air and took a step toward Pastor Avery. "You knew about that?"

He shrugged. "Only in complete confidence," he said quietly. "He said he was frustrated that he couldn't get you the pages faster." The pastor touched the large cross that hung from his neck. "He knew it would be a mystery to you at first, but he hoped it would all make sense to you in the end."

Jonathan could barely find words to start talking, start questioning. "But . . . but it's still a mystery." He looked the pastor square in the face. "Why would Clyde do something like that? Why would he write those things down?"

The pastor's face glowed with sincerity. "The decision was made through a lot of prayer. That you can count on. You know Clyde wasn't a man who took anything lightly. You know the type of man he was."

Jonathan tried to hide his frustration and anxiety. "I thought I did. Maybe I didn't."

The pastor smiled. "He lived a quiet faith indeed."

Jonathan shook his head and asked, "But . . . but how did he . . . did he let you read it?"

"No. I never asked to. It wasn't for me, though I must admit I was quite curious."

Jonathan swallowed. "Did he tell you how he knew? How he knew all that about me?" Jonathan blinked hard to keep the emotions that were swelling inside of him down where they belonged.

The pastor's eyes found the stained-glass window at the top of the chapel. "Clyde always had a way of seeing things differently than the rest of us." His eyes found Jonathan again. "He always seemed to know things. Didn't you ever get that feeling?"

Jonathan shrugged and turned away a little.

"I remember one time I had been angry with God. I felt cheated and betrayed by a man in my congregation, and I hadn't understood why things had not worked out how I thought they should. Clyde had approached me after service one Sunday and told me I needed to let it go, so to speak. I wasn't even sure what he was talking about, but Clyde knew I was holding on to some bitterness that would eventually cause more damage than it already had."

Jonathan's fingers stroked his tight lips. "I just don't see how . . ." He looked over at the pastor's peaceful face. "I'm just not sure what Clyde wanted me to get out of it. That's all."

The pastor smiled and said, "You will, son. Trust me." He took Jonathan by the shoulder and said, "Shall we go to the reception? I hear they have those little barbeque weenies. Clyde loved those."

———

Jonathan couldn't even pretend to drink the small glass of punch Kathy had brought him. He watched her fuss over the children's satin dresses and Sophie's insistence on licking her plate. In the corner he kept an eye on Pastor Avery, who at present seemed to be hearing some awful confession from Nellie while Mark guarded their privacy.

He felt a hand laid heavily on his back. He turned and found Carl Osburg. "You okay?" Carl asked.

Jonathan shook his hand. "Yes, I'm fine. Thank you for asking."

Carl glanced over at Nellie. "Nellie's not looking too good."

"Grief management isn't her strong point, if that's what you mean."

Carl and Jonathan exchanged knowing smiles and then were joined by Austin Sable, the new marketing genius hired out from under Random House and paid twice as much as he was worth. Besides being an egomaniac, he was also annoyingly handsome, with dark skin, high cheekbones, and spiky hair that was gelled to perfection. Every woman in the office knew everything about him. He offered his hand to Jonathan, then Carl.

"Austin," Jonathan said politely, finding an excuse to raise the cup of punch to his lips.

"Jon, man, this must be a real downer for you."

Jonathan stared him straight in the eyes. "I'd say more than just a downer, Austin." He glanced at Carl and then said, "What are you? Twenty-seven or so?"

Austin smiled tolerantly. "Thirty-three."

"Ahh."

The three men stood in a corner for a while and watched everyone mingle. Soon enough Kathy made her way from the other side of the room to Jonathan.

"Honey, can I get you something else to eat?" Jonathan asked.

She shook her head. "Sophie just spilled an entire plate of some sort of dip onto the front of her dress. Leesol is miserable. And Meg can't stop crying." She dusted off her black skirt. "I think I'll take the girls home since we took separate cars. Is that okay?"

"Of course. Do you need help getting them to the car?"

"No, Meg's taking care of that right now. You take your time. I'll see you when you get home."

Jonathan kissed her on the lips, and Kathy's hand made its way to his cheek, touching it lightly. She smoothed out his hair, then smiled as she walked away.

Austin shook his head. "Man, I don't see how you do it. Being tied down like that."

"It's worth it. Every moment." Carl and Austin both looked at Jonathan. "What? I'm in love with my wife."

Carl raised his punch cup to him. "Good for you. Those gushy feelings left a long time ago for me."

Austin watched a young female editor from nonfiction walk by. "How long have you been divorced?"

"I'm still married."

Jonathan laughed and Austin had a disturbed expression on his face. "How can you stay with a woman all that time and not love her?"

Carl crunched the cup in his hand. "It's called commitment. Most people don't know what that means these days, right, Jonathan?" Jonathan smiled as he continued. "Don't get me wrong. I still love my wife. But I have to admit, she's not the babe I married back in 1968."

Suddenly from a small table about twenty feet away, a plump woman with her blond hair tied up in a bun, yelled, "Carl! Can you fetch me some more of them weenies?"

Carl's face blushed the color of a rose garden. "It's amazing a man in my profession has a wife who still uses the word *them* incorrectly, isn't it?" He glanced at Jonathan and Austin and then said, "She's from Arkansas."

"Oh," they both said together, and Jonathan gave her a quick wave.

"Excuse me," Carl said, making his way back to the long table of food. Austin let out a whooping laugh.

"Man, Jon," he said, holding his gut, "you're lucky your wife's still hot."

"Careful," Jonathan said.

"What? I'm just saying, how would you like to be Carl and married to some woman who yells at you across the room to go get you barbequed weenies?" He laughed again, tears filling his youthful green eyes. "I mean, that's my worst nightmare, you know?"

Jonathan and Austin watched together as Carl dutifully brought his wife a plate, kissed her on the cheek, and joined her at the table.

"Ugh!" Austin gasped.

Jonathan smiled. "You know what, Austin? Marriage has nothing to do with beauty. Those feelings you're obviously looking for eventually fade. No matter if you marry a supermodel. Carl still loves his wife because of who she is, not what she looks like."

"I dated one once, you know. A supermodel. Back when I was at Notre Dame. She works in Paris now. Her name is Samantha."

Jonathan rolled his eyes. "Good for you, Austin. I'm sure you have many trophies."

Jonathan looked up just in time to see Sydney sliding past a group of people and walking toward them. Jonathan's heart raced. "Excuse me. I have to go get . . . something."

But it was too late. She had reached them. "Jonathan," she said and wrapped her arms around his neck. He patted her lightly on the back. Austin stuck out his hand.

"Austin Sable."

Sydney smiled. "Oh. Hi. You're new in marketing, right?"

"Marketing director," he said confidently. "You're in fiction?"

"Hoping to be," she said with a playful glance at Jonathan. Jonathan, though, had found something else to focus on. The last place he wanted to be was in the presence of Sydney Kasdan. "Jonathan, I need to talk to you."

Jonathan glanced up at Sydney, then Austin, whose curious stare caused Jonathan's fingers to fidget.

"About the meeting Monday . . ." she added with an urgent, professional tone.

Austin buttoned his suit coat. "Ah, the business of publishing never ceases, not even for death, does it?"

Sydney smiled graciously but not friendly enough to indicate he should stick around.

"I'll see you at the office, Sydney," he said and then pretended to spot someone important across the room.

As soon as he was out of earshot, Sydney's expression grew grim. "Jonathan, I'm so glad I found you."

"What is it?"

"Jeremy . . . he's so mad."

Jonathan guided her away from the crowd and pretended to be interested in the plate of vegetables at the food table. "Sydney, I'm sorry, but I can't help you. You need to get a restraining order if you're worried about it."

"I'm not the one who needs it." Her voice was strained and

angry. Jonathan looked up as he was about to stack broccoli on a plate. "You do."

"Me? What in the world for?"

Sydney's hands clenched at her side. "What do you mean, 'what in the world for'?" She looked around. "You know how mad he is at you."

Jonathan set his plate down. "Are you trying to tell me that your fiancé is so upset with me that I need to get a restraining order on him?"

"He's not my fiancé, Jonathan," she said in a forcefully quiet tone. "And yes, that's exactly what I'm saying. He's a violent man. Have you already forgotten what he did to me?" Her dark eyes teared.

Jonathan hung his head. "Good grief, please tell me you're kidding." He looked up at her. "Are you doing this to get my attention?"

She half laughed. "Please! Do I look that desperate?"

Jonathan stood taller and scanned the room for any onlookers. "No. But I want to make it clear once and for all to you that I want nothing to do with you. I know that's harsh, but it's the way it has to be."

Sydney folded her arms and her eyes narrowed to slits. "So you'd rather be killed than have me walk over here in a crowded room and tell you your life's in danger? Is that it?"

Jonathan closed his eyes and took in a breath. "Look, I'll take what you said into consideration. I'll watch my back. But, Sydney, whatever it was that happened between us is over. For good. I've made my decision. It's the right one."

Huge tears rolled out of her eyes and she started to say something, but then she suddenly turned and disappeared between two large men near the end of the table. Jonathan let out a breath.

"Is everything okay here?"

Kathy appeared on the other side of him but was watching where Sydney had disappeared to. She then carefully studied Jonathan's face.

"Um . . . honey. I thought you'd left."

She opened her hand and inside were his keys. "I forgot I had them."

Jonathan took them and wrapped his arm around her shoulder, guiding her through the crowd and out the door. The cold air relaxed his muscles and bathed his hot skin. He barely noticed the press photographers gathered on the lawn. He focused on Kathy as they walked through the parking lot.

"Kathy, that wasn't what it looked like. Whatever it looked like. And I know it must look awful to you."

She wrapped her arm around his waist as they continued walking. "I feel as if I can trust you."

"I've made it clear to Sydney that . . . I've just made it clear that I don't want to be around her."

"She's beautiful."

Jonathan stopped Kathy and tilted her head up to him. "*You're* beautiful. You're the one I love." Kathy blinked slowly and took it in. "And Austin thinks you're hot."

Kathy's eyes opened. "Who?"

"The frat boy who's now in charge of major marketing decisions for my department."

"*Him?*" Kathy laughed. "Is he out of college?"

"Thirty-something," Jonathan said, smiling. "Apparently he's better at marketing than making an impression."

"He's got an ego the size of Texas," Kathy said with disapproval.

"Well, most marketing people do."

Kathy shrugged. "I'm not worried about him. I'm sure he'll see that you're a brilliant editor and you won't have any problems with him."

Jonathan walked her a few more rows and then they came to the van. Meg gave him a short wave and he blew her a kiss. "I probably need to go talk to Nellie again. But I'll be home soon, okay?"

She nodded and kissed him and then got in the van and backed out. Jonathan headed back toward the funeral home. Before he crossed the small street back to the sidewalk that led up to it, he spotted Austin and Sydney sitting on a bench talking and obviously flirting. His stomach turned at the thought of having to cross either one of those two again, so he decided he would just head home. He had a lot of reading to do before Monday, not to mention two proposals to pull together, though he'd done most of the legwork for both of them.

The sun, now high in the sky, warmed the top of his head enough that he felt comfortable taking his time walking to the other side of the parking lot. Carl and his wife invaded his thoughts, but he couldn't stop smiling as he thought of them. She had no idea the power that man held or the high esteem he was held in. He was just "her Carl," and she loved him. He felt disappointment that he would not have a flawless record as a husband. But he was sure he wouldn't make the same mistake twice. If out of fear only, he would never cheat on Kathy. But if he ever thought about it, Clyde Baxter wouldn't be there to send him pages chronicling every sinful move. He convinced himself that was a good thing.

He rounded a large, oversized Chevy pickup and walked from the rear of his car to the front. With his remote he unlocked the doors and was just about to climb in when his blood froze in his veins and his throat swelled so tight he started choking.

Underneath the driver's-side windshield wiper was a manila envelope.

CHAPTER 24

"Jonathan . . ."

The voice, distant and hollow, was thousands of miles away, spoken from a black hole.

"Jonathan . . . Jonathan . . ."

The pain was heavy and deep and suffocating.

"Jonathan . . ."

Darkness. Thick and inky. Then a harsh light, stinging his eyes.

"Jonathan . . ."

A shadow softened the light a bit and he managed to focus on it, though it was no more than a blurry scribble.

"Are you okay? Let me get you some water."

He tried to sit up but fell back onto a soft surface, presumably a bed. He waited, shutting his eyes, and then felt a hand on his, guiding it to a cool glass. He brought the glass to his lips and poured the water into his mouth without regard to neatness. He sat up a little and opened his eyes. The light was still bright, but the shadowy figure in front of him had now transformed into his wife.

"My head . . ." Jonathan whispered. He feared anything louder might cause something inside to erupt.

"I'll get you some aspirin," she said and went to the bathroom again.

Jonathan took another drink of water and gazed out the window. The sun was high in the sky, still strong enough to heat the room.

Kathy appeared again and dropped two aspirins into the palm of his hand. She sat on the edge of the bed and watched as he pushed them down his throat with the rest of the water.

"You look terrible," she said softly. "Do you want something to eat?"

Jonathan rubbed his eyes with force. "What time is it?"

"Four o'clock."

Jonathan looked down and realized he was completely dressed, minus his tie and shoes. He unbuttoned three buttons of his white dress shirt and leaned his tired body against the headboard.

"Are you hungry?"

He was. He didn't know why. He'd just eaten a ton of food at the reception. "Sure." He closed his eyes and tried to think.

"Does anything sound good?"

"Whatever is fine, honey."

She touched his face. "You were so exhausted."

He smiled a little. "I guess so. It's rare that I take a nap at all, much less a four-hour one."

"A four-hour one?" Kathy asked carefully.

Jonathan opened his eyes. "I got home about noon, didn't I?"

"Well, yes . . ."

"It's weird. I don't even remember coming home. Everything's a blur."

Kathy took his hand. "I guess so. I think you're more torn up about Clyde's death than you're willing to admit."

"Look, it's just been a hard day. Tomorrow's Saturday. I'll sleep in and then I'll feel much better."

Kathy paused, looked away nervously, and then said, "It *is* Saturday."

"What do you mean?" Jonathan asked.

Kathy stood near the end of the bed. "Jonathan, you've been asleep since yesterday at noon."

"What?" He wasn't sure if the question was even audible.

She swallowed. "You came home from the funeral and went straight to bed." She nervously smoothed out a wrinkle in the comforter. "You didn't even stir when I came to bed last night. And you slept through all the racket the girls were making this morning." Her expression showed worry. "I tried to rouse you but you just mumbled you wanted to sleep. I figured you probably needed it."

Jonathan forced a smile. "I think I will have something to eat."

"Of course," she said as she relaxed. "Anything you want."

"Whatever you make is fine." He rubbed his temples.

"Is that aspirin kicking in yet?"

"I'm sure it's just a matter of time. I actually feel pretty good and rested," he lied.

"Good. Come down when you're ready." She patted him on the leg and left the room.

Jonathan collapsed against his pillow and shut his eyes tightly. What in the world was going on? What had happened? It was like the last twenty-four hours was a blank slate. He thought back as hard as he could and remembered the funeral, though it felt as if his mind had sunk into a thick haze. He took a few deep breaths to try to calm himself. His knee kicked something hard underneath the covers and he threw the sheets back, revealing the picture frame of his children that normally set on his nightstand. He vaguely remembered holding it against his chest as he went to sleep. He picked it up, and as he set it back on his nightstand, he noticed a small bottle of over-the-counter sleeping medication sitting near the lamp. The bottle was open and a few blue pills lay scattered across the dark wood.

Yes. He had taken two pills, then two more. He remembered fighting the urge to chase it with liquor. But why? Why had he—

A numbing tingle started at his head and blazed down his body like a white fire. He held his breath, clenched his jaw, and then felt underneath his pillow. His hand emerged with the manila envelope he had found on the windshield of his car. He didn't have to open it. His mind was clear now. He remembered exactly what it said. Still, it almost had the power to command him to open it again, and so he pulled up the flap and removed the single white sheet of paper from it. He reread it.

You have attended a funeral today.
Yet this is not the end. Only the beginning.
For some, death is final.
For others, it is not.

You have forsaken the one you love.
And the one who loves you.
Your death, if not eternal,
is immediate.

Though how can death sting one who is already dead?

There is life.
But life only through death.

Embrace the death that is required of you.

Jonathan's hands were shaking so badly he was afraid the rattle of the paper might draw unwanted attention. He attempted to shove the paper back in the envelope but couldn't find the coordination to do so. Instead, he folded the piece of paper and stuffed it in his shirt pocket.

He managed to stumble across the hardwood floor into the bathroom, where he ran his toothbrush across his front teeth only, and then mindlessly swallowed the toothpaste before splashing his face with ice-cold water. His head pounded in sync with his heart. He felt as if he were in a tunnel.

Combing his hair to the wrong side, he buttoned one button on his shirt and closed his eyes for a moment. He had to pull himself together. No matter what, he couldn't let Kathy know anything was wrong. Not now.

He didn't even know what all this meant. He couldn't imagine how to explain it. And the more he thought about it, the more he feared the worst. His death was imminent. And there would be nothing he could do to change it.

"Everything has come true," he whispered as he looked at his red, wrinkled, tired face in the mirror. His eyes were puffy and bloodshot. His five o'clock shadow looked like dirt on his face. Deep creases where the sheets had been looked like a road map on his skin. But the more he stared at himself in the mirror, the more he knew what he was looking at reflected perfectly what he was feeling inside. Hopeless. Helpless. Scared.

Maybe the riddle meant something else. Maybe it didn't mean he was going to die. Maybe it . . .

His thoughts swirled together in a heap of emotions that let itself out in a quiet, angry cry. So many questions. So much confusion.

Was Clyde writing from his grave now? Impossible. Yet this last page had said that it wasn't the end for him. Only the beginning. What did that mean? And he thought he'd reconciled with Kathy. Why, then, did it say he did not love her? He did love her. He'd seen the error of his ways. Wasn't that good enough? Did he have to shed blood as a penalty for his mistake?

He picked up his razor and thought about shaving, but with the way his hands were shaking, he quickly put it down.

"Pull yourself together," he commanded through his tears. "You've got to."

The mirror image perfectly repeated what he said to himself, yet it was as if he were looking at a man he did not know. He studied the face and knew each line well, yet the eyes were different. The eyes were distant. Sad. Gone.

He sat down on the edge of the tub and buried his face in his hands. His muffled cry sounded like a child's, scared of the dark, needing a parent, helplessly feeble. For the first time in his life, he wasn't in control. For the first time, someone else had the answers, and someone else ruled him. Why fight it anymore? Why not embrace it?

Because he wasn't ready to die. Not yet. Not now.

He came up for air and wiped his tears away swiftly with each hand. Somehow, some way, all of this had to make sense. There had to be a logical explanation for it all. Clyde could not be writing this.

"Clyde is dead," he said out loud, as if that made it more of a fact.

Then someone else was writing it. That was logical. What didn't make sense was why, and how. But he had to answer those questions. He had to find this writer before . . .

He couldn't bear to think of it, so he removed it from his mind and focused hard on the facts. The writer knew him, inside and out. The writer knew things from his past no one else knew. The writer had watched him every single day for the past month. The writer had the ability to predict what he would do. The writer was trying to tell him something.

The writer wanted him dead.

Jonathan laughed a little. This writer had saved his marriage and now wanted more. Wanted his life. Why would the writer care about his marriage if he was to die in the end anyway?

Outside his bedroom door, he could hear the girls rumbling down the hallway to the stairwell. He stood, grabbed the Visine out of the medicine cabinet, squirted a drop into each eyeball, and then tucked his shirt in. He brushed his hair one more time and headed downstairs.

At the kitchen table, Kathy had a display of waffles, sausage, eggs, and biscuits lined up like a buffet. Jonathan slid into a chair and felt like he might throw up. His appetite had disappeared as quickly as it came. But for her sake, he shoveled some eggs and a sausage link onto his plate.

Leesol came in from the living room. "Breakfast for dinner! Cool! Hi, Dad. Are you sick? Can I have a sausage, Mom?" Kathy nodded, and Leesol pulled a chair up next to her father. "Dad, are you sad about Clyde?"

Jonathan glanced up at Kathy and then said, "Of course I am. Aren't you?"

"Sure. But I know he went to heaven. I'll be there, too. So I guess I'm not that sad. God's probably got him a big pond next to his mansion. He's probably fishing."

"Probably." Jonathan patted her on the back.

Meg came in next and sat at the table, but she didn't even look at the food. "You slept forever, Daddy."

"I know. I'm sorry."

"Don't be. Mom says you needed it."

"True. I'm paying for it now, though."

She shrugged, her eyes cast down at the table. "I know Clyde's in heaven, but I miss him already."

Kathy came in with another batch of scrambled eggs. "That's normal, honey. We all miss Clyde."

Meg looked at Jonathan. "Do you think he can see us?"

Jonathan looked away and rearranged his eggs on his plate.

"Dad?"

"Sure."

"Does he have a body?" Leesol asked with a mouthful of sausage. "But better? Thinner? Clyde was fat, you know."

"Lees, cut it out," Meg said sharply. "It's not nice to talk about dead people like that."

Kathy sat down at the table. "Honey, Clyde's fine. And he probably is looking pretty good up there in heaven."

"Can I talk to him?" Leesol asked her mother. Jonathan watched Kathy think the question over.

"Well, I don't know. Maybe it's better to just talk to God about him, and maybe God will give him a message for you."

"That's a good idea," Leesol said as she snatched another sausage. "God will probably take the message down just like I said it. Right? God's a good notetaker. Right?"

The chatter continued as Jonathan mulled over Leesol's last statement.

"Jonathan?"

Jonathan looked up to find everyone at the table staring at him. "What?"

Kathy pressed her lips together and like a schoolteacher to a young student said, "Meg asked you a question. Aren't you going to answer it?"

Jonathan looked at Meg. He had completely missed it. Everything about him was far away and almost nonexistent. "I'm sorry, sweetheart. What was your question?"

Meg paused, glanced at her mother with worry, and then said, "Why do good people die? Bad people should die. That's how it should be."

Don't cry, you idiot, Jonathan scolded himself. But he felt he could answer no other way, in light of the last page he had received. "Bad people do die. Every day. Maybe even today."

Leesol and Meg exchanged questioning glances and then Kathy said, "Children, remember you need to pick up your rooms. Why don't you go ahead and do that."

Leesol grumbled, but Meg took the hint and took her sisters up the stairs. When they were alone, Kathy took Jonathan's hand across the table. "Jonathan, is everything okay? Really? You seem . . . weird."

Jonathan looked up at her. She was beautiful. The late afternoon light glowed in her skin. He squeezed her hand and nodded, unable to say anything that was truthful. She waited, then released his hand and began clearing the table.

"What are you going to do right now, honey? Can I help you with anything?"

Jonathan's hands lay limply in his lap. He stared out the small kitchen window near the table. That, he could answer honestly. "I don't know." Did he say that out loud? He wasn't sure. His thoughts and actions didn't seem to line up appropriately.

"Oh. I almost forgot. Nellie called early this morning. She said she wanted to push Monday's meeting up to eleven A.M. She sounded horrible."

"I'll do that." He stood up with a newfound energy. "Yes. I'll read the rest of Clyde's manuscript. I've got to write the proposal tomorrow. It should've been done last week. That's what I'll do. Perfect."

Jonathan caught Kathy staring at him with odd curiosity. He challenged it with what he hoped was a graceful smile. She went about clearing the table, and he shut himself in his study.

At his desk, he found the manuscript. The aspirin was kicking in and he felt a little better. Perhaps he could concentrate enough to finish reading it. Time was running out. Monday would be here too soon anyway.

"Hello." Donomar's voice greeted me before he came into view. I nodded at the guard to leave us alone and then took three more steps and came into his view.

"Dietrich." I folded my arms as he stood from his desk. "I suppose you've heard the news."

"Of course I have, Keaton." He smiled graciously. "Lincoln Smith will be released. Joseph James will be executed."

I pulled up the plastic chair near the cell and sat down. "They've linked you to the murder of Mamie Smith. You lose. We win. Are you going to be a sore loser?"

Donomar laughed a little but didn't respond. I pulled my chair a little closer. "Oh, come on, Dietrich. I mean, you did do a good job of hiding the evidence. Whatever evidence it is that proves you killed the girl. I've got to say, I'm awfully curious." I tried to smile lightly. "I had my best men in here. Couldn't find a thing. Had you strip searched, so I know the evidence wasn't with you." I clasped my hands together. "Are you going to show me what it is? After all, all bets are off now."

He leaned against the wall of his cell and stared at me with narrow eyes and a hint of a smile. I watched him as closely as he was watching me. For once, I had the upper hand with Donomar. I just wondered how he was going to respond to getting beat.

"Well?" I asked. "Are you going to show me or not? You must know how curious I am."

Donomar stood still for a while longer, I guess stringing my curiosity along, and then walked to the front Plexiglas. He was only inches from me, and I felt the need to back up, even though there was nothing he could do to me. I tried to remain cool.

"I guess it's time." He looked at the clock on the wall outside his cell. "Yes, it's perfect timing."

I smiled, as if I were following.

"The truth of the matter, Agent Keaton Spade, is tonight a guilty man will be set free and an innocent man will be executed."

"You're wrong. They're releasing Lincoln Smith as we speak. They have all the evidence linking you to the murder. Is it that hard for you to accept?"

Donomar's eyes suddenly flashed with such evil that it took

my breath away. I stood up and backed away, though I didn't know why.

"What is going to be hard to accept, Keaton," he hissed, "is that I have won and you have lost."

I clenched my jaw. I held nothing back. "Prove it," I stated defiantly.

He stood motionless and stared hard at me for a few moments. I stared relentlessly back.

Then, suddenly, he began unbuttoning his shirt. He was careful with each button, as if he were handling a delicate creature. When his shirt was completely unbuttoned, he removed it, and then looked at me, grinning like a Cheshire cat.

I couldn't imagine what he was doing. "Impressive physique. Is that your supposed clue? You're big enough to kill a small female?"

"No," he said smoothly. "This is."

He turned suddenly and extended his left arm toward me. At first I saw nothing but bulging muscles. Then it hit me and I gasped. I saw it as clear as day, and as soon as I did, Donomar laughed hard, as if someone had just told him a good bar joke.

On the shoulder of his left arm was a tattoo in the shape of a heart. It perfectly matched the tattoo on Christy Krennel's arm. I looked up at him, speechless. His laugh rolled into a quieter chuckle.

Then he said, "It's been here all along. No one has ever mentioned it. No one has ever found the connection." He touched it with two fingers. "Here is your clue, Keaton. Stained on my arm. Here to stay. You missed it."

"No," I said. "No!"

"Yes," he said. "Joseph James is innocent. And tonight he's going to die."

I froze. My mind couldn't imagine what I needed to do. All that spilled from my lips was, "Why?"

He was buttoning his shirt back up. He answered in a casual tone. "Why not? I love evil. And what can I say? I was bored."

I couldn't imagine how he had pulled all this off. I stood in dumbfounded awe.

"Well, are you just going to stand there, Keaton? Or do you need a shoulder to cry on?"

I turned and ran down the corridor. His laugh chased me all the way to the steel gate.

"Open it! Open it!" I demanded. A guard rushed over, assessed the situation, and then opened the gate.

"Agent Spade, is everything—"

I ran past him and made my way outside as fast as I could. I looked at my watch. I had an hour before Joseph James was to be executed.

It took me twenty minutes to get home. The five-o'clock traffic was thick as mud. I cursed myself all the way home for not bringing Esther's number or having a cell phone. I had stopped at a pay phone and tried her through the general number but was told she wasn't available.

My car came to a screeching halt on the curb outside my apartment. I ran the steps up to my door, and before I got to my door, I remembered the small white envelope that had been on my welcome mat. I took it out of my coat and opened it cautiously.

Written in neat printed letters with a light blue ink pen was:

Keaton Spade:
  Let this be.
  Lincoln Smith will find a new life, a better life, than before. This is what I want for him. I give it to him with confidence and peace.
  This is what I choose. Grace makes a poor man wealthy, and an unworthy man more thankful.
                    Joseph

I reread the letter quickly and then froze with indecision. Should I take this to the governor? He wouldn't reconsider without more evidence. What about Esther? She already believed they were both guilty. How would something like this alone persuade her?

Then I looked at the letter again. He was asking me to overlook this? To let him die without a fight? What kind of insane person was this? I didn't know and quite frankly didn't care. The truth contradicted the governor's decision. My instincts had been right all along.

Without more hesitation, I got back in my car and drove as

fast as I could to the governor's mansion. I gambled he would be there. With an execution less than thirty minutes away, where else would he be?

The governor eased himself into a large, plush wingback chair and crossed his legs with smooth elegance. "Care for a cigar?"

I steadied myself. "A cigar? Sir, did you just hear me—" I had just spilled out all the evidence in my possession.

"I heard you, Agent Spade. Sit down. Take a load off."

I randomly found a place on the sofa across from him. "Sir, we've got less than thirty minutes."

He checked his watch and then pulled a cigar from his pocket. "You're sure? They're Cuban. I know, I know. Illegal." He smiled. "But well worth the risk. You're not going to turn me in, are you?" He snatched a lighter off the table and clipped the end of the cigar.

I swallowed, trying to focus on the situation in front of me. "Donomar showed me a tattoo on his left shoulder. It matched the tattoo that Christy Krennel had on her left shoulder. Exactly."

Governor Wallace twisted the butt of his cigar in the flame of the lighter. "It's important how you light a cigar. Did you know that? You don't just light and go. It's much slower. You light the entire end. Turning it, like this."

I stood up. "Are you hearing anything I'm saying? An innocent man is about to be killed!"

The governor smiled as if I'd just complimented his pansy garden and then rose from his chair and walked toward the television. "An innocent man is being released even as we speak." He turned on the television. A picture came up quickly. It was Lincoln Smith being interviewed outside the gates of the prison.

"I cain't believe it. I cain't believe I'm free," he said in response to an unheard reporter's question.

"Are you mad at the system? You've been in prison for over ten years."

Lincoln Smith formed his words carefully. "I ain't mad. I'm gettin' outta this place. I'm gonna go find myself a good job. Maybe get a wife."

"Do you have anything to say to District Attorney Caladaras?"

He paused. "Nothin' to say."

"What about to anyone else?"

He paused again. "I guess I thank the govern'r. Fer makin' this decision in my behalf." He looked around at everyone and his eyes fell as he said, "I'd also like to thank a special friend. He is one good man. One good man." Lincoln Smith teared up, his emotions so evident that even the governor took more notice. "He knows who he is. He gave me this gift. I'm here 'cause of him." He then backed away from the microphones and refused to take any more questions, wiping his eyes and turning from the cameras. I looked at the governor.

"What about this?" I opened the envelope and let him read the letter Joseph James had sent to me.

He folded it neatly and handed it back to me, avoiding my eyes. "Sounds to me like he wants to die."

"That's not the point! The point is that there is hardcore evidence proving James didn't kill that girl!"

The governor turned toward me. "Who do you think you are, coming in here and questioning me like this! I've made my decision! It's based on evidence!"

"I'm telling you the evidence right now!"

His eyes cut into me. "You don't tell me anything. Not one, single thing. You think you're going to go out there and convince the world that I'm wrong? That we released the wrong prisoner again! Think twice. I'll smear you. I'll ruin you forever. Do you understand that?" His face was red and sweaty. I couldn't believe what I was hearing.

"I don't, sir. Not at all."

Suddenly his wife came back in. She glanced at me and then said, "The president is on the phone for you." She smiled. "He sounds happy."

"I'll be right there." As his wife excused herself again, he said, "Get one thing in your head right now. Don't try to be the hero. Don't try to change this. Lincoln Smith is going to remain a free man. Joseph James is going to die as scheduled. And everyone's going to be happy. Our state will be commended for its bravery in reopening the case and finding the right evidence. I will be reelected and will draw votes from both parties." He blew a ring of smoke from his cigar. "And I could care less which criminal is released."

I could hardly remain standing. "Are you saying that you believe Lincoln Smith is guilty and you're releasing him anyway?"

"You're putting words in my mouth."

I shook my head. "This is all a political move for you after all, isn't it?"

The governor gently set his cigar in a nearby ashtray and said, "Excuse me. I can't keep the president of the United States waiting any longer. You'll see yourself to the door?"

The two security officers stepped my direction and indicated that I was to leave immediately. I checked my watch. I had one more option. I had to go see Joseph James myself. Maybe, just maybe, I could convince him to change his mind.

"Honey?" Kathy stood in the doorway of Jonathan's study. Jonathan flipped over the last page of the manuscript.

"That's all . . ."

"What?" Kathy came to his desk.

He sighed and stared at the ceiling. "This is it. This is all that Clyde has written." Kathy stayed still as she eyed his desk. Jonathan laughed out loud a little. "I don't even know how it ends!"

"The manuscript gives you some indication, doesn't it?"

"I don't know, I don't know, I don't know," Jonathan said as his head fell onto his desk. "How am I supposed to write a proposal for a book that's three-fourths of the way finished, with no clue of how it's supposed to end?"

"Clyde didn't leave any notes?"

Jonathan threw his pencil down in frustration. "No. I thought so. He had a folder labeled *Notes*, but it was just filled with some sort of Bible study or something."

Kathy started to say something but paused instead.

Jonathan looked up. "Did you need something?"

"Yes. A Francis Flowers is here to see you."

CHAPTER 25

Jonathan sat up in his chair. "What? Zippy's *here*?"

"Yes."

"What's he doing here?"

"I don't know. I opened the front door to take the garbage out and there he was, standing on the porch. Scared me to death. But he seems nice enough."

"No one's ever described Zippy as 'nice,'" Jonathan sighed as he stood. "How does he know where we live?"

"We are in the phone book, you know. He's in the living room. I sent the girls upstairs. Should I make coffee?"

"No. He's high-strung as it is. You might just stay out of the room. He has a habit of offending just about anyone he comes in contact with."

Jonathan followed Kathy out as he straightened his shirt. "He can't be that bad," Kathy said. "I'll bring in some water, at least." Kathy went in the direction of the kitchen as Jonathan slowly made his way into the living room. Zippy was sitting on the couch staring into space.

"Francis," Jonathan said, extending a tired hand. "I'm surprised to see you."

"Is that so? You shouldn't be. You're proposing my novel Monday, are you not? You haven't changed your mind, have you?"

Jonathan smiled and offered him a seat back on the couch. Zippy chose to stand, so Jonathan sat in the recliner. "Everything's ready to go."

Zippy seemed stunned. "It is?"

"Yes. I've just got a little tweaking to do. Nothing major. I'm looking forward to it."

Zippy sat down and pushed his glasses up his nose. "If this is just another line to put me off—"

Jonathan laughed. "Why would you think I'm lying?"

"We haven't talked. I thought you'd blown it off."

"No. Not at all." He leaned forward in the recliner, his forearms resting on his knees. "I have been preoccupied. I apologize for not returning your phone calls."

Zippy seemed defensive and understanding all at once. "Oh. Well. I suppose Clyde Baxter croaking has been one factor."

Jonathan silently reminded himself Zippy wasn't worth getting upset over. "Yes. And Thanksgiving. I took my family upstate for a small vacation. A needed one." Jonathan caught Zippy's eye.

"Oh. Sure." He smiled suddenly. "It's going to committee!"

Jonathan couldn't hide his surprise in Zippy's glee. "Yes. Of course it is. Francis, it's a good novel. I'm looking forward to getting feedback from everyone else." He paused before saying, "But I must be honest. There is some reservation from those who think that you won't be able to cross over."

Zippy leaped up from his seat. "But you know I can!"

"Yes . . . that's why I'm proposing your novel. Francis, this is going to happen. Rest assured. Your book's going to committee. Beyond that, I can't promise anything."

Zippy's eyes moistened and he hid his face in a handkerchief. Jonathan stood. "Are you . . . okay?"

"Fine. Fine. Allergies. Always make my eyes water. Just allergies. Nothing else." He glanced over at the coffee table. "Look at the dust on that thing! No wonder my air passages are closing. Look at the dust."

Kathy appeared with glasses of water. "Mr. Flowers, would you like some water?"

"Yes, thank you," Zippy said, snatching a glass from her. He gulped it down as Jonathan collapsed back into his chair. He wiped his eyes one more time. "Ma'am, I'd recommend you get busy with some Endust in here. Or next time I'm going to have to bring my inhaler."

Jonathan smiled as Kathy shot him an astonished look, then quickly left the room.

Zippy folded his handkerchief back in his pocket, wiped his nose with his hand, and looked at Jonathan through his thick glasses. "You look terrible."

Jonathan managed a half laugh. "Thanks."

"I hope you're not sick Monday. You've got to be on top of things."

"I'm not sick, Francis," Jonathan said with deliberate heaviness. "I'm trying to figure out what to do with the other proposal I'm expected to present."

"Bad writing? Bad plot? Bad dialogue? Why the heck did you pick it?"

Jonathan tried to be patient. "It's actually none of those. It's Clyde Baxter's last book. He didn't finish it. I'm sort of at a loss as to how it's supposed to end."

"Did you look at his outline?"

"He apparently didn't have an outline or notes or anything. It was like he sat down and wrote chapter one and kept going." He sighed and shook his head. "I don't know if it's a masterpiece or if the man lost his mind."

Zippy took a seat near the end of the couch that was closest to Jonathan. "Is it a good plot?"

Jonathan shrugged. "So far. It's based around a serial killer. That's always interesting."

"If he's the protagonist you've got a problem."

That made Jonathan laugh, a tired laugh that released a little stress. "No. He's definitely the bad guy."

"How much did he get finished before he went riding off into the wild blue yonder?" Zippy smiled at Jonathan's questioning look. "Before he went to heaven in a blaze of horse dust glory?"

"The whole story revolves around three men on death row. And the serial killer actually killed one of the victims one of the men is accused of murdering. So this FBI agent and the district attorney are trying to figure out which one it is before the first execution." Zippy cleaned his glasses on his shirt sleeve, revealing fat, bloodshot eyes. Then he looked intently at Jonathan as he continued. "But what I don't know is how the story ends. It's been suspense all the way so far. But the question is, does the innocent man live or die?" Jonathan smiled as he said, "He sort of left me with a massive cliff-hanger that I have to pick an ending to."

Zippy's glasses sat neatly on the end of his nose now, and he was brushing the stray crumbs from some previous meal off his lap. "I can take a look at it."

"Pardon me?"

"You seem to be in some sort of a crunch here, Jonathan. Ghostwriting is my specialty, you know."

Jonathan thought for a moment. "You have time to read it by tomorrow?"

Zippy's eyes lit up. "Well, I'll have to cancel all my dates with all the womenfolk, but I'd do that for you." He smiled at his own joke. "That was funny, wasn't it? Cancel my dates!"

Jonathan laughed as a gesture of kindness and added, "Well, as long as you refer to them as 'womenfolk,' you're sure to have a pretty poor dating life."

Zippy's mind was reeling. "Yes. Yes. I'll read it for you. We'll come up with an ending. I'm sure if I look at it, I'll know how he intended on ending it. I'll read it. Did you know that I wrote the entire middle of Alberta Stowey's book on grandparenting? Yes. She had a stroke and somehow chapters six through eighteen had gotten lost in the mail. When they went to search her house for it, they never found it. Not on a disk. Not in her computer. Not even a hard copy. It was very strange. So I ended up filling in the blanks, as it were. Not even a hard copy. Got paid well for that job. And I don't even have children, much less grandchildren! Can you imagine me writing about grandparenting?" He smiled satisfactorily. "Let's just say I saved the bacon of a few thousand people. And I don't even have grandchildren!"

Jonathan leaned forward in his chair and looked hard at Zippy.

"Francis, would you be willing to ghostwrite the rest of Clyde's book? I mean, when we figure out the ending. If I can say that I already have a ghostwriter lined up and I can give them the ending, there's more of a chance this could fly."

Zippy blinked curiously at Jonathan. "You're worried a Clyde Baxter novel might not fly?"

Jonathan hesitated. "Well . . . it's just that . . . sure, it'll go. I mean, I just need it to have an ending, that's all."

Zippy's lips curled into a sly smile. "He's changed genres. This isn't a sure sell for you, is it? And now that he's worm food—"

"Enough with the metaphors."

Zippy straightened his thin cotton dress shirt and adjusted his belt as he stood. "All right, Jonathan Harper. I will agree to that. If we find an ending we both agree upon, then I shall ghostwrite the rest of Clyde Baxter's novel. As a personal favor to you. For proposing my novel. I will write the rest of Clyde Baxter's novel."

Jonathan was confused but delighted all at once. "Francis, you don't owe me. Your novel's good. I'm not proposing it as a personal favor to you."

Zippy's face exposed confusion, but he hid it quickly with the allergy act. He blew his nose and blotted his eyes. "I know that. I was just joking."

Jonathan stood. "Thank you, though. This is a personal favor. And I *will* owe you for it."

"Good. I have a second novel I've been wanting to discuss with you."

Jonathan smiled and guided him toward his study. "Great. Let's concentrate on Clyde's book first."

Zippy's eyes lit up with the light that Jonathan turned on. "Goodness gracious, Jonathan. The house must be paying you well." He scanned the books in his study. "You read all these or are they just here for show? Editors tend to be a little showy about their knowledge of books."

Jonathan laughed. For some reason, Zippy's abrasiveness wasn't rubbing him the wrong way today, which was odd, all things considered. Jonathan stacked the manuscript as neatly as possible and handed it to him.

Zippy, though, was focusing on something on his desk. "What's that?" he asked, pointing to a crinkled file folder sitting near the edge.

Jonathan picked it up. "Oh, this is just something from Clyde's office. I thought it might be some notes or something for the book, but it's just a bunch of Bible passages."

Zippy glanced up at Jonathan and then said, "May I?"

Jonathan shrugged and handed him the folder. Zippy looked at the label. "It says 'Notes.' "

"I know. I think he just used an old folder or something. Trust me. It's not significant."

Zippy flipped through the folder quickly, closed it, and stuffed it underneath the rubber band of the manuscript. "I'll be needing this."

"But—"

Zippy held up a defiant hand. "Jonathan, either you let me do this or you don't. You want your bacon saved or not?"

Jonathan sighed. "Fine. Take it. Throw it away. Do whatever you want with it."

"Thank you. Now, without further ado, I'll go home and take a look at this."

Jonathan walked Zippy to the front door. "Francis, let's meet at the Coffee Bean tomorrow morning. Let's say ten?"

Zippy's face dropped like a wounded puppy's. "I'm busy. Shouldn't you be?"

Jonathan wasn't following. "I'm sorry? Would there be a better time?" Jonathan tried to smile graciously.

"I would say so. You shouldn't be available at ten either." His eyes narrowed scornfully. "Don't you go to church, Jonathan?"

Jonathan was so surprised by the question he barely had time to recover. "Oh. Tomorrow *is* Sunday, isn't it? Of course. Then one?" Again, he mustered a confident smile.

Zippy eyed him suspiciously but said, "Fine. One. At the Coffee Bean." Zippy wrapped his arms around the manuscript and ducked into the wind, running toward his car, a beat-up, rusted-out Volvo station wagon. The wind prickled Jonathan's skin like sharp needles, and he waved one more time at Zippy.

The rest of the evening, Jonathan went through the motions of normalcy. He played Chutes and Ladders with Leesol. He discussed school with Meg. He gave Sophie a bath and, later on, sat near the fire with his arms wrapped around Kathy as he explained the paradox of Francis Flowers and their plan to salvage Clyde's manuscript.

But what none of them knew, or could possibly know, was that fear had gripped him like a vise, and he wondered if they would wake up and find him dead in his bed the next morning. He thought about telling Kathy he had received one more page to the nightmare that had plagued them, but he couldn't even imagine how he would, so he kept the secret to himself, and rather well, he thought, considering Kathy had so far suspected nothing.

She yawned from the comfort of his arms and then stretched hers up and out, pulling her body up off his. "I'm tired. I think I'll head to bed. Are you coming?"

Jonathan smiled as if undecided, though he knew very well that he would not be coming up. "Oh, I'm really not tired yet. I slept until four, as you know," he said with a wink.

"Okay." She lingered in the room a little bit before she said, "Tomorrow . . . are you . . . coming?" She hardly waited for an answer. "To church?"

Church. It seemed to be the word for the day. But things were going well with them, and he didn't want to fuel the fire for any disagreements. Not now, anyway. "Of course," he said. He tried not to appear stiff. "Make sure I'm up."

The delight in her face warmed the room even more. "Thank you. Thank you."

He nodded and watched her prance up the stairs like a little girl. It made him smile. Soon, though, he rose from the couch and walked to his desk in his study. With a key inside a book on his shelf, he unlocked the drawer that held the gun he had purchased the week before. He checked for bullets and then turned out his study light and walked back into the living room.

The fire sounded like a wind tunnel, and even the wind outside had picked up. He randomly grabbed a book off the coffee table and opened it as if he were reading it. He turned out all the lights but one and tucked the gun underneath the cushion of the recliner. Sitting down, he tuned his ears to any outside noise.

And then it hit him. It hit him so hard it was as if someone had punched him in the stomach. He had a loaded gun in the house with three young girls. Was his paranoia worth all this? Was it worth risking their lives? His head fell into his hands, and then he made a snap decision. He rose, took the gun, emptied it of the bullets, and grabbed three trash sacks. He dropped the gun in one, then placed that one in the other trash sack, and then wrapped the whole thing in the third. It was disguised now. He went to the garage and dropped it into the trash.

He went back to the chair and sat down. His eyes scanned the room for makeshift weapons. Fireplace tools. Lamps. Statues.

Maybe he was destined to die soon. But it wasn't going to be tonight.

A soft giggle tickled his eardrums, and he batted away an imaginary object until he opened his eyes and realized morning had come and Leesol now stood beside the recliner with her hand over her mouth.

"Daddy! You fell asleep!"

He rubbed his eyes and welcomed the morning light. He couldn't remember when he had been happier to see it. "Good morning. What time is it?"

"Early," Leesol whispered. "Mommy's not up yet. I'm getting myself some cereal. Mom lets me on Sundays. But I have to eat it before I get dressed so I don't mess up my good Sunday clothes. Get it?"

Jonathan smiled. "Sure. Go on. I don't want to hold you up."

Leesol ran out of the room, and Jonathan was thankful the gun was gone. What could have happened if she'd found it? He went upstairs. As he rounded the corner into his bedroom, Kathy was just waking up. She peered at him through tired eyes.

"You're still in your clothes?"

He shrugged guiltily as he sat next to her. "I kind of fell asleep in the recliner downstairs. Reading."

"Oh. Well, as nice as those clothes are, you've had them on for more than forty-eight hours, so you'd better pick out something else." She kissed him on the cheek. As they say, the morning always brings unexpected new beginnings. If only he didn't have to fear unexpected endings.

The drive to church was delightfully bright and wholesome. Kathy quizzed Leesol and Meg on Scripture verses while Sophie tried to remember the song she had learned the week before. Everyone was talking at once, except Jonathan, who simply listened gratefully. It was good to be with his family again, in spirit, in mind, and in heart. Maybe this church thing wasn't so bad after all. It brought them all together, and that's what mattered to him the most.

During church, Jonathan felt his mind wandering. He wished he could've concentrated, but heavier things weighed on his heart. He wondered how he was going to survive the last message from the writer. He wondered what it meant. Several times throughout the sermon, he felt Kathy's stare, but he managed to greet it with an assuring smile and then somewhat attentive ears and eyes. Soon, though, the pastor's words would fade to the loud, clanging noise of fears and uncertainties inside his head.

Finally he felt Kathy's hand on his knee as she leaned over to his ear. "Are you okay? You're pale. Are you sick?"

He squeezed her hand. "I'm feeling a little woozy. Maybe too many pancakes. I just need a drink of water."

"Do you want me to come with you?" she asked quietly.

"No, no. I'll be okay. I'll be back."

Jonathan ducked and tried to inconspicuously make his way down the pew and out to the aisle. A few people stared, but most everyone else kept their attention on the pastor. His chest felt tight, and he tried to make a graceful exit without breathing hard and looking stressed. But as he reached the second to the last pew before the doors that led outside the sanctuary, he froze in his tracks and had to turn around. The pastor's last words sent a chill up his spine.

"Yes, my friends, there is life. But only through death. It is the seeming paradox of our faith that astonishes and confuses so many, yet there is no other way to find life."

Jonathan couldn't believe what he was hearing and became unaware of the fact that he was standing in the middle of the aisle while everyone else was seated in pews.

"So, my friends. Are you willing to die? Are you willing to give up the life that is so precious to you? Then, and only then, will you find life. And these are the words of our Lord Jesus Christ. Amen."

"Amen," the entire congregation responded. It startled Jonathan and he backed out of the sanctuary as if he'd seen a ghost. He went to the bathroom and vomited so hard he thought he would pass out. What was happening to him? Everywhere there was a message! Everywhere the writer spoke to him! About everything! And now through people! Through the pastor!

The bathroom door opened and someone came in. Jonathan flushed the toilet and opened the stall door, greeted an elderly man with a small smile, and then splashed his face with cold water. Maybe he had misunderstood the pastor. Maybe he only thought he heard that. Yes, that must've been it. He was hallucinating in a sense because he was short on sleep and those words were in the forefront of his mind.

He stepped out into a crowded hallway and looked for Kathy. He figured she'd gone to get Sophie, and he decided to stay nearby so they wouldn't miss each other. As the crowd in the hallway died down, a hand found its way to his shoulder and he turned around. It was Pastor Gregory.

"Jonathan, I was so glad to see you in service today. Where's Kathy?"

"The kids," Jonathan said with a shudder. "I think. Went to get."

Pastor Gregory could not hide his concern. In a low voice, he said, "Jonathan, why don't you step into my office? You look like you need to talk."

Jonathan resisted at first, but he didn't want to make a scene, either. Inside, Pastor Gregory shut his door and offered Jonathan a seat on a large, cheap-looking couch.

"I must admit I was surprised to see you. I had hoped to see you sooner since our last talk."

Jonathan played with the sleeve of his coat. "Been busy."

Pastor Gregory tried to catch Jonathan's darting eyes. "Jonathan, something is bothering you. What is it? You know you can trust me."

Jonathan's eyes found his. "I'm not sure whom I can trust, quite frankly."

The pastor's compassionate eyes urged him to continue. Jonathan tried to sit taller on the couch, but he felt as if he were drugged. His life was spinning out of control, and there was nothing he could do to stop it. He looked the pastor in the eye as best he could.

"Someone told me that I had to die." Jonathan blinked, trying to arrange his thoughts. "I messed up. I didn't love her like I should have." His own voice seemed far away. "So I have to die."

Pastor Gregory was quiet, trying to understand. Jonathan looked away.

"It probably doesn't make sense to you. But maybe it does. You said so in your sermon. Even you said it. That I have to die."

The pastor cleared his throat. "Well, yes. If you want the kind of life God wants for you." Pastor Gregory was opening his Bible. "Jonathan, your wife has been praying for you a long time. Praying that you would find your peace with God. Praying that you would know Him. Is that what's happening?" He looked up at Jonathan with caring eyes. "Are you realizing that your life without Him is empty?"

Jonathan swallowed the emotions that were creeping up through his throat. "Can someone speak from their grave? Maybe someone who has died and is in heaven? Can they talk to me?"

Pastor Gregory rubbed his forehead. "Jonathan, I'm not sure what you're—"

"Sounds stupid, doesn't it?" Jonathan interrupted with a sad laugh. "Like out of a horror movie. But it's happening. It's like a ghost following me everywhere I go. Knowing everything I do." He glanced up at Pastor Gregory. "Knowing everything I will do."

"Jonathan, please tell me what's going on."

Thick tears balanced on the rims of his eyes. "You wouldn't believe me if I told you." The tears dropped as Jonathan laid his head in his hands, his heavy body leaning forward, braced by his arms on his knees. "Maybe God wants me dead."

The pastor rose and joined Jonathan at the couch. "Why would you think God wants you dead?"

Jonathan looked up at Pastor Gregory. "Doesn't He? I've messed up. I thought I'd saved myself in time, but I guess I didn't. I'm supposed to die. To embrace the death that is required of me." Tears flowed rapidly from Jonathan's pleading eyes. "But how am I supposed to embrace a death that I don't want? I'm not ready to die. And I don't want to know that it's soon. I can't live my life day to day, wondering if this is the day that it will all end for me."

Pastor Gregory paused, his hands folded neatly together, his face peacefully concerned. Then he said, "Jonathan, are you talking about a literal death or a spiritual death?"

Jonathan blinked the tears away. "I . . . I thought . . ." He looked at Pastor Gregory with quizzical eyes.

The pastor's voice was calm and soothing. "Today, in my sermon, I was talking about dying to one's self. That means that we die to our desires and our wants, and we follow what God wants for us. We die to our old self and embrace the new life God has for us. We don't literally die. Is that what you thought I meant?"

Jonathan's mind snapped into consciousness, and he thought of the exact wording on the page he had received from the writer. "Pastor . . ." Jonathan said carefully. "How can death sting one that is dead?"

The pastor studied Jonathan's face. Then he said softly, "Are you dead, Jonathan? Spiritually?"

Jonathan swallowed. "I don't know. I don't know anything. I feel like God is closer than my shadow and farther than the sun." He looked at Pastor Gregory as he wiped a few stray tears away. "Does that make sense?"

"Sure, Jonathan. Everyone feels that way sometimes."

Jonathan stood and towered over him. "The death that is required of me . . . it's spiritual?"

"It is."

"Am I spiritually dead, Pastor?"

The pastor placed a gentle hand on Jonathan's shoulder. "Only you know that. Only you and God."

Jonathan managed to smile a little. "And one other person."

"Excuse me?"

"Nothing." Jonathan let out a breath and held out his hand to the pastor, who took it graciously. "I'm sorry. I'm sorry to . . . to fall apart on you."

The pastor frowned. "Are you sure you're okay? I'm not completely sure I follow what just happened here."

"Thank you for your time."

Jonathan left the office and walked down the hall toward the outside doors. As soon as he hit fresh air, he drew as much of it as he could into his lungs. Was this what the writer had wanted from him? A spiritual death? A renewal toward God? Not a physical death?

Then there was the overwhelming question of who—and why? He felt inspired to pray to God and run from Him all at once. Everything seemed so supernatural, yet all of the logic he knew told him there was a reasonable explanation for what was happening.

An arm reached around his waist. And then another one. He looked down to find his beautiful daughters clinging to him.

"Daddy! Daddy! We're hungry! Can we go?"

Kathy walked up next to him. "There you are. Are you feeling okay?"

Jonathan smiled as he played with Sophie's hair. "Yes. Fine. Let's go."

As they walked to the car, Jonathan looked back just once to see Pastor Gregory watching him from the dark window of his study. He wondered who else was watching him, too.

CHAPTER 26

Jonathan had dropped his family at the house and gone to the Coffee Bean early. He needed some time to think. But when he arrived, Zippy was already waiting for him and flagged him down at a corner table near a window. Jonathan sat across from him.

"Yuppieville, USA." Zippy sneered as he sank into his seat and guarded his coffee. "They think they become smarter by drinking coffee while sitting next to a bookshelf." He put a finger in his mouth and pretended to gag himself, then apparently stuck it too far down and did gag himself. "Sorry," he managed after an ineloquent recovery.

A waitress took Jonathan's order and then he said, "Tell me. How did the reading go last night?"

Zippy seemed to suddenly focus and his expression became serious. He pulled the pages out of a dirty old backpack. "I finished it. Every single word."

Jonathan smiled with delight. "Wonderful. Any thoughts on the ending?"

Zippy arranged the pages mindlessly. His thoughts were elsewhere. Finally he looked at Jonathan. "Yes. I know how it ends. I'm surprised you don't."

Jonathan frowned and cocked his head to the side. "You are? Why is that?"

Zippy's eyes dropped to the pages beneath his hands. "Nothing. Never mind."

"No, Francis, please. What is it?"

Jonathan had never seen a more sincere face on Zippy during their entire acquaintance. He seemed disturbed and anxious and gently determined. He scratched his head and said, "Well, this was obviously the first draft. Lacking a lot of character development. Missing some important plot points. Not unusual for a first draft from Clyde Baxter, from what I hear."

"Repairable, I'm assuming?"

"Yes, of course. Nothing I can't manage. For the right price."

"Always." Jonathan leaned forward on the wobbly table. "So? Are you going to keep me guessing? How does it end?"

"He dies."

Zippy's voice was strong and his words had a rare finality about them. Jonathan paused, then tore a packet of sugar open and poured it into his mug. "He dies. Okay. Sort of a downer ending, isn't it?"

"Well, in one sense, yes. In another sense, no."

"What do you mean?"

Zippy removed his glasses before he began. "It's not a downer for the man he's set free, now, is it?"

Jonathan thought about it. "So we're supposed to be happy about the murderer denying his knowledge of this guy's innocence and taking a freedom that didn't belong to him in the first place?" Jonathan shrugged. "Not exactly bonding material for the reader, is it?"

Zippy's fingers traced the edges of the pages. "It's a fascinating story, really, if you look close."

Jonathan was intrigued by Zippy's sudden abating offensiveness. He seemed real and normal in a way that surprised Jonathan into a curious stare.

Zippy continued. "The innocent man is set up by incarnate evil, yet it isn't the schemes and plotting of this that kills him in the end anyway. It's his silence. It's his love for this other prisoner." Zippy looked up at Jonathan. "He chose to die so a guilty man could go free."

Jonathan wanted to laugh, but a disturbing motion of rationalization stirred his spirit. He kept his voice quiet. "A little farfetched, wouldn't you say?"

Zippy put his glasses back on his nose and said, "Depends."

"Depends on what?"

"Depends on if it's ever happened to you." Zippy pulled his perpetual handkerchief from his pocket and wiped his nose. He remained silent, inviting a moment to think for both of them.

Jonathan tried to follow. "I see. So . . . has it ever happened to you? I didn't realize you had a prison record, Francis." Jonathan smiled at his own joke. Zippy found nothing funny about it. "Lincoln Smith isn't exactly what you'd call 'likeable.' That's what I meant."

"It has happened to me, actually. And I thought it had happened to you." Zippy's bloodshot eyes seemed to stare deeper into Jonathan's. Jonathan shook his head and laughed a little.

"I'm afraid not."

Zippy folded his handkerchief as he said, "Fascinating approach, really. Very strong marketing points . . . making the serial killer the beginning focal point of the book. People love stuff like that. Look at *The Silence of the Lambs*. The movie won an Oscar, for crying out loud." Jonathan couldn't take his eyes off Zippy. "The FBI agent and his sidekick DA lady make for interesting characters. But I do find it odd that we never meet the character that the entire book revolves around. Don't you?" He stirred his coffee and glanced up. "Don't you want to know this man more?"

Jonathan took out a note pad from his briefcase. "Well, I guess. Isn't the main character the FBI agent, though?"

"I suppose we do follow a man's journey to try to stop evil only to find a man who turns evil for good and makes the ultimate sacrifice for an unworthy prisoner's freedom."

"Maybe the angle Clyde was taking from here on out is what effect it has on this Spade character. What do you think? Does it affect him?"

"Sure."

Jonathan sipped his coffee. "Why can't the Spade fellow save him? Wouldn't that be a more exciting ending? A better one? He could get there just in the nick of time."

Zippy didn't miss a beat. "I guess that depends on who you want your savior to be."

Jonathan felt a strangeness in the air, but he dismissed it and continued. "Okay. So the hero, you mean?"

"You're uncomfortable with the word *savior*?" Zippy asked with directness.

Jonathan felt defensive. "*No*. I'm just clarifying here. Besides, why are you so sure the death of the innocent prisoner was Clyde's intended ending?"

"I read his notes."

"He didn't have any notes."

Zippy pulled the folder he had taken the night before out from underneath the manuscript. "These were his notes."

Jonathan took the folder and glanced at the contents. "A bunch of Bible verses?"

Zippy took the folder back, straightened the notes, and bound the manuscript in a rubber band. "That's the conclusion I came to. I feel quite certain that this is the ending Clyde wanted. But it's in your hands now." He handed the pile over to Jonathan. "Let me know what you decide."

"You're offended, Francis?" Jonathan asked carefully.

"Offended. No. Yuppies offend me. I'm perplexed."

"Perplexed. Well, I must say I am, too. I'm still wondering why Clyde wrote this manuscript. He told me before he died it was something he had to do." Jonathan shook his head. "Something he had to do before he died. I guess he started a little too late."

Zippy stood and gathered his things. "Actually, I was talking about you. You perplex me."

Jonathan frowned. "Me? Why?"

Zippy shrugged. "Because I thought you would know this story. I thought it would be as clear to you as it is to me."

Jonathan stood, too. "Francis, if you feel this strongly about the ending, I will consider it. I've got the afternoon to think about it. I'm not completely on board with the idea, but it's growing on me."

Zippy took one last look at Jonathan before adjusting his glasses. He had begun to move around Jonathan toward the door, but Jonathan stopped him with a gentle hand. "Francis . . . I . . . I want to thank you for this. For helping me out. I'm . . . I guess you could say I'm on my last leg with the house. I just . . . really need this."

Zippy buttoned his stained cardigan that looked like it would perfectly fit a schoolgirl and said. "That's not what you need, Jonathan. Not what you need at all."

The afternoon and night, until the early hours of the morning, were spent locked away in his study, typing out proposals, contemplating Clyde's manuscript, rewriting, and then tossing it all and starting over. Jonathan's head pounded with pressure and his muscles ached with stress. But he was relentless. This had to get done. His job, his reputation, and even a little bit of his sanity depended on it.

His process was slowed down, though, by the looming thoughts of the page the writer had sent and the words of Pastor Gregory that morning. He was beyond answers and knew it, but his mind convinced him to keep trying to find that single clue that would lead him to an answer. And his mind was not about to let him forget the death threats that Sydney's fiancé, Jeremy, was supposedly making toward him. Was it just a coincidence that the writer had told him to embrace his death? Was it as close as the angry young man in leather? Did Jeremy really intend to kill him?

And then there was the odd conversation with Zippy that afternoon. He had never seen Zippy like that. It was as if he'd found his element. But the question was, what exactly *was* that element?

Jonathan warmed his hands against the fresh cup of coffee he had poured and leaned into his chair. He contemplated Clyde's story line with the ending that Zippy had offered—insisted upon. It wasn't such an unlikely ending. Many classics were made famous by their disturbing endings.

But Nellie didn't want a classic. She wanted a bestseller.

If he chose that ending, he knew much of the book would have to be rewritten. He would have to find some motivation for the James character to die for Lincoln Smith. After all, the man was a filthy, lying, no-good criminal who was hardly worth the clothes on his back. What in the world would make someone like Joseph James give his life for him? Maybe they knew each other. Or maybe Smith had done something kind for James a long time ago. That would need to be resolved.

Secondly, he would need to know more about Joseph James. If not, then it was just a shell of a story. It wasn't real. But he was sure Zippy could handle that. He did think it was odd that Clyde hadn't developed him more. He was a great writer. He knew better than to leave a character underdeveloped like that, even in the first draft.

Jonathan's thoughts drifted to the character of Dietrich Donomar. He wondered what inspired Clyde to write such a purely evil character. And why did the whole story revolve around him, instead of the James character? If you're going to have a hero, at least get to know him.

He pictured Clyde at his desk with a yellow note pad, writing illegibly, drinking iced tea. Why had this story been so important to him? A serial killer? A hero we know nothing about? A prisoner set free for no good reason? The story itself was as perplexing as the motivation for writing it.

Still . . . something about it kept him rallying for it. Maybe it was just his desperation for two good sells. Maybe it was clouding his judgment. Maybe Clyde Baxter's book was nothing more than an old man's attempt at one last hurrah.

No. It was more than that. This story had a meaning. If only to Clyde. But now Jonathan had to make it have meaning for everyone other than Clyde.

The clock read 1:43 A.M. Jonathan moved to his computer and began to type. He was surprised how fast and easy the ideas flowed out of him. With each passing minute, Jonathan Harper felt he was creating a masterpiece. And an hour and a half later, he knew beyond a shadow of a doubt that the strange story about the serial killer, the prisoner, and the innocent hero would pass with flying colors.

But shades of gray quickly colored over his confidence in the form of doubt. A battle inside him brewed. He had to make a decision by morning.

"How do I look?" Jonathan nervously asked the four women at the table.

"Wonderful," Kathy said.

"Very professional," Meg offered.

"I like your tie!" Leesol chimed in.

Jonathan looked at Sophie. "What about you, sweetheart? You think Daddy looks good this morning?"

"Daddeeee!" Sophie squealed, then took a handful of oatmeal and hurled it at Jonathan. It splattered on his tie and white shirt as if he'd had a bull's-eye painted there.

"Sophie!" Kathy scolded, rushing over to a stunned Jonathan. "Honey, here, let me help you." Kathy carefully removed his jacket. "It missed this, at least. Let's go upstairs and get a new white shirt and tie." Kathy glanced back at the table. "Meg, watch your sisters."

Upstairs, Kathy went to the closet and came out with a new white shirt and dark-colored tie. Jonathan sat on the edge of the bed and removed his stained clothing. "This was my lucky tie," he said with a heavy sigh. "I've worn it every time I've had a big proposal." He looked up at his wife. "And this is my biggest day ever."

Kathy handed him the tie and shirt. "You'll do fine. You don't need a lucky tie."

Jonathan stood and put on the new shirt. "I feel sick."

"Do you need breakfast? Breakfast would help."

"No. I can't eat."

Kathy touched his face. "Jonathan, you're going to do fine. This isn't life or death."

Jonathan tried to hide the fact that a cold chill ran up his spine. He pulled away from her and went to the bathroom, pretending to need to check his hair. "Okay, I guess I'll get going."

Kathy followed him downstairs and helped him on with his coat. She kissed him and then wrapped his scarf around his neck. "Knock 'em dead."

"Enough with the death analogies, okay?" Jonathan said half jokingly. "Sorry. I'm just nervous."

She laid the collar of his coat down. "All right. Break a leg. Does that work?"

Jonathan smiled and kissed her. "I'll take that over being dead any day of the week."

Jonathan looked at his three girls, who sat at the table with encouraging, bright smiles on their faces.

"Good luck, Daddy!" Meg said, and the other two nodded.

"Thanks. I love all of you."

Jonathan walked outside and down the sidewalk. As he unlocked his car, the lump in his throat grew bigger. "Please, God, let me see them again," he whispered, his breath freezing in front of him and then blowing away in the strong north wind.

The drive to work was slow. A heavy snow had fallen the night before and the salt trucks lined the main streets, slowing traffic down even further. Jonathan didn't mind. The meeting wasn't until eleven, and he was in no hurry to get anywhere fast.

He was on three hours' sleep. He'd pitched proposals on less. But, as hard as he tried, he couldn't rid himself of the events in his life.

As if the strange manuscript about his life wasn't enough of a mystery, the last page seemed to have a mystery of its own. Jonathan had assumed the death it said was required of him was a physical death. But Pastor Gregory had spoken the same words and meant a spiritual death. What was the difference? And which did the writer mean? Jonathan's thoughts darkened as he wondered if there was a difference at all. Many men had died a physical death to keep from dying a spiritual one.

Perhaps the guilt he still felt over Sydney brought him to the conclusion that he should die a physical death. It had been many, many years since adultery was punishable by death, yet the guilt that came with it was enough to condemn him alone.

A car in front of him slid sideways and then recovered, causing Jonathan to use greater caution. Unless, of course, the writer controlled the weather as well and this was how he was to fulfill those mysteriously prophetic words.

His thoughts mingled together like old friends until he reached the parking lot of the publishing house. He parked his car in his reserved spot and sat with the engine running. The tall building loomed over him, and he realized he'd never noticed much about it before. He'd walked in and out of it, had failures and successes in it, made friends and enemies inside the doors, but he'd never really noticed how dark the windows were or how red the brick was. He never noticed the landscaping that was now covered in white snow. He smiled a little. It was amazing how beautiful snow made everything. Even the dirty parking lot, stained with oil and tire marks, glowed like a white cloud underneath a hot sun. The snow blanketed everything and made it pure. If only he could be covered like that. If only he could be made pure.

He turned off his engine and wrapped his scarf tightly around his neck. He started to button his coat until he glanced out of his window. Snow had begun to fall again. It fell lightly, as if not heavy enough to even carry it to the ground. Jonathan looked up to find a small cloud from the west moving in, nearly covering the sun, but not quite.

Stepping out of his vehicle, he planted his foot firmly into the snow so as not to slip, then buttoned his coat and covered his face with his scarf. He grabbed his briefcase and shuffled his way up the sidewalk and into the building. The monotony of his routine brought him little comfort, and he was barely aware the elevator doors had opened to his floor until Nellie walked by and said, "Don't forget the meeting."

Jonathan nodded and walked exactly seventeen paces to Edie's desk, picked up his memos, avoided Edie's eyes, and went to his office. He set his briefcase down on his desk, removed his coat, threw it over a chair, then pulled up the shades.

He pressed his hands against the window. The snow was falling harder now. The sky was almost entirely white. Everything below was dusted completely by it. Nothing was left untouched by its beauty. Except him.

It was out there. And he was in here. He was separated from it by an invisible piece of glass that let him look and yearn . . . but not touch.

C H A P T E R 27

Jonathan felt energized. The round table held the people who could make or break him. They were putty in his hands. Zippy's proposal had flown without a hitch. Nellie had even winked and said, "You sold me. I can't believe it. But you sold me."

It was like old times. The mood was light. The trust was in him. Everyone was laughing and joking. Things couldn't be better.

Robert Huff, another senior editor, was passing croissants around the table. "The big dog is back!"

"Woof, woof!" Peter Strong, managing editor, added. "I gotta hand it to you, Harper, we've been joking for weeks about this."

Jonathan smiled smoothly, passing on the croissants but pouring himself a glass of water. "You doubted me?" he asked with a charming grin.

"We doubted Zippy," Peter Strong replied and everyone laughed.

Austin Sable pushed half a croissant in his mouth and, before chewing, said, "Va name is a huve provem."

Nellie agreed. "Francis Flowers isn't exactly a catchy name."

"Unless you're a romance novelist," Lisa Potter, the newest senior editor, added.

Jonathan held up his hands to quiet down the laughter. "I know,

369

I know. I've already discussed it with Zippy."

"Did you come up with a good pen name?" Austin asked, finally swallowing the food in his mouth.

Jonathan clasped his hands behind his back. "Not yet. But I'm sure we'll come up with something agreeable."

"I trust Jonathan. It's not an issue." Ezra Arnott, vice president of Bromahn & Hutch, was in his seventies. His hair was so silver it was almost reflective, and he had a tan that seemed to last all year round. For thirty-nine years he had sat in on committee meetings. He had started in the mail room, moved to a low-ranking editor, and worked himself all the way up to vice president. His suits were Armani. His friends were famous. He had final say on everything that happened in fiction. And he trusted Jonathan. Jonathan smiled.

"Thank you, Mr. Arnott." Jonathan glanced at Nellie, who was smiling and relaxed. Nellie was never relaxed at committee meetings.

"Okay, Jonathan, one down, one to go. Tell us about Clyde's novel," Nellie said, then added somberly to the rest of the group, "As all of you know, Clyde's death has put this house in a precarious position. We were counting on revenues that will not happen now. However, this final book could be very big for us, especially if we market it right." Nellie looked at Austin. "So let's listen carefully and give Jonathan our full attention."

The room quieted and everyone sat forward in their seats. It had been a long time since he had held a room so captive.

"Thank you, Nellie." Jonathan took the stack of proposals in front of him and passed them around the room. "As all of you know, Clyde had retired from writing when he approached me about one final work—that was not a western." A soft murmur swept the room. Jonathan laughed. "I know, I know. I was skeptical as well. As our fine editorial director pointed out to me, crossing over to a new genre has ruined more writers' careers than demon agents. But, nevertheless, I felt I . . . we . . . owed Clyde at least a look at it. And it's here today because I feel like it deserves more than a look. I feel it deserves publication."

Peter Strong flipped through the pages of the proposal and laughed out loud. "A serial killer. Are you serious?"

Jonathan smiled confidently. "Well, Clyde wanted to sail uncharted waters in children's books."

Nellie's face paled. "It's a children's book?"

"I'm kidding," Jonathan said, and the group all laughed, except Nellie, who was shaking her head and asking for water. "Actually, people, it's a little hard to describe. I would say it's a thriller. But it's much more than that. You could say it's a drama, but you've got the creepy serial killer. And there's a little humor in there, too."

"Gee, you're making my job easier," Austin quipped sarcastically as he bit off the end of yet another croissant.

"Get used to it, Sable," Jonathan said with a wink. "This is just the beginning."

The group laughed again, and even Nellie managed to smile. "Go on, Jonathan. I want to hear this," she said.

"Basically, the plot centers around a serial killer who is crazy like a fox and smarter than NASA. He's one of the most prolific serial killers the country has ever seen. And, like the book says, he's bored. Three men are about to be executed on death row, and one is innocent, accused of a crime the serial killer has actually committed. So his goal is to kill the innocent guy."

"Why?" Robert asked.

"It's simple. He's evil incarnate."

The room sank into silence until Austin said, "Wow. There's a complex character for you."

Nervous laughs were followed by stares at Jonathan. "*Anyway*, the serial killer lures in an FBI agent by the name of Keaton Spade to fall for his setup. Spade becomes obsessed by the whole thing and is determined to stop the serial killer's plan from happening. Spade gets the DA involved. To make a long and complex part of the story short, they release a prisoner they believe is the innocent one. Unfortunately, they are wrong. They've released the wrong prisoner. So there are two prisoners left. And time is running out for both of them. But the serial killer isn't going to make it easy. He's got a single clue that proves who is innocent and who is guilty. Unfortunately, he won't reveal the clue until they've decided which prisoner to release.

"The media and agenda groups are pressuring the DA and the

governor to make a decision. Three recent executions of innocent men fuel the fire. The heat is on. The DA decides both are guilty and refuses to look into it any further. However, the governor then gets involved and comes to a decision. He has decided which prisoner to release."

"Which one?" Lisa Potter asked anxiously.

Jonathan smiled. "His name is Lincoln Smith. Accused of killing his prostitute girlfriend. A real lowlife."

"Is he the innocent one?" Peter leaned forward on the table.

Jonathan had them and he knew it. "Well, we don't find out until he's released. And he's released the same day the other one is to be executed. So the FBI agent goes to the serial killer's cell and demands proof that they've released the right prisoner. But to his horror, the serial killer shows him otherwise."

"What's the proof?" Robert Huff asked, glancing around at the other captive audience members.

"A tattoo on his arm. It matches the tattoo on the victim's arm the other prisoner is accused of killing. Everyone missed it. Even the FBI."

"What happens?" Nellie's eyes widened.

"Agent Spade rushes home to try to call the DA, but when he gets there he remembers he found a mysterious note on his door before he left to see the serial killer. It is from the innocent prisoner. It tells him not to try to save him."

"He wants to die?" Austin asked with genuine curiosity.

"No. But he wants the other prisoner to live."

Everyone in the room glanced around the table. Jonathan continued. "So the FBI agent has one chance left. He races to the governor's mansion and begs to see him. When he finally gets to speak to the governor, he realizes the governor's reasons for releasing the other prisoner were strictly political. He doesn't care who lives or dies. And he doesn't care who is innocent. All he cares about is that he's gotten votes from both parties, and he's in good political standing."

Jonathan stopped and looked around the room. Everyone was holding their breath. He waited for a moment and finally Nellie said, "Well, come on, Jonathan, let's hear the ending."

Jonathan cleared his throat and sipped his water in a casual manner. "That is the ending."

Eyebrows raised and heads turned. "*That's* the ending?" Peter asked with a disapproving laugh.

"Well, death does have a way of leaving things a bit unraveled. That's where Clyde left off when he died."

Nellie's expression turned to worry. "That's not good."

Jonathan smiled at her. "Never fear, dear Nellie. It's Jonathan Harper to the rescue. I have hired a ghostwriter, and we have come to a conclusion as to how Clyde intended to end the book."

Nellie reached for the pitcher of water. "Thank goodness, Jonathan. I thought you meant that's how the whole story ended. The innocent guy dies."

Jonathan scratched his ear. "Well . . . um, there's a little more to the story than that. I mean, the agent tries to get there in time, and he does, but the innocent prisoner refuses to see him." Jonathan paused. His heart began to race. Suddenly the six pairs of eyes that were on him seemed like a hundred. The hot air from the vent above him started making him feel a little sweaty. "And so . . . he dies. And the other prisoner goes free."

You could hear a pin drop in the room, and soon a pen did drop. Nellie's. Straight onto the table with a loud thud, then rolling several feet to the other side. She blinked twice, looked down at her notes, and glanced around the room.

"Jonathan, are you trying to tell me that the ending to Clyde's novel is that the serial killer wins? The innocent man is executed?"

"Oh no. Not like that. See, the serial killer *thinks* he wins. But the truth of the matter is that the innocent prisoner chooses to die."

More silence was followed by Robert saying, "What's the difference?"

Jonathan gulped his water. "The difference is that he chose this for himself. He wanted the other man to live."

Lisa looked down at her notes. "A man accused of killing his prostitute girlfriend?"

An annoying and sharp itch moved over Jonathan's scalp. "Well, yes. See, the innocent prisoner has a positive effect on everyone he comes in contact with. Even the warden says so. He's an extraordinary human being."

"So extraordinary that he dies in the end? On purpose?" Austin looked around the room at the others. "I'm not seeing the appeal here."

Nellie was tugging at her French twist. "It's a sad ending, Jonathan."

"Not if you're the prisoner set free."

Austin laughed out loud. "What does that mean?"

Jonathan's undershirt was soaked. "If you're the guy that gets set free, it's a good deal for you."

Peter and Robert exchanged glances and then Robert said, "Sure. But who's going to want to read a story about some loser who needs to be executed being set free by a man who doesn't deserve it?"

Austin's laugh grew louder. "Yeah. I can see the catalog copy now. 'Warning: Ending of this book may make you want to hang yourself.' "

A mild chuckle grew into a louder laugh. Jonathan glanced at Nellie, who had poked an entire pencil straight through her twist. She looked up at Jonathan, her eyes filled with uneasiness.

"Everyone settle down," she said sternly. Jonathan noticed Austin was the last one to stop laughing. "Let's take this seriously." She looked at Jonathan. "Jonathan, you realize we've got a huge problem here."

Jonathan swallowed and wanted to drink more water, but his glass was empty. And so was the pitcher next to Nellie. "We do?" he said in pretend confidence.

Nellie flipped through some pages of her notes. "First of all, when do we meet the innocent prisoner?"

"Meet him?"

"In the story."

"Oh." The back of his shirt was soaked through. "You don't."

Everyone was shooting questions and answers.

"The main character is the FBI agent?"

"So the hero fails."

"But he's not the hero. The prisoner is."

"That doesn't make sense. We've got two heroes and both fail."

Jonathan tried to chime in. "He doesn't fail. It's his choice."

"And our hero lets a murderer free. Wow. That's reassuring as I lock my door and load my gun," Lisa said as she shook her head.

"But the prisoner is changed by it . . . by him. . . . You see?" Jonathan added, though no one heard him.

Austin toyed with his croissant. "And what else happens? The serial killer gets elected president?"

"Cut it out, Austin," Nellie snapped. She calmed everyone down, then looked at Jonathan. "If we never get to know the man, how do we know why he dies for this other prisoner?"

Jonathan could hardly breathe. His palms were as slick as oil. He cracked his knuckles and said, "Well . . . because he . . . he loves him."

Austin's snicker was met with a sharp eye from Nellie, who then said, "They knew each other? They were friends?"

"Well, no."

"The other prisoner did something for him? Maybe saved his life once?"

"No."

Four out of five of Nellie's fingers on her left hand were in her French twist. Jonathan met the stares of everyone in the room. "None of you are getting this?" he asked.

Peter looked down. Lisa began writing in her note pad. Robert just stared back at him with lost eyes. Austin was laughing under his breath and picking at his croissant. Nellie had added another three fingers from her other hand into her hairdo. But worst of all, Ezra Arnott's eyes were filled with pity.

Jonathan leaned forward on the table, trying to find a way to recover. His eyes found Nellie's, and for a second they locked. Then Nellie said as she looked away, "I'm sorry, Jonathan. I just don't think we can make this fly."

Jonathan straightened up. "Why? Sure, there are some holes in the story. But it's nothing that can't be fixed. I've got Zippy as the ghostwriter. You've seen what he can do with fiction. He can fill in the blanks. He can make it happen."

Austin tossed his croissant on a napkin. "This isn't going to happen. Not with an ending like this. Not with a name like Clyde Baxter."

Nellie's sad eyes found Jonathan's. "Jonathan, you know what Clyde's readers expect from him. I mean, I wasn't opposed to Clyde switching genres. But a story like this would kill us. We can't let Clyde's last novel be something like this."

"But . . ." Jonathan's voice cracked. "This is what he wanted. He told me. He had to write this before he died."

"The guy was like a hundred or something, wasn't he? He probably wasn't thinking straight. It happens to the best of us." Austin looked at Jonathan and winked. "Right, buddy?"

The blood that was pumping into his heart suddenly made its way to his face, turning it a bright red and pushing beads of perspiration out of his pores. "You think you're smart, Austin? You're a kid. You wouldn't know a good piece of literature if it read itself to you. Can you even read?"

Austin sat up in his seat. "Look, I'm not the enemy here. I'm just saying this is a marketing nightmare. From every conceivable angle." He looked at Nellie.

"Why don't you stuff your flapping tongue back into that big mouth of yours before I stuff a croissant down your throat."

Austin's condescending laugh resonated off the walls. "I'd like you to come over here and try."

Before Jonathan could move, Peter had hopped up and grabbed his shoulders. He looked him in the eyes. "Jon, it's not worth it. He's not worth it," he said in a soft voice that was intended for no one else.

"Sit down! Everyone sit down!" Nellie's shaking hand brought an empty glass to her trembling lips. She slammed the glass down and everyone took their seats. Half her hair was now falling down, and her fingernails nervously clicked against the side of the glass. "This isn't a war room, for crying out loud. What is wrong with all of you?" She drew in a breath and tried to put her hair back in place, an impossibility even with hairpins. She looked around the room. "The question here is, do we think this book is right for our house? Do we think it will sell well? Do we think it has something to say?" Her eyes roamed the room. "These are the questions we ask of every book, do we not? Is it good writing? Is it a good plot? Is it the type of fiction we want to put our name on?"

Everyone in the room focused their attention on Nellie. Except Jonathan. All he could do was look down at his feet.

"Now. I want everyone here to focus. To focus on the issue at hand here. We have a famous author that our house represents. He's written one final book that is not in the genre that made him famous. It has an ending that hardly makes sense to anyone sitting in this room. What are we going to do about it?" Nellie's voice was stern and direct, and everyone became a professional again.

Lisa was the first one to speak. "I have to say, I wish this wasn't his last story. I mean, *Mahogany Hills* was so great. His career ended on a high. Do we dare mess with that?"

Peter Strong clicked his pen rapidly. "I agree with Lisa. The ending kills it for me. And the plot, though fascinating, has a few holes in it."

"But that's something that a ghostwriter can fix," Robert added. He then looked at Jonathan. "But the ending . . . that's the real problem. Doesn't everyone agree?" A couple of people nodded, though Jonathan knew everyone agreed with him. Robert leaned forward on the table. "What about changing the ending? Making the FBI agent rescue him at the last second? That's more along the lines of what Clyde writes."

The room came alive with hearty agreement. Jonathan felt so tired he couldn't even stand. The noise died down as everyone focused their attention on Jonathan, who sat down slowly.

"Well?" Nellie finally asked. "What about changing the ending? Then it could possibly be salvaged."

Jonathan felt a pain inside himself. Not a physical pain. Something deeper. Something stronger. It was as if his soul had been cut. It confused him. He'd never felt anything like it. It was like something inside of him was grieving. His hand moved over his trembling lips as he tried to hold himself together. He looked down at the table and said, in a babbling manner, "But . . . it doesn't really work with a different ending. It's about sacrifice . . . and freedom. Freedom that isn't earned but given. It makes you richer . . . and you appreciate it if it's not yours to have. . . . It's not about the serial killer and the FBI agent. It's about this prisoner."

There was a long silence. The whole room had come to a complete standstill. "Then why does the whole story revolve around the serial killer and FBI agent?" Nellie finally asked.

Jonathan didn't know. He didn't know anything at this moment. It was as if he had been swept into space and didn't have any oxygen. The room tilted back and forth, and he closed his eyes to try to refocus.

"Jonathan, are you saying you're unwilling to change the ending of this book?" he heard Nellie ask.

Jonathan swallowed. His mouth was dry as cotton. He finally looked up at Nellie, and Nellie only, and said, "That's what I'm saying."

Nellie's disapproving eyes might as well have cut his throat.

"All right," she said in a forceful, professional tone. "Then let's vote. Peter?"

Peter's eyes were downcast on the papers in front of him. "No, Nellie."

"Lisa?"

A pause, and then, "No."

"Robert?"

"No."

"Austin?"

"Nope."

The last one left was Ezra. Jonathan looked up at him. Ezra met his eyes, and then in a regretful voice said, "No."

It was as final as death. Nellie jotted down a note or two, then said, "The meeting is adjourned."

The group rose slowly, gathered their things, and left, each eyeing Jonathan as if he were a freak show at a circus. Nellie was the last one out, and she lingered in the doorway.

"Why'd you do this, Jonathan? You know what this means to your career."

Jonathan looked up at her, his eyes red and his face splotchy. "I don't know. I guess I don't have a lot to lose."

Nellie tilted her head and frowned. "What do you mean by that?

You've got so much, Jonathan. This was your big chance. You had a lot to lose today."

Jonathan hung his head. "Not so much, really."

Nellie shook her head. "I don't get it. You used to be my shining star. Now you're like a black hole. I don't understand what's happening to you."

"Neither do I," Jonathan managed before his throat swelled so tightly with emotions that he had to turn away. He heard Nellie step out of the room and close the door.

A black hole was right. He'd never felt deader inside.

———

Five o'clock came and went, and around five-thirty he noticed most of the office had left due to the heavy snow that had fallen. He finally managed to get out of his chair. Quietly unlocking his door, he peeked to make sure no one was around.

He went back to his office and grabbed his coat and briefcase. The elevator arrived quickly at his floor and made a quiet descent. When he got off, he started toward the exit where his car was. He didn't want to go home. But he didn't know where he needed to go. No certain "place" was going to make him feel any better.

He sighed and decided to go outside at the back of the building, where they had landscaped a small parklike area where editors, writers, agents, and whomever else could come and talk or think. It was quite beautiful in the spring, when the flowers were blooming and the grass was green.

Jonathan walked to the back exit and went outside. The snow covered all the benches and sidewalks, and the pond was glassy ice. It was a winter wonderland that meant nothing to him. Right now it was just a cold place to sit.

He swept off a bench with his bare hand and sat down, hunching over to try to stay warm. He wanted to cry. Hard. But the cold, adding to his already numb body and mind, kept anything from happening other than a tired, old body sitting on a soggy, wooden bench.

A hand touched his shoulder. Jonathan turned around to find Zippy, bundled in a snowsuit, looking down at him.

"Jonathan Harper, what in the world are you doing out here in this weather?" Zippy reached up to swipe at his drippy nose.

Jonathan didn't bother to continue looking at him. "If you're wondering about your book, they took it. With flying colors. They loved it."

Zippy was blowing hot air into his mittens. "You don't seem too happy about it."

"I need to be alone right now, Francis. I'm sorry. I'm happy for you. But I need to be alone."

Zippy plopped his padded form down on the bench next to Jonathan. "I don't think you need to be alone."

"I really do." Jonathan tried to keep his body from shaking.

Zippy arranged himself better on the bench and said, "Clyde's proposal didn't go well, did it?"

Jonathan looked up. "How'd you know that? They've called all the authors in the house and told them, too?" Jonathan looked away angrily.

"No. It was just a hunch."

"A hunch? Well, if you had that hunch yesterday, why didn't you say something? It could've saved me a lot of grief."

He zipped up his snowsuit as high as it would go. "What happened?"

Jonathan sighed, realizing Zippy wasn't going anywhere soon. "It just . . . it didn't fly. It was like I had them, all the way to the ending. And then it fell to pieces. They were asking questions I couldn't answer. I was practically laughed out of the room." He looked down at the snow. "They asked me to change the ending. And I said no. Isn't that crazy? I must've lost my mind. I said no."

Zippy wiped his nose with the thumb of his mitten. "Why didn't you change the ending?"

Jonathan shrugged, a cold shiver crawling up the skin over his spine. "I don't know, exactly."

A light snow began to fall, and Jonathan welcomed the small flakes on his face. Then after a long silence, Zippy said, "I do."

"You do what?"

"I know why you refused to change the ending."

"You do, do you?"

"Yes, I do." Zippy's glasses fogged up, but he continued. "It was because it made sense to you. The other ending didn't. Sure, it would've been a better sell, but you would've lost something important in the book."

Jonathan swallowed and dusted the snow off his face. "You're right. That's exactly how I felt." He looked at Zippy. "How did you know that?"

Zippy smiled and pushed his fogging glasses up on his bright red nose. "It's because that's how I felt about it. That's how I knew the ending."

Jonathan sat on his hands and stared out at the frozen pond. "But . . . why? Why does it make sense to us and not everyone else?"

Zippy paused before saying, "Don't you see, Jonathan? Clyde Baxter didn't write this book to be another bestseller. He wrote it because there was a message he wanted to send."

Jonathan blinked away the snow on his lashes. "A message? Well, the message I got from my fellow editors today is that this book is missing a lot of pieces."

"Like?"

"If the story revolves around this innocent prisoner, why do we never meet him? And what exactly is his motivation for exchanging his life with a guy like Lincoln Smith? Why is the entire story based on a serial killer and his whole plot to kill this guy?" Jonathan shook his head. "I couldn't answer any of those questions today! I looked like an idiot!"

"I can answer all of them." Zippy took his glasses off and wiped them with his sleeve.

Jonathan was stunned. "You can?"

Zippy nodded humbly. Then he said, "I can answer those questions because the book wasn't ever written to be published. I believe, Jonathan, it was written for you."

Jonathan held his breath. "For me?"

"Yes. Clyde wanted you to see something about your life."

Jonathan could hardly speak. "What?"

Zippy adjusted himself on the bench and pulled at his mittens. "It's a story about your life, in a sense."

"My life?" Jonathan laughed.

"Yes. You see, I believe Clyde was trying to show you a picture of your life without God." Jonathan swallowed hard. Zippy continued. "The innocent prisoner represents Jesus Christ. The reason you never meet the innocent man who sacrifices his life for the guilty man is that you, Jonathan, don't know that innocent man. You don't know Christ. It doesn't change the fact that He's willing to die to set guilty men free, to die in their place. But to you, you're looking from the outside in, like a shell of a story that doesn't have any meat or motivation. You can see what's happening, but you don't know why, and it's not personal to you." He rubbed his mitten across his nose.

Jonathan frowned and listened carefully. "Why . . . why is the story told from the point of view of the serial killer?"

Zippy's glasses fogged over again. "I believe the serial killer represents Satan. Satan is a distraction to us all. His plan is to get rid of the one man who represents everything he is against. But, like Keaton Spade, we all get caught up in his plan and forget to look at Christ's plan for our lives. But what Donomar intended for evil, the innocent prisoner turned to good. And even though Donomar thought that he had control over the situation, in the end it was the innocent man's *choice* to give his life away that caused the events to happen. At any time he could've proclaimed his innocence and stopped the execution. There was more than enough outside evidence to do that. But instead, he died quietly for another prisoner."

Cold tears dripped down Jonathan's bright red cheeks. "But why would he die for someone like Lincoln Smith? A murderer! Who hung out with prostitutes and drug users?"

Zippy's eyes focused on Jonathan's. "Well, I can't imagine any of us are close to worthy enough to let an innocent man die for our sins, are we? Lincoln Smith represents what all of us look like on the inside. And that's exactly what Christ died for."

Jonathan let out a soft cry and turned away, blotting his tears with the edge of his coat. "This is unreal. . . ."

"It is very real. It was obviously real to Clyde Baxter. Real enough for him to write an entire story about it." Zippy leaned forward to see Jonathan's face. "And I suspect that this story touches you in a way that is very personal, doesn't it?" A loud sneeze exploded into Zippy's mitten, but he wiped away the evidence and sat quietly.

Jonathan couldn't answer. He was stunned and crushed and revived and grieved all at once. He just nodded his head as the tears poured out of his eyes. He felt Zippy's mittened hand pat him on the back.

"This is a wonderful thing this man has done for you. He wrote a story that would make sense to you. He knew it would eventually, though I imagine he thought he would be the one to interpret it for you when you looked him in the eye and told him his story had some major holes in it."

Zippy squeezed Jonathan's shoulder and said, "He wants you to see there's a man who was willing to die for you. In place of you. You're not worthy of it. But He loves you. You just don't know He loves you because you don't know Him. He's just a character in a story to you. But you know of Him, and you know that it is *His* part of the story that is powerful. It is His part of the story that is worth telling. You've been distracted a long time by the enemy and his plot to keep you away from this man and keep your attention on him. But now you've come face-to-face with this extraordinary man. You've come face-to-face with the truth. With what matters."

Jonathan's tears flowed faster. "What do I do?"

Zippy smiled and wiped his nose again. "You get down on your knees and you accept what He's given you. That's what you do. And then you pray that you would understand why, and understand Him more, and know Him more." Zippy stood. "That's what He wants most. For you to know Him."

Jonathan looked up at Zippy. The snow had begun to fall harder. "Thank you," he whispered through his tears.

Zippy nodded, unfogged his glasses, and walked slowly down the sidewalk and back into the building, sneezing and hacking all the way.

Jonathan cried harder than he had ever cried in his life, and before he could stop himself, he fell to his knees in the cold, packed snow and clasped his hands together. No words came.

None that were verbal, anyway. He knew he didn't have to say anything. He knew the prisoner in that cell heard his heart.

But what he didn't know was that, as he knelt down on the ground and gave his life to God, a soft blanket of snow had covered him. He was finally pure.

CHAPTER 28

You will go to the old park.
You will follow the path into the trees.
There you will meet your Maker.
Be there. For your family's sake.

Jonathan was completely soaked, even through his coat, but he didn't notice. His frozen hand held a single sheet of paper that he had pulled out of a manila envelope he found underneath the snow on the windshield of his car.

He reread the four sentences carefully. He knew the old park. It was twenty minutes from his house. He and his family used to go there all the time, until they built the newer one three miles away from their home. Now this one sat on the outskirts of town, barely used. Not too many people even knew it still existed. In fact, he and Kathy hadn't even taken Sophie there. It had only one piece of playground equipment. The new one had fifty-two pieces, plus a gigantic rocket slide.

The path into the trees was always off limits. At least to the children. It led to a thick grouping of trees that always seemed ominous. One time Meg had run in there and gotten lost for ten minutes.

Jonathan swallowed hard as he looked at the paper again. *There you will meet your Maker*. Jonathan couldn't help but laugh a little, and he said out loud, "I just did." But the humor faded at the very real possibility that the writer meant that this would be the night he would die. He thought he had it all figured out. He thought his death was spiritual. Now he wasn't so sure.

Jonathan managed to move his stiff body enough to get into his vehicle and turn on the heat. His nose was still running from all the cold and emotions he had just experienced. The heavy, invisible burden that had hunched his shoulders for so long was gone. He'd never felt freer. He'd never felt more loved.

And now he never felt more scared.

Be there. For your family's sake. Would something happen to his family if he didn't go? The thought sickened him. He needed God now more than ever. Tonight was the night that the writer had destined for him to die. Just when he had found life. Jonathan shook his head at the irony, then carefully set the sheet of paper down next to him on the passenger's-side seat.

He leaned his head against the steering wheel. There was no choice to be made. If something were to happen to his family, he would never forgive himself. If this is what he had to do to save them, then he would go.

He backed out of his parking space and drove three miles to the highway that would take him to the park. He wanted to call Kathy. He wanted to tell her everything. But he didn't want to frighten her. Not knowing what to expect, he wasn't about to tell her his life had been threatened and he was on his way to see if the threat was real.

The drive in the snow took forty-five minutes. He exited off the highway onto Sandler, then made a right and drove north on Ashley. The park was a mile away. On the right.

Jonathan slowed his vehicle down and turned onto the small gravel road that led into the parking lot of the park. There was no one else around, and the park wasn't even lit anymore. The moon's light bouncing off the snow gave an eerie glow to the night.

He shut off the engine and opened his briefcase. He took out a piece of paper and pen and wrote: *Kathy, I love you. If you are*

*reading this, it probably means I'm dead. But I want you to know
that if I am dead, I'm still alive. In heaven. With God. I did it
today. I kneeled down and did it. I love you. And the girls, too.
Always know that. J.*

He placed the note on the seat beside him, then cautiously got
out of his car and locked it. He looked around and saw the path
that led into the trees. As he started to go toward it, he noticed
something. Taped to one of the swings on the swing set was a manila envelope. It swung slightly in the evening breeze.

Jonathan buttoned his coat, still wet from the snow, and walked
over to it. He yanked it free and opened it. A single, white sheet of
paper read:

Don't forget your briefcase.

Jonathan was stunned. His briefcase? Why would he need his
briefcase? He looked at the paper one more time, then went back
to his car and got his briefcase. He locked his car again and slowly
continued up the path into the dark woods. The moon was filtered
more by the trees now, and the snow didn't reflect as much light.

The trail wound a little. His feet crunched against the icy path
and dead leaves. If someone was waiting for him, they certainly
would hear him coming. If not for the crunching snow, then for his
pounding heart. The cold air made it hard enough to breathe without the fear of losing his life. He clutched his briefcase in front of
his chest and slowly made his way deeper into the woods. He had
no idea how thick the woods were, but the light was becoming
scarcer.

He rounded a large tree and stopped. Sitting in the middle of a
small clearing was a hurricane lamp with a small votive candle in
the middle of it. Around it were some small stones to keep it from
falling over in a strong wind. That tiny flame illuminated everything
around it, including a small Bible set on a white cloth in the snow,
held open by two tiny rocks.

Jonathan approached slowly and looked around. Three sets of
footprints led away from the candle, each in opposite directions
and into the darkness of the woods. A bush nearby wiggled and
crackled. A small rabbit hopped out and then ran for his life.

Jonathan ran his hand through his hair and closed his eyes. He was shaking terribly. He managed to refocus on the Bible in front of him. He walked past the candle and toward the Bible. Kneeling down in the snow, he slowly removed the rocks. The print was small and he had trouble seeing anything but blurry letters. He moved toward the light of the candle. Several verses were highlighted on the page that was opened:

For the wages of sin is death, but the free gift of God is eternal life in Christ Jesus our Lord.

Another one read:

He who has died is freed from sin. Now if we have died with Christ, we believe that we shall also live with Him.

And then:

For God demonstrates His own love toward us, in that while we were yet sinners, Christ died for us.

Jonathan kneeled down in the snow and reread all the verses. He couldn't believe what this had all led to. A Bible open and sitting in the snow next to a small candle in the middle of the woods. He smiled as he read the verses again. Now they meant something to him. Death and life had new meanings in more ways than one.

He gently set the Bible in the snow and lowered his head, silent before a God he knew was nearby, unafraid of anything else that might be. His life was in God's hands now. He was no closer to solving the mystery of the writer. But he prayed that whatever was intended for his life tonight, it would happen as God wanted it to.

A cold wind moved the treetops and caused their shadows to dance on the white snow below. The tiny flame of the candle flickered but held its life. For the first time since he had walked outside his office building, he was cold.

Jonathan stood and scratched his head. So this was it? Three Bible verses and a candle? He glanced around to see if anyone was there, and then he saw it. Nailed to the tree he had first come around was another manila envelope. Jonathan looked around again and then shuffled through the snow to get the envelope. He laughed a little. It had almost become old habit. He wondered what this envelope held. More Scriptures? An instruction to go home and be with his family? Maybe more secrets from his life?

His hands were so frozen he had trouble opening it up. He finally managed to pull out another single white sheet of paper. Back at the candle he held the paper close to the flame.

It's time to meet your ghostwriter.
Walk toward the light.

Jonathan gripped the paper as if he were trying to hold on to the leash of a running dog. Meet the writer? He stood and looked all around him. Did he want to? He had dismissed ever solving the mystery. And now it was time to know who had been doing this. Jonathan couldn't move. A part of him didn't want to know. Another part of him expected Clyde's ghost to walk out of the woods. And yet another part of him had almost believed that God had written all the pages.

Jonathan looked at the page again. He stood, his muscles and joints beginning to feel the effects of the cold weather. *Walk toward the light.*

He looked around. There was not a single light around, except the flame below him. Even the moon had now ducked behind a thin, long cloud. Jonathan looked around him again. Maybe he had missed it. Nothing. Not a single light.

Wait.

There was one. Deep in the forest. A white light. Small and seemingly in the limbs of some far-off trees. Should he go? Was that the light he was supposed to follow?

Jonathan's body was barely taking direction from his mind. He snapped open his briefcase and put the pieces of paper inside. He closed it and stood, his briefcase feeling as if it weighed a ton.

The trail he had walked on continued, so he glanced around one more time and decided this was the only light to be seen. He found the trail underneath the snow and followed it. His feet hurt from the cold, and now his fingers were red and swelling. He breathed warm air into his free hand and continued to follow the light for about forty more yards.

Suddenly, without warning, he came to the edge of the woods. And to his surprise, the white light had been a light in the parking lot of the restaurant at the bottom of the small hill he stood on.

Without further hesitation, he decided to go down the hill. But the snow was thick and a little slick, and before he knew what had happened, he was tumbling down the embankment. He hit the bottom hard, his briefcase landing on his head.

He was now covered in wet snow again, and his body began shivering uncontrollably. A couple who had parked their car nearby got out and stared for a moment, then walked across the parking lot and into the restaurant.

Jonathan didn't bother dusting himself off as he looked up at the sign. *Piora's.* He had never heard of it before, but he was so cold he knew he needed to get inside. And very quickly. His legs barely moved and his feet plowed through the small bit of snow that had managed to avoid the tires of the cars.

He finally got to the sidewalk that led to the front of the restaurant. He noticed the people going in and out were dressed in cocktail-type evening wear. He was still wearing his suit from work, but it had been wet, had dried, and had gotten wet again. His hair was soaking and plastered to his forehead. A well-dressed man at the door opened it for him.

"Good evening, sir," the man said, a questioning look on his face.

Jonathan couldn't even answer. His jaws were frozen. Inside, the heat immediately hit his face and he was able to catch his breath a little better. He looked around the restaurant. It was intimately elegant and definitely high-class. He took off his heavy coat and pushed his hair to the side.

From where he was standing, he had a good view of the restaurant. He quickly scanned the room but saw no one that looked familiar. The maître d', a tall man behind a small podium, eyed him carefully.

"Sir, may we help you?" he asked in a drawn-out, haughty voice.

Jonathan wasn't sure what he should say. "Um . . ."

"Do you have a reservation, sir?"

Jonathan scratched his head. "Well, um . . ."

The maître d' grew impatient. "Your name, sir."

Jonathan stepped closer to him. "Jonathan Harper."

The maître d' checked his list and then smiled warmly. "Yes, of course. Right this way."

Jonathan couldn't believe it! He was at the right spot. And someone had already made a reservation in his name. The maître d' led him to a table for two in a quiet corner of the room. In the center of the table a small candle was lit, creating a warm atmosphere. The maître d' took his coat, and Jonathan slid his briefcase next to the table, then sat down. The maître d' started to walk away.

"Sir?" Jonathan said.

"Yes?"

"Will . . . anyone be . . . joining me?"

The maître d' smiled slightly. "Yes, sir." Then he walked back to his small podium.

A waiter then appeared holding a manila envelope. Jonathan couldn't even act surprised. "For you, sir."

Jonathan looked around and said, "I didn't order this," but the joke was only to himself. The waiter was gone.

He tore open the envelope and pulled out a single piece of paper. It was blank. Jonathan flipped it over twice. Nothing. Just stark white staring back at him. The waiter reappeared with a steaming cup of coffee. "Here you are."

"Um . . . I'm sorry, but I don't have any money with me. I wasn't expecting to, uh . . . "

The waiter smiled patiently. "I believe your tab will be picked up by the lady over there."

Jonathan looked to where he was pointing. At first no one stuck out. But then he saw her. His mouth dropped open and his heart stopped.

It was Kathy.

She was dressed in a long, red, strapless silk dress and her hair was tied on top her head with small, light wisps hanging down on either side of her face. She met Jonathan's eyes, smiled warmly, and then rose.

"May I join you?" she asked, standing above him. Jonathan was speechless. "I'll take that as a yes." She took a seat across from him. "You're all wet."

Jonathan's eyes were so wide they began to dry out. He blinked and shook his head all at once. "Kathy?"

She shrugged and laughed. "Yes, well, I suppose I'm a bit unrecognizable with a fancy dress and makeup on." She smoothed her dress and crossed her legs. "How do I look?"

Jonathan tried not to stutter. "Fine. Beautiful." Jonathan looked around and whispered, "Kathy? You're the . . . the writer?"

She never took her eyes off him. "Yes."

A thousand and one questions filled his mind, but only one escaped to his lips. "Why?"

Her eyes moved to the candle on the table and she casually rested her chin on her hand. "Isn't it obvious? It was the only way to reach you."

"Reach me?"

"Yes. Books are your life. I couldn't get to you any other way. So I wrote a manuscript that was sure to grab your attention. That's how to get to an editor, right? A story with real punch?"

Jonathan was finally starting to feel his toes, but he was so stunned everything was starting to go numb again.

Kathy continued. "I wanted to save our marriage. I wanted to save your soul. And I couldn't even get you to tell me how your day was. So I decided I had to find another way."

Jonathan rubbed his face and peeked out at her between his fingers. "How?"

"How did I do it?" Kathy asked.

Jonathan nodded. "How did you know all those things about me? In my past? I never told anyone."

She smiled and drew a playful line on the tablecloth. "No. But your mother did. The last Thanksgiving she was alive. Your aunt Eleanor almost told on me by accident when she talked about how we had stayed up late one night and talked. Your mother had so many regrets, and most of them centered on your relationship with your father. She started mentioning it that night, and I asked her questions. She had a lot to get off her chest, and I had a lot to learn. You never talked about your past, and it was so much a part of who you were . . . and your relationship with your father . . . so much of why you gave up on believing in God."

Jonathan swallowed. "What about all the other stuff? How did you know what was happening in my life from day to day?"

"I actually got the idea from Leesol. Uncle Earl sent her a mini-recorder, so I sort of borrowed it without permission and recorded you. It has a feature that only records if there's noise, so most of the time I had enough tape to last the whole day."

"The tape recorder was in my office?"

"No. In your briefcase."

Jonathan paused. Then he picked up his briefcase and opened it. "Where? I don't see anything."

Kathy stood. "May I?" Jonathan handed her the briefcase. She set it on the table and slid her fingers along the fabric on the inside lid. She then revealed a small hole, taped together with fabric tape. She unstuck it and reached in. Her hand revealed a tiny voice recorder a little bigger than a pocket calculator. "The microphone was powerful enough to pick up sound through the leather."

Jonathan rubbed his temples. "I can't believe it." He looked at her "What about all the future predictions? How did you know what I would do?"

"They only seemed like predictions. But I was actually controlling the situation. Each prediction revolved around me, so I made sure to write down exactly what I knew we would be doing."

Jonathan's temples pulsated with confusion. "I don't get it. You knew about Sydney? When I came home and you were reading the pages . . . you knew all along?"

Kathy's bright face faded a little. "I had my suspicions about your being involved with someone at the office. I wasn't sure. But I did a little undercover work, which wasn't hard, since Edie has a hard time keeping her mouth shut about anything."

"Why didn't you just confront me about her?"

"I did. In the bathroom when you accused me of not cautioning the girls about strangers. But you denied it. You were closed off.

And distant. I knew I had to find a way to bring it to your attention and scare you into stopping." She looked him square in the face. "I was willing to do anything and everything to save our marriage. I loved you so much, and I didn't want you to throw what we had away. But I also knew that unless your heart changed, Sydney wouldn't be the first or last 'other woman' in your life."

Jonathan stared into the glow of the small candle. "I thought I was going to die tonight." He looked up at her. "I thought that Jeremy kid was going to kill me."

Kathy smiled. "Yes, well, he was definitely an easy suspect. But I overheard Sydney talking with a girlfriend of hers at the funeral. Jeremy was actually in jail and would probably be there for some time. Drugs, I think. Anyway, he wasn't a threat, even if she told a different story. I used it to my advantage."

Jonathan raised his eyebrows and squeezed his eyes shut, fighting off a maddening headache that threatened to pull his focus away. "I have to ask—did Clyde know about this?"

Kathy shook her head. "No. Not until the end. A few days before he died. I felt guilty that you suspected him. I had sort of contributed to that suspicion. I finally went to his house and told him what I was doing. He didn't agree with it and told me I should just talk to you about it, but he told me he wouldn't interfere with what I was doing." Kathy moved uncomfortably in her chair and adjusted her dress. She looked away and said, "There was a part of me that wanted you to suffer. To be scared."

"Well, it worked."

"It was wrong of me, but I wanted you to pay for your fling with that girl. And the more I saw what the pages I was sending you were doing to you, the more it made me feel better. But then there came a point when I realized it was wrong. I was being deceitful and you were going insane. Seeing you suffer like that was breaking my heart. That's when I decided to use the manuscript to point you to God. That's what I had wanted from the beginning, anyway. Just to point you in the right direction."

Jonathan laughed and frowned all at once. "So you just sat up one night and thought all this out?"

"Well, it wasn't quite as organized as an outline or anything. I thought I'd write down your past and send it to you. Make you confront your demons. But the more I wrote down, the more I realized you needed God. It just kept working, so I kept doing it."

Jonathan shook his head. "Apparently you're not the only one." He looked up at her. "Clyde wrote his last story for me. It was all about Jesus Christ and my relationship, or lack thereof, with Him. It was incredible. I've never been so touched by anything in my whole life."

Kathy smiled. "Clyde told me that he was writing that book for you. The day that I went over to tell him what I was doing. We both sort of laughed about it, then prayed that something would work and that you would give your life to God."

"I did. Today. At the office." Both their eyes teared and then Jonathan laughed a little and looked at his briefcase. "So everywhere this briefcase went, you were there, too?"

Kathy grinned. "Yep. It was like putting a handle on me and carrying me by your side." Her expression turned serious. "Are you mad? You should be. You can be. I'll understand."

Jonathan wasn't mad. He was tired. And still a little cold. He took her hand from across the table. "I didn't realize you were such a prolific writer."

"Well," she said, squeezing his hand, "I did major in journalism."

He laughed. "It showed. You're actually a terrible storyteller. No consistent description. No flow. Just choppy bits of information."

She locked eyes with him. "An editor's worst nightmare."

"You have no idea," he said, his eyes never leaving hers.

She shook her head. "In the end, it wasn't my story that led you to God, anyway. It was Clyde's. I suppose we all know what our demons are. No one needs to tell us, right?" Tears came from nowhere and dropped down her face. "I did this because I love you. I know it got a little out of hand. But I did it to try to save our marriage. It was my last hope." She laughed a little and added, "There were so many times when I thought you knew. You'd tell me about the pages you found, and I was sure your next sentence would be that you knew it was me. That's why I always looked so scared! A few times I even tried to tell you it was me. I started to. But something always happened and I never got a chance."

Jonathan felt tears forming, too. "No. I'm glad we're here. I'm glad it ended this way." He reached across and touched her face. "You look beautiful." He laughed through his tears. "But did you have to traipse me through the woods and into the snow?"

She laughed, too, and more tears fell. "I wasn't counting on this much snow."

He wiped her tears away and then his own. "It doesn't matter. What matters is that I'm here with you. And you still love a man who is totally unworthy of that love."

She leaned across the table. "I always have. I always will."

Jonathan sat a little taller and drew in a breath that released every bit of tension he had felt over the past few weeks. Then he said, "Tell me something."

"What?"

His lips turned upward into a half smile. "How does the story end?"

A deep glow radiated from within, shining through the sparkle in her eyes. "It's kind of funny."

"Is it?"

"Yes. You see, the story doesn't have an ending."

A huge smile found its way to Jonathan's lips. "Is that so?"

"It's true."

Jonathan stood and said, "Well, then, I think I know what happens in the next chapter."

"Oh, really?"

"Yes. The sorry low-life excuse for a husband asks the beautiful, talented heroine of a wife to dance."

Kathy blushed and laughed. "We haven't danced in years."

Jonathan took her hand. "Then here's to another fifty chapters of dancing the night away."

She took his hand and he led her to the quaint dance floor in the middle of the restaurant. A soft, slow piece of music filled their ears, and he held her close to him.

"Thank you," he whispered in her ear.

"You're welcome."

And that's how it happened. It sounds unbelievable, and maybe it is. But God used what I loved so much—books—to help me find Him. And to help me find my way back to the right kind of life that I had lost many years ago. And so I wrote it all down, so that maybe someone might read it and know that life has a lot to offer. But if God isn't offering it, then it's really no life at all. I was changed that day. Changed for good. My life went on. My children grew. And I eventually left the editorial world and became a writer so I could tell the many more stories about God that Clyde Baxter had to leave behind. But I never forgot the story he wrote for me. And I never forgot what my wife did, either. Never again did I forget God. Ever.

Jonathan Harper
New York

Acknowledgments

The author would like to give special thanks to the following people:

Sean and John Caleb, thank you for making the sacrifices so I could do this. I love you both. Mom and Dad, thank you for all the baby-sitting time and for buying me my first computer so I could discover my passion. Wendy, thank you for being a supportive sister. The Gutteridge clan, your support I'm unworthy of. Amy, thank you for an incredible first edit.

Jim Lucas and family, you're a mentor writers only dream of. Dr. Terry Phelps, Dixie Jordan, and Darrell Reed are all extraordinary teachers. Your dedicatin and support along the way gave me the confidence and skill to do this. Dr. P—the endless time and energy you spent molding me as a writer has paid off!

Steve Laube, much thanks for believing in my vision and helping to make it happen. Dave Horton and Sarah Long, you are an editorial team that exceeded my greatest expectations. Ron Wheatley, your expertise gave much dimension to Clyde's novel—I'm grateful we met!

God the Father, thank you for everything that you are. May you take this feeble attempt and use it for your glory.